HOLLOWOOD FALLS

the series

HOLLOWOOD FALLS BOOK 1-4

WILL FORREST

Contents

HOLLOWOOD FALLS

Book 1

48 Hours in Hollowood

Graeme doesn't know me like he thinks he does. There's a secret I've been keeping since we met. A secret big enough to destroy our marriage. A secret I can't hide if we have to spend two days in Hollowood Falls. It's not that my family's overbearing (spoiler: they are) or that I left home at seventeen because they were about to ruin my life (spoiler: they were.) The problem is that we're werewolves.

But there's only so long I can lie to the man I love. And there's more to my hometown than meets the eye. If I have to deal with that arrogant, asinine, mouth-watering Pierce Platter, my ex-best friend and so-called fated mate, then forty-eight hours is just long enough for everything to go wrong.

One

Birds

I'm sitting on the back deck daydreaming about my husband's ass when everything goes to hell. Just when I've figured out how to be happy. Who wouldn't be happy? We're living the American Dream: Gay All Day edition, in a nice midcentury bungalow on a treed street in a great neighborhood, with completely normal neighbours who bring us banana bread and watch our cat when we go out of town. Ordinary, maybe even boring, and it's a little slice of heaven.

All thanks to Graeme, who not only healed my mangled heart but makes our backyard a paradise. Even in the heat of summer, it's shady and green, and he's planned it so there's always something blooming, something bright and happy to see first thing in the morning.

We get tons of birds too. Finches and jays and more things I can't name. Even a few white-capped crows, like the ones where I grew up and that I've never seen anywhere else until a trio moved into that dead tree on Mr Richardson's lot. He's been fighting with the city for years about that rotten old thing. One day a storm is going to bring it down, right on top of him.

But there's no talking to some people. Sometimes listening is the hardest thing you can do. I could write a book about the things I haven't said because certain people weren't ready to hear them. Not today, though. Today is perfect.

Or it will be once Graeme gets home. He loves living here, so close to that little shopping district, where they still have a green grocer and a butcher shop like they did where he grew up in Anstruther, a painfully quaint village on the east coast of Scotland. He'll go down nearly every day like his mum might have, to nose about as he says. Sometimes he brings me flowers, which made me feel really weird the first time and is now just a thing he does. Just a man in love with his husband.

It's so good to be able to say that, to have a husband, to have this much. To never have to hide our love. We don't fly any rainbow flags on our lawn, but everyone knows who we are and no one gives a shit. Like I said: a slice of heaven.

Even with the clouds rolling in, the sky to the west darkening before my eyes. No big deal, and the garden could probably do with some rain now that the hot weather is here. Far away thunder rolls, a low, treacherous murmur that makes my hair stand on end. A sudden gust of wind tears through the treetops, ripping off leaves and snatching at my soul because all of a sudden here it comes: the fear.

White hot, all-consuming, my heart hammering at my ribcage, my mouth too dry to scream. Another growl of thunder and I'm on my feet, running blind, running for my life, and I don't know why. I hit the garden gate, and I mean hit, run into it full speed, the pain spiking through me and waking me from my panic. I haven't felt like this in years. Not since leaving Hollowood. Feeling like this, hating these feelings, is exactly why I left.

"My lights, Evan, what's happened?"

Graeme. My hero, my husband, coming up the walk with a grocery tote and a bunch of flowers and my heart. Holding my gaze, his gorgeous brown eyes full of worry, he sets down the bag of groceries to key the code into the gate lock. He knows I get like this. It hasn't happened in a while, but he knows just what to do, how to save me.

I let go of the gate so he can open it and then he's holding me and God, it feels so good. He's my home and he's here and I hate looking weak but he knows me, he saves me, he's mine.

"Love, what's wrong? Is it a panic attack? Come in the house, then," he says when I nod. "Come on, let go of me, we'll get in quicker." He hooks the shopping bag over his arm holding the flowers then takes my hand and leads me back inside.

"I don't know what's wrong with me," I rasp as he slides the patio door shut.

"Not to worry, love. Sit and I'll fetch you a drink."

He leaves me on the couch, where I watch the wind silently beat the hell out of the trees through the patio doors. Graeme comes back with a glass of water, stepping over the back of the low couch to settle beside me.

"Oh look," he says, pointing at the pair of crows as they touch down on the deck. "Spicks and Specs must be worried about you." He's convinced the pied crows know us, and named the mating pair after a show we bonded over. A show no one I knew had seen until I met Graeme, which is why we kept on talking the night we met as our friends left the bar one by one, until we were the only two left at the birthday party of someone we haven't seen since.

The crows on the patio sure look like they're here for a reason as they hop towards the door. Spicks, the bigger one, tilts its head, blinking at us through the glass. And there it is again, that fear, but I'm not giving in, not letting it rule me. I'm stronger than the fear, stronger than my past, my pain. I'm not afraid.

"Jesus, Evan!" Graeme jumps up from the couch, his jeans soaking wet, broken glass on the floor. The other half of the glass is still in my shaking hand, and I drop it on the carpet. "I'm calling the paramedics," Graeme murmurs, backing towards the kitchen counter where he left his phone.

"I'm not sick," I say, my throat so dry it comes out like an angry bark.

"Well, something the fuck is going on," he bites back, his hands on his hips. "Can I call Doctor Vanian?"

My therapist, and the only other person who can deal with me when I get like this. I nod and Graeme grabs his phone and disappears down the hall. I turn around and there are more crows. Half a dozen, more, and as I'm trying to count them another one lands. Then another. A murder. A sign.

I know what's wrong. It's not a panic attack. Not anxiety or PTSD or a manic episode or anything that Vanian or even Graeme understands.

It's Hollowood.

It wants me back.

Two

The Letter

I talk through my shit with Doctor V. At least the parts I can tell her. She doesn't know the truth about Hollowood Falls, only that my hometown messed me up pretty badly, broke my trust a hundred ways and made it hard for me to let my guard down around anyone. When I met Graeme, he had to coax me out of my shell, and if I ever believe in my own worth it's because I trust his opinion.

When I get off the phone Graeme has started defrosting dinner in the microwave, and is kicked back on the couch, upgrading one of his characters' armor options. Beside him on the couch is an envelope. "It's for you," he says, thumbing through the menu. "Dunno how I missed it when I left for the shops."

"Maybe you went out by the garden gate."

"But still. That means you walked past it like five times."

"I can walk past a running sink five times," I say, as I step over the back of the couch. "I've burnt microwave pizza."

He snickers but doesn't say anything. Neither do I, happy to be near him, to be normal. "Are you not going to open your letter?" he asks after a minute.

The letter I forgot. The letter I'm sitting on. I pull it out and look at it for a full five seconds, then toss it on the ottoman. There's no return address but from the handwriting I know who it's from. Someone I swore on my life I'd never talk to again. "Nope."

"Are you shitting me?" As the microwave dings Graeme saves his character, then shuts down the game and drops the controller beside the letter. "Who's it from?"

I almost don't tell him. Almost lie to the love of my life. But if anything's going to survive what's coming, I want it to be us. "My brother."

His eyes wide, Graeme looks from me to the letter and back. "A brother you completely failed to mention even existed? And you're not going to open it?"

He's giving me that look, that slant-eyed stare he picked up from his mother. I love my mother-in-law but in twenty minute doses. Her son I see every day and he's a pain in the ass when there's something he wants. I put up with maybe ten seconds of that piercing look before I snatch up the envelope. "I hate you sometimes."

The envelope looks like any other, the corners dinged, the postmark blurred, like the rubber stamp slipped. Who still rubber-stamps their mail? There's a normal digital postmark across the bottom, the numbers a code but not the sender's zip code. I open it and pull out a page torn from a kid's school primer. The letter looks like Chase wrote it with the pencil between his teeth.

Ev
Granny passed. Big tumor, nothing doing. Funeral on the 11th.
You're expected.
C.

Classic fucking Chase. "Granny passed away."

"Shit." Graeme slides nearer and puts his arm around my shoulders. "I'm so sorry, Evan."

"My brother wants me at the funeral."

"Of course we'll go," he says kindly, giving me a squeeze.

"You don't have to come with me."

"Don't be daft. You shouldn't have to go through that alone."

"I don't know what they're going to think of you."

"I don't much care. I'm going, end of discussion. Besides, it'll give me a chance to wear that new bow-tie."

"The red one with the cow skulls? Can you not?"

"I'm joking," he says, dropping his arm to hug my waist. "I'm not so disrespectful. It's full dress kilt, all the way."

"You're an ass," I groan but it's too late, I'm laughing. I love him in a kilt. I love him in anything. I love him.

But will that be enough? Graeme's so good to me I can't help worrying what might happen when he meets my family. Being gay's not the problem. If it was, this would be so much easier. I'd breeze in for Granny's ceremony, drop a white rose on her casket, maybe a rainbow flag when she's already in the ground and it's too late to retrieve it, just to piss them off. Instead my family were happy when I came out at twelve. I'd made their lives a lot easier, they said. Or at least I would have if I'd stayed.

Graeme wakes up the next morning even earlier than usual. I'm sure I haven't slept at all, but in what seems seconds later he's shaking me awake.

"Gi' th' hie, love. The car's packed, I've made coffee, I left a message with Joanne about coming over to feed Dolly and change the litter, and she's still got our spare key."

"Wha' time is it?"

"Half six. Traffic'll be murder if we put it off much longer."

Grumbling the whole way (a right I defend to the grave, because me and mornings have permanent beef) I go through the motions: sit-ups, shower, shave, caffeine. Another man might be mourning Granny. I haven't seen anyone in my family since I left Hollowood, did all my grieving at the time. I never planned to go back.

It's not even seven when we hit the road. Graeme drives for the first few hours while I doze. We switch back and forth, talking about nothing, about the color of the sky and the chance of Mr Richardson's tree falling on our house while we're gone, which isn't much of a chance as he's at the corner and we're at the top of the cul de sac. Anything to avoid the conversation I know I need to have. The one I've never had with Graeme. The one I can't avoid, because I can't let him find out from someone else.

We're no more than an hour away when the pressure gets to me, when the need to confess burns hotter than my fear of what happens when I do. "There's something I should tell you about my family. You know, before you meet them."

"You think?" he says without looking up from his phone.

"Don't be sarcastic."

"Sorry," he says, putting his phone away. "You were saying?"

"Right." My hands are shaking on the wheel, and for a minute I think about pulling over and letting him drive, but every second I delay only makes this worse. "You're not going to believe me," I say weakly.

"You don't know that. How about if I guess?"

"Good luck."

"Alright." He twists in the passenger's seat to look at me. "You're straight. Alright, alright," he says with a grin as I burst out laughing. "You're a bigamist."

"A what?"

"You married twice and didn't tell either of us."

"No."

"A Mormon? No, because then you'd probably be a bigamist too," he muses, looking me up and down. "I know, you're one of those escaped Amish."

"You're getting colder."

Graeme says nothing for a few miles, but his eyes are moving the way they do in a tense Pub Trivia match. "I've got it!" he says triumphantly. "You're a serial killer, aren't you?"

"I'm not even going to answer that."

"Well, you're either a serial killer, a cult member, or, I don't know, a werewolf."

This is the bit where I nearly drive off the road. Because I'm so fucking subtle. Every marriage has its challenges, those moments that make or break you as a couple (or throuple and God bless you if you're trying to manage more.) Skidding out on the graveled shoulder of a country road at eighty miles an hour while my husband hollers at me to keep my fucking eyes on the fucking road as we'll never sort out this werewolf shite if we're fucking dead, was definitely one of those moments.

I get out as soon as the car stops. So does Graeme, and we lean on the roof of the car and stare at each other. I love this man more than anything in the world, and I've lied to him every day since we met. "I thought...I thought I could leave it behind. I thought I'd never have to go back to Hol—to my hometown."

Saying the name out loud when we're this close feels like a summoning. Another fifty miles and it will be. Graeme is studying my face. Does he want some sign of the truth? "If you're looking for the pointy ears—" I start.

"Don't be an arse," he snaps. "I'm doing my fucking best here."

"I wish I was joking. I wish none of this was happening."

"You and me both." He blows out his breath, then straightens. "Oh well, nowt to be done about it, is there?"

"Nothing."

"C'est la fucking vie, love. Now come here." He's moving around the front of the car, his arms open to me. I want to run to him but I can barely breathe. Then he's holding me, and he's everything. "Go on, then," he says as I start bawling like a little bitch. "Have it out."

"I'm sorry..."

"Hush. We'll sort it out."

"You aren't safe here."

"Then neither are you."

"No. This is where I'm from. This is where I belong."

"You belong with me. Honestly, Ev, even if you are...that, we're not moving here, are we? We're in and out. Two days, tops. Forty-eight hours. Nothing's going to happen."

And I want him to be right. I want it to be true. But two days in Hollowood Falls? Anything could happen.

Three

The Dew Drop Inn

The first time Hollowood Falls shows up on the road sign, I nearly grab the wheel to force a u-turn. I don't want to be here, don't want to feel this helpless. There's nothing I can do to stop this feeling except not be here.

Another sign, this one for the entrance to the state park. The Falls aren't in Hollowood itself but about five miles from town. A natural wonder, one of the longest straight drops of any waterfall in North America, and they closed the path to the top because of how many people have tried jumping off it.

We pass another sign, then the old gas station with the Sinclair dinosaur sign. A modern micro-turbine spins freely on a tall pole nearer the building, another conquest for my uncle Trace's distributed power installation firm. Then the steep gravel switchback that leads to Humboldt's sawmill. In less than a mile we'll see the billboard that reads *Welcome to Hollowood Falls.*

I close my eyes. I hope for a miracle.

Graeme touches my leg and I startle awake, hitting my head on the seatbelt mount. We're parked in front of the Dew Drop Inn and it's like I've gone back in time. The ten-room motel was dated when I left. Now I guess it's retro, with its curving stucco walls and red and yellow striped aluminum awnings and that neon martini glass on the roadside sign.

"Is this place alright?" Graeme asks, squeezing my knee.

"The Dew Drop? It's clean, if that's what you're asking."

"Are you alright?"

"No. Yes. Maybe?"

"I went ahead and booked a room. We got in at the right time, he said it was the last they had."

"Awesome. I don't want to have to lean on Chase." For all I know, my brother isn't even in a situation to be leaned on. You might think I'm a handful; Chase is a full-blown disaster gay. And not even nice about it, he's just...Chase. I can't imagine how he's dealing with Granny being gone, because she was the only one who put up with him at his worst. And now I'm crying again because my little brother is a disaster and I'm so much like him, a goddamn liar. And I just know I'm going to take it out on the man I love.

Somehow Graeme gets me out of the car and into the motel room, where I stand leaking tears until he makes me lie down. I wake up alone on top of the covers. There's a lamp on but the room is dim, and if I didn't have to piss I could go straight back to sleep. I can hear water running which only makes it worse, but that means Graeme's in the shower.

I love him, so much it sometimes hurts to look at him. I can't let anything happen to him this weekend. Can't let Chase start a fight, can't let my dad or my uncles and their friends goad me into anything. Feeling stale from the long drive, the lack of sleep, I strip off my wrinkled clothes. Graeme's left the bathroom door unlocked so I go in.

"Don't flush," he says from behind the shower curtain when he hears me washing my hands. "The water pressure's shite."

But the bathtubs at the Dew Drop are nice and wide. I brush my teeth quickly then peek around the curtain. He's standing under the spray, his head thrown back, water and little streams of soap cascading down his back and his gorgeous ass. I step into the shower and he goes to turn but I put my arms around him, my head on his shoulder, my chest to his back, my cock nestled in the cleft of that gorgeous ass.

"Feeling better?" Graeme asks, arching to rub against me, his skin slippery with hot water and the traces of soap.

"Much better." I slip one hand up to brush over his nipples, making him suck in his breath and thrust his hips back. The little bottles of shampoo and conditioner are standing on the edge of the tub, and I'm inspired to empty the conditioner into my hand then smear it over my cock and between his buttocks. Fifty miles a week on the treadmill does something magical to a man's ass, the clench of Graeme's muscles almost like a hand, except thicker and softer and so much hotter as he braces himself with one arm and begins to work his cock in time with my pumping hips. I'm not even in him and it's still so hot, the way he responds to my touch, the way we fit together.

"Sweet Jesus, Evan, I'm done for," he groans.

"Yes. Come for me."

He hisses a laugh through his clenched teeth because I don't say shit like that in bed. Because that's what you say in porn and this is true love, like I've told him before, probably too many times. But it's too late, and his laugh turns into a deep, throaty moan as he comes, fucking into his own hand, the shove of his incredible ass against my cock pushing me to the brink. I pull back just enough to reach my cock and in seconds I'm there, my spunk dousing his lower back, the shower's soft rain carrying it down his ass crack and away.

We should have dinner but I didn't sleep worth a damn the night before and when I say I'm going to bed he doesn't argue. I'm not just tired, I'm angry, at myself for letting Hollowood get to me. And sad, because Granny was a good woman who deserved more than life gave her. And hungry, now that I have nothing on my mind. And scared, but of what? I don't live here anymore. I'm not a frightened kid but a grown adult, with a mortgage and

a husband and a life that has nothing to do with Hollowood. Nothing's
going to happen.

Four

Hollowood At Night

I hear them in my dreams first. Not just their howls but the breath steaming from their red mouths, the swish of a pelt past an evergreen's sharp-smelling bough, the click of claws over cold stone. They gather in a great swirling mass of jaw and tooth and fur and eyes of depthless gold. And I run but they have me, are all over me, are me...

I sit up before I'm even awake. The room is pitch black, not enough streetlights in Hollowood Falls to do much about the darkness. I nearly lie down when I hear it. The howl. The chorus. My cousins, my kin, my nightmare, and I grab my pillow and jam it between my teeth because the same howl lives within me, waiting to erupt and destroy everything I've made for myself.

Graeme murmurs in his sleep as he rolls towards me and I wonder how I will protect him. It's one thing for him to know the truth. It's another thing to slap him in the face with it repeatedly. My uncles and cousins, my parents, everything in this town turns to the pack for guidance, leadership, protection. Protection from shit that wouldn't affect them if they didn't live in Hollowood.

So much for sleep. Wanting not to bug Graeme I get out of bed and put on the bathroom light. Can they tell from outside the room that I'm awake? Do they know I'm here? Or is this just another moonlit night in the werewolf capital of Colorado?

I can only imagine. I never stuck around long enough to run the streets. Standing by the window, I fight the urge to pull back the curtain and look outside. There'll be nothing to see. The wolves (not werewolves, not my cousins, my parents, my old next door neighbour) have to be miles away, the valley walls reflecting the sound to make them seem closer than they are. Nothing to see, and even as the howling starts again, first one then the whole pack in dissonant harmony, I go back to the bed. Back to Graeme and sanity and the life I've clawed out of my history. I'm just climbing in beside him when the chorus cuts short, the howling now snarling as the animals turn on each other, or on some intruder.

I'm at the door before I know it, my hand on the knob. Like my place isn't here but out in the streets, as if that fight is mine, my body shaking with the urge to run, to leap, to bite and tear and taste blood, raw and living.

"Ev?" Graeme's just a shape in the blackness as he sits up. "Where are you?" The edge of fear in his voice breaks through my sickening need and I stumble to the bed, the springs poinging as I drop onto it.

"What's happening?" he murmurs, patting the covers to find my hand. I make it easy by pulling him into my arms. "Are those dogs?"

"Wolves. I'm guessing, I haven't exactly gone out there to ask."

"Are they—"

"I don't know. I don't know what's going on. We shouldn't have come here. I should have sent a card and some flowers and done like I said and never come back to Hollowood—"

"Shh, love," Graeme murmurs, holding me tighter. "It's alright. I promise, I won't anything happen."

"You don't understand—"

"Hush. We'll get through this together."

"I love you so much."

"I love you too, sweetheart."

He kisses my cheek but I need more. I need everything he can give me, to drive away the fear and the darkness and the doom that's breathing down my neck. I turn to kiss him properly, dirty breath and everything. I don't care, he's still so sweet. He's mine.

We're naked and I stroke my fingers down his spine. Moaning, he arches towards me as I trace down the crack of his ass. "Can I fuck you? Please Graeme, you're so gorgeous when you take my cock."

We don't play this way very often. Something about being in charge makes my skin crawl and my cock deflate, but sometimes it's all I want, to have him under me, giving in to my cravings, mine, mine, mine.

I feel more than see him nod as I kiss him again. He wants it, his body rocking in time with the thrust of my tongue deep into his yielding mouth. In the dark it's all feeling as I grope my way across the nightstand for the lube, then grope my way across the bed to find him already lying on his front, his legs apart. He wants it as bad as I do, as he reaches back to hold his ass cheeks apart for me.

"Fuck, you're gorgeous," I groan, and I mean it, even in the dark. The satin feel of his skin, the raw smell of his sweat and the funk of his ass as I dip my head down to stroke my tongue around the pucker. Graeme swears, some rank Glaswegian curse he picked up at university. Laughing, I do it again, making him shiver and hump into the mattress. This sort of sex knocks him right out, takes over his brain, makes him mine in a whole new way. It's a gift and I treat it that way, cherish everything he gives me.

By the time I work him open my cock is leaking onto my leg and his moans are one long sound of pleasure. I can't hold out, and leaving my two fingers deep in him I stretch my body over him to kiss the nape of his neck. "Kneel for me?" I whisper.

Graeme falls quiet, his back pressing against my chest with his heaving breath. Even when I want him this way, sometimes he likes to have more control, but as I start to move my fingers inside him again he groans like he's coming. "Yes. Fucking have me. I love you every way, Ev. Just get to it before I unload. I want you in me when I come."

As I withdraw my fingers he shoves up onto his hands and knees. I wish I could see him better, but it's enough to feel him—his hairy thighs against mine as I get close, his buttocks flexing then softening as I stroke my cock over his hole. And then to feel it take my cock, so tight and slick I just about lose it right there. Oh, but I want more. Want to fuck until we forget our names, until there's nothing in the world but us.

Grabbing his hips, I thrust deeper, his ass sucking at me as he pushes back against me. He's everything I've ever wanted, and he's mine, all mine. I push down on his ass, changing the way I fill him, and he swears again, calls me a devil, and maybe I am because it only makes me fuck him harder.

As he reaches for his cock I feel the change in his balance. "Did I say you could touch that?" I bark, slapping his ass cheek.

"Jesus, Ev, you're wild tonight."

"And you love it."

"I do. I want this. Want you to make me come just like this."

"With me drilling your sweet ass?"

"Aye..."

"Spreading you open like the slut you are?"

"Fucking hell, Ev, when did you get such a filthy mouth?"

I'm only saying what we're both thinking, that this is the best fuck we've had in months. A catharsis, raw and truthful, something we both needed more than we knew. "Fuck, I'm going to come so hard," I groan. Somewhere inside me I cringe, because who talks like this? Me, when I'm fucking the man of my dreams, who's trembling with joy at the feel of my cock taking him apart.

"Yes..." he gasps, his hips jerking. "Do it..."

"Not until you come. Until you're screaming."

Close, as he groans from the bottom of his soul, shoving himself back onto me. Wanting more of me and I give it, my own orgasm rising fast, but he's so goddamn gorgeous when he's full of my cock. I turn one hand so my thumb is between his sweating ass cheeks, the tip stroking the rim of his hole where it stretches to take me. One touch and it pushes him over, and he screams like I want him to, his muscles squeezing around my cock and shredding my self-control as I shoot my load, the pleasure scorching me from the inside out as I spill into him.

Then I hear it. The scuffle and whine, the scrape of claw and paw across concrete as some huge beast paces at our door. I'm on my feet before I know it. By the time Graeme understands what's happened, I'm in the bathtub. Shaking.

Five

Breakfast

Graeme tells me the noises stopped right away, but I can't even make myself get out of the tub. Around three in the morning he brings me a spare pillow and bedspread and leaves me to sit it out. I'm not upset. He knows there's only so much he can do with me when I'm like this.

After a few hours of thinking very hard about not thinking about anything at all, I take a shower. When I hear Graeme brushing his teeth I poke my head around the curtain. "Sorry about last night."

"Don't be," he says around his toothbrush. "It was great until the Warren Zevon fan club showed up."

"The what?" I ask as he rinses his mouth.

"You know, Werewolves of London? You must have heard it at least once or twice."

"I hate that song."

"Sook."

"Dog-fucker."

"Wow," he says, shaking his head as he catches my eye in the mirror. "Just...wow."

"Too soon?"

He snorts a laugh. "I'm sorry, who you and what have you done with my husband? You're not meant to be this funny."

"Must be all this fresh mountain air," I say as I pull the shower curtain closed.

"Or the sleep dep," he shoots back. "And hurry up, I'm starving."

The motel restaurant is a cinderblock addition with a diner's glass front. Everything is decades old, from the glitter-flecked vinyl cushions in the booths to the wallpaper design of ducks and daisies. The menu too, which doesn't have a single thing on it that Graeme can eat.

"Toast it is," he sighs in continually frustrated vegan as he shoves the menu away from him. "There's not even peanut butter in the jam rack."

I'm too tired to do more than nod. It doesn't matter anyway. We'll be gone by tonight, away from Hollowood Falls and on our way back to reality. The whole town is a time capsule, like a Disney executive's idea of a logging town, with everyone dressed in plaid flannel and scuffed boots, though the last time I checked all these kings and queens of the wild frontier worked for remote call centers, booking redeye flights for worn-out executives and confirming Zappo returns.

The waitress shows up with food I don't remember ordering. As I rip through a Spanish omelet Graeme picks at his toast. I'm just about to apologize to him again when something catches my eye.

"Well, I'll be damned!" Someone is standing at the door, staring at us. Someone I know.

"Shit," I mutter as Reed starts towards us. Graeme does a double take, which is unsurprising because Reed is six foot two and built to last, his gingery hair in a thick braid over his shoulder, his arms inked with every kind of tattoo, from stick-and-pick stars to a massive python winding its way around the other flash, its head stretching onto the back of his left hand. The hand lands heavy on my shoulder.

"Evan Culver, who'd have thought. You're here for the funeral."

Not a question. Everyone knows how I left. "Yep. Fast in, fast out."

"That's a real shame. Some people here would sure love to see you."

"They can see me this afternoon," I say, sounding like a complete ass-hole. Which is just how Reed looks at me, his big nostrils flaring. Then he notices Graeme.

Here's the thing about Graeme. He's...hot. Like the kind of hot that makes people walk into stuff because they're looking at him. I'll admit his looks went a long way when he picked me out of the crowd at that awful birthday party like I was Baby in the corner. You can't help but want to look at him, so I had until he broke through my front of *go-fuck-yourself*, that shield I'd been wearing around my heart.

Yep, big tough Evan slayed by pristine skin and cheekbones to make Timothée Chalamet seethe with envy. As for his dick...well it's not on display at the moment but Graeme might as well have whipped it out on the table from the killing look Reed's giving him.

Reed looks down at the ring on Graeme's left hand. He looks at me, at the matching ring on my hand, white gold inset with chips of onyx. Reed snorts, his nostrils literally flapping, then he turns and shoulders his way through the group of people who have just come into the restaurant.

Sinking low in the booth, I grab the dessert menu and hold it in front of my face. "Do you know them as well?" Graeme whispers across the table.

"I don't know, but I'm not taking any chances."

"Was that a cousin or uncle or something?" He grabs the other lit-tle menu from behind the napkin dispenser as the new people pass us, but from their puffy jackets and shiny new hiking boots I know they're day-trippers from Vail, here to pose for selfies in front of the falls.

"Look, it's not just my kin you have to watch out for," I say as I sit upright. "Pretty much everyone in town thinks of themselves as one big family."

"That's a bit...incestuous? And did you just say kin?"

"It's a figure of speech," I say, a blanket statement because I'll be damned if I'm explaining anything in detail. "Just don't be surprised if everyone we meet here already knows."

"That you're gay?"

"That I'm married."

He tips his head, his perfect brows pinching over his honey-brown eyes. "They're okay that you're gay but not that you're gay married?"

"I was meant to marry someone else."

"So you are a bigamist after all," he says, his lips twitching.

"Shut up."

"Sorry," he says, propping his elbows on the table to put his head in his hands. "I don't mean to be salty but I'm starving, and exhausted, and I kind of wish we hadn't come."

"Too late now. And I'm sorry too. I didn't mean to snap at you."

"Ach, we'll get through it," he says with a shrug. "It's the middle of day one, so we're already a quarter of the way there. Nothing bad's going to happen."

"Don't say that out loud."

"I'm not going to jinx us," he says, rolling those honeyed eyes. I want to believe him, believe his hope and his faith in me will survive the rest of the weekend. "Now finish your breakfast and we'll us find a grocery store," he says, reaching for another packet of jam. "This close to Vail someone's got to be selling oat milk."

A Meeting in the Aisle

On the surface, Graeme should be right, because the town of Hollowood Falls looks an awful lot like an ecovillage. Nearly everyone out here is on solar, wind, and rainwater, there's a community arts hub with a gallery and a kiln, and right before I left the town had signed onto a zero-plastic pledge.

"I can't believe with all this green power and other woo that there were no vegan options on that menu," Graeme says as he stands on the curb, looking both ways even though we can see up and down the empty street half a mile in either direction.

"What can I say, people out here like their meat."

"Still....if they're getting Vail kids, there should be a keto raw bar on every corner."

"Colorado, a land of contrasts."

"Is there even a grocery store?"

"Is a general store good enough?" I ask, pointing across the street to Sutherland's Dry Goods.

"We'll see, won't we?"

Sutherland's is another Wild West theme park building: shaped like a barn, the plank siding silvered by a hundred winters, the heritage hitching posts out front protected by yellow safety poles to keep SUVs from driving into them. It's the same vibe inside as out, the rafters hung with old timey crap like kerosene lanterns and two-handed saws. The hand-built wooden shelves hold basic convenience store stock: cereal, canned tuna, boxed macaroni. The coolers standing along the back wall are full of pop and juice and bottled coffee. On the front counter, the old black book of products to order has been replaced with a tablet, and there's a shelf behind the counter full of white and blue bubble envelopes and smiling boxes. While Graeme scours the shelves for anything worth eating I lurk around the coolers, reading the labels on the canned iced tea, keeping my back to the store in case anyone else recognizes me.

And then I smell it. What it is I don't know. All I know is that it's calling to me, like a song you forgot you love that you hear from far away. I take a deeper breath and it grabs me, like someone shoved their hand through my chest and is caressing my heart. I follow it, that scent of sugar and sap, that cologne I'm going to buy six gallons of for Graeme because I want to fuck whatever smells like that.

Like I'm sleepwalking, I come around the corner of the potato chip aisle. Another man is there, his head tipped back, his nose in the air. He turns and I realize I know him: Pierce Platter, my best friend growing up and the reason I left town.

The colour draining from his face, he's staring at me like I've risen from the dead. Maybe he thinks I have, because who knows what they told him about the reasons why I left. He was the reason, but not in the way they all think.

I want to speak. I have no words. I want to grab him and kiss him, shove him against the shelf of Cap'n Crunch and shove my tongue in his beautiful mouth because of course he's gorgeous, of course he grew into those lips and those eyelashes, which he's fluttering at me. No, he's trembling, and as I step towards him he bolts for the door.

Like a fool, like a starving dog, I chase him. I burst out the door to see Pierce ducking down the grassy alley between Sutherland's and the building next door. I run after him, because after all these years I owe him an explanation.

"Pierce," I call after him. "Pierce, stop and talk to me. Let me explain."

"I don't want to hear it."

"I didn't mean to hurt you."

"Then why the fuck did you leave?" he shouts as he turns on his heel and with both hands shoves me away from him. I hit the other wall with a heavy thud. Panting, we stare at each other. He's so much like his old self but totally new, the sweet face of his boyhood sharpened, hardened.

"It wasn't about you," I say when I can breathe.

"How was I supposed to know that?" he shoots back. "Do you know how I felt when you left? Like a piece of trash. Like the thought of ending up with me was so gross, so totally impossible that you had to run away. Like all those years we'd been friends, you'd just been putting up with me."

I start to explain, how my parents sprung my fate on me an hour before Pierce was due back from the airport, but he's too angry to hear me, his face red, his eyes full of fire. "I'll bet that model guy's your boyfriend, isn't he?"

"Husband."

He goes still, then looks at my ring. "You asshole!"

"Come on, Pierce, you know what it was like, growing up out here in the middle of nowhere," I say as he turns his back on me and carries on down the alley. "No clubs or bars, not even a mall. Nowhere to go where everyone didn't know everything about you. And then to be told before I was even an adult that they had my whole future mapped out, down to the last detail. Our parents set us up, Pierce. Our parents thought about us fucking. Didn't that ever bug you?"

I'm shouting now because he's so far away, but this makes him come storming back to me. "Why do you think I left?" he hisses. "So I could have a life of my own before everyone else's plans kicked in."

"You could have told me," I say, hearing the whining words in my sixteen-year-old self's pitchy voice. "Instead you left me on my own when I needed you. I hated you for leaving."

"So you understand how I felt when I came back and you were gone."

He had me there, and all the reasons that seemed so sure, every explanation I crafted for betraying my friend fall apart in my mouth. "I couldn't let them control me," I say weakly.

"We could have been amazing," he says, a sad smile distorting his lips. "You and me. We could have left Hollowood together."

"Did you stay? Please tell me you didn't. Not all these years. Pierce, tell me you didn't wait for me."

His smile twists, and my heart twists with it. "What was I meant to do?" he says in the same hurt tone.

"The same thing I did. Leave. Find someone who meant something to you." I cover my mouth as the cruelty of that strikes me, though not as hard as it hits him. "Sorry. I don't mean that you didn't—"

"Fuck you, Evan Culver," he snarls. "You know, I can't wait for you to leave town again. So you and that pretty little husband of yours can go back to your perfect fucking life, and I can go back to hating your guts."

"Pierce, wait," I say as he shoves past me and returns up the alley. "Will you please talk to me?" Without looking back he flashes his middle finger and keeps walking. That would be a *no*.

After a minute (or two or three, which I totally don't spend crying then wiping my eyes on my sleeve) I make my way to the front of the store, where Graeme is standing eating a Clif bar.

"What happened to you?" he asks around a mouthful.

"Saw someone I knew."

"Friend or enemy? Or frenemy?" he adds when I don't answer.

"Friend. Ex-friend, I guess. He didn't take it so well when I left town."

"I wondered, the way you went bolting out of the shop."

"Sorry. I wasn't thinking. I was just..."

"Going on instinct?"

"I guess."

"Is this a…you know," and Graeme holds up two fingers on either side of his head and twitches them like a dog's ears. "That sort of thing?"

"If you mean werewolf," I mutter as we start walking, "probably, but please don't ever do that again."

"Fine," he replies way too cheerfully. "You're the expert here."

"I'm not, though. I took off when I was seventeen."

"So it's been a few years. No stress. I expect it's like riding a bike, you never really forget."

I should laugh. Graeme's funny as hell and I need to laugh but my guts feel like they're going to turn inside out if I so much as open my mouth, so I settle for a smile. At least he's still here.

Seven

Waiting

When we get back to the Dew Drop three kids are out front playing mini-golf on the crumbling 9-hole course. I say kids, but when you're coming up on thirty that's what people in their early twenties start to look like. One of them waves to me and I recognize my cousin Sunny. Graeme follows a pace behind as we meet at the fence around the course.

"Good to see you, Ev," she says, grinning. She's had some orthodontic work done or maybe just her head caught up to her two front teeth.

"Hey, Sunny." I reach out to ruffle her short blonde hair and she ducks away with a laugh. She's got to be twenty-one now, not that little tomboy who used to follow me around town but a grown woman with a scar on her chin and a barbed-wire armband tattoo. Her other bicep is bandaged with a roll of gauze. "Get some new ink?" I ask.

"Accident. No big deal."

"Yeah, you should have seen the other guy," her brother Ash calls from the fourth tee. Sunny flashes him a dirty look and he blushes then goes back to his ball. He fans on it, sending it trickling down the slope instead of ricocheting off the little log cabin, the only way to nail the fourth hole in less than three shots.

Before I can remember, Graeme does his Graeme thing and introduces himself. "Sunny, did he say?" he asks her as they shake hands over the fence. "A pleasure to meet you. Name's Graeme."

"Are you like his boyfriend?" Sunny asks, her eyes lighting up.

"Husband, actually."

"Oh, that's so cool!" she squeals. "Omigod, I'm so happy for you! Omigod, Ev, why didn't you tell me?"

"How was I going to tell you?"

"I do still look at my email sometimes. Or you could, I dunno, text me like a normal person? Ash, River, get over here and meet your cousin-in-law."

And then it's like when we were kids, as they swarm around me and Graeme, asking questions all at once and not waiting for answers. River was maybe eight when I left town. Now they're a pimply teen with a hoodie and a home-done tattoo of a star on their wrist. Ash was always tall but he's bulked up, his one-armed hug crushing my lungs.

His other arm is in a light sling. River has a limp though they're trying not to let on. They've all been injured but something tells me not to ask. For all I know it was them last night messing around. Not a fight but just kids being dumb after dark. They didn't need to know that their cool older cousin had been so freaked out he locked himself in the bathroom.

"Sucks about Granny," Ash says in his big booming man voice. "But I'm glad you made it."

"Wouldn't have missed it for the world."

Graeme has the grace not to laugh or even look my way while Sunny explains to him the meaning behind her thigh tattoo. About five minutes into the drive yesterday, I nearly got out of the car at a stop light and walked home. We then had what Graeme would call a 'proper row' that left us both feeling pummelled, but the prick was right and so I gave in and here we were.

"You sticking around for the party?" Ash says. "I mean, wake. I guess it's not supposed to be a party if someone, you know…"

"We'll be there."

"Awesome. Me and Sunny made snickerdoodles."

"You made cookies?" The last thing I remember this kid making was snowballs with dog-shit in the middle to drop off the overpass onto the sunroofs of passing cars.

"I make great cookies, dude," Ash replies with a friendly punch to my shoulder that stings like I walked into a wall. "Hey, I'll bring you some special cookies tonight at your hotel. You know, to share with your dude. You know, special cookies?" he says with an obvious wink before turning serious. "You know weed's legal here, right?"

"Yeah, I read the news, Ash."

"Cool, cool, he says, shoving his hands in his pockets. "Well, I guess we'll see you in a bit."

"It starts at eleven, right?"

They climb all over us again then jump on their bikes and ride off, waving. They've left the golf stuff laying on the green so we go to pick it up.

"Want to finish their round?" Graeme asks as I pick up Ash's ball.

"Nope. I want you to take me back to the room and take me to fucking pieces."

He looks around then glances at his watch. "Did you say it starts at eleven?"

"We'll make it work."

You know how you believe things about yourself that turn out to not be true? Maybe you enjoy olives after all, or you really do like rom coms but were always ashamed to admit it. I never thought I was a size queen but then I met Graeme.

It shouldn't matter, just like him being so ridiculously good looking. It shouldn't matter, and it doesn't really, I was into him long before we fucked. It doesn't matter, but his cock still fascinates me. It's not even envy. Just lust. And maybe a bit of masochism because to take him is always a test of my limits.

But I want it. Want him to take me to pieces then fuck the pieces. I settle for him stripping me and shoving me down and fingering my ass until he has me sobbing into the pillow. He asks if I'm ready and I don't know if I am but I nod because I need him to fuck me right now, before all these contrary pressures crush me. Only this pressure matters in the moment, as he gets me on my knees and starts to rock the fat head of his cock against my stimulated ass.

"Come on, sweetie," he coos, bumping his hips forward. "Open for me. Open that lovely arsehole for your man." He could say anything, it's the accent undoes me, the way he gets all husky when we're in bed. "Yes...yes, sweetheart, let me have it..."

He groans as I push out then let my muscles draw him in. I can barely breathe, from the shock and the aching stretch, from the overwhelming sense of being possessed. Being his, and that's what matters most, that it's him behind me, his cock splitting me open, his hands gripping my hips, his voice praising me, coaxing me to take a little more, a little more.

I'm whispering *please, please*, but I don't know what I want, if I want more of this or less, if I want him to blow his load fast, or fuck me until the heat death of the universe. Probably the second one, because now that he's all the way in me I'm good, so good.

"Fuck, you feel divine, baby," Graeme sighs, rolling his hips and stretching me in every direction. "I wish we weren't in a hurry, I want to make you fucking sing."

I come pretty close, not shouting exactly but making some wordless, senseless noise as he pounds into me, his cock hitting so deep I feel it all the way up my spine. It's all I can do to stay on my knees, stay open, give myself up to it, let him take me to pieces.

With a savage groan he grabs my waist and rides me even harder. I'm going to shatter, going to die, his cock too much, too thick, too hard. It's everything I wanted as he comes with a wild cry, bucking into me fiercely as he fills my aching ass with his cream.

I fall forward with him still inside me. After a few seconds he peels himself off and stretches beside me. I roll onto my back, needing his kiss, not expecting him to slide down the bed and take my cock in his mouth. I'm too wrecked to argue, to ask or encourage, and again take what he gives me, let him suck me until I'm as hard as I've ever been. Then he takes me beyond...

When the room stops spinning he's lying beside me again, propped up on his elbow to look at me, a silly little smile on his pinkened lips.

"Wha' so funny?"

"I was thinking," he says, tracing a finger around my nearest nipple. "I hope there's something for me to eat at this thing."

"You mean other than me?"

With a laugh he pinches my nipple, making my whole body lurch off the mattress. "I'll save the rest of you for dessert."

Eight

The Culvers

At 10:54 I'm still shaving. Graeme's hollering at me to hurry up, which is all good for his silky skin but if I go too fast I'm going to show up to Granny's funeral covered in blood.

At 11:02 we get to the Lodge. Graeme insisted on driving so we didn't sweat, and it takes us at least five minutes to find a spot because the small lot is full to capacity. At the end of the row, a hoodie-wearing friend of River's is listlessly waving a glow stick and Graeme heads that way. We end up parked between a blacked-out Suburban that looks bulletproof and a rusting pick-up with a payload of actual dirt, the hulking pair making Graeme's bright blue Volkswagen look like a toy.

We are definitely not late. There's still a good twenty people milling around outside with more gathered at the doors. Located at the top end of Main, the Lodge is visible as soon as you come around the bend, watching over the town from under its deep eaves. It's both the biggest building in town and its most recognized symbol, displayed on ashtrays and shot glasses and other tourist junk in Sutherland's and the state park gift shop down the road, usually comped with the Falls and the peak of Ragged Mountain, which you can just see from the top of the ridge.

Nearly everything important in town happens here, from dances and weddings to elections and, well, funerals. My great-great-grandfather (I think) helped to build it, as did members of every old Hollowood family.

Graeme's right, we are hillbillies, the family lines so tangled it's amazing we don't all have six toes.

We're hanging back waiting for the crowd to thin when I hear my name. "Hope you're ready," I say to Graeme. "Because here comes my dad."

I've only seen my folks a few times since I left. It's been five years since the last time, at that weird Olive Garden that time forgot, where the stucco walls looked like blocks of parmesan and everything smelled like wet laundry. I didn't tell them about Graeme that day. I was still holding part of myself back from him, even though at the time I'd been seeing him for almost two years and was secretly shopping for rings, and it all seemed too fragile to bring into the open. I'd left because of who they wanted me to marry. I didn't need them complicating my feelings about the man *I* wanted to marry.

From a distance my dad doesn't look like he's aged. He's always been fair so the grey hairs blend in. Only when he gets up close do I see the deeper wrinkles, the loose skin under his chin. Otherwise we look like brothers, a resemblance that hasn't faded as Graeme stares back and forth between us.

"Evan. Glad you could make it," Dad says, giving me one of those two-handed salesman handshakes.

"Happy to be here. Well, not really. Because Granny...Dad, this is Graeme Knight. My husband."

He's going to be my widower in a minute, my heart rattling in my chest as I stand back for Dad to give Graeme the same meaty handshake.

"It's a pleasure to meet you at last, Mr Culver," Graeme says with a steady smile. "And may I offer my deepest condolences."

"Call me Leif," Dad says, flashing me a look. I'm meant to do that bit, say his name, but ten seconds in his presence and I might as well be seventeen again, or seven, surly and tongue-tied, missing my cues. "And to be fair," he goes on, "she wasn't my mother."

"You called her Granny," Graeme says to me.

"She was kind of everyone's granny," I explain.

"Her family's lived in Hollowood since it was founded," my father continues, because what I said clearly wasn't good enough. "She left town when she married but came back after she lost her husband."

"It's a very pretty place," Graeme says cheerfully. "A nice place to retire, I expect."

"A great place to live. If you can make it work." Unlike me, he meant, who pretended that I belonged somewhere else.

"Well, I'm doing really well," I say, cringing inside at my crappy vocabulary. "We have a really nice house, and really great neighbours. I'm really happy." *May lightning strike me down...*

"That's good to hear," he says evenly. "Maybe next time don't wait so long to let me know."

I hate this town. I don't hate my dad because he's my dad and it's not his fault because he's practically a boomer but it's moments like this that remind me why I left. Before I can think of something witty but not hugely offensive, I hear Pierce Platter's laugh.

"Haven't you seen Pierce yet?" my dad asks as I shudder.

"Yeah, I saw him, but I don't think he wants to see—"

"Pierce!" my dad shouts, waving across the crowd. When Leif Culver shouts everyone hears it, so twenty people watch as my fated (ugh, try hated) mate escorts my mother towards us.

By the time I hug my mom and let her fix my clothes (which were fine but it makes her happy) Pierce has got my dad in conversation off to one side. The first decent thing he's done since I got here, not making me make small talk with him when I don't know how I even feel. Having him this near, smelling him with each and every breath, is doing stupid things to my brain, blotting out my other senses so I totally miss my mother meeting my husband for the first time.

No harm done, the two of them laughing together like old friends. With a happy sigh my mother turns to me. Like my dad, she's showing her age in the depth of the creases in her cheeks when she smiles, the white strands easy to see in the dark hair I inherited.

"Where's Chase?" she says.

"Why are you asking me?"

Her smile slips. "He said he was coming with you. That he was meeting you at the Dew Drop. Though I didn't really get why he would go all the way down there just to come back up," she ended with a little frown.

"Um, maybe because he lied to you?" How many times? How many more times did he have to betray them before they understood he was never going to stop?

"Oh Chase," she says, her shoulders sagging. "Today?"

"I'll find him."

"Okay, but hurry," my mother says, gripping my wrist. "The service starts in about twenty minutes."

Fuck. "Well, now I'm going to find him and kill him."

"Honey," she says in that voice only moms have. "Don't kill your little brother."

"Can I at least, I don't know, injure him?"

"Just find him," she says, squeezing my hand, and I can feel the shake in hers. Every time we lose Chase could be the last time.

"Are you okay with this?" I say to Graeme.

"Of course. Just go."

I kiss him on the cheek then I'm gone. I know where Chase is. That lying little prick, always on the run, always fucking off when the going gets tough. Running back to Granny's with his actual tail between his legs because he lost a guy, lost a fight, lost his shit.

At this end of town the street slopes up hard, and I'm sweating by the time I reach the old graveyard, closed around the time I was born when they ran out of flat ground. The tiny Methodist church is even older than the graveyard but it's a ruin and has been for longer than anyone remembers. When we were kids we used to dare each other to go in and run the length of the chapel to touch the back wall. The roof has fallen in since, splintered beams clogging the doorway, the back wall half toppled. Chase will be in the woods behind, and I only have to go a dozen yards past the graveyard before I find the pile of his clothes. So much for talking it out. Fine, if he wanted to do this the hard way.

Stepping behind a tree, I ditch my clothes, folding them as neatly as I can and stacking them on top of Chase's messy heap. This is too nice a suit to get forest crap all over it. Feeling self-conscious as ever, only half convinced that it's going to work, I close my eyes, quiet my mind, and...

It's like falling without ever hoping to land, a full body feeling that borders on terrifying. Like the ache after a brutal gym session, like the sting of my ass after Graeme's drilled me hard except everywhere all at once, my skin prickling as the hairs thicken, lengthen, my bones and ligaments stretching, bending, swelling until I drop to all fours.

Though I've told myself a thousand times that I hate it, it feels like coming home.

Nine

The Funeral

With Chase's scent in my nose, I trot into the forest. It really is like coming home. Growing up, we spent more time in the woods than in town. The town was the same, day after day, but there was always something new to see in the forest. A rockfall that revealed a cave, or formed one. A fallen tree, its huge pan of upended roots like a mass of fleshy snakes. Winter brought its own changes, with the evergreens protecting the ground from all but the heaviest snowfalls.

Our powers (or is it our curse?) awake with puberty, and I've only been in the forest a few times in this form and that was years ago. Now the deluge of scents and sounds floods my heightened senses. I can hear not just the creak of branches and the wind that drives them, the flitter of birds and small creatures, but the sounds of the funeral a mile down the valley: the hubbub of voices, the squeak of rubber chair feet over pine floorboards. Sharper sounds reach me from farther away: the slam of a screen door, even the buzz of Denver-bound airplanes high overhead. Nearer, the skitter of animals as they dart into their burrows or freeze under the leaf litter, fearing my jaws.

A crow sweeps past and lands on the stump of a broken-off tree branch just ahead. I've been told these crows are only found in this watershed. You can tell them from other types of crow not just by their little white cap but by the prominent yellow rings around their eyes. Some old folks call them 'pastor birds' and it's not hard to picture them as a country preacher with a bald head and gold-rimmed glasses. Trust Hollowood to have its own crows, to add that extra spooky touch to a town whose lycan population outnumbers the humans.

The crow is looking straight at me. Okay, as much as a bird can, the way their eyes are positioned. It caws then flies another ten yards down the path. Like it wants me to follow it. I'm already going that way, but when I reach the tree it flies off again, this time a little to my right. One sniff tells me the bird knows what I'm hunting as I catch a stronger trace of Chase's scent of wet leaves and powdered milk.

I find him curled up under the hollowed out log of a fallen tree. A giant in its time, its hollow could fit a small couch. Or one asshole werewolf, who raises his head as I lope into the clearing. He meets me in the middle and we touch noses.

What the fuck, dude?

My brother sits on his haunches, whining like a puppy. Shit, he's really making me work for it. I lay my paw over his.

This isn't helping anyone. Least of all you.

What am I going to do now, Ev?

How about think about someone besides yourself for a change?

Don't start. Not now. She's not even in the ground, Ev. The thoughts we share, they're not like words. More like pictures, and in this picture Chase's chest has been torn open and his heart is gone.

I'm sorry.

Fuck you.

He pulls away from me, trots to the edge of the clearing, throws back his head and howls. It's devastating, the saddest sound I've ever heard, full of loss beyond words, the mortal ache of a severed kinship. I can't help but join him, let him know he isn't alone in his hurt. Bad idea, as he breaks off and he lunges at me with a snarl. I spring to one side and he crashes into the undergrowth. He rolls to his feet then takes off through the trees, heading further up the mountain.

Fuck him. I did my best. I don't need my face bitten off. If he can't deal with having feelings, that's his problem, even if he is family. I've hauled his ass out of the fire so many times, you'd think I'd have learned not to bother.

I run back to where I left my clothes. Shifting takes effort, mental and physical, and I'm light-headed by the time I get back to the Lodge. They're playing sad organ music in the main hall and I sneak in just as Uncle Trace takes the podium.

My mom glances back from a row one from the front. I look around and see Graeme two rows from the back. He notices me and points to the empty seat beside him, the only one I can see. I give my mom a quick wave then slink to the seat by Graeme.

"Is everything alright?" he whispers as I fan myself with the program. "Where's your brother?"

"Off being an asshole. Forget about him."

Trace is fucking around with the mic. As the organist starts another hymn Graeme leans near again. "That was him, wasn't it, that your mother was with. The man you were meant to marry."

I nod, my tongue glued to the roof of my mouth, my stomach a lake of acid. Not even twenty four hours in Hollowood and my whole life is going off the rails.

"Not bad looking," Graeme mutters as he settles in his seat. "Bit of a ponce, I'll expect."

"A what?" I don't always understand his slang.

"An entitled little shit."

"Oh. Yeah. Nailed it."

The funeral is a funeral, with a closed casket, a memory board, a parade of eulogists who had known Granny better than I ever did. Chase should be here, should be speaking, should be thanking the ground that woman walked on, for all she did for him. Though I want to keep looking over my shoulder to see if he's maybe standing by the doors, if he scraped together enough guts to at least be present, I push him out of my mind and concentrate on the feeling of Graeme's hand in mine. We have a second night booked at the Dew Drop but I'm determined to leave town tonight, even if I have to drive the whole way myself.

As soon as the service ends, I'm on my feet, dragging Graeme towards the doors. The crowd bottlenecks, and I'm about to suggest we sneak out the side door when my dad catches my other elbow.

"I'm talking to you, Evan," he says with that half frown he wears when he's testing me.

"Sorry I didn't hear you. There's a lot going on."

"I thought you went to find Chase."

"I did. He ran off again."

"Why didn't you go after him?"

"What was I supposed to do, knock him out and drag him here? There was nothing I could do."

"You're his older brother."

"And you're his father!" I'm getting shrill and people are looking but I don't care what anyone in Hollowood thinks of me. They already think I'm a joke. A coward. Half a man, because I ran away. "Chase isn't a little boy, he's a grown up. Don't make him my responsibility. And you know what, he isn't yours either. You should let him fail now and then so he can find out what he's made of."

If I stay I'll say worse so I walk away, not outside where everyone is but downstairs to the toilets. Graeme catches up as I'm splashing water on my face. He says nothing, lingering near the door with his hands in his pockets. Waiting for me, like he always does, because he's perfect and doesn't deserve this shit.

"I'm sorry," I say to his reflection.

"Don't be. I'm sure you did all you could."

"I didn't mean to yell."

"I'm not surprised. Your father hasn't spoken a nice word to you yet."

"He had a point."

"No, he didn't," he says with a bitter laugh. "I've got brothers. They're fucking useless. Somehow it was always on me to sort things out. Why do you think I emigrated?"

Ten

Pierce

When Graeme and I get upstairs the hall has been switched from an auditorium to a dining room. There isn't a lot of decorations, not even flowers, because Granny had asked for donations to the Sierra Club in lieu. Like every event here the meal is pot luck, the dishes set out on a long table to one side. A few early birds are already picking over the spread of picnic classics: mac and cheese, fried chicken, meatballs, chili. Every salad has mayo or cheese or bacon or chicken, every dip is sour cream.

"Fucking hell," Graeme mutters as we stroll past the table. "They don't even have fucking hummus. Sorry, I shouldn't swear, it's your nan's funeral and all."

"Swear all you like. This whole thing is fucking brutal."

We skirt the growing crowd and slip outside where we sit on the bottom steps. The town's so pretty when you see it from here, the afternoon light gleaming like gold off the roofs of the houses nestled among the trees, the lower valley hazy with distance, the air sweet with sap and the absence of exhaust fumes. A feast for the eyes but no help to Graeme, who leans forward on his elbows and covers his face, pressing his fingertips against the pressure points over his eyebrows.

"I've never wanted a fucking faro bowl so badly in all my puff," he moans from behind his hands.

"We'll be out of here soon."

"Every fucking salad had something in it."

"Country life, man."

"Yeah, but with all this other business," he says, sitting up to gesture at the houses and few shops that dot the valley, most with solar or wind units on the roof or in the yard. "The PVs and the thing about banning plastic and all, you'd think the place would be crawling with vegans. Instead it's like when I was growing up."

"Have you ever eaten meat?"

He shrugs uncomfortably, making a sour face. "Fish was alright. Anything else it was only ever to keep from getting smacked. But that only worked for so long. The school decided it was easier to figure out how to serve me a dinner I'd eat than to have me vomit chicken nuggets on the headmaster's shoes while he's trying to cane me."

"Jesus."

"That's what he said."

There's a burst of noise as the doors swing open and someone comes out onto the broad deck that circles the lodge. A couple someones who go around to the side of the building to carry on with their argument.

"I said, I don't care what you want. He's an asshole." Pierce, damn it, following me around like a bad smell.

"You don't know that," says his mother. "What if he's changed?"

"What if he hasn't? You still want your only son to pledge himself body and soul for all eternity to an asshole?"

"It's not about what I want or you want, Pierce," says Mr. Platter. "This this is bigger than all of us."

Graeme goes to stand up and reveal us but I grab his leg, shake my head. Maybe this is eavesdropping but I need to know what Pierce says next, need to know if we're on the same side or if he's buying into the myth like everyone else.

"It's a crock of shit," he says with even more venom than usual. "Some made-up archaic bullshit. Why'd you even wait if you knew I was meant to be with him? Could have got us hitched at fourteen, isn't that legal limit in this state if both families sign off?"

"You're making too big a deal of this," his father says.

"Oh sorry, I'll just let you, my parents, decide how I, a grown adult, spend the rest of my life."

"I told you, this isn't up to us."

"It never is, is it? It's always about Hollowood. Well, fuck your laws and fuck the alliance and fuck this backwater shithole."

No one speaks for several agonizing seconds. Then two pairs of feet cross the hollow planks of the deck. "You'll be here for Thanksgiving, right?" his mother asks as the door creaks open.

"Of course I'm coming to Thanksgiving," he answers in the same angry hiss.

As the door swings shut Pierce kicks the nearest deck post, sending a shiver through the stairs. We look up and he's standing at the top of the stairs.

"I'll bet you heard every word," he says to me. "Well I don't give a shit. I'm sick of this town and its bullshit mythology and if they think I'm giving up everything I've worked for to marry you of all people…" He honest to God rolls his eyes and I come really close to jumping up and grabbing him by the throat and choking some manners into him. "No offense, but I can do better."

"Fuck your *no offense*," I say as he stomps down the stairs. "You haven't changed a bit, have you?"

"Why would I?" he shoots back, one hand on his hip. "I'm happy with who I am. You probably are too. I mean, your guy looks like he has his shit together."

"I like to think I do," Graeme says, straightening his shirt cuffs.

"So then why would you quit him," Pierce asks me, "to hook up with someone like me?"

Not what I thought he'd say. "Why, what's wrong with you?" I ask.

"Let's see. My family's straight out of a holiday movie, my career just got erased, and once a month an ancient curse turns me into a monster straight out of some other kind of movie. How do you manage it? How does he?" He gestures at Graeme, whose lethal expression should tell him to shut up.

"Excuse the fuck me," he says crisply. "I can hear all the words you're saying about me so why not try saying them *to* me?"

"Fine," Pierce says. "How do you deal?"

"Spa night."

"What do you mean, spa night?"

"It's the bedrock of our marriage," Graeme says as if that's an explanation.

"It is?" I say. "Not love, or trust, or...really? Spa night?"

"Without it I would have found out about this a lot sooner, no?"

"What the hell is spa night?" Pierce says.

"God, you're basic," Graeme replies with a toss of his head. "Once a month or thereabouts, I take a night off from everything and everyone. Go to a hotel by myself, binge Gilmore Girls, and eat vegan ice cream until I want to puke. Sometimes I make a little video for Ev."

"Video?"

"Forget the video," I say quickly as my face gets hot. "The point is that he's out of the house for a night."

"And so what do you do?" Pierce asks me.

"I lock myself in the basement and ride it out."

"And he's never...he's like..." Pointing back and forth between us, Pierce frowns harder. "And you've never figured it out?"

"If I have to work the next day I go straight from the hotel," Graeme replies with a shrug. "The times I've come home in the morning, I'm usually so relaxed I wouldn't notice if the house caught fire."

"How long have you been together?"

"Six years, married for two."

Pierce cocks his head. The way he used to when we were kids, right before saying something that was likely to get him—and me—in huge trouble. "So are you dumb," he says to my husband, "or were you just ignoring the evidence?"

"I beg your fucking pardon?" I know this sign too, when Graeme's fists clench and he arches his neck and whoever he's talking to better start apologizing straight away. Pierce doesn't notice or maybe doesn't care as he looks down his sleek nose at us.

"I should have told you," he drawls. "I have this thing where I'm awful. To everyone. All the time."

"Ugh, why bother?" Graeme says, his fierce tension dying away.

"Are you serious?"

"It's because he can get away with it," I say, tired of the back and forth, of watching Graeme fall for his game. "Seriously, Pierce, you don't give a shit about anyone. You never have. You do what you like, and you use your pretty face and your name and your sense of entitlement to sweet-talk your way out of taking responsibility for your actions. It's a good thing you're not going along with all this fated mate bullshit because I don't want you anywhere near me."

"Good. Same."

"Good. Have a nice life."

He's staring at me, and though I know I should look away, break the connection, there's something magnetic about him, the lift of his proud chin, the wildness hidden in his eyes. The sounds of the party have died down and suddenly all I can hear is the wind whipping through the pines and the knock of my heart against my ribs. He takes a deep breath and turns and starts walking away and something in me screams out for me to stop him, to catch him in my arms and...

I put my head between my hands and squeeze. Graeme slides closer and puts his arm around me and I lean into him, wanting that feeling of safety he always brings me. A feeling that won't come.

"Let's go back to the hotel, love. We've done damage enough here."

Eleven

Missing

I don't remember walking back to the Dew Drop. When we get there I lie down and immediately fall asleep. I wake with a start but not much time has passed, the sky still bright. Graeme's sitting against the headboard flicking through his phone with a surly expression.

"Can we go home now?" I croak.

"I'd say yes if I thought you could drive." He grunts in disgust, sticks his tongue out at his phone and sets it aside. "The signal's shite out here."

"What were you looking up?" I ask as I haul myself upright.

"How far it is to the nearest salad bar."

I slide closer and rest my head on his shoulder. "Sorry. I really thought things might have progressed."

"Never mind," he sighs, butting his head against mine. "We did our duty. One more night and we can put it behind us."

"You haven't eaten since we got here. There was peanut butter at Sutherland's, I can at least make you a sandwich so you don't pass out."

"And maybe another Clif bar. And an Odwalla. Anything but the green one."

"What's wrong with the green one?" He looks at me like I'm basic and I jump up and start for the door. "I'll just go."

Graeme's right not to want to drive home tonight, for the sun is setting and it's a good six hours drive along some really bad roads. The lodge is shining at the top of town like a star on a Christmas tree, the sound of music drifting from its open doors. At least with everyone at the party (wake, whatever) no one's around to try talking to me.

Or so I think but as I'm about to go into Sutherland's someone says my name. Chase, human again and lurking in the alley. He's barefoot and shirtless, his jeans rolled at the waist and cuffs. Like he lost his own clothes and stole someone else's jeans off a wash-line. Again.

"Why aren't you at the party?" the dick has the audacity to ask as I join him in the shadows. Instead of punching him through the wall, I count to three. Twice.

"I'd seen everyone I wanted to see," I answer, keeping my voice light when I want to snarl.

"How's Pierce?"

"You know what, go to hell, you—"

"Sorry, sorry. I wondered if he'd still be mad at you."

"I'm sure you've done nothing to fix that."

"What, haven't sold him on the idea of my big brother who fucked off from town ten years ago and never came back? Remind me again of why you don't suck."

I take two big steps back, because the next thing he says is going to break my self-control. "What do you want?" I grate through my teeth.

"I need your help."

"You picked a funny way to ask."

"Sorry, but I'm still kinda pissed at you too. I love you, so it's sucked not to see you."

Shit. The asshole does this all the time, make you feel bad for making him feel bad and though I still want to wring his neck, I hug him. He's my little brother and I'm not even sure it's his fault that he's such a mess. I was a mess before Graeme. I still am sometimes, and every neurospicy thing in me got magnified in Chase.

"I love you too," I mumble, the words catching in my throat. "But if you skip out on Mom or Dad's funeral I will end you." He laughs, even though I'm dead serious.

"Can we talk?" he asks when we get our shit together.

"What's on your mind?"

"I mean, really talk?" he says, more urgently. "Like top secret?"

"You can come back to the hotel and—"

"No, that's too obvious." He glances up and down the alley. "Plus I don't want anything to happen to your guy."

"What's wrong, Chase?"

"I don't know, but there's some really weird shit going on over the ridge."

"Are you kidding me?" He's always been obsessed with the land on the back of the ridge. It belongs to some insanely rich guy who bought up as much land as he could so he could hide away there when the 99% show up at his Manhattan condo with pitchforks. No one lives there, no one goes there, except for Chase, illegally.

"This time it's for real," he says in a tense whisper. "I swear to God, Evan, there's something fucked up going on over there."

"Whatever. Go tell someone who cares."

"You ought to care."

"Don't tell me how to feel. You should have been there today."

"I couldn't."

"You fucking coward. Were you scared someone was going to see you cry?"

"I couldn't do it, Ev." His face is screwed up with emotion and part of me wants to forgive him, but the part that had to strip naked in the woods and run after his dumb ass still wants to punch him. I settle for being horrible. "You need to get over yourself, Chase. You're not proving anything by running away."

"I can't believe you said that. You of all people."

"This is different."

"No, it isn't and forget about that. Listen to me, I think Granny was murdered."

"You're out of your mind."

"No one will believe me but it's true. She was poisoned."

"She died of kidney failure."

"I used to go with her to Denver to her doctor and he never said nothing about her kidneys. Evan, she was poisoned." He starts explaining and at first I'm too angry to tell him to shut him. And then I'm terrified.

"I'm meant to get the well water samples back next week," he says at the end. "But then what?"

"Duh, go to the cops?"

"And say what, let's dig up my Granny who we just buried and who's not even my blood relative?"

"Why haven't you told anyone?"

"I have. I've told them and told them. Mom, Dad, Uncle Trace, the coroner's office. But I'm a waster so they just think I'm high."

"Are you?"

He steps back, and the last rays of sunset beaming along the alley catch his face and paint it blood red. "Unbelievable," he says in a heavy voice that drives home the fact that he's not some kid but a man in his twenties. "Fucking unbelievable. I come to you for help and you..." He breaks off, shaking his head.

"I'm sorry. I shouldn't have said that."

"Forget it. I'll figure it out myself."

"Chase—"

But he's already running, away from me and into the darkness. I hear the shredding of fabric as he shifts without taking off the jeans. By the time I get there he's gone.

I barely remember to buy the peanut butter and bread but when I get back to the motel Graeme's asleep. But nothing can happen if we don't leave the room. Not wanting to wake him, I tiptoe around as I get ready for bed. I don't expect to sleep with all I have on my mind, but the long day has caught up and I'm out before I know it.

I wake to the sound of gunfire. No, it's someone hammering on the door. Graeme rouses first and peek out the eyehole. "Just a minute," he calls and the hammering stops. "It's your mate, Pierce," he says to me.

"He's not my mate," I mumble as I force myself upright.

"I meant frenemy," Graeme says. He must have woken up at some point and undressed because he's only in his boxers, and we fumble to put on the bare minimum of clothing.

I'm about to open the door when I hesitate. "Did he look drunk?" I ask.

"He looked terrified."

"Shit." Graeme goes into the bathroom and I let Pierce in. He's white as a ghost, rubbing his arms and looking around like someone's about to jump him.

"What's up?"

"Have you seen your brother."

"Earlier. Why?"

"He's missing."

"What else is new?"

"No, I mean he was meant to stop in at my place and I haven't seen him."

"Again, this is not news. I don't trust that shithead to show up any-where on time."

"You don't understand."

"I understand perfectly. You're fooling around with my little brother because I'm not here to keep you entertained—"

"Jesus, stop being such a fucking narcissist, Evan. This isn't about you."

I'm so shocked it's like he's punched me in the chest. "Did you just call me a narcissist? You? You stuck-up entitled ponce—"

Twelve

Uphill

Graeme won't stay in the motel alone. "Not after last night. Scared the daylights out of me, all that howling and carrying on. Can I not call on your parents?" Pierce says no at the same time I say yes and Graeme rolls his eyes.

"I wasn't talking to you," he says sharply. Pierce blushes, and my brain skips a beat because Pierce Platter just took a hit. Nothing critical but you normally can't shut him up.

"But if you go over there," Pierce says, "they're going to know something's up. They'll know he's missing."

"As far as they know, he's been missing since the funeral," I tell him. "They might be glad to know someone gives a damn."

The three of us walk up to my folks' place, on a side road halfway up the hill along with a few other houses. Pierce is a few steps ahead of us and Graeme takes my hand.

"Don't lose time coming in," he says. "I'll explain everything to them."

"Do you understand everything?"

"Do you?" he says with a half-smile. "Ev, your brother is missing. You and a friend of the family are trying to find him. That's enough explanation."

"You're right. You're so smart."

"Just be careful."

"Shut up and listen," he hisses, and the fact that he's not yelling makes me pause. "I think your brother's in real trouble. He was going to go over the ridge tonight—"

I mostly understand Graeme's slang. I understand the swear words perfectly and I let loose with a string of blasphemy that makes Pierce's mouth fall open and makes Graeme start applauding from the bathroom. "...fuck-witted gobshite arsehole, I will tear his fucking throat out!"

"Woah," Pierce says. "Take it easy."

"Fuck easy. I'm sick of his shit. He came to me earlier with some bullshit about weird things over the ridge and Granny being poisoned."

"He told you?"

"Don't tell me you believe him. Do you?"

"There's something fucked up going on over the ridge. To be honest I'm not sure what I believe anymore."

"Either way we gotta go find him, don't we?"

"I think he's in real danger."

I want to say no. I want to tell Pierce to get lost. I want to pack the car and drive home immediately, but it's my little brother. Even though spending all night running around in the forest with Pierce is the last thing in the world I want to do, I will.

My little brother is missing and if anybody hurts him, they're going to have to deal with me.

"I will. I love you so much."

"I love you too."

We've reached my parents' corner, and I stop here to kiss him rather than risk them catching us making out on the front steps. The chalet-style house hasn't changed much from the outside and as I watch him walk up the path I wonder if they've kept my room the way it was when I moved out, with the wallpaper border of mallards in flight that I'd felt super grown-up for choosing out of the sample book at the big box store in Colorado Springs, and whether Graeme will like me less because of it.

The sort of stupid thought you regret forever if it's the last thing you think about someone you love, and I run to catch up with him, hold him close and kiss him once more, so that if this all goes to shit, if I don't come back, he's got something to remember me by.

"Don't want him to see this?" Pierce says as I rejoin him on the sidewalk.

"It's not a pretty sight."

"I think it's cool. Kinda hot."

"You would."

We've agreed that the best place to start was where Chase met me, at Sutherland's, so when we hit the corner we keep on up the hill. "Look, I get that we're not friends like we used to be," Pierce says, "but can we try being nice to each other?"

"I can try."

"What happened, Ev? How'd we go so wrong?"

"Speak for yourself. I have a great life."

"I mean you and me," he says, kicking at pebbles. "Did you mean it, what you said before? Do you really think I don't care about other people?"

"I don't know. I don't really know you anymore, do I?"

"I haven't changed that much. I'm still a smart-ass."

"Do you still hate potatoes?"

"They're creepy murder-roots that taste and feel like sand. Do you still bite your nails?"

"Only in my sleep."

As we slip down the alley Pierce is already unbuttoning his shirt. It's been forever since I've been around him in his other form and I undress with my back to him and a weird guilty feeling in the pit of my stomach, like I'm cheating on Graeme by being here. Luckily it's dark behind the store, and we leave our clothes in two piles on the edge of the landing dock.

"I'd like it if you didn't watch." I say as I back into the shadows.

"No problem," Pierce says with that grin I remember. "The last thing we need is me thinking you're hot."

I haven't eaten since that omelet and the shift leaves me with a heavy head, and I twitch away from Pierce's seeking nose before I realize what it is. We circle each other, imprinting the scent of each other, the way our tails move, the pattern of our footfalls. He lifts his head, and I catch the same thread of scent, the faint trace of leaf-mold and dry milk. With a single low growl Pierce is off and running, and I follow him into the night.

There's never been a time I didn't know Pierce. We were the only two kids born in the valley that year and for a few years after, so I never really had a choice. Whenever he pissed me off, when he got us in trouble or broke something of mine, all I could do was forgive him, because I didn't want to be alone.

This forest too is something I've always known. My playground and my refuge, the trails and slipways branded on the pads of my feet. Pierce is headed towards the ridge that divides our valley from the next. Going over the ridge, trespassing onto the neighboring property, was a kind of heresy when we were young, and if the adults found out you'd done so you paid for it for a long time after. Naturally you couldn't keep Chase away from it, and his scent is all over the trail.

There's a rift in the trail ahead where the rocks below it have fallen away, but we clear the three-yard wide gap without breaking our pace. Pierce runs with his head low, a sleek shadow in the shadows, ducking and weaving through the pale trunks of the aspens like it's broad daylight and this is a game and not the midnight forest and a race against time.

Nothing's happened. Chase is fine. Chase is probably eating carrion somewhere, playing wolf to relieve the pain of playing human. I repeat this again and again as we run, always uphill, not faster than a man but without tiring. The trees are thinning as we approach the summit of the ridge and for a second I think Pierce means to go right over and keep on running. Instead he stops so suddenly I collide with him, and for a tense second it's all snapping teeth and raised hackles, the lycan version of *you wanna start something, bro?* as we get untangled.

With a glare and a last chesty growl he sits to look down the valley. I sit beside him, trying to ignore the heat that blazes up inside me as his scent fills my nose. I follow his gaze with eyes and ears until I pick out what interests him so much.

Two miles away at the heart of the narrow valley is a single-story industrial building about the size of a grocery store. What little light it lets off glows not white but pink. I lean against Pierce's flank.

Is it a grow-op? I ask.

A grow op wouldn't need to be so well hidden.

I don't want to go down there.

Me neither.

Yet something says we must. Something's down there that matters to us, and I'm about to say so when we hear a bark from further up the ridge. A single yip, the sound a wolf makes in lonesome frustration.

I don't reply because I don't want the other valley to hear how many we are. I don't want anything to do with that glowing building now that I know Chase isn't down there, and I take off along the ridge, Pierce close behind.

The swing from frigid winter to the spring thaw can be fast enough to crack rocks in half, and a big section of the ridge ahead has collapsed, boulders the size of houses littering the slope below. Chase's scent is everywhere, not on the ground but in the air, like he's up in the trees, and we hunt around the fall of rocks for a few minutes before Pierce lets out a yip.

Chase goes off, his barking amplified by the walls of the crevice where he's trapped, little better than a gap between two slabs of mountain rock. About ten feet deep and six feet across, it angles nearly straight down, Chase visible at the bottom as a tongue and a pair of panicked yellow eyes. A human could scramble up the jagged walls without more than a few scratches, the rock eroded in bands that have made plenty of foot- and handholds.

Pierce shoves his head against mine. *Why won't he shift and climb up?*

Who knows? He's not usually this stupid.

Is he injured?

Why are you asking me?

Because if we want to ask him one of us has to shift.

Yeah, him.

He pulls away from me and trots around the gap once more. Chase is whining, and though my heart aches for him I'm not giving in. Let my dumb-ass brother spend the night in the dark. Dad can come up in the morning and yell at him until he does what he should have done as soon as he fell. What he should have done was not go screwing around in the forest in the middle of the night, and I can't wait to tell him so.

I look up and Pierce is gone.

Thirteen

Downhill

No, Pierce has shifted, and he's climbing down the crevice, his bare skin starkly pale against the gray stone. I can't do anything to help, can't do anything except pace back and forth at the edge, my ears pricked for the slightest sound that doesn't belong in the forest stretching around us for miles. As Pierce reaches the bottom, Chase growls softly, and I answer with a growl of my own. Both of them are trigger happy, both habitual shit disturbers when they were kids, poking sticks into hornets nests, jumping in the river. So many times, I was the only one standing between my brother and Pierce's fists, when Chase had pushed him too far.

"See? That was nothing," he says to Chase, his voice echoing off the narrow walls. "You're not injured, so what the fuck are you waiting for?"

Easy... I growl again, a warning to them both, but it's lost in Chase's savage snarl.

"You can knock that shit off right now," Pierce shouts. "I can't believe you're making me do this, you little..."

And then there are two wolves in a space that could barely hold one. I can't tell them apart, can't see a thing, only hear the grunts and snarls and snapping teeth as they shove against each other. There's a sharp yelp then the sudden bloom of pale skin as Chase gives up his wolf form.

"Alright, alright! I'm sorry. It's not like I meant for this to—" Pierce snarls again and Chase jumps back, then turns and starts to scramble up the wall. In about thirty seconds he's hauling himself onto the table sized boulder where I wait.

"Wow, that was easy," he says, dusting his hands. His smile drops as he peers down the crevice at Pierce, circling below. "Are you okay? Shit, you guys must have been running around all night. He's probably tired. Can he shift or are we going to have to wait it out? Or do you want to go get someone—"

I snarl and he jumps back in fright, nearly falling off the boulder. I won't, I can't leave Pierce like this. There's something evil in the other valley, something so dangerous we're at risk every minute we spend on the ridge. Pierce feels it too, whining as he sits on his haunches, but there's only one way he'll make it out of that hole.

Watching him climb, naked and exhausted, is like the twist of a blade in my heart. If I'm as tired as I am I can only imagine how he feels. There's stories of lycans dropping dead from shifting too often in too short a time, and every one of them replays in my mind as Pierce climbs, one shaking handhold at a time.

It seems to take hours. It's probably ten minutes, but at last he's in reach of the top, sitting on a chunked out ledge on the far side of the crevice with his back against the rock and his legs dangling in free space. And yet so far away: too far for him to jump, too far for Chase to reach.

"If I was a wolf I could clear this no problem," he says with a tired chuckle.

"You can't shift there," Chase says through his chattering teeth. "You'll fall for sure."

"I can't shift anyway. I'm wrecked." He doesn't have to say it for me to know, I can hear the shake in his voice, sense the cooling of his skin. There has to be a way. A way we can save him.

Though the rock wall behind him stretches higher than he can reach, there's a substantial crack leading from the ledge where he sits. There, two fallen boulders form a vee, a narrow shelf poised above the crevice. He'll have to stand up then hope that crack is wide enough for a foothold, but how can I tell them?

If I shift I'll be in as bad shape as Pierce. If I leave to get help, he'll fall long before we reach him. Or am I seeing what isn't there, a path where there is none? I pick my way over the loose shale littering the edge of the crevice to the break where the shelf of boulders stretches back. Carefully, so carefully, I creep forward on my belly. As I near the lip I see him. He's figured out where I am and is on his feet, edging towards me, pressed flat against the wall of rock, hands extended to either side. Closer, closer, don't look down, don't think about the drop, the pain, the end of something that's only just begun. Closer, one tiny sideways step at a time, his gaze fixed on mine, his hand so close I could lick it.

"There's nowhere else to go," he breathes. "I'm holding on by my fucking toes, man."

He laughs but I can hear the terror in his voice, smell it in the cold sweat rolling down his bare back. I want to reach out and grab him, save him, protect him from death. "I'm going to have to jump," he says. "You can't get any closer can you?"

What do you mean jump? There isn't time, there just isn't and I creep nearer until my head is hanging over the edge. Until I could catch his fingers in my mouth, and I realize what he's about to do as he bends his knees, twists and throws himself across the last distance.

I keep my head down and my feet braced as he flings his arms around my neck. His weight jerks me forward a few terrifying inches, but I manage to drag him far enough onto the shelf he can crawl the rest of the way.

He struggles upright, his torso lacerated by being scraped over the cruel rocks. A sad whine escapes my throat as he buries his face in my ruff. He's alive, he's alive and the relief is so extreme I have to give voice to it, have to throw my head back and salute the night, because Pierce is alive and I don't know how I would have lived if he wasn't.

We crawl together away from the black hole. Chase is there to help him over the piles of rocks. "You got any more wolf in you, kid?" Pierce asks him.

"Sure thing, old man," he says, grinning like he hasn't spent the night trapped in a hole.

Pierce snorts, too tired to laugh. "If I wasn't mostly dead I'd make you sorry for calling me that. But seriously, it's for your dumb ass that I'm mostly dead, so do me a favour, get down there and tell them we're coming. Make sure we have clothes, make sure there's coffee. Make sure your folks know your brother's a hero."

"So are you," Chase says, sidling out from under Pierce's arm. "So thanks. Thanks for, you know, well, just thanks and stuff. Okay, I'll see you in a few minutes." He jogs away, dropping into the shift between strides then streaking away down the mountainside.

It takes Pierce and I the rest of the night to walk what I could run on my own in an hour. Pierce is bleeding, exhausted, and cold, so our pace is torturous. Slopes are a problem for him, even going downhill, and I can't take the same routes I would if alone.

After an hour of picking our way down a gravelly hillside in the pitch dark, we reach flatter ground where there's a groomed trail. We're still a mile from town and Pierce is stumbling like he's drunk as he walks beside me, his hand buried in my thick fur.

"D'you remember..." he slurs. I make a soft growl he takes as the yes it is and goes on. "D'you remember when we went to Denver? You'd just got your license and we stole my mom's Lexus. And we tried to get into that gay bar. That was just before I left."

I growl again, the memories a tangle of expectation and reality, our longing to be seen set against our total irrelevance to the sort of men we hoped to be seen by. Simply because of our age, but at the time we took it hard.

"That's where I went when I left Hollowood," Pierce continues in that same punch-drunk slur. "That bar. I found the cheapest hostel I could and hung around outside the bar every night until people started talking to me. I never took them up on most of it. But some guys were okay. They knew I just needed friends."

He stops talking while we get around a boulder that's blocking the path and while I wonder why he kept it secret at the time. Maybe he senses this because he starts talking again once we're back on the trail. "You were...you were too Hollowood, Ev. I couldn't go through with it. It was like giving up on myself. Never going anywhere, never seeing the world. So I get why you left. I'm sorry I did it to you first."

I stop walking and he stops with me. I don't want to break this gentle quiet with my howl but I'm too full of feeling to know what else to do. But Pierce puts his arms around my neck and leans into me, breathing deeply. He needs me, and I want him to need me, want to shift so I can put my arms around him and make him know that he's forgiven. But then we'll be two naked idiots lost in the forest, and so I simply let him take what he needs, breathe in my scent, warm himself with my body. Steal my heart.

After a few minutes he sighs. "I think I'm okay to shift now," he murmurs but I shake my head. I know where we are, how close we are to home. If he shifts and collapses, I'll have to carry a wolf home instead of a man, and I jump up and run a few paces along the trail.

"Are we almost there?" he says. "I can barely see you." I run back to him and he grabs my fur again and lets me lead him as above us the outline of the trees emerges against the paling sky of dawn.

It's another stumbling half hour before we reach a part of the trail Pierce recognizes. The sky is turning blue, the light glinting through the trees, and I realize that Graeme might be waiting for me.

"What is it?" Pierce asks as I halt. "We're nearly there."

I'm not ready for my husband to see me like this. Not ready to make him confront the truth of me. Not ready to find out how he'll take it, if this is what breaks him, seeing my other side. I'm also kind of not ready to come waltzing out of the woods naked, hand in hand with someone that Graeme assumes I hate.

I nudge Pierce with my nose, urging him further along the trail. He gives me a funny look as I back away from him, then the understanding dawns. "He hasn't seen it yet, has he? Your fursona."

You asshole... I think as he snickers. But I forgive him. He rescued my brother and he's not a bad person and even if this fated mates mythology is just that, a myth, I want to forgive him. Want to love him, even if only like a brother, like the friend he once was, because hating Pierce Platter has been too big a part of my life for too many years. I'll never get those years back. But I can give us a better future.

Fourteen

Destiny

Like I expect, Graeme is there behind the general store with Chase and our parents and the Platters. Dad brought his new truck down and has the coffee maker plugged into its outlet along with a couple of electric blankets that are too hot for me but just what Pierce needs.

I'm still doing up my jeans when Mom grabs me in a hug, ugly-crying into my chest. "Chase told me what you did and I want you to know I love you but don't ever do something like that again without coming to see me first. Do you know the last time we talked was at the funeral? If you died—"

"I was never going to die."

"Don't argue."

"Fine. I promise, next time I have to haul Chase's dumb ass out of a hole in the ground, I'll make sure to swing by your place first."

She laughs, wiping her eyes. "Don't say that about your brother. Yeah, I know, figure of speech. Be nicer to him, Evan. He really loves you."

I have nothing to say to this. I don't doubt it, but it doesn't make it easier, knowing he's always looked up to me. With a last parental squeeze of my arm she leaves me and then there's only Graeme. Before he can speak, I pull him close and kiss him with everything I've got.

"Gee, I'm glad you're alright," he murmurs when I come up for air.

"So am I." I'm about to kiss him again when Pierce starts shouting.

"I don't care what you thought. We haven't agreed to shit. And how can you even be asking right now?"

"We just thought—" Mrs. Platter says with a nervous glance at me but he cuts her off with an angry gesture.

"You only thought about yourselves. Again."

"But son—" his father starts.

"I don't want to hear about it, okay? I'm fucking done. Don't bring it up again."

"You can talk about it later, D.W.," my father says to Mr. Platter. "These boys are exhausted." I bite back the urge to say we're not boys, but I don't want to interrupt as Dad puts a firm hand on Mr. Platter's shoulder and steers him and his wife away.

"They're obsessed with their stupid inter-coastal alliance," Pierce mutters only half talking to me. "I'm not their puppet."

"You can stay with us if you need to," Mom says to him.

"Are you sure?"

"Pierce, you're always welcome, you know that."

News to me, but I let it pass. It's none of my business what goes on in Hollowood when I'm not here. She pats his arm then gives me a tight smile and goes to help Graeme unplug everything. Leaving me with Pierce.

He's still only wearing the blanket, holding it closed over his scratched chest. He's clutching a camping mug of coffee in his other hand. I've never seen him looking this rough, and he's never been hotter.

"Thanks," he says as I stare at him like an idiot. "For getting me home, getting me out of there. For believing me last night."

"It's cool. He's my brother, I know what he's capable of. Sorry to make you take care of him."

"He's not your responsibility."

"He isn't yours either."

"But he is my friend."

"I gotta say, you went pretty far out of your way to help someone who's just a friend." I don't mean a thing by it but Pierce blushes, the coffee cup shaking in his hand.

"Don't worry," he says urgently. "We're not—"

"I don't mean that I think that you're—I only meant he's lucky to have a friend like you," I finish, my face just as hot.

"Right. I guess he is."

There's nothing left to say. Everyone's gone except Graeme, sitting on the loading dock to wait for me. There's nothing to say but I don't want to be the one who walks away.

"Are you coming back to your parents' place?" Pierce asks.

"I hadn't planned on it. They're going to want to talk to me and I just kind of want to pass out."

"Me too," he says with a half-smile. "Well. Okay. Guess I'll see you?"

"I'll stop in before we leave. See you one last time."

"I'd like that," he says, and my heart leaps as he smiles. When did he get such a beautiful smile? "Okay. We should keep in touch."

"For sure. And thanks for being so honest tonight."

"In the woods? I wasn't sure you were listening."

"I was. So thanks. And you don't have to apologize for leaving. I'm sorry I did it to you." I want to hug him but I'm scared that I'll never let him go. Shaking hands feels like a slap in the face so we just stand there like idiots who may or may not be in love, neither ready to say goodbye. This morning I wanted to kick him down the mountain. How did I get to this moment, to being terrified of him walking away in case I never see him again?

What if all this crazy shit is real, and this is my destiny?

"Pierce," says Graeme before I can find the words for any of this. He's standing near but doesn't meet my gaze. "Can we have a talk?"

It takes me a bit to understand what's going on as Pierce stammers a yes then follows Graeme across the empty lot. Not knowing what else to do, I stand there and watch them, wishing I could hear them, terrified of what I might hear.

After a few minutes I feel like I'm eavesdropping, so I go around to the front of the store and sit on a bench. The valley faces north, so the sunrise is like the sunset and happens only in the sky, which changes from velvet blue to silvery grey as I wait for the two most important people in my life to finish talking about me.

It really is pretty here, with the mist rising from the trees as the sun warms the air. A nice place to live if you were happy with not much happening. I can't see Graeme wanting to ever move here. Not unless the Dew Drop gets a juice bar. Even then, would we be happy with so little? With seeing the same few people day after day, with Westeros-grade winters and werewolves play-fighting in the streets in the middle of the night?

Why am I even thinking about it? We're going home today. Back to the suburbs, our cat, our yard. Our ordinary lives, Gay All Day edition.

Except we can't. Not now that Graeme knows what I am. We can try, but I don't know if we'll ever be the same.

Fifteen

Only One Bed

I'm still trying to think myself back to normal when they come around the corner. Pierce is dressed, though he's wearing the blanket around his shoulders. I stand up, then sit down again as a wave of nausea passes over me. I need sleep, or a steak, or both. I need Graeme to explain why he's smirking at Pierce, who toddles over to the bench and sits down beside me.

"I've had time to come to terms with what's going on between the two of you," Graeme starts.

"I swear, there's nothing—"

"Hush," he says to me. "Let me speak then you can tell me what you think. Now, I won't say I'm familiar with all the ins and outs, but I'm sure that it's real. And I'm sure that you two are fated, and that there's nowt that I or anyone can say or do about it."

"We don't have to follow—"

"Hush, you," he says sharply but not unkindly. "I've made up my mind, so you'd better come with a good counterargument if you hope to change that."

"I don't know what you decided."

"To let this play out," he says, his eyes flicking between the two of us. "If this truly is fate, if there's something greater than all of us driving this...scenario, then nothing any of us do is going to change it, right?"

I sneak a glance at Pierce, who is looking into his coffee cup, his expression carefully blank. "I guess not?"

"So either I sit back and watch the man I love put himself through hell denying what his soul calls out for, or I get okay with the thing he needs, which may well turn out to be him." He jerks his head towards Pierce, who tenses but doesn't reply

"But I don't need—"

"Hush," he says firmly and I do, because he's so rarely wrong. Because he's not angry or sulking or confused, because he's the only one of the three of us who seems to have a clue. "There's no good saying more about it tonight. Or this morning, if we're fair. Let's sleep on it, and we can talk it through when we're all in a better state of mind."

I don't want to argue. I want the night to have never happened. I want everything to be like it was two days ago, before the funeral, before Chase's letter. When Pierce still hated me and I hated him. Except that's not what I really want.

Numb, wordless, we follow Graeme down the alley and across the empty street and so to my parents' house. I expect we'll drop off Pierce then keep going but Graeme hustles me inside, which hasn't changed a bit in a decade. Same geeky studio portraits hanging on the wall of me and Chase with bowl-cuts and matching turtleneck sweaters. Same floral print couch with plaid blankets on the seat cushions.

"Can I make you something to eat?" my mom says as I stand swaying in the door to the living room. "I know, time's gone out the window, but if you're hungry—"

"I just want to lie down."

"Good idea," says Pierce, leaning heavily on the doorframe. He pushes himself upright and heads for the stairs.

"I'll help," Graeme says, starting after him. "He won't know where he's going."

"And you do?" I say, following him.

"I've been here all night," he says over his shoulder as he starts up the stairs. "I've figured out a few things." He bundles the two of us through a door on the landing. Not my old room but a guest room done in alarming shades of apricot.

"There's only one bed," Pierce says pointlessly as Graeme closes the door.

"And? Go lie down in it."

"Okay." As he stumbles towards the bed I turn to Graeme, who takes me in his arms.

"And as for you," he says with that rough purr that makes me shiver. "You can have one of these."

With that he kisses me. A proper kiss, starting slow and building, one hand cradling my face and the other on my ass, his tongue tasting, tempting, and then demanding. The way we kissed at our wedding as a symbol of our union, the depth of our love for each other.

"There," he says. "Now into bed with you."

"Okay." I climb in and settle in what would normally be Graeme's spot on the left, very conscious of Pierce lying an arm's length away even though he's fully dressed. Graeme meanwhile has stripped to his shorts.

"Shift over, love."

"But I—okay." I roll on my side and he gets into bed behind me and pulls the covers over all three of us, the first time I've ever been in bed with two people.

"I'm so glad you're safe," Graeme says, snuggling closer and slipping his arm around my waist.

"I was never in danger," I mumble.

"I didn't know that, did I?"

"Gray...this thing...Pierce..."

"Hush," he says, his breath a caress on the back of my neck. "It'll keep."

Maybe I'm just that tired, but I fall asleep right away and stay asleep, unbothered by my dreams, oblivious to the world. I wake alone in the bed and lie there for a little as the other two talk softly somewhere nearby.

"Look, we're good with the fated mates situation," Graeme is saying. "We're good with the werewolf thing. But there's not a chance in hell I'm going to live all the fuck the way out here. I'll fucking starve. Plus I've got a wicked cedar allergy, so that's going to be a hard no from me."

"Fair enough," Pierce replies. "As long as you think you have room for me."

This makes me sit up. "Where him? I mean, where going him. I mean…"

They're sitting on the edge of the bed and both turn to look at me. Pierce is wearing one of my dad's old shirts which hangs off him like a tent. With the shadows under his eyes and his dark hair sticking out everywhere he looks like a flood victim. Or emo. Graeme is Graeme, dressed appropriately for the drive home in clean chinos and a nice blue shirt.

"Do you mean, where are we going to put him?" he asks as I yawn. "I thought the study."

"My study?"

"You don't use it much," he says, which is true but totally not the point. "And besides, it's only temporary. He's just coming for a visit."

"I…ugh, okay. He can stay in my study. Temporarily."

He grins at Pierce. "Like I told you, not a problem."

They're smirking at each other like they have something to hide. A weird feeling twists my stomach. "You two didn't…no. You wouldn't."

"Do you think we've been fooling around?" Pierce asks me. "While you lie there?"

"No. I mean… No."

"I've got to say, though, I wouldn't exactly boot him out of bed," Graeme says, waggling his eyebrows.

"Excuse me?" I sputter as Pierce's face turns red.

"He's got a lovely arse," Graeme says with that silky smile he wears when he's about to win a game of cards. "What? You do," he says as Pierce groans and covers his face. "Stand up and give us a twirl, let's have a peek."

Pierce drops his hands to glare at Graeme. "Are you serious?"

No. He can't be. He's fucking with us as he holds up a hand to inspect his fingernails. "I've got to say, for great big hairy monsters, you're a bit stuck up, no?"

"Excuse me, great big hairy—"

"I am not stuck-up—"

"Bit of a diva though—"

"Takes one to know one—"

"Wait, how long are you staying—"

We all fall silent as someone knocks firmly on the door. "What time are you meant to hit the road?" asks my dad in his ninety percent serious voice. "Because you know it's nearly noon, right?"

My dad takes Pierce to get his things, though I don't know what kind of trouble they think the Platters are going to start. They're getting what they want, which makes me wonder if it's what I really want. It's all too easy, all happening too fast, and I had no say in any of it.

Graeme's bustling around the hotel room, checking under the bed and the dresser for loose change or charging cables while I sit zombified in the only chair.

"Gray..."

"Hmm?"

"What's going on?"

"I'm packing our bags and we're—"

"No, I mean..." *What are we doing to our perfect life?* "Stop and talk to me, please." He leaves the suitcase half zipped and sits on the end of the bed nearest me. "Why are you okay with this? Why am I?"

"I can't speak to your reasons," he says gently. "But I've had some very enlightening conversations with your mother over the last twenty hours."

"And?"

"And I think it's premature of us to place any conditions on him or ourselves."

"Premature? You invited a man I was meant to marry to stay at our house. Without asking me. I would kind of like some conditions."

"Like what?"

"Like...I don't know. I don't know what's supposed to happen now. I don't know if I...if having him in my life will get in the way of how I feel for you. And I don't want that. But I'm scared it's going to happen anyway." I shove away my tears with the heel of my hand. I can't freak out now, not in the middle of the most important conversation of my life. "What if I don't even like him?"

"That's why he wanted to come. Low stakes, no pressure. Maybe he hates the suburbs."

"Maybe I break your heart."

"I'm not going to let that happen."

"How can you stop it?"

He looks at me hard, in this way he has that isn't aggressive, it just makes you pay attention. Then he smiles, shaking his head a little, like I'm missing the point. It reminds me of when we met, when I was so closed down that I didn't even know he had a crush on me until he gave me this exact look then leaned across the table at the coffee shop and kissed me. My mouth is open like he's going to kiss me right now, but he's there on the bed and I'm in this chair and I don't think I can make my legs work enough to get to him.

But he gets to his feet and gives me his hand and I stand so he can put his arms around me. "If you think some ancient tradition handed down in a line unbroken is going to get in the way of me loving you," he says with that soft purring voice he saves only for me, "then you forget what I gave up to marry you. I betrayed everything I was meant to stand for, because none of it was as powerful as what I feel for you."

"I'm sorry."

"Don't be sorry. We need to have these talks. But I'm not worried, not in the slightest. I won't let you forget me."

Sixteen

A Kiss

How are we going to fit Pierce into our lives when we can't even fit him into our car? "Should have thought of this before you invited him over," I say as Graeme folds himself into the ungenerous backseat.

"I didn't realize he was mainly leg."

Seated behind the wheel, Pierce smirks but says nothing. He lost the rock-paper-scissors shoot out for who had to drive. Graeme and I got to fight over who had to cope with the back, which is made for stoic German children and not a full-grown Scotsman, though he stops complaining when we get him an oat milk latte at the Starbucks at the new service station.

"I don't get why you didn't move further away," Pierce says to me as we pull back onto the highway.

"I didn't want it to be a hassle if I had to come home for something like this."

"You didn't move out-of-state just so you never had to pay for airfare? Dude..." He laughs through his teeth.

"Maybe I was pining for you."

"Shut up," he says by reflex, trying not to break into a grin.

"Maybe I was pining but I didn't know that's what I was feeling."

"That'd be you all over, missing the big picture."

I smile but say nothing. I think I'm right, that the sense that never left me that I was leaving something out was because I didn't have him. He rests his hand on my knee while he drives, the warmth travelling up my leg and easing something frozen in me. A denial I can stop defending. I haven't lost Graeme, I've found myself.

Pierce doesn't say much after this, smirking at our shit-talk but keeping his thoughts to himself. Maybe he has changed since I left, but that's no surprise. So have I. Graeme might have been the one to kiss me first, but I'm the one who proposed to him, and I never used to be that brave.

I'm in the back now and Graeme's driving, and he glances back when he feels me looking. "It's nothing," I say. "I'm just happy."

Pierce is sleeping in the front seat, the setting sun lighting his face. I think about what it must have been like to come back to Hollowood to find out I was gone. I've never let this sink in: the loss, the shame. Wondering if he'd ever known me. Waiting for me to come home.

"Are you sure you're happy?" Graeme says as I wipe my eyes.

"It's a lot to think about."

"I know." He glances at Pierce who shifts in his seat, curling into himself. "I hope we're doing the right thing."

"It was your idea."

"Does that make it my fault if it goes poorly?"

"No. He'll have no one to blame but himself."

"You arse," he chuckles. "God, I love you." He reaches back to take my hand and drives like this until there's too much traffic and he needs both hands on the wheel. But that means we're almost home.

I'm surprised the house looks the same as when we left. The past two days feel like a lifetime. As Graeme goes about opening blinds, talking to the cat, I show Pierce to the study.

"Give me a minute," I say, grabbing an armful of books and shirts and whatever else I've let pile up on the futon beside my desk, which is also piled with books and whatever. Pierce tidies this to give me more room for other junk, while I silently pledge to watch every *Queer Eye* episode I can find about decluttering. If it works on straights, it's going to work double on me, right?

Pierce helps me unbend the mattress and then there's an awkward moment where we're standing beside a bed and I'm glad he's here but still not sure why that is. He has to be thinking all the same things, as he blushes and picks at his sagging neckline. We've changed but we haven't and when I look at him I don't see all the hurt we caused each other. I see that livewire kid who never turned down a dare. I see a proud young man standing up against his suffocating parents. I see the person whose friendship I mourned even when I told myself that all I felt towards him was anger.

"I missed you," I say, and though it doesn't cover everything I need to say it's a start.

"Me too," he replies with a catch in his throat. "I'm sorry I left."

"You don't need to apologize anymore. I forgive you. And I get it. I mean, I did it to you."

"So we're even?"

"Yep."

He sighs, his whole body softening, as if all these years he's been waiting for my forgiveness. I want to touch him, hold him, let him lean on me, depend on me the way he couldn't before. I don't know what the rules are, what Graeme expects, what Pierce wants, but when I reach out he goes into my arms.

That's all. A hug. He's my friend and in need and I'm giving support. He's my friend and I love him because that's what friendship is, another way to give love. He's my friend and I've loved him all my life and maybe that's why I can't let him go. Because he feels like home.

"Do you think it's true?" he says quietly, his hands tensing on my back. "That we're made to be together?"

"I don't know. I know I've only ever felt like this about one other person and he's out there feeding our cat."

Pulling back to look at me, Pierce laughs, that shushing giggle through his teeth. "So what are you saying?"

"I don't know." Maybe there aren't words for why this feels right. Why this doesn't feel like I'm tearing my marriage apart. I don't make stupid choices. I don't rush into big decisions with my heart in the lead. Graeme's never been jealous, but then again I've never made him doubt me. "Am I allowed to want this?" I say. "To want you?"

"Your husband's the one who asked me to come. What do you think?"

"I think if I don't kiss you right now I'm going to pass out."

It's not a pretty kiss. It's ten years, twenty, a lifetime of waiting. It's hunger and fear, loss and forgiveness, his hands tearing at my clothes, his mouth locked on mine, our tongues at war over who can taste the other deeper. It's our hearts beating in time as our bodies seem to meld into each other. It's nothing like kissing Graeme and not because it's new but because this is the pinnacle of so many things. So much feeling and longing, so many unanswered questions, my past and our future, our fate.

It's happening while my husband muddles around the living room making our lives perfect. Though my cock has already decided what it wants, which is Pierce all over it and right now, I put my hands on his shoulders and push him away. "Okay, we are making too many assumptions."

"Right," says Pierce, blinking hard, licking his lips bruised pink by our kiss. "You're right."

"Graeme's the best thing that's ever happened to me. If you hurt him, I'll kill you. Simple as that."

"O...kay."

"So let's go see what he thinks about this."

"I think your mother owes me a hundred bucks," Graeme says from the doorway.

You know that thing dogs, foxes, wolves do when they suddenly jump six feet in the air because something scared them shitless? Pierce does this now, letting out a terrified whoop and ending up on the futon, his back against the wall, his chest heaving. "How long have you been there?" he asks, pointing an accusing finger.

"Long enough." Graeme's not angry, not a bit, smirking as his eyes linger on my hard-on.

"Wait, what do you mean, my mother owes you money?" I ask him as Pierce climbs down from the bed.

"I bet her a cool hundred you two wouldn't last the night."

"I'm sorry," Pierce starts, but Graeme quiets him with a raised finger.

"Ah-ah-ah, we'll have no more of that," he says. "I've done my research. I know this isn't just about love or lust. This is fate."

I have no words. Maybe there are no words for how much I love him. He knows me like no one else and he still loves me, which is so much more than I deserve. "Besides," he says with a spark in his eyes, "there's plenty of me to go around."

"Hey, you're not part of the deal," I call after him as he leaves the room. I want to follow him but Pierce won't let go of my hand. "He is not part of the deal."

"I don't need him," Pierce says with a soft laugh, laying his other hand against my cheek. "I need you."

He pulls me closer but I'm not ready to kiss him and I lower my head to rest my forehead against his. "Is this crazy?" I ask, the only word I know for the manic rush of emotion, the fear and the longing racing through me.

"We're werewolves, Evan," he says like the two things equate.

"So?"

"So crazy's what you make it. Most people don't believe we exist, yet your adorable human is willing to not only believe you but accept you in all your supernatural weirdness. That's not crazy. That's love."

"He's amazing."

"So are you."

"You can't know that," I say, and it's true, Pierce doesn't know me like used to. Hasn't seen me at my worst, crippled by panic, lost for direction. I hid all that from him by running away. Denied him the chance to know me.

"We can never know another person completely," he says. "That's part of being alive. But if someone as good as him loves you that much, you must be worth something."

All I can do is believe him. Believe him, and try to live up to his faith in me. Believe that we can make this work, because the thought of letting Pierce go is sickening. I need him like he needs me, now and forever.

Seventeen

Ours

Again, to kiss him feels like coming home. Like everything good and true in the world is here in this room with us. Like every fear and failure I've known on the way to this moment was to teach me how much this moment is worth.

"Holy shit..." he breathes as I kiss my way along his stubbled jaw. "Why does this feel so good?"

"Maybe it's all that fate." Graeme's at the door again. "Oh, don't stop on my account," he says, coming farther into the room as Pierce tenses against me.

"I thought you weren't part of the deal," he says, looking between us.

"Deals can be changed," I murmur as I wake to the possibilities. Deals can include Pierce's gorgeous mouth choking on Graeme's cock. Can include any number of things, things that live in the deepest, dirtiest parts of my mind, things I've never said out loud that can now come true.

"I wasn't planning for this to happen," Pierce says, looking urgently back and forth between us. "I swear."

"But do you want it?" I ask. I do, shamelessly, am ready to push all my limits. This has to be fate, has to be real, because right now there's nothing I wouldn't let these two men do to me.

"Don't make me decide," he says in a whisper. He's shaking in my arms, and something in me opens up, like a gate rusted shut for years that suddenly swings free and lets me into a new world.

"I'll take care of you," I say, running my finger along his trembling jaw to tip his head up. "We're going to make you feel so good."

"Kiss him again," Graeme says, something tender yet deadly in his voice. He wants this as much as I do. As Pierce gasps I cup the back of his head, pull him harder against me, and claim that gorgeous mouth.

"Aye, that's it," Graeme says from somewhere behind Pierce. "Fuck, I'm going to come just watching you two." Pierce groans into my kiss, molding his body against me, his cock shoving against mine, his need unmistakable.

"Tell me, sweetheart," Graeme says to him in that luscious purr that sets me off every time. "How do you like to fuck? Slow and soft? Hard and ugly? Can I tell you what I want?" Both of us nod, moaning into each other's kiss.

"I want you naked. I want you naked and mounted on this one's cock. I want to see you bring him off with your sweet arse and nothing else. I want you to watch me fuck his mouth so you can see how hard I'm going to make you work. Does that sound nice?"

Whimpering around my thrusting tongue, Pierce nods. He wants this, wants us to take him to pieces. Knowing this, knowing I don't have to stop, don't have to second guess, breaks through my last barricade of self-control.

Pierce Platter is finally mine. And I'm going to make sure he knows it.

No, Pierce is ours. Ours to touch, tease, love, enjoy. He's everything I fantasized. The shadow of Graeme's sunlight. The slashing blade to Graeme's stony strength. The boy I remember in a man like no one I've known, and I want to make him scream my name.

Now that we're committed to it, I don't hold back. Pierce is still wearing that shirt of my father's, the fabric worn to a tissue from being stretched over my old man's massive shoulders. Still kissing him, I run my hands up his chest, knot my fingers in the thin fabric, and tear it in two. He gasps again but so do I as I feel the scratches across his torso from the harsh rocks. My instinct is to pull away, but he earned these marks protecting my brother.

"Does it hurt?" I ask, lightly touching the skin alongside one of the rough red marks.

"Not enough to stop me."

"Good. Because I don't want to stop." The bed is behind him and with a mostly gentle push I shove him down onto it. He scrambles back to give me space but before I get my jeans undone Graeme's arms snake around me,

"D'you remember what I wanted?" he asks, one hand covering my cock, the other gripping my face, his index finger plucking at my lips, his hard-on jutting into my back.

When I nod he lets me go and I sink to my knees, my mouth watering. Ignoring Pierce's soft moaning, I unzip Graeme's beautifully tailored slacks. Like I expect, he slips out of them and drapes them, creases matched, over the back of my chair.

"Are you fucking kidding me?" Pierce gasps as Graeme pulls his shirt over his head and shows himself for the first time. "Okay, I totally get it. I get why you married him."

"That's not why I married him," I say. "That's why I fucked him. I married him because he's the greatest thing that's ever happened to me and I was smart enough to realize it."

"It was a bit like this though, wasn't it?" Graeme says as he stands before me. "You on your knees, me about to get my mind blown."

"Except it was at Comicon."

"I still would have fucked your darling mouth," he says, stroking his fingers through my hair while his other hand works his thick cock to maximum hardness. "Right there. With everyone watching."

This shouldn't be such a turn on. It's weird enough that Pierce is here, never mind if there was a convention center full of people... A jolt of pleasure shoots up my spine as Graeme moves closer to stroke the slick head of his cock across my cheeks. Marking me, taunting me, making me want to open up and take him.

The distance between wanting and having is the width of my husband's cock. I want to suck him dry, swallow him down to his balls, but there's just so much of him, my cheeks and jaw stretched to their limits, the thick head alone almost filling my mouth. I want more, want to feel this tomorrow, and I arch up and relax my neck, take him deeper. His hand tightens in my hair but the sting can't compete with the ache of my jaw, the choking pressure of his cock, the helplessness I shouldn't want but love to feel.

"A little more, love," Graeme purrs. "I know you can take me. Show Pierce how good you are at taking cocks."

Another startling bolt of pleasure rockets through me. I've never been so hot without someone's hands on me, like it's my cock getting sucked. I'm drooling and choking and I can't take him all but I can take more, until it feels like he's inside my brain, until I need air or I'll pass out. He reads me, knows me, pulls out enough I can catch my breath.

"Goddamn..." Pierce groans.

"You want a go?" Graeme says to him as I sink back on my knees.

"Me?"

"No, that other lad over in the corner." Pierce fucking looks, and I let out a messy laugh, my mouth numb.

"How about we come back around to that later?" Graeme says as Pierce glares at me.

He's kneeling on the bed in those tight black jeans, his shirt ripped to ribbons, the marks on his chest making it look like I did it with my claws. He's angry and gorgeous and he's all ours, and I want him to never forget it.

"You're right," I say, climbing onto the bed. As I crawl towards Pierce his frown fades, replaced by shivering want. I keep moving towards him and he leans back, then falls, and still I keep coming until I'm lying on top of him, face to face. "Wasn't there something about you mounting that pretty ass of yours on my cock?"

Eighteen

Slice of Heaven

First a kiss, so Pierce can taste Graeme on my lips and tongue. Straddling his thighs, hoping that I'm getting it right, I catch his hands and stretch them over his head. He groans into my mouth, arching his hips off the bed like he can fuck me through his jeans. How did ever I walk away from him?

The answer is in Graeme's strong hands running down my back, over my arse and between my thighs. It's in his love, so strong that this isn't breaking him, it's only making us love each other harder. Pierce and I might be fated, but I chose Graeme and he chose me. It's because of him that I'm brave enough for this.

I need him now, to show him with my body what's so hard to say in words, that I still belong to him. I roll away from Pierce, who sits up as I pull Graeme down to me. He's nude and I'm not and I want to feel his skin, feel it burn against mine. As we kiss I reach for my zipper but someone else beats me to it.

The two of them strip me, taking turns to kiss me as the other works my jeans past my hips and off. Then Pierce, his tight jeans clinging to his sweating legs, so that I end up holding him around the waist while Graeme peels them off. It's a gorgeous mass of male body parts, of steaming skin and dripping cocks and this is my life from now on if I want it.

Pierce is on top of me, his tongue deep in my mouth, our skin welded together by our mingled sweat, when his whole body suddenly stiffens. Graeme is behind him with a bottle of lube and as I watch he squirts more between Pierce's ass cheeks. As Graeme strokes him he relaxes more and more, his eyes closing, his weight settling on me. Sighing, shaking, his dark hair falling over his flushed face, he's the most beautiful thing I've ever seen and I want to make a mess of him.

Graeme is hot. He's fire and stone, he's magnetism, a hot comet blazing in the night. Pierce is cold, but a blazing cold, a wild wind tearing through my soul. I can't believe this fate is mine.

"Aye, that's it, darling," Graeme coos as Pierce shoves back against his penetrating fingers. "You want this so much, don't you? I bet you're right bonny when you ride. Will you show me?"

"Yes...please...I want..."

"I know, darling," Graeme says in that filthy brogue that makes me shiver deep inside. "You want Evan's cock to split you open like the slut you are."

"Yes."

"Good. You're such a good boy. He's going to make you fucking sing."

If I live, because Graeme's dirty talk has me shaking head to toe. We taunt and tease but this is something new, a depth in him I've never tested. I'm not stopping him now as Pierce sits up, straddling my hips, my sheathed cock sliding between his buttocks.

"This is not how I imagined this," he says to me, breathing hard. "Because you should know I did."

"I won't ever leave you again."

'You asshole," he hisses, halfway to laughing as his face turns even pinker. "Don't make me cry when I'm naked."

"Shut up and fuck me, Platter. Like you've always wanted to."

"Like this?" Grinning, he arches his back, riding his ass against my shaft, and I groan, moving to meet him. "I'll take that as a yes."

Yes, as he pushes back, increasing the friction, the pressure. Yes, as he rises up and reaches beneath himself to fit my cock against his slick hole. Yes, as he sinks down, taking me inch by thrusting inch, as Graeme runs his fingers through Pierce's hair then jerks him down hard so I'm all the way in him.

Have I imagined this? Yes, but not with Pierce in the middle. The third man never had a name, was a figment of my dirty mind. It would have been a stranger, some man we picked out of a crowd, or more like Graeme picked while I watched because I wouldn't have the guts. It was never going to be someone who mattered. This is better, even if it isn't fate, if all of that is a lie. This is enough to unite us, this sense that this is exactly where each of us are meant to be.

And Pierce is good, so good, winding his hips, screwing down onto me slow and deliberate. He lifts himself then winds back down and between the clenching heat of his ass and the ecstasy on his face it takes all I have not to come. Graeme's beside him, his hands all over Pierce's sweating body, toying with his nipples, nipping at his shoulder as he rides me. I gasp his name and he leaves Pierce and bends down near my face. We kiss, and it's like we've never kissed before as I cling to him, moaning to the rhythm of Pierce's rocking hips as I suck at Graeme's tongue.

"How about you finish what you started?" Graeme says to me, running his finger over my lips. "As you are, with Pierce riding your cock and me riding your face."

In answer I lick his fingertip, words beyond me. His eyes rolling closed, he groans then falls on me, biting at my lips until I open to his tongue again. When he's had his fill he leaves me panting and whispers to Pierce, who stops moving as Graeme straddles my head. They're both facing forward, Pierce leaning back on me as Graeme dips his hips down to rub his cock across my lips.

Like I do in my dreams, I open my mouth to take the fat head of his cock. It seems even bigger when I'm this helpless, when his whole body presses down on me and my breath is his to give or take. Slowly, Pierce starts to rock his hips in time with Graeme's, working my cock inside him as Graeme works his cock deep in my aching throat. It's all too much and not enough and I grab Graeme's ass with both hands to give me leverage, help me bend to take him deeper.

"Yes, love, that's it," he urges me as I gasp breathlessly. "Choke yourself on me, the way you like. You're a dirty fucker, Evan Culver. You and your slutty friend. I'm going to have him next. You hear me, Pierce? I want you next."

"Shit…" Suddenly Pierce is riding me hard, Graeme's filthy talk pushing him to the brink. If I could breathe I'd be shouting as the pressure in me builds and builds. As Pierce shouts again Graeme shoves in deep, bruising the back of my throat. Nothing can stop this, as a hot flash of pure sensation strikes like lightning, the orgasm ripping through my core like I'm closing the circuit between these men, like I'm what unites us, like this is the moment my whole life has led to, their love my reason for being.

Pierce suddenly shivers, grabbing onto Graeme's shoulder, his body jerking over me as he strokes himself. With a groan and a strange shudder, Graeme pulls back, leaving me gasping as he works his drool-slick cock until his hot cream douses my face. They're leaning against each other and as Pierce raises his head Graeme kisses him. Deep and hard, wrapping his free arm around Pierce's neck when he tries to pull away. Fucking Pierce's mouth with his tongue, and I've never been more in love.

Slowly, carefully, we get untangled. My ears are still ringing as Pierce stretches beside me. "What the fuck is that beeping noise?" he groans, throwing his arm over his eyes.

"You hear it too?"

"That'll be the eggplant casserole," Graeme says brightly. "I'll just go put the cheese on your end." He hops off the bed like he hasn't just come all over someone's face and starts for the kitchen, his bare feet slapping on the hardwood.

Pierce meanwhile looks like the end scene of a porn, every bit of him covered in kiss marks and bites and sweat and come. He looks perfect in other words, my stinging cock lurching back to life as he props himself up on his elbow. "When did Graeme have time to make a casserole?"

"He made it last month and froze it. He must have put it in the oven when we got home."

"Wow," Pierce says, flopping back again. "He's kind of amazing."

"Welcome to my slice of heaven."

I show him the towels and soap and leave him to shower then go do the same in our ensuite. I thought it was a bit much buying a place with two full bathrooms. Now it feels like Graeme was planning ahead for exactly this, but that's my brain running wild. This is new for all of us.

My husband's in the bedroom when I come out in my robe. He's shoving the empty suitcase under the bed and I step up behind him quietly to bump my cock against his ass. He laughs, low and dirty.

"See? I was right," he says as he stands upright.

"About what?"

"You are a bigamist."

"Ha ha, and fuck you."

"What, again?"

"Seriously though," I ask as he slips his arms around my waist. "How are you okay with any of this?"

"I could ask the same of you. But I had quite a long talk with your mother while you were gone. Plus I did a bit of research on my own."

"What kind of research?" I ask as he blushes.

"You know...books," he replies in a wavering voice.

"Books about what?"

"About...things..."

"Proper books? Or smutty romance books?"

"Bit of both. Cut me some slack, will you?" he says as I start to laugh. "The first sort was hard to come by, I had to make do."

"And so what did your research tell you?" I say, completely unprepared for the romantic assault of his reply, as he gazes into my eyes like I'm the best thing he's ever seen.

"It tells me that if your love for me is so strong it overcame everything in your nature, ever instinct, every bit of your upbringing, then you must be even stronger, and worth every bit of my love in return."

I can only stare at him, at the depths he keeps revealing, his bravery beyond anything I've known. "Either that," he says, "or you're obsessed with my enormous cock."

"You ass..." I have to laugh. I want to laugh. I want to love him for the rest of my life, and that's what I'm going to do. There's fate and then there's love, and sometimes they intersect. When they don't, sometimes you make it happen, and I don't care if I'm crying because these are tears of joy.

"I love you so much," I say.

"You fucking better."

So that's it. That's how forty eight hours in my home town of Hollowood Falls changed my life. If you ever come down from Vail, make sure it's only a day trip. Unless you want to bring home a werewolf as a souvenir.

NEXT

WHAT HAPPENS IN HOLLOWOOD
(HOLLOWOOD FALLS BOOK 2)

Book 2

What Happens in Hollowood

We're the typical 21st century American family. My dad's from India, my mom's a religious cult refugee, and I'm Black, Bi, and adopted. Nothing I haven't been able to rise above, even if I'm always the new kid in class. But school's behind me now and all I've got on the horizon is the question of what to do with my life, and a mountain.

I don't know what I'll find up there. If the town of Hollowood Falls is where I belong or if my past is better forgotten. If my feelings for River are real or a fantasy. Like River themselves: a myth, because unless my parents are lying to me, I've just fallen in love with a werewolf.

What happens in Hollowood Falls doesn't always stay there. Sometimes it follows you home.

One

Suspicions

There are more than thirty species of crows, whose habitats span the globe from Scandinavia to the Solomon Islands, and whose diet includes snails and insects, fruits and vegetables, carrion, garbage, and the nestlings of other birds. I'm watching a gang of them—technically called a murder—hop around the backyard of our new house in this new development on the edge of a town called Hollowood Falls.

Mom says these crows are endemic to this bioregion, that you can tell them from other crows by the patch of white feathers on the top of their heads and the band of gold around their eyes. Her job at the university has taken us to Borneo, Vietnam, Sulawesi (bet you don't even know where that is) and a bunch of less interesting places like Dorset and Copenhagen. This subdivision with no city attached is probably going to be the most boring out of all of them.

A racist teacher, the pandemic, and my own bullshit added up to me not graduating on time. Now I'm stuck in semi-rural Colorado with a GED, a weak-ass resume, and sweet fuck all else, not even the prospect of college on the horizon. The only thing on the horizon is a mountain.

There's not really any part of Colorado that isn't mountain. But there's living at high altitudes and then there's living beside actual mountains, green with trees that have never been logged, their bare stony, peaks stretching another quarter mile into the sky. About the only thing I have to look forward to is riding that mountain.

Gazing out the kitchen window at it as I dry the plates my mom is washing (they look clean to me but what do I know?) I think about whether there's trails or if I'll get to blaze my own. Whether other people in the area ride and if any of them are worth knowing, or if the cycling scene here is just another clique of middle class white people who'll give me side eye like I stole my bike and I'm planning to steal theirs next.

"Remind me why you took this job," I say as Mom slices through the tape on the next moving box.

"You know there aren't a lot of opportunities in my field," she says, looking over the contents.

"Never mind your being a woman," I add, knowing what she's gone through to get this far, starting her masters in her thirties while working at Waffle House and the library.

"You know it. It was Hollowood Falls or Norfolk Island."

"I don't even know where that is," I say as she starts unwrapping coffee cups.

"Neither did I," she says with a grimace. "Trust me, Marcus, I did us favour."

Dad won't join us for another week and a half. The pandemic ankled his career until he found a payroll firm looking for a junior executive who didn't mind oil rig hours. That is, he works from home three weeks out of four, then spends a week in Denver going to meeting after meeting. If that's what it takes to get the bills paid, alright, but I'm not exactly thrilled about entering the job market. What job market? There's not even a grocery store nearby, and the gas station can only need so many cashiers.

I'm lying on the couch the next day scrolling through community college options and feeling sorry for myself when I decide to go for a ride. If my brain's turning to mush I can at least keep my body fit. I pull up Maps and plot a route, straight along the highway then up the switchback side road that leads up to the little plateau where the village of Hollowood Falls sits. The waterfall is in the state park and there's a fee to get in, but I'm sure I'll find a few backroads once I get used to the area.

The weather's just right, the sun softened by a wispy veil of clouds. I keep a steady pace on the lowlands, saving my strength for what turns out to be a brutal climb. My legs are on fire by the time I reach somewhere safe to pull off the road, as I've been hugging the guardrail for the last mile. The old gas station is giving major *Fallout* vibes but the bald man behind the counter smiles and waves through the glass then leaves me alone. Sitting on a bench beside the phone booth, which is not only free of graffiti but looks like the phone might actually work, I swallow half my water in a couple big gulps then dump the rest on my steaming head. I'm used to weak-ass trails through city parkland, and this mountain just made me its bitch. Not for long. I've had my fill of losing. From now on, it's nothing but wins.

When my heart chills out I ride on, knowing I'm past the worst of it. I'm still climbing but it's a gentle grade and before long I reach the village. It looks just like the postcard our real estate agent left on the kitchen counter with a cheerful *I love referrals!* written on the back. Hollowood Falls kind of sells itself, with its houses like blinged-out log cabins tucked in among the soaring trees, the hotel like a P.T. Anderson set, all 1950s stucco with a diner to one side and a mini-golf course out front.

I cross the road to the little row of wood-sided shops, the big one in the middle shaped like a barn. A couple of bikes are propped against the wooden bars out front. Nothing special, both bikes ridden hard, the black worn off the pedals, the grips on the heavier Schwinn held on with tape, the green paint chipping off the frame of the little BMX hybrid.

As I'm trying to decide if I need to lock up my bike or if that makes me look suspicious as fuck, a couple of people pass me. The one woman does a double take, then nudges the other, who sees me and gasps before the first hustles her into the store.

The fuck? If this is some hillbilly bullshit where no one's ever seen a Black person before, then me and my mom are about to have a hell of a talk. Leaving my bike leaning against the front of the store in case I want to get out fast, I go inside. I need water, should have thought to bring my canteen pack, but I didn't think the ride was going to kick my ass like that. The white women are in the corner by the cooler and I wander up and down the aisles waiting for them to leave, my tongue feeling like leather and sweat dripping down my ass crack. I don't feel like starting any shit today. When they head for the cash I grab a couple bottles of water, one for now and one to get me home.

It happens again when I go up to pay, the cashier looking my way, then looking again harder. Maybe it's just my jersey which I only ever wear when I ride because it's neon Barbie's-dream-car pink. Fuchsia, my mom calls it, but whatever, it makes my arms look mad cut and gives cars no excuse for not seeing me coming. I pay for the drinks and am about to leave when the bell on the door jingles again. A huge guy with a ginger braid down to his ass and motherfucking snakes tattooed all over his ripped arms is standing there gawking at me like I'm the weirdest thing he's ever seen. Enough of this creepy ass town, but as I get ready to tell him to get out my way, he steps aside, nodding to me as I pass like he knows me.

The other bikes are gone from the front of the store. Not stopping to drink the water I just went through all that to buy, I jump on mine and use gravity to get me the fuck out of there. Fuck Hollowood Falls. I don't need this shit.

The sun's starting to drop by the time I get home. Mom's out back grilling chicken wings, because Dad can't grill a wing to save his life but totally thinks he can, and when he's away me and her go to town.

"You rode all the way to Hollowood?" she says as I wheel my bike across the yard to the door that opens onto the back of the garage.

"How do you know?"

"I started following a few hashtags."

"So?"

"So there were a few pictures."

"Of what, me?"

"Look for yourself, she says, nodding to her phone on the cushion of a nearby chair. "My hands are greasy."

Of course I know her unlock code—who do you think set up her phone? There I am, the same three blurry pictures of me through the window of Sutherland's Dry Goods, shared across a dozen accounts under the hashtags #hollowoodfalls, #hollowoodlife, #teamhollowood, #fierceinthefalls, #foundlingsFTW…

"Okay, but why take my picture? Everyone was staring at me. I thought I was gonna get jumped."

"We should have told you sooner," Mom says over her shoulder. "This is where you're from."

"The fuck?" It's no secret I'm adopted. It's no secret to anyone because I don't look a thing like my parents, both born in India, my mom to white South Africans who were there as missionaries. But they've always said they didn't know a thing about my past. Which means they've been lying since day one. "Why wouldn't you tell me? Why would you do this to me?"

I'm shouting but that's nothing compared to the pressure in my brain as she calmly puts down the tongs then lowers the heat on the BBQ. "Your father and I talked and talked about this but we could never decide what was right. And then it was moving day and now…"

"And now I'm fucking famous."

"Sweetie," she says in a warning tone, but I'm too mad to check my mouth.

"Forget it. I'm fucking angry and I'm using one of my passes, god-dammit. I'm fucking famous and you didn't fucking tell me?"

"Sweetie, you're not famous—"

"When people stop and stare at you and take pictures of you and post them online where other people freak out? Yeah, that's basically famous."

"Your family is fairly well known around here."

"I have *family*? Fuck this noise. You can tell me the rest later."

"Marcus—"

"Later." I have to get away. Get some air, some space, but where can I go? Back to Hollowood Falls to find out *why* I'm famous. I'm too mad at my mom to want to hear her version. I want the truth from the people who abandoned me. And nothing's going to keep me from getting it.

Two

Relations

I get as far as the gas station before my machismo gives out. It's getting late and I'm going to run out of daylight too and I'm really not thrilled about dealing with these roads after dark. But as if I'm going to go home and admit to my mom that I rode off without thinking and then couldn't make it all the way into town.

Feeling every push on the pedals I make it back to Hollowood. It's the same postcard perfect scene as before, a few people strolling on the sidewalks, the lights on at the big log house at the top of the hill that overlooks the road. At Sutherland's I leave my bike against the wall like before then go in, my stomach in a knot, my heart in my mouth.

"So what's the deal?" I ask the elderly white man behind the counter. "I was in here before and everyone acted like they knew me but were scared to talk to me. What is it about me that's got all of you so freaked out?"

Sucking on his dentures, he looks me up and down. The bells on the door jingle and he glances at whoever it is over his wire-rimmed glasses. "If you want to hear it from the horse's mouth, you might ask them," he says in a gravelly New England accent.

He nods towards the door and I turn to find the most beautiful person I've ever seen in my life. Deep brown eyes, pale lashes, a narrow, pointed jaw supporting a pair of sweetly curving lips. I don't care that their skin is white, that their forehead has zits, that I've never met them before and know nothing about them, I *want* to know them. Want to know their name, their favorite band, the parts of them that are ticklish, the smell of the curve of their neck.

The current between us breaks as their friends bump into them on their way into the store. Not hard to do, for the two men are each over six feet tall and seriously built. It's not my color that's making people stare, because one of the big guys is darker than me, his locs coiled up on the back of his head. The other person—the perfect person, the stunner, my god—is still staring at me. One of the men whistles and they flinch then pull their hoodie up and head for the back of the store.

"Like I said, you might as well ask them."

The smallest and palest of them, the stunner is talking softly to the big guys, their hood shifting like they keep trying to look at me as I stand wordless at the front of the store. The bells on the door jingle as someone else comes in, and I make myself move. I'm halfway down the household goods aisle when the hoodie turns all the way around.

I stop, because I can't feel the ground under my feet. What the hell is wrong with me? I don't fall like this, don't get random crushes, but I can't stop staring at them, soaking in the details, the slope of their nose and curve of their eyebrows and the shaggy auburn curl that's snaked its way out of their hood. I have to speak, have to tell them they matter, that they're beautiful, that I need to know everything there is to know about them right now, but before I remember how words work, the big white guy growls, a low rumbling sound from deep in his massive chest. Hoodie flinches then drops their head and follows him to the front of the store where the Black guy is waiting.

And then they leave. My answers, my everything. The reason I'm here, and I bolt for the door. They're halfway across the street but stop when I shout. The big white guy nods to the others, and they keep going, Hoodie glancing back a couple times.

"What can I do for you?" the man asks.

"You can tell me what the hell's wrong with this town."

He chuckles, looking up and down the street. "Where should I start?"

"By telling me why you all are staring at me? Everyone whispering behind their hands. Posting up pictures of me without my permission, so what's going on? If I left here when I was a baby, how the fuck do you all know who I am?"

"That's quite a lot of questions," he says warmly. "I don't know if I can answer them like this. It's better if you come back tomorrow."

"You got to give me something. I came all the way back from Cattail for this. What about my family?"

"You have no blood relations in Hollowood, I'm sorry to say. Your family came from back east."

"Did you know my parents."

"I did."

"And?"

"We can't talk about this here."

"Why not?"

"Because it's going to hurt." He says it gently, and for some reason that's scarier than if he shouted. "Come and see us tomorrow. I'll explain what we know."

"I got nothing going on right now," I say weakly as he turns to go.

"I'm sorry, but it'll have to be tomorrow."

I want to argue more, but I'm only going to piss him off, make him that much less likely to tell me what I want to know. "What time's good for you?" I say instead.

A trace of a smile pulls at one corner of his stern mouth. "We're busy in the morning. Come after lunch."

"See you then." I'm calling on everything I remember from Mr Wickramasinghe's business ethics class to keep from freaking out, because this guy could tear my head off without breaking a sweat. He knows things about me that I don't. Maybe he's a link to the past I never knew, and I need to stay on his good side, so like a grown man and not the sweating, shaking only-just-a-man I truly am I put out my hand and we shake.

"What's your name?" he asks, which is probably way more important than the fact that I shook his hand.

"Marcus. You?"

"Call me Robin."

Thank the good Lord for Mr Wickramasinghe because I manage to take this gigantic man's soft little name for what it is, his name and nothing more. I don't even ask the name of the other person, not the Black guy but that small pale flame to the moth that is me, because I'm an adult and I am totally not in insta-love with a person I've never even met.

I am totally in control of my senses. Totally sure of my body. Totally sure as I mount my bike that I'm going to wipe the fuck out if I try to ride, my heart fluttering in my chest, the road ahead of me disappearing into twilight. All I have to do is coast, but I haven't charged my headlamp battery and I'm so tired as it is from climbing this mountain twice in a day.

"I'm happy to give you a lift down the hill," Robin says, for he's been watching me all this time.

"It's cool."

"It won't be so cool when the mist comes up. It would make me feel better knowing you got home safe."

I'm kind of an asshole to say no at this point, so I dismount and wheel my bike over to his beautiful new truck parked in front of the store. "I don't want to scratch up the flatbed," I say as he picks up my bike with one freaking hand and straight-arm lifts it over the side.

"I'm going to wreck it sooner or later," he says with a chuckle in his massive chest. "Might as well be for a good deed."

The electric truck sails down the road, the lack of engine noise a bit spooky as we glide through the mist. He doesn't say anything and neither do I, but somehow it doesn't feel weird even though I could be asking him all sort of questions. Questions I'm coming back tomorrow to ask, but if I get the answers now, I lose my chance to maybe see that person again.

I need a name. I can't think about them all night as Hoodie-bae, but I can't think of how to ask without wrecking this chill vibe. We soon reach flatter ground, leaving the mist behind.

"Do you mind if I leave you here?" Robin asks as he pulls off at the service station. "It's about five, six miles to Coat-tail—I mean Cattail Crossing, should be an easy ride."

"Why'd you call it that?" I ask as we get out of the truck.

"The subdivision? What else is there around but us? If there wasn't a Hollowood Falls there'd be nothing here."

"So we're riding on your good name, is that it?"

"Pretty much," he says, setting down my bike. "See you tomorrow, Marcus."

I give him half a wave as he pulls onto the highway. It's brighter here than on the mountain but still later than I like to be riding on a major road, but there's hardly any traffic and I'm home before I know it. After stashing my bike I come into the house through the door from the garage. Mom's curled up on the sofa under a blanket, cradling her big I'm-stressed-but-hiding-it handmade ceramic mug, an old ep of *Riverdale* playing on the tv with the sound way down.

"Sorry I walked out like that," I say, bending over the back of the sofa to kiss her forehead.

"I understand why you're upset. We really let you down."

"That's okay. It's not like I've ever asked you about this sort of thing."

"Still, we shouldn't have let you walk into this unprepared."

"Tell me the truth, though. Did this have anything to do with why you took this grant and not the Norfolk Island?"

"Kind of the opposite," she says, making a sour face.

"That would have been worse? What, am I the king there?"

"No, see, then we would have definitely gone there. What?" she says as I start laughing. "I'd make a great Queen Mum." She does that closed-hand wave like a British queen.

"Wouldn't you be a King Mum?"

"Either way, your highness, your dinner's in the fridge."

"You better have left me some flats, woman."

Do I forgive her? I don't know yet. I'll figure it out tomorrow when I go back and talk to Robin. Is he Hoodie's dad or uncle or none of the above? Does he know what happened to my parents, and if he does, am I ready to hear it?

Three

Revelations

I expect to lie in bed staring at my new ceiling all night but the riding knocks me out fast, my dreams a blur of noise and heat and chaos, of running blind, seeking silence. I wake with my pillow crushed to my chest, the corner wet like I've been chewing on it. In the last house, the night table was on the right. Now it's on the left and it takes me a bit to find my phone and figure out what time it is. And what day, because I don't have school to keep me tethered to the real world.

Mom's door is shut but I can hear her on a call so I go out to the garage and start bringing in unopened boxes. We've moved enough times that every box is labelled with a shipping manifest listing the contents, thanks to the app Dad built a few years ago. I fill the first two bookcases in the living room with books but also photos and little statues and cool shells and all the stuff we've picked up in the places we've been, and the room feels a lot more like home by the time I'm done.

I make a few grilled cheese and bring one up to Mom. I've been thinking about Hollowood all morning, but I manage to wait until nearly one, then pack a t-shirt, a towel, and a few bottles in my pannier and hit the road. I want to look half normal when I see my not-my-bae. And their ripped dad, and maybe people who knew my birth parents. I need to look like I know what I'm doing.

It's only when I get to Sutherland's that I realize I don't know how to tell Robin that I'm here, though for all I know he's following the hashtags. I duck into the restroom to change my shirt and when I come out he's talking to the cashier.

"Good timing," he says to me. "I came for the mail." He nods at the pile of padded envelopes and smiling boxes on the counter.

"I can help carry some of those," I say as he starts stacking them.

"What about your bike?"

"It's cool. I have pannier bags, even."

"I think I'll manage," he says with an easy smile, scooping up the pile with one massive arm. He gestures to the door and I hustle to open it for him.

"What's brought you back to Hollowood Falls?" he asks as we start across the road.

"My mom. She's a behavioral ornithologist."

"She studies birds?"

"Yeah. I guess the crows here are some rare species. She's leading this big Jane Goodall immersive study so we're here until next summer."

"And you've come with her?"

"You mean, why am I still living at home?"

"Not exactly," he says. "All my grown kids still live at home, and I don't see them moving out any time soon."

"I guess that's how it is now. I just didn't want to go into debt going to school when I didn't know what I wanted to do once I got out."

"And now?"

"I still don't know what I want to do. But I'm not in debt, so that's something."

"I'll drop these off and then take you up to the Lodge," Robin says. We're standing on the driveway of a big log house set back in the trees, the spur of the mountain so close it seems to start in their backyard. "You can leave your bike on the porch with River's."

He points to a beat-up green BMX as a thrill runs through me. Is that their name, my hoodie-bae? It suits them, but I can't start thinking like that. Robin has a few kids, and I don't even know that he's my crush's dad. I don't know anything about them.

Robin and I walk further up the hill to the big log building at the bend in the road. With its angled roof, wide stairs, and veranda running around the outside, it reminds me of traditional houses in Sulawesi. I tell Robin this and he spends the next couple minutes quizzing me about everywhere we've been. I take it for granted but by the end he's looking at me with a little more respect. I hope. I hope he's River's dad and I'm impressing the hell out of him.

Inside it looks like a log cabin except huge, with a big mezzanine running around the upper floor of the main room like the veranda in reverse. Banners and flags hang from it, some of them faded or missing their felt letters, though I don't know any of the acronyms. Rows of folding chairs and a few tables are leaned against the far wall. Robin stops at a big photo on the near wall, a wide shot of a party. A banner on the mezzanine reads *HAPPY NEW YEAR 1998*.

"Your folks are in this one. There." He points to a couple in the foreground seated at one of the long tables. They're smiling as they lean into each other, neither of them looking at the camera, as if there's more than one person taking pictures. They're real, and for a second I can't hold my head up, can't even breathe. Robin rests his big hand on my shoulder.

"I should have waited," he says.

I shake my head. I need every bit of this, even if it hurts. "I don't mind. I knew this was going to be hard."

He leads me to an office upstairs where he gets out a huge old book with leather corners and starts explaining the families of Hollowood Falls. He might as well be explaining the British royal family. This shit goes back generations, though it seems like five main families are what keeps the town going, with enough newcomers that no one had to marry their cousin. It's too much to take in, even when he starts talking about my folks, who had come from a similar town on the east coast. All I can think of is that photo. My birth parents, young, happy, and alive.

"So that's Hollowood," Robin says as he closes the book with a thud. "Do you want to know what happened to your parents?"

"Might as well get it over with, though it doesn't sound like it's good."

"We don't know the whole story. If we did, it's likely someone here would have adopted you. What we do know is that the three of you were going back east so you could meet your grandparents. So they could meet you, really, because you weren't even a year old."

As he talks, I start to feel cold. He pauses, looking at me with concern, but I nod. As much as I don't want to feel like this, if he stops I might never be brave enough to ask again.

"They never arrived, and they never returned. We, and I do mean we, spent a lot of time on the phone calling police departments, city after city, looking for records of a car crash or...violence. Something where they didn't know the next of kin, anything. It was like they'd vanished. You too. About three years later, someone turned up a news report about an infant found abandoned at the scene of a car crash."

"So then they are dead," I say, my voice sticking in my throat.

"That's the thing," he replies carefully, watching my face. "We still can't say for sure. There weren't any bodies. Just the car, burnt to the frame. No luggage, no license plate, no VIN plate, nothing."

"What are you saying? What happened to them? Where are my parents?"

"I don't know. Marcus, I'm sorry."

"Do you remember them?" I ask when I can breathe again.

"I do. And I think they would have been proud to see the man you're becoming."

That hits too hard, my throat closing, eyes burning, but I'm not going to break, not in front of this man. It was so long ago and I never knew them and he doesn't know me, this man telling me that my parents vanished off the face of the earth. This doesn't change a thing so why should I cry, or feel any different than I did this morning? I should be grateful that I have a family, but I should have had a different one. I should have known this man all my life, grown up with his kids, known River since birth, and the sense of lives unlived has never felt so real.

"You don't need to be brave for me, Marcus," he says, hoarse with feeling. "I lost friends. You lost everything."

I've spent my whole life not breaking. Not letting other kids see how much their words hurt me. Not letting on how big a hole there is in my heart. Robin's the strongest man I've ever met and he's crying like...like a man having feelings. Fuck that voice in me that says he's weak, that I am. If I was weak, I wouldn't have made it this far.

Four

Dangerous Things

When we get ourselves together he puts the books away and we go back to his house. I feel wrung out but lighter, like my soul was dirty and the tears washed it clean. My bike is where I left it by the green BMX, and it's only when I'm stepping through the door that I remember what that means.

They could be here. They could be close. Or that bike belongs to whoever, no one that matters to me. But there's something familiar about this house, this place I've never been, that's not like any house I've ever seen. The huge logs that make up the walls glow like hot honey. Stairs hug the wall to my right, and the doorway in front of me leads to the kitchen. The living room is to the left and down two steps, and as I take a deeper breath, wondering what flower has such a sweetly pungent scent, I see a pair of pale legs sticking out from the deep cushions of a nearby recliner.

The chair is turned and I can't see the person's face, but those legs are too familiar. The delicious smell suddenly meets up with the shape and skintone of those legs and turns into me standing in the doorway to the living room with my mouth hanging open because it's them.

"River," Robin says. The hoodie in the recliner grunts in reply. "Why don't you put your laptop away and show Marcus around town?"

Because it's a livestream," they say absently, their nails scraping the bottom of the chip bowl wedged beside them.

"Just do it," Robin says, in that voice dads use when they know your reasons but don't give a shit.

"Ughhhhhhh..."

"Riv..."

"You know I'm like an adult, right?"

"By about five months."

"Still, legally—"

"River Croft," calls their mother from the kitchen. "If your father has to tell you again—"

"Fine! Whatever. It's going to take like ten minutes anyway because there's nothing to see in this dump." With a groan of irritation they make no attempt to hide, River hauls themself out of the armchair, dusting cheese powder off their bare thighs. Blushing, I look up at the same time they do, and bam...

From across the store they were magnetic. Face to face, River is without a doubt the most beautiful person I've ever seen. Not in a filtered way but real, living beauty standing right in front of me. The word *puckish* drifts through my mind, a memory from Ms Bellingham's grade eleven English class. A Shakespearean for life who spent her summers doing stock theatre in the park, she had an almost fangirl thing going with *A Midsummer's Night Dream*. River could pull it off, be a sneaky, teasing fae, with their deep-set eyes and wild tumble of soft auburn curls. They absently wipe a smear of cheese powder off their cheek and I want to follow their fingers with my tongue.

I'm staring, but so is River, who startles as their dad puts a huge hand on their shoulder. "This is Marcus," he says to River. "Marcus, River."

"Yeah. That's me," River says vaguely. "And that's you. Wait, what am I doing?"

"Marcus wants to know a few things about Hollowood. I've got work but you don't so—"

"Sure. Yeah. Whatever."

"Off you go, then," Robin says in the voice of a parent encouraging a toddler at a wading pool. "Have fun."

And then we're outside, both of us blinking in the afternoon sun. "So...did you like move here?" River asks, shoving their hands in the hoodie's front pouch as we start down their driveway.

"No. I mean I live in Cattail," I add as they give me a weird look. "Cattail, um, whatever."

"Coat-tail Crossing?"

"Yeah, real funny."

"Hey, I didn't name it," they say, kicking gravel as we climb the hill. "I've never been there even."

"There's not much to see. Not like here." I turn to look down the hill. The afternoon sun is lighting up the trees on the east of the valley, little clouds drifting across a sky so blue it hurts. The bend in the road at the bottom of town makes it look like the place has nothing do to with the world outside. "This is really pretty."

"It's boring as shit." River kicks another pebble that goes skittering down the road end over end. "All I want to do is get out of here. Go somewhere I can get a real life."

"Did you graduate?"

They give me a disgusted look. "How old do you think I am?"

"Hey, no shame. I lost a year. I ended up graduating remotely."

"No prom?"

"I went, I just hadn't graduated. Why, do you wish *you* went to prom?"

"I *did* go. It's not a big school but—" With a dramatic sigh they turn their shoulder on me and gesture indifferently at the valley. "Anyway, this is Hollowood Falls. Big wow, everything is made of wood, everything smells like trees, and...that's about it."

"Do other people our age live here?"

"Oh god, you're sick of me already?"

"No, I'm just wondering what you do for fun."

"Other than drag townies around?"

"You're the townie."

"Ugh, whatever." They throw up their slim hands and their sleeves slide up their arms, showing their other tattoos, a gudetama fried egg chibi passed out on a bowl of rice on their left wrist, and on the inside of their right arm the leopard boy from the cover of *Zaba*.

"Is that your favorite album of theirs?" I ask, pointing at the tattoo.

"Glass Animals? I mean all their stuff's amazing. You know them?"

"I saw them live."

"Shut up!" they cry, punching my shoulder, which stings more than I expect. "I tried so hard to go to Red Rocks last year but I wasn't allowed to go on my own and no one would take me."

"Next time it won't matter, you can just go."

"Right? We should totally go. I mean if you're around."

"Yeah, right. It's not like they announced dates."

"There's not even a new album yet."

The little flare of hope in me dies as River shoves their hands in their hoodie then keeps climbing. I want to tell them all about the concert but then I'd be rubbing it in that they didn't get to go. I want to ask them a million questions but their hunched shoulders and quick steps tell me what I'm likely to get as an answer. So I follow without speaking as they lead me past the Lodge then along a little raked gravel path to a graveyard. The headstones are ancient, crusted with lichen and hard to read, some of them leaning forward at such an angle I can't see the face at all as River leads me between them.

"You should know," they say as they step around a canting stone angel, "there's weird things in this forest. Dangerous things."

"Bears?"

"Wolves. Big ones, and they don't take shit from humans."

"My house is made out of brick, so I'm good."

"I'm serious. They could be watching us right now. Thinking, mm-mm, that boy looks tasty."

"You going to protect me?"

"Maybe. Maybe I'll let them eat you."

If they're flirting, they suck at it, because River's glaring at me like it's true, like they hate my guts and they'd throw me to the wolves and laugh while I got torn apart.

"You can't scare me," I say, trying to keep my voice level. "My parents vanished off the face of the earth. Now *that's* fucking scary."

Five

The Escort

I was wrong. I was seeing things. I wanted that first look in the store to mean something, for River to mean something to me, but I was wrong, they're just another asshole kid, and I'm done.

"Wait," they call after me as I start back downhill.

"I can find your house myself."

"I didn't mean to...it's just that my dad...will you let me fucking apologise, you ass?"

"Not when it's not going to mean anything."

"But I'm sorry."

"For what? For wasting my time, for trying to freak me out, for staring at me?"

"You're the one who keeps staring at me."

"See? We're both wasting our time."

This whole day was a waste. If anything I know even less about my birth parents, because I didn't get any answers, only more questions. What happened to the family out east? Why did no one look for me? Why do parents think that if young people are the same age that's enough to start a friendship?

"I'm sorry," River says again, and they sound like they mean it, a hitch in their voice as they scuff along behind me in their slides, which must be hell to walk in on these damn hills. "I wasn't trying to freak you out."

"You took me to a graveyard and told me the forest was full of man-eating wolves. I kind of think you were."

"It's just... you need to know these things if you're going to be hanging around Hollowood."

"Fuck Hollowood! You think I'm coming back here after the way I've been treated? People taking my picture through the window, talking behind my back. My birth parents evaporated or some shit, and now you've ruined Glass Animals, because every time I go to listen to them from now on, I'm going to think of you!"

"I'm sorry—"

"You're not. You're embarrassed because I'm not buying into your shit. Game over."

"Fine. I tried. I tried being nice—"

"The fuck you did."

As the echoes die away I realize everyone in town has heard me shouting. They'll have heard me in Denver, the way the valley walls reflect the sound. My throat hurts, and my heart, and my brain because what the hell was I thinking? There's no such thing as love at first sight.

We still have to walk back to River's house together so I can get my bike. Robin is on the front porch with a red-headed woman who must be River's mom. The door is open and River tries to blow past them but Robin stops them with a hand on their chest. River mutters something I don't hear.

"You haven't given him much of a chance," Robin says.

"Why bother?" River shoots back. "He doesn't even live in the Falls. Six months, he'll be gone. Well, you will," they say, glaring at me over their shoulder. "Like anyone with brains would stick around this nowhere town if they had a choice."

"Mind your manners," Robin says coldly.

"Make me."

My shoulders hurt, and I realize how tense I am waiting for it to get ugly, because if a man built like Robin told me to watch my mouth I'd shit myself then goddamn do it. River is unshook, glaring at their father, their little fists clenched at their sides.

"You're going to ride him home," Robin says evenly.

"You're kidding! What about my livestream?"

"River, please do what your father wants," says Mrs. Croft, though I swear she rolls her eyes.

"Yeah, because why break with tradition? I'm going, I'm going," they snarl at their dad as he opens his mouth. They grab their bike and are at the end of the driveway before I know what's going on.

"Thanks, Mr. Croft, for telling me all that," I say as I wheel my bike off the porch. "Nice to meet you, Mrs. Croft. I guess I gotta go." They wave but say nothing as I pedal off after River, who is already a hundred yards down the road. I pump a few times to catch up.

"Why does he think I need an escort?" I ask once we're riding.

"Because it'll be dark sooner than you think, and the roads out here are fucked, and if you fall off you're dead and they'll make it my fault somehow."

"I'm not scared to ride down a mountain."

"Whatever. You just better ride fast," they say, their hood billowing with the wind. "I don't stop for anything." They rise up on the pedals and take off, picking up mad speed on the downhill straightaway, but I'm not falling for their shit. It's a single road from here to the tableland and then a few miles along the highway. I don't need anyone's help.

We blow through town in less than a minute. It's getting cloudy, the forest to either side growing darker and darker. Swinging around a switchback I see the mist gathering in the hollows below us. A few more turns and we're in it, clumps of fog drifting across the roads like the silvery ghosts of clouds.

I'm riding River's slipstream, leaning into the curves, the only sound the wind whipping past my head and the hum of tires on asphalt. River's legs flash white in the gloom as they rise up on the pedals again. I've never seen anyone rock a BMX like it's a road bike. Picturing River on the civic trail, that battered green frame shooting past the weekend warriors on their composites and the hipsters on their Flixis, I have to laugh.

Despite the speed, the dark, the very real danger, River glances back, their teeth and eyes flashing. It is one of the greatest rides of my life, and as I realize this we pass the twin teeth of jagged black rock that mark the start of Hollowood Road, and it's over.

Riding the highway pretty much kills the vibe. There's hardly any traffic but it's a boring straightaway that leads to saying goodbye, and I can't remember why I was so angry. Can't remember why I was so eager to get home. We ride silently through the flat and dusty subdivision, past nearly identical homes with under-watered saplings on every third lawn, motion-sensing lights on the garages flicking on as we pass. I nearly miss my place, but it's the only one that doesn't have a massive SUV in the driveway.

"I guess I'll see you around," I say, because there's not much else to say. River's face is in shadow, the red smear of sunset along the horizon shining through the mess of angles that is their legs and the frame of their bike.

"I guess," they echo. "I don't come this way much."

"I meant if I come to see…the Falls." I almost said to see you but we're not friends, not at all. We're nothing to each other.

"Right," they say, and though they weren't out of breath on the way they're breathing hard now as we stare at each other down the length of the driveway. "Sure. I guess…"

They shiver, making a funny little noise in their throat, and I'm about to ask if they need some water when they're off, gravel shooting from under their tires, bare legs pumping. At the bend in the road they look back and we wave at each other once, and that's how I meet River Croft.

Six

Not in Love

I stay away from Hollowood for the next few days. Mom's on calls for a lot of the time so I go on unpacking the house and get it mostly right. When Dad calls after dinner I keep it light, telling him about the neighbourhood, the clouds, the shit-show that was the last NBA draft. I do not mention River.

Do I think about them? What do you think? And it's bad. I've never been so shook. Never had someone come up in my thoughts twenty, thirty times a day. Making a sandwich, I wonder what they like on theirs, if they eat peanut butter or if they're allergic. Swapping the wet laundry into the dryer, I think about that hoodie and whether they have just the one or a whole bunch the same and if I just happened to see them in the same one twice.

Nights are worse. The nights make me question my integrity because I've never fantasized about someone I know. And not just that vague kissing-and-then-some feelings way because I can't quite imagine ever getting to bone Janelle Monaé. I mean full Hollywood-production-level stroke scenes that if you wrote them down would be the kind of smutty erotica that housewives read when no one's looking. I'll be lying there wondering what they like on their pizza and suddenly it's us drifting down a Venetian canal in a gondola, dressed like dukes in silk breeches and frilly shirts, River draped over me with their lips wrapped around my cock. Then we'd go back to the room with the high ceilings and that big bed with the canopy, where I'd use their cravat and mine to tie them to the bed posts and...

Every night for three nights, and good thing I'm not working or in school because unpacking boxes is about all the brain I have left by Thursday. So when the new follower notification pops on my phone around two in the afternoon, I follow River back instantly.

But don't I hate them? Didn't I go off on them, throw their apologies back in their face, decide I never wanted to see them again? Don't they hate me for that? It's too late, I can't unfollow, not right away. Maybe later, after I see if their feed is even interesting.

And...it's adorable. It's River and their siblings and their cousins and friends goofing off in the forest, in Sutherland's, in River's living room. In another room lit with pink and blue lights that must be River's bedroom because there's always someone in the shot wearing a comforter. Blurry pictures through a screen door of birds in the backyard, and deer and rabbits and squirrels. Their pencil crayon art—hyperreal drawings of those animals leaping through archways of fantastical flowers—which makes me tremble and catch my breath each time one slides across the screen. Selfies, with or without other people: River cross-eyed, with their tongue out, with the cat-ears filter, with wolf ears and nose.

That one has more reactions than most, some kind of inside joke. Maybe everyone in Hollowood is scared of the big bad wolves. When I get to the reel where River is in literal tears, pleading for someone to help them crowdfund a ticket to the Red Rocks concert I realize I've scrolled through a year of their life.

But I'm totally not in love.

Neither is River, or so I tell myself, but the next morning they're in my DMs with a playlist. Without a thought, I click through to it. As the soft scratching beat and plucked guitar of *Heat Waves* by Glass Animals begins to whisper from my phone speaker, I realize this is the high school romance I never had. I was never anywhere long enough, was usually gone by summer, on to the next school. Never knew anyone I wanted to screw up my life for, break my own heart by falling for them and then leaving.

I don't want to leave. I want to ride to Hollowood right now blasting this song like that old movie where he holds up the big cassette player outside the girl's window until River comes out of their house and we meet in the middle of the road so I can apologize for treating them wrong. I want to ask everyone in town everything they know about my birth parents, see all the photos, cry all the tears.

I want this to be where I belong.

The playlist is a sign. Maybe an ask, but I don't message them before setting out for Hollowood the next morning. Even if they're not around, or if they don't like me after all, I can get in a good ride, maybe check out a few trails. I gear up like I'm going to be gone all day, even packing a shell jacket in case I'm out late or it rains. It doesn't add much weight and we've seen every kind of weather this week, from sunshine to hail.

It's already getting cloudy by the time I reach the side-road, but the extra effort soon warms me up. As I'm nearing the gas station a cyclist comes whipping past, heading downhill. No, it's River, wearing short shorts and shell-toe sneakers and that same hoodie. They skid to a stop way too close to the guard rail, but before I can shout a warning they're up on the pedals again and speeding towards me.

They stop so close I feel their tailwind sweep over me, carrying a trace of their weirdly interesting herbal perfume mixed in with the smell of their sweat. Like a dog, my dick sits up and begs, and I say a silent prayer of thanks that I wore cargos today and not bike shorts.

"Hey," River says breathily after almost a minute of us staring at each other.

"Hey."

"So...if I was shitty last week—"

"So was I." Not that I don't want their apology. But we were each other's problem, and what I want is for the problem part to go away.

"Right," River says, nodding slowly. "So does that mean we're cool?"

"Um...sure."

"Cool, cool. So you want to ride, maybe?"

I look down at the bike I'm straddling. "Sure."

"Cool. There's a trail just behind here."

"You take that thing on trails?"

They smile, and the tight feeling in my chest opens up. "I take it wherever I want," they say. "You sure yours isn't too high end for off-roading?"

"Show me what you got."

"Alright. Let's rip it up."

And it's unreal. Peak biking. Real back-country riding, the trail only a suggestion, branches whipping my arms and legs and smacking off my helmet. River rides hunched low over the handlebars, making up for the lack of shocks on their bike by jumping every slope, every ridge, sometimes seeming to skip down the hillsides, tires barely skimming the ground, their hoodie cinched tight around their face so it's like I'm chasing a game avatar through the endless trees, only it's real.

It's the toughest ride I've ever been on and it's the best feeling in the world. No one can catch us, no one can stop us. Maybe gravity, but even that's negotiable as I clear a three-foot gap like I'm hopping a curb. This is where I belong. This is our forest. Our home.

Look, riding's a trip. You go hard and fast enough and your brain takes you other places. Sometimes it's work to stay rooted in the moment, but you have to or you'll wipe out, break bones or worse. In this moment, on this ride, my brain and my body are working as one. Time disappears in the flow of adrenaline and altitude as we rise and rise and fall and fall through the forest.

It's not until we stop at Sutherland's for energy bars and water that I feel how far we've ridden. River's feeling it too, their hands shaking as they pay for the bars, and we sit on the bench outside and restore our blood sugar in what books like *Bridgerton* call companionable silence (sorry not sorry but Regé-Jean Page is a goddamn snack and I'd heard the book was even dirtier.)

It's nearly five o'clock and if I don't start home soon I'll be riding in the dark. Maybe River's thinking the same because we set off downhill without discussion, but before we reach the gas station they turn up a side road. At the top of a sharp climb is a big stone building with a caved-in roof. It stands on the edge of a ravine, the wooden posts sticking out of that side of the building rotting into oblivion.

"This used to be a sawmill," River tells me as they dismount. "Back when there was a creek running behind here, before they built the big dam." Aspens ring the clearing, their fluttering leaves bright against the dense canopy of evergreens. The sky has cleared again, sunlight filling the clearing like a bowl of honey.

"It's really pretty," I say.

"I can't believe they haven't fucked it up with a gift shop and an interpretation walk."

"Fridge magnets."

"Someone who loves me went to Hollowood Mills," River starts in a prissy voice, and we finish it together, "and they bought me this shirt."

Have I ever seen them smile? Maybe not like this, because it's such a joy, seeing them happy, making them laugh. "I'm sorry again for being an ass the other day," they say.

"You don't need to apologize anymore."

"I want to, though. I was a shit-head. I shouldn't let my parents get to me. Well, it's mainly my dad, but she doesn't back me up much. That's why I can't wait to get out of here."

"It's nice though."

"I know I should be grateful. People pay a lot of money to live in places like this."

"Yeah, but usually not until they're too old to do much."

A weight lifts off my heart as River smiles again. "You want to see something special?"

Seven

The Other Valley

I follow River up the hill, past the mill and into the woods. From the way they keep glancing back with that shy smile, I start to worry that *something special* is code for making out. Then I wonder why I'm worried when I should be overjoyed. Or am I imagining everything, painting this scene in the wrong colors, wanting what isn't there?

In a couple minutes we reach the crest of a ridge. Here they stop, and it's not hard to see why because it's beautiful. It's not the brilliant beauty of New Hampshire in the fall, or the drama of a snowy peak, but the view is still magnificent, the undulating waves of green and gold pierced here and there with huge fingers of stone. We're so high up I see eagles coasting the thermals below. Far away, lost in the blue haze of pine sap, another great peak rises, its summit cloaked in cloud.

"Not bad, hey?" River says. Their hood is down and the sunlight is catching every bit of red in their tangled hair. I want to comb out each tangle, one by one, so I can run my fingers through it, and I turn away before the feeling overwhelms me.

"It's pretty good."

"Don't look down, though. I said don't look!" They put their hand on my chest as I do exactly that. Good thing because we're standing at the top of a hundred foot drop.

"Shit!"

"We're good, just step back a bit." Their hand over my heart, their heat soaking into my skin, they give me a little push and I step back from the edge, the rocks I've dislodged bouncing from outcrop to outcrop before disappearing into the trees.

Nearby a rock stands free of the undergrowth with space for us to sit side by side. Once my heart stops hammering the quiet is immense. It's not silence, with the wind whistling through the evergreens and the rustle of softer leaves, the birds twittering in the treetops below us, the sun so bright it's almost a sound in itself, an electrical hum underlying everything.

Now that I hear it, I can't stop hearing it. River is staring at something in the valley and I follow their gaze to the only unnatural thing in the valley, a wide flat roof painted a murky green, half hidden by the trees about a mile away across the valley.

"What's that building?"

"I don't know," they reply softly, and something in their voice makes me shiver like the wind has turned ice cold.

I don't like the building, not at all. I don't like it being there, even though it blends into the landscape so well it's hard to see unless you're looking right at it. Is that what's giving *Black Mirror* vibes?

"I've heard things..." River says in the same low voice.

"Rumors?"

"Noises."

"Like what kind of noises?"

"Like noises I didn't want to hear."

That's it for asking questions. The less I know the better, and I stand up when River does. I don't want to turn my back on the building, but not as badly as I want to get the hell away from it. We've hardly gone two steps when River steps on a loose rock and stumbles sideways. Towards the edge, towards death, and I grab their arm and pull them back.

They fall against me and we stand like this, my hand tight on their wrist, my other arm around their waist, the pink shell of their ear next to my mouth, the sunlight glowing on their soft cheek. If they were facing me I'd kiss them. I should kiss them anyway, brush my lips over their cheek, let them know how I feel, but that means taking advantage of an accident that could have been a disaster. I let them go, and hiding behind their hair they squeeze past me and start down the narrow path to the mill.

Shit. Too much touching, and it's a good thing I didn't kiss them. Or not enough touching and I *should* have kissed them no matter what my brain was telling me. But it doesn't matter what I've fantasized, they're still a stranger to me, even if their mouth looks like strawberries and their smell makes my head swim.

I'm still beating myself up when we reach the cleared ground around the mill. River falls into step beside me and as we walk their hand brushes mine. Just like an old romance, when a touch meant everything, and when they do it again I catch their fingers in mine. I'm holding hands with my crush on a perfect sunlit day in the forest, and maybe they're a stranger but they don't have to stay that way. Maybe this is how forever starts, with two people who aren't sure what they want or what they mean to each other, reaching out across a distance and taking a chance.

I stop and they stop with me. "Thank you for showing me that view," I say.

"Sorry I had to wreck it by almost dying."

"It's all good. We made it out alive." I do what I keep wanting to do and brush back that one loose curl that falls over their face. As my fingers brush their skin River gasps, their lashes fluttering, which I didn't know happened outside of books. It's so hot I moan as I trail my hand down the side of their neck.

"Is this okay?" I whisper, and I hardly know what I mean, if I'm asking permission of them or myself.

"I don't know," River says in the same breathy whisper. "I don't know what this is."

"Then why—"

"I don't care why." Their hands are on my waist, grabbing at my shirt and I rest my other hand on their shoulder.

"Can we—"

"Yes."

I've kissed some people. Not many but enough. Enough that this, this kiss, this moment is explosive. A real kiss, driven by real passion and not teenage desperation. An adult kiss, as in adult entertainment, as in River's hand sliding down to cup my ass, pull me hard against their body. I moan again and River takes advantage of my open mouth to plunge their tongue deep.

What the fuck am I doing? Last week I wanted to punch this kid in the face. Now I can't stop kissing them, and it's not just the shock of them kissing me but desire, strong and raw. A want beyond kissing someone who's cute. I want my body inside theirs, their mouth under me, their legs wrapped around my waist. I want everything they're ready to give me.

River hooks a leg around my hip. They're so light I might pick them up, and as River's leg tightens around me I do just that, grab them by the waist and shove my thigh between theirs and hold them against the stone wall with the weight of my body. River lifts their other leg, grinding against me, and I don't need to think about what's doing the grinding to know that this is the best kiss of my life.

Still, we're outdoors in a forest full of bugs and snakes and hikers. We've been riding all day and there's not a bit of me that isn't either sweaty or dirty or both. I want to stand here kissing River until the end of the world, but even while I'm thinking this they make a sound like they're in pain and unhook their ankles from around my waist.

"Wow," they sigh when their feet are on the ground again. "Okay, that answers that."

"What answers what?"

"Doesn't matter. Come on, this is about as much as I want to do in a forest with someone I really only just met.

"But...okay."

"Don't worry," they say, laying their hand against my hot cheek. "I have plenty more where that came from. Enough to last a lifetime."

Eight

Fated

I ride home alone. I'm not ready to introduce River to my parents, and my dad's meant to get back from his week in Denver tonight. I hear his laugh as soon as I walk in, but I need a shower badly and he lets me off with a hug, which fucks up my plans to jerk off while thinking about River. When I come downstairs Dad's caked out on the couch, some dancing show on the tv that he's not watching.

"Rough trip?" I ask as he mutes the tv.

"Rough everything," he says, laying his arm over his eyes. "You ever heard the saying, this meeting could have been an email? This whole week could have been an email."

"That sucks."

"And you? How are the trails around here?"

"They're great. I met someone."

"To ride with? Or..."

"If you're tired, we can talk later."

"No, no, I want to hear this," he says as he struggles upright. "Tell me about your someone."

"It's...complicated."

"It always is with young people. You should do like I did, order off Amazon, that's how I got your mother." The guy can't stay serious, which has been a real problem for a few of my teachers who took everything he said at a hundred percent face value. "How old is this someone?" he asks.

"My age, I guess."

"You don't know?"

"A bit older. But not old like you. I mean…I don't know exactly," I say as his eyebrows shoot up.

"And what do you say to letting me and your mother meet this someone?"

"You might already know their family."

"Keep going," he says, rolling his hand, but River's name sticks in my throat.

"Can you maybe get mom in here so I only have to say it once?" I ask after a few painful seconds.

"Pattycakes," he calls out, "your son wants to tell you something."

"Thanks, Dad, real smooth."

"I'm just cutting to the chase. Did you know, that's from film-making, where they—"

"Yeah, you've told me."

"Excuse me, Einstein. I forgot you knew everything."

"I don't…ugh…forget it." This is hurting my head and I haven't even got to the difficult part.

"What's up sweetie?" Mom says as she comes around the end of the couch.

"He's got a person!"

"A person! Well. Isn't that sweet?"

Why did I think this was a good idea? "We just met. I don't know what's going to happen."

"And that's fine," she says kindly, sitting down on the ottoman and patting my hand. "It's fine if you're still figuring things out for yourself."

"I'm not figuring anything out. I know I'm bi. You know I'm bi. Everyone knows, alright? It's the emotions part that's freaking me out."

"What about it?" says my dad.

"You know…having some."

"You've had Special People in your life before," Mom says, and I can feel the capital letters.

"Yeah but this is different. This feels…unavoidable."

"They…or is it he or…" She trails off, glancing at my father, who has just about swallowed his lips trying to keep quiet.

"*They* is fine," I say, realizing I need to ask River and not just assume.

"They're not pressuring you into anything, are they?" she says.

"No."

"Is this someone you met in Hollowood?" she asks with another odd look for my dad.

"Yeah, but I'm not related to them."

"What's their name?" he asks.

"River."

He sits up straight, the twinkle fading from his eyes. Mom moves from the ottoman to sit beside him.

"River Croft?" she asks in a tight voice. A sick feeling is churning in my stomach as Dad puts his arm around her.

"Why? What's wrong with them?"

"A few years ago," Dad says in a nervous voice, "we had a visit from a Mr Croft."

"The fuck?"

"We didn't take him seriously," he says quickly.

"It sounded ridiculous," Mom adds. "I told him he was out of his mind."

"You said that to *Robin Croft*?"

"He had no proof. No contract, no papers of any kind. Just some disintegrating book that he showed us then took when he left."

"What are you telling me? What did he say to you?"

She looks at Dad, who squeezes her hand again and nods sadly. She turns to me, closing her eyes briefly as she exhales through her nose. "He said to us that you and his second child are fated mates."

The words set off something in me, some deep panic as I jump off the couch. "Ah hell, no. If that's what that sounds like, you are...ah hell, no! I'm not some Beverley Jenkins heir to the fortune you get to marry off to whoever!"

"Mr Croft was very insistent," my father says, and if he laughs I will snap, so help me Lord.

"And you never thought to tell me this?"

"We did, we thought about it a lot, but..." My mom trails off, looking to Dad for back up. He claps his hands together like this is a pep-talk on track-and-field day.

"Think about it from our position, Marcus," he says. "Imagine you're in your room, I don't know, gaming, and me and your mom come and say, we want to have a talk, and we tell you that a thousand year old legend says that you're destined to fall in love with a person you've never met who happens to be a werewolf."

I don't know that I've ever seen a face-palm in real life but Mom does it now as Dad turns ashy. "Goddammit, Hal..." she groans.

"How could I know you haven't told him that part?"

"Because we haven't told him anything!"

"Hang on," I say sharply before they start to argue. "Go back to the bit where you said *werewolf*, because if that's what you said then that is the worst dad joke you've ever told. Or I'm asleep. That's gotta be it. This is a dream. This isn't real, my parents are not out of their damn minds and I did not just make out with a goddamn werewolf on the side of a mountain!"

This pulls my mom up short and she gives me one of her start-explaining looks. "I'm sorry, Marcus, you did what?"

"I'm allowed to make out with whoever I want. You don't have a say about that anymore."

"But...on the side of a mountain?"

"It happened really fast. We were riding, and then we stopped, and how is that the most important thing? A motherfucking werewolf?" They're lying. They're out of their minds. They're fucking with me because this is impossible and insane and River is just a person.

"So. When do we get to meet this River?" my mom says in a sugary voice I've only heard her use on elderly relatives.

"Who, the werewolf? I don't know, when's the next full moon?"

"Wait, I thought he had a person, " my dad says, like he missed the whole damn talk.

"I do! They're not a werewolf, they're a person and their name is River and I kissed them on a mountainside and even if they are a werewolf, you don't get any say about how I live that part of my life, remember?"

"And do you think you and River will be spending much time together?" Mom says in that same ass-kiss voice.

River the werewolf. River the liar, except I hadn't asked because who asks their crush, *by the way, are you a monster?* River, golden in the sunlight, pinned against the wall, sighing into my kisses as I... "I don't know. But the trails in Hollowood are lit. I'm looking forward to riding that valley."

Nine

On the Trail

My parents are joking. Or they're suckers. Fated mates is a thing in romance books, a fantasy. Nothing to do with the real world, with River and the rest of the Crofts. River is not a damn werewolf.

But the fate thing…I can get with that. It's pretty much already happening, because after a really uncomfortable dinner I go up to my room and spend the night with River. Virtually: I like all their posts, I follow all their friends and they start to follow me back. I wonder how my old friends will feel about watching this happen, then decide I don't give a fuck because not one of them has reached out to me. Around ten, River sends a DM, and three hours later we've covered politics (I'm Black and we're both queer so you can guess what side we're on,) pop music (not completely evil but used by evil people,) AI (same) and block chains and makeup on straight men and Leigh Bardugo and my eyelids grate against my corneas and my thumbs are maybe a little numb and I want to ask them to Facetime but it's two in the morning and everyone is asleep and I don't want to wake them by shouting River's name when I come. Because I want that too, want to see them so I can touch them, want to gaze into their eyes and feel them tremble under me and…

uhhh lemme sleep or I cant c u 2mrw I tap, the screen doubling in my aching eyes.

shit sorry shit ok bye

They follow with a pile of emoji: rainbows, kisses, unicorns, stars, a peach. I want to shoot my shot, type those three little letters and let River figure out what to do with them. But if I tell them to their face, I get to see their reaction. I don't care what River really is. Werewolf, weirdo, whatever. All I care about is that River is mine.

Then next morning I wake up at eight feeling like a superhero, though I'm running on maybe five hours of sleep. My bike is hurting from the crazy ride yesterday and I spend an hour with it, changing the tubes and getting the grit out of the chain. One of my brake grips is starting to seize so I'll have to think about ordering some parts.

When I come in from the garage my parents are cuddling on the couch. They're all about the PDA, not just because Dad's gone so often but because it's part of Mom breaking free of her hardcore conservative past. I very deliberately turn my back as they rearrange themselves, pretending I don't hear my dad zip up his fly. At least they like each other.

"Didn't think you'd be out of bed this early," Mom says over the back of the couch. She's got that funny smile on again, like I need to be handled with care. "Weren't you up kind of late?"

"I feel alright. I'll probably go for a ride in a bit. I don't know if I'm seeing River," I add as they swap parental looks. "I'll let you know if I won't be home for dinner."

I hurry upstairs before she comes up with a reply. Not that I expect a fight, but her encouragement is, well, creepy. She of all people should not want to buy into an arranged marriage, seeing as her own folks had planned to set her up with one of their church elders when she was only fifteen.

So why am I buying in? Because everything I feel for River, I started feeling before I knew. Everything I'm feeling right now, I'm feeling despite that knowledge. Maybe Robin did visit my parents to warn them. They still chose to move here, so how scared could they have been?

I'm closing the garage door when I get a message from River: *at mill u bored?*

I send back a selfie, the roofs of Cattail in the background, the phone reflecting off my sunglasses.

ok so c u 2mrw maybe River replies.

duh im coming 2 cu now

ohhhhhhhhhhhhhh im dumb ok cusoon!!!!!!!!!!!!

I laugh, picturing River's thumb twitching on the keys. Their smile as they figure it out. Their eyes, gazing into mine as I tell them all the things I want to do with them. And to them.

The bike flies along the highway and before I expect it I hit the switch-backs. The mill's halfway to town but as I sweat up the steep driveway I hear voices. Three or four bikes are standing against the stone wall, the voices coming from behind the mill, but as I dismount River comes around the corner wearing that same damn hoodie. They squeal, clapping their hands inside their sleeves, then run down the slope, stopping short of jumping on me.

"Who else is here?" I ask as I wheel my bike over to the building.

"My cousins. And my brother Drake. He wanted to meet you."

"Why?"

"Because...I don't know," River says, screwing the toe of one shoe in the gravel. "Because he's my older brother, he's supposed to do stuff like that?"

"Whatever. I'm cool."

"Okay but before you go up there..." They beckon urgently, like they want to tell me a secret. I glance around but no one's watching. I lean close, but instead of whispering, River whips up their hood so it shrouds my face too and kisses me, quickly but hard, licking my lips then swirling their tongue over mine when I open my mouth. Just as suddenly they step back, leaving me with my mouth open and my body on fire.

"Was that okay?" River asks, twisting their fingers together uncertainly.

"Yeah. That was hot."

"It was?"

"*You're* hot. You're amazing."

"Shut up I am not."

"I wanted to see you alone. I want to—"

Someone whistles. "Riv, what're you doing?" they call.

River sags, groaning. "Nothing," they shout in reply.

"I'll tell you later," I say. I kiss them on the cheek then step back as three people come around the corner. Two are massively built like Robin, though the light-skinned kid is shorter than me. The third is a pretty blond girl with super short hair and tattooed thighs who River introduces as their cousin Sunny.

"Is that your ride?" Sunny says, seeing it behind me. I'm getting ready to explain how long it took to save the money to buy it when I realize it's not an accusation that I stole it, it's awe as she brushes past us to kneel beside my bike like she's going to start praying.

River's brother Drake looks like you put his dad in the dryer too long, with the same huge build but shrunk. He shakes like we're grown-ups, with both hands and a serious face. The other kid is called Baz and looks like the guy with locs that was with River's dad. A close little family, but found family if they were meant to all be cousins.

River tears Sunny away from her worship and we start riding, not on River's crazy trail but a smoother trail that leads us higher and higher until we reach a cattle wire fence. A huge tree lays across a section, crushing it flat. Drake and Baz are the first across and disappear into the woods.

"It's cool," Sunny says to me. It's the state park. We just say we paid and they always believe us."

"I'll stay with you if you don't want to go," River says, leaning their elbows on their handlebars.

"I'm cool. The worst they can do is kick us out, right?" I don't need Drake chasing after me because I ran off with his sibling. Before I change my mind, I dismount then carry my bike over the flattened fence.

"You don't need to impress my bro," River says quietly as we wait for Sunny.

"What if I'm trying to impress you?"

Choking, River pulls up their hood to hide their red face. "You goof," the hood mumbles. "You don't have to *try*."

"You mean, you're already impressed?"

"Why yes, Mr...wait, what's your last name?

"Gupta."

"Really?" Sunny says as she joins us.

"My dad's from India."

"Oh right, you're adopted. That sucks, what happened," Sunny says with a sad grimace. "I'm glad you found a family."

"They found me but yeah, I'm pretty lucky."

"And now you're back. That's kinda cool." One of the others whistles from the woods and Sunny whistles back. "We hitting it or what?" she asks us.

"Let's tear it up."

Sunny grins then takes off down the trail. I lean over to kiss River's cheek, then follow.

River's Room

I expect we'll ride to the falls then maybe turn around to go back the way we came. Instead we bypass the falls, though I can hear them in the distance. We then cross the fence again and ride the trail to where it ends, in a gravel parking lot behind Sutherland's. I buy us all ice cream bars and we hang out on the lawn beside the next building to eat them.

River's face is pink and dotted with sweat, that misbehaving curl glued to their cheek. As the other three argue about something that happened last summer, River looks straight at me, mouths their whole ice cream bar in one and pulls it out with a luscious slurp, leaving a ring of creamy white on their lips.

Not to be beaten, I run my tongue around the tip of mine then close my lips over it like I plan to do to River's nipples. Their eyes grow enormous, and the droplet of melted ice cream that has been gathering on their bottom lip falls, spattering on their bare thigh.

Much more of this and we're going to accelerate climate change. But River's fam are getting to their feet, Drake having said exactly nothing to me this whole time, making me wonder if this was his idea or River's. I'm not complaining; a brother who doesn't care who his sibling hooks up with is way easier to deal with than one who cares too much. River gets up to hug Sunny, their hoodie riding up as they do so I see exactly how short their shorts are, the shape of their ass and the sweet curve of their thighs.

As they leave River waves, then does a little spin. Grinning, they spin in place again then go racing off across the lawn. As they dance back towards me they do a messy cartwheel, their bare stomach flashing. They flop down beside me panting, then lie down with their head my lap to look up at me.

"Thanks for being okay with that," they say. "I mean like, for not minding that I threw all those people at you."

"No problem. I would have met them sooner or later."

"Yeah but...what if you wanted to be alone with me?"

"We're alone now."

Their eyes flick to the side, where my cock is doing all it can to join in the conversation. "We *are*. But it'd be better if we weren't, you know, *here*."

"If we were in bed, you mean?"

Their shock is as great as mine, though I hide it better as their eyes fly open. It felt so adult to say that I nearly take it back but if we're going to follow through on these feelings then we should be brave enough to admit it.

I want to fuck River. I want them to want me. I want us to want each other and for it to be good and I know your first is usually no good but I want this and I don't want to wait. I should be saying these things out loud, saying them to River, so they know I'm as freaked out as they are. With another glance at my hard-on they carefully sit up.

"I really want to kiss you," they say with a sweet huskiness to their voice that makes me shiver. "But I think I want to wait a couple minutes until we're...uh..."

"Not out here?"

"Yeah."

"Okay."

"Okay maybe just one kiss."

A kiss that I wish would last forever, their mouth sweetened by the ice cream, their scent spilling over me, their fingers tugging at my hair. The world falls away, until all that exists is us and the kiss, the point where we meet, a rip in the thin membrane separating the possible from the real.

They've climbed onto my lap and are straddling my thighs. My hands are up the back of their sweatshirt, stroking their bare skin, and if this goes on much longer I'll nut in my shorts. River suddenly stops, shoving themselves away from me. "Okay, we really need to not be outside," they pant.

"What are we going to do?"

"Be legal adults."

"I thought we were going to be adults," I whisper as River eases shut the door in the side of their garage.

"We are being adults," they reply softly.

"Then why are we sneaking in?" I ask as they lead me on tiptoe across the garage.

"Because do you really want to have a conversation with my parents at this exact moment?"

They carefully open the inside door and we slip through into a little room full of coats and shoes, then down a split staircase at the other end and through a partly finished basement with three chest freezers and a row of domestic batteries mounted on one wall. We go through a door in a partition wall and the sight takes my breath away.

This wasn't in the pictures of River's room. That's what this is, their bedroom, their world, and the whole place is decorated. I don't mean they have an aesthetic, with succulents and framed prints and pretty lamp-shades. I mean River has painted every wall and even the ceiling with a vast swirling, flowing, connected explosion of flowers and trees and birds and clouds, unicorns and scarlet macaws and luminescent puppies with stars in their eyes, the same style as their pencil art but at huge scale. I'm staring about like I'm new, but I guess I am. New to knowing someone who lives so openly, who thinks to paint rainbow dragons on their ceiling.

"It's weird, I know," River says, tracing a swirl of silver paint outlining a purple leaf. "I get bored easy."

"It's beautiful."

"Is it?" They stare at me, astonished, like no one's ever said it before.

"It's more than beautiful. It's...incredible. You're incredible."

Twisting that loose curl around their finger, they duck their head, but I know they're smiling. "Can I put music on?" they ask, pulling their phone out of their pocket.

"It's your house. Do what you want."

"But you're my guest," they say with a smirk as they flick through songs. "I'm meant to make your stay pleasant."

"Then play *Heat Waves*."

Their thumb stills and they look up. "I thought Glass Animals made you think of me."

"They do."

As the song starts to play through a pair of speakers on the dresser I take River in my arms. We kiss, swaying to the pulse of the song, the lyrics hitting a whole new way now that I have someone to lose. I can't make sense of it, how that first day lead to this. None of the other stuff matters: my parents or theirs, my future, my past. Everything that matters is here in my arms.

We kiss, and we dance, but when I slide my hand down to their ass they tense. "Too much?" I ask.

"No, just...is this the first time you've done this?"

"Not *first* first."

They raise an eyebrow. "How is that a thing?"

"I tried a few times with this one girl."

"Girl?"

"I'm bi."

"Are you sure?" River asks, both eyebrows raised. "I mean, if you couldn't, you know…"

"It was her. I think she was out to prove something, but she didn't really like being touched."

"That's kind of a problem."

"What about you?"

"I like being touched."

"I meant am I your first?"

They roll their eyes. "It's not like there's a lot of options out here."

"So are we…what are we doing?"

"I don't know. What do you think?"

"I think…I think that I really like kissing you. And if you want to do more we can but we don't have to."

"But like what more?"

"You're going to have to tell me that. It's your body."

"Right."

"I want you to feel okay about whatever we do. So what do you want to do?"

"I think…I think we should lie down."

Eleven

Paradise

Part of me wants to strip River bare, lick them all over, discover everything about them. The other, stronger part of me wants them to reveal themselves when they're ready. I don't even care that they're still wearing that old hoodie, because it's a part of them and because more than anything I want them to want this. To feel safe with me, feel like they don't have to hide any part of themselves.

They're on top now, my hands on their thighs, fingertips slipping under the edge of their sweatshirt, brushing the hem of their shorts. River moans softly as I slide my hands up and under their sweatshirt to stroke their bare skin. As I run my fingers along the waist of their shorts they moan again, grinding on me, but I don't care about myself, I want *their* pleasure, want to touch them, feel them, cherish them.

They stop moving when I dip my fingertips inside their waistband. "Too much?"

"No…"

"We can do whatever you want. We can stop—"

"Nononono, that's not what I meant," River says, grabbing for my wrists. "Keep your hands where they were."

"Or maybe you want them here?" And I slide my hands down to cup their ass. River groans, working their hips like they're trying to grab my fingers with their cheeks.

"Marc..."

"Yes?"

"Will you—"

"Yes."

They laugh giddily and nuzzle into my shoulder. "You don't know what I'm going to say."

"Say anything. Whatever you want, that's what I want."

"I just...I want...ugh. I want you and I want this but I don't know how to say the...things." Their body is doing the asking as they grind against me, the slippery fabric of their shorts sliding over the sleek muscles earned on that messed up old bike. Knowing how I feel when I touch myself like this, I splay my hands and squeeze their ass harder.

"Fuck!" As River shoves their face into the curve of my neck I do it again. They groan, their whole body shaking.

"Tell me, River. Tell me to do it and I will."

"Ugh...you're mean."

"And you're perfect."

With a hoarse cry between a shout and a whisper, River grabs my jaw and wrenches my head towards them for a kiss. A kiss that undoes everything all over again, their lively tongue tasting every part of my mouth, their grip on my face almost painful but so, so good. I creep my fingers inwards and they break off, panting.

"You want me to touch you here?" I ask, stroking between their ass cheeks.

"Yes..."

"Do you want me inside you?

Trembling, they whimper softly, closing their eyes. "Yes...I don't know...yes...I...just..."

"Be gentle?"

River laughs again, a dry, nervous giggle. "No. I mean yeah, but...I might get kind of crazy."

"I think that's what's supposed to happen. If I do it right."

My dick wants to start right away but River has other plans. "We've been riding all day. I'm way too gross. Gimme two minutes."

"Okay."

"Okay, that means you gotta leave," they say, bumping my shoulder with theirs when I don't move.

"Where am I supposed to go?"

"There's a bathroom out there. Maybe wash your hands?"

"Good idea."

I try not to make any noise. I don't need Robin coming down looking for a burglar. Or for some kid about to pop his kid's cherry. When I get back in the room, River has changed the lights to green, making the fantasy paintings on the walls and ceilings look even more like a magical forest. A glittery lunch box lays open on the bed.

"Making plans behind my back?" I ask, looking over the stash of neon silicone sex toys and sample packs of artisanal lube. Nothing too freaky, except maybe that tentacle, but what do I know about what people are into?

"Hello? I'm a horny eighteen and a half year old living in the middle of nowhere. You should see my search history."

"You'll have to show me."

"Like right now?"

"No. Right now I want to see how hot you are when I'm in you." They reply with that soft whimpering moan as they fall back against the wall. We kiss like this, like we did at the mill, their body pinned, their arms tight around me, their mouth mine. As River wraps their leg around me and pulls me nearer I slide my hand up their thigh to grab their ass and...

Are they naked under the hoodie? That's for sure River's naked body, revealed to my hand but not my eyes. Touch is all I need, as I slip my lubed fingers between their cheeks. River makes a gasping groan and I press deeper, seeking the sweet pucker of their ass.

They want this, they have to, the way they're pushing back to meet my fingers. Circling, stroking, I play them like this until they're shaking, then gently push one fingertip inside. River makes a strangled cry, shoving their hips back like they want me deeper. I do it, but only a little as their muscles clamp down on my finger.

"Is it okay?" They nod, their eyes screwed shut, their lips pinched closed, and when I try moving my finger they moan in what sounds like pain.

"Why can't I relax?" they whisper.

"You don't have to prove yourself to me."

"But I want this. I want you. I want to belong to you."

"We don't need to fuck for that to be true."

"But...really?"

"I want this because I want to make you feel good. You don't owe me anything."

"It's not owe, it's just...I want you to like me."

"I already do," I say. "This is extra."

"A bonus level?"

"A side quest?"

They make a face. "Ugh, what does this look like, Baldur's Gate?"

"Nah, they're way bigger skanks than you."

"I'll show you skank," River says with a wicked grin, locking their arms around my neck. They angle their hips back sharply, shoving themselves onto my stiff finger. If their ass feels like this to touch, hot and tight and soft and deep, I can't imagine how it's going to feel when it's my cock in them. We're going to fuck, I know it, not tonight but soon. We're going to use every last freaky thing in that lunchbox.

We kiss again as I play in them, working them open until they take two fingers. I twist my hand, sucking River's moan right out of their mouth. Their other leg is trembling, all their weight on it, and I lean closer, holding them against the wall with my body. Whether it's the pressure or the changed angle or who knows what luck, River's ass seems to bloom around my fingers, letting me get even deeper. I want to stroke them until they can't see, until they know that they're mine forever.

River pulls away from our kiss, but I don't mind because now I can see their gorgeous face, their lips open, eyes half shut, a swooning fae in a magic forest, and me, the mortal fool who wants them beyond reason. Every romantic feeling or want I've ever known come together in this raw touch, the physical reality of finger-fucking River's ass. It's glory and the gutter, paradise in a basement bedroom. It's River rocking against my hand to let me fuck them harder.

I feel the change in the way their ass seems to suck at my fingers. I slow from a thrust to a push, and as I work a third finger into River's soft, hot hole they're gone, fucking onto on my hand, their whole body rocking as a wild heat blooms across their face. A sight so intensely erotic an echoing wave of pressure rises from my balls up through the core of me, not an orgasm but not far off, and I bite my lip to keep from fucking up everything by saying the words that are crowding my throat.

I love you, River Croft. Even if you are a werewolf.

Twelve

Surfacing

It's nearly six by the time we surface. I text my mom a bunch of apologies for not texting earlier, even though it's not really her business what I do. We're all still getting used to that way of living, and it's throwing them off because I've always been a good kid. Or was I just lonely?

"You staying for dinner?" River asks, kicked back on the other end of the couch, their sock toes nudging my thigh. "We're not like vegan or anything, so…"

"I should go home."

"Don't want to look my dad in the eye?"

"Um, kind of?"

"Whatever," River says, spreading their thighs to look at me down the length of their body. "You'll be back."

"You think so?"

"Now that you had a taste, don't you want the main course?"

I have to look away. I want to fall on them, shove my head up inside that hoodie and lick them everywhere. "Imma head out now before any trouble starts."

"Aw, but I love trouble." They push their hand between their legs, rocking their hips like we aren't in their parents' living room.

I glance around to be sure no one's near. "Unless you're ready to have all of me up in you and not just my fingers, you can chill."

"You saw what's in the toy box, right?"

"Yeah, and you and Cthulhu can sort yourselves out. My parents are already bugging about fated mates and shit, I don't need them getting ideas."

Their sly grin fades as they sit upright. "They told you?"

"Are you saying you knew? Since how long? Is it longer than since yesterday?" I add when they don't reply. "Have you known the whole time?"

"Depends what you mean by *the whole time*."

"Do you even like me or are you just playing along with our parents bullshit?"

"I *do* like you. I really do."

"Yet you kept this secret from me?"

"Ugh, because I wanted to just *like* you," they plead, their eyes shining with tears. "I didn't want you to think I was hanging out with you just because I had to."

"Except that's how it was."

"No! I wanted to get to know you without all this other stuff getting in the way. Without you thinking I was just with you because I had to be."

"Without me knowing the truth."

"No!" They cover their face with their hands, lost in the sleeves of that hoodie. Saying this is like twisting the knife in my own stomach but if I can't trust River to tell me the truth then what's the point?

"Tell me, how long have you known?"

"Forever, okay? For fucking ever." They jump off the couch and they're gone. I hear a door slam, leaving me, the asshole, alone. Before I can figure out how I'm going to get out of the house without being seen, River's brother Drake wanders in from the kitchen.

"You here for dinner?"

"I should probably go."

He shrugs his massive shoulders and drops onto the couch beside me. "Give Riv an hour. They'll paint another bird. They'll get over it."

He's handing me the other game controller and maybe he's right. I just made his sibling burst into tears, and he can't need my help in his campaign to judge from his character's stats, but he knows River better than I do, so I gear up and we go and shoot fascists, while the smell of their dinner wafts from the kitchen and I let the focused mayhem distract me from the mess I'm making of my life.

"Can I ask you something?" I say as we slip down a shadowed alley, the walls pocked by small arms fire.

"What about?"

"Hollowood. This valley. The shit I heard."

"From who?"

"My parents." As we step out of the alley, a bullet ricochets off the brick beside my head and we fall back. For a couple minutes it's a firefight, but we subdue the offence and carry on.

"I know this place doesn't make sense to outsiders," Drake says. "But that doesn't mean a thing. You don't know, you didn't grow up here, living the myth, seeing your name on Old Mother's letter, knowing they got it all planned. Knowing that you don't belong to just yourself."

"That's kind of fucked up."

"I don't know," Drake says in the same low rumbling voice. "Seems like everyone wants to belong somewhere. Maybe it's not so bad to know that life has a plan for you and you don't have to figure it all out on your own."

"What about you? Who's your mate?"

His lip curves in a smile that transforms his face, the blank mask of maturity falling away as he blushes. "None of your business."

It's amazing how having your hands full frees up your brain. I'm only half in the game, following Drake's lead as the rest of me thinks about love. About all the weird and unexpected ways that people find it. Because you like the smell of the other person's shampoo, because they're nice to your dog, because they're funny and adorable and brilliant and alive. People in arranged marriages can build a love, in books and in real life. If this is fate, then fate's being kind to me, because I don't know what more I could wish for than what I already have.

If I didn't mess it up. This thought brings me down again and again, until the only thing that will break the cycle is if I tell them how I really feel, that this chance is too rare, these feelings too precious for me to ignore.

Another fragrance cuts through the meaty warmth of dinner, the scent of fresh herbs and pine and skin. River is peering around the doorway, just their eyes and the top of their hood visible. Drake grunts as my avatar takes a bullet in the neck and dissolves into the bloody concrete floor of the abandoned penitentiary.

"Sorry," I mumble as he saves his progress.

"It's cool," Drake says as he powers down the game. "I usually get iced breaking in here so at least you got me past the checkpoint." He leaves and then it's just me and River. Chewing on the end of their loose curl, they perch on the couch arm furthest from me.

"Aren't you mad at me?" they say in a tiny voice.

"That doesn't mean I have to leave you."

"Don't leave me," they say, lurching forward to kneel on the cushion. "I mean...no, that's what I really mean. I don't want you to go."

I open my arms and they launch themselves at me, throwing their arms around my neck and burying their face into my chest, not crying, just breathing hard. Holding them I feel the release of a tension in me I hadn't known was there.

"I'm sorry I didn't tell you," they sniff. "I didn't know how. Then we were getting along and I didn't want to wreck it and—"

"It's cool. It's okay. I'm here." Stroking their back, I kiss their hot forehead. They shiver, then pull themselves up to kiss me on the lips. It's hard not to keep kissing them, and I'm about to ask if we can go downstairs when someone in the doorway clears their throat. Drake, his rigid mouth twitching like he's trying not to laugh.

"Dinner's ready," he says. "Looks like you already had the appetizer."

Robin is up at the big lodge house on 'pack business' as River's mom Dawn puts it, so dinner is chill, with me and River sitting across from Drake and the youngest Croft, Crystal. Dawn sits at the head of the long but simply built table. One wall of the dining room is all windows, giving me a view of the backyard and the rabbits and skunks and countless squirrels who pass through on their little animal business. Dawn is easy to talk to, with a dry sense of humor and a leprechaun smile that goes with her faint brogue. We end up talking about the British ex-prince and the high costs of fame and all the while, River's foot is stroking mine under the table.

"It's so sweet," Crystal is saying. "Like that king from whenever, from before, when he married that American."

"Wallis Simpson," River offers.

"Was that her name?" Crystal says, wrinkling her nose. "But she's so pretty."

"A weird name doesn't make you not pretty."

"I didn't say that, ugh!"

"When your father was courting me," Dawn starts, to the groaning disgust of her kids.

"Courting?" Crystal says, making a face.

"Would like it more if I said, when we were shagging but I hadn't let him propose to me yet?"

The Croft children lose their shit, Crystal shrieking, River covering their face, even the unshakeable Drake setting down his knife and fork to glare at his mother.

"You should show Marcus the poem he wrote," River says from behind their sleeves.

"No," Dawn replies firmly, though she's smirking. "No, I should not."

"Ooh, you should play that song he wrote you," says Crystal.

Dawn groans, putting her head down on her arm for a second. "Only if I get to show Marcus the video of you as Sailor Mercury."

Thirteen

Lost

After dinner, Drake drives me home. I have a hundred questions but they can wait for the next time I see Robin, and I promise myself I'll make a point of visiting just for that. It's not fair to make Drake explain what I should have heard from my elders,

It's so late I won't be hearing much from my elders tonight, except stuff I totally don't want to hear through their bedroom wall, which is apparently as thin as in the last house. I get ready for bed wearing noise cancelling headphones. I check my phone one last time and River has sent me another playlist. Funny, I was already planning to think about them for the rest of the night.

I bounce out of bed the next day like I have plans to be somewhere. I guess I do, because even though I didn't tell them so, I'm going up to see River. I need them to know that last night wasn't a one-off, that I want that every night.

My parents are still in bed, like they usually are after Dad gets home. I leave them a note then pack my panniers and start riding. The highway is busier than usual this early in the day but the traffic dies off once I take the turn for Hollowood. My plan is to ride up through the state park lands to where we crossed the fence yesterday, and when I pass a service track that branches off the park access road I turn and start climbing.

Half a mile along I reach a fence that cuts across the road, which continues on the other side. The fence wires have been cut close to one of the poles and it's easy to lift my bike through the gap. The road climbs gradually up the mountain's spur, the forest falling away to my right. After about twenty minutes I realize I haven't seen any other bike tracks on this road. Just the twin tire marks of a heavy jeep. I'm jolted back to reality as my front wheel strikes a big rock and I nearly go over the handlebars.

A puncture. Worse, this brake lever is starting to split. Just what I need halfway up a mountain with no one to complain to. There's a squat green shed a little further up the road, and carrying my bike I start in that direction. This deep in the forest it's hard to tell if it's cloudy or sunny or even what time of day it is. Maybe it's going to rain, because I can't hear any birds. Isn't that a sign that the pressure is changing and the weather is about to turn?

The shed is at the top of a steep slope, so I leave my bike leaning against a tree. No one's around to steal it. The silence heavy in the air, I scramble up the slope. The green building has no windows, only a metal door with a padlocked deadbolt. It's not nearly as interesting as the hole in the ground.

About twelve feet deep and maybe twenty feet across, the circular hole is edged with plate steel, the poured concrete base stained with rusty brown spatters. Four doorways have been cut in the blunt wall, each sealed with a heavy steel door. If the rundown gas station gives *Fallout* vibes, this is the entrance to one of the vaults. A place where violence happens.

I sense eyes on me and look up, and so help me, I scream, because a row of skulls mounted on stakes is watching me from across the pit. Half a dozen dog skulls, or are they wolves, because those are bigger than a dog's head. Worse are the human skulls on the right...

No. What's the very worst is the ones in the middle. The ones that look like a wolf's skull in the middle of melting, the snout too short, the skull too round. Like the wolf was halfway to human...

My guts churning, I hear the snap of a twig. As a cold sweat breaks across my back, I look to my left and see a wolf. Another is approaching from the right, its head lowered, black lip curling to show its fangs. A movement among the distant trees catches my eye and then I wish it hadn't as a black shape like a man but with a horrible blob for a head and two red eyes emerges from a bunker just like this one and starts towards me.

I'm going to die. I'm going to die from being a dumb-ass because what's the first rule of back country? Don't go alone where you've never been. I can barely breathe as I start backing down the slope towards my bike, the wolves matching me step for step, the one on the right crouching like it's about to pounce. At the rustle of leaves behind me I freeze. Despite all I'm facing I can't stand not knowing and I chance a look.

River is standing by my bike, wide eyed in horror. Shit, now we're both going to die. The wolves are growling, heads lowered, teeth bared. The black blob man has been joined by another and they can't be more than a minute away. We're going to die, right here, and I still haven't told River that I love them. How romantic, to declare my undying love and then die, but when look back River's gone. Now there's just another wolf.

A wolf with a streak of ruddy fur down its spine...

Snarling, the two wolves hurl themselves at the third, which dashes away into the woods so fast all three are out of sight in seconds. The cryptid men are closing faster so I race down the hill, snatch up River's fallen hoodie, and keep running. That bike's worth a lot but my life is worth more.

When I pass the fence I keep going. I can't stop seeing any of it, the horrors bleeding into each other until I feel like I'm being pursued by a wolf in a red-eyed demon's mask. I reach the road to Hollowood Falls and though my legs and chest and heart are on fire I keep running, up the hill towards the village. I have to find someone, Robin or Dawn or Drake. Find them and tell them that River's in trouble. But I'm so tired. So tired and so scared, because now I'm doubling back up the slope I just ran down. The blob men could be just over that rise, waiting to drag me to that pit and chuck me in and...

I nearly throw myself into the ditch as a big blue pickup comes sailing down the road. It does a screeching u-turn then pulls up beside me. The driver reaches over and pops open the passenger door. He's as built as River's dad but blond, with a pale scar down one side of his nose.

"I'm Leif, I'm a friend of the Crofts," he says. "Let me give you a lift up the hill."

"I have to find River."

"We're on it, trust me. We'll bring them home safe."

"I didn't mean to go over there. I didn't know."

"It's alright, Marcus, you're safe now," he says and though he's smiling his eyes are searching the forest behind me. "Those things never cross the fence-line. Get in and we'll go see if River's back yet."

"Was that real?" I say as I climb into the cab. "Did all that even happen?"

"Tell me," he says, and I do, feeling sick, feeling stupid.

"It's gotta be just some old wartime thing, a decommissioned missile base or something," I say at the end. "And there's going to be wolves in the forest, right?"

"Don't gaslight yourself, Marcus," he says firmly. "This is important information. We'll need you to remember as much as you can."

"We?"

"There's a lot about Hollowood Falls you don't know yet."

We're at the bend in the road at the bottom of town. We'll be at River's in less than a minute. "So then is it true?" I say before I lose my nerve. "What my parents told me. Is River...forget it. it's crazy."

"Go on."

"My folks said...they said the craziest thing. I mean it's impossible. There's no way." Then why am I clutching River's empty sweatshirt? Where did that wolf come from? How did River know to be there and where did they go?

What if it's all true?

Fourteen

Found

Is the whole town here? I recognize nearly everyone gathered in front of River's house. Baz and his father and a regal woman with a golden warmth to her skin who must be his mother. River's cousin Sunny, the guy with the red hair and snake tattoos, even those two Karens who took my picture through the window of Sutherland's that first day. A couple people are wrapped in blankets like they're victims of some natural disaster, River's mom moving among them with a tray handing out steaming mugs.

They all turn as I get out of the truck, but no one says anything as Leif ushers me into the house. We go into the dining room, where four of the largest men I've ever seen, Robin among them, are sitting looking at the contour map spread on the table. The place has the feel of a war room: the grim, determined faces, the smell of coffee and damp leaves.

I don't want to ask about River. Instead I tell them what I saw—the pit, the skulls, the wolves, the dark men—waiting for one of them, any of them to stop me. To tell me I'm wrong, that I'm out of my mind, that I imagined everything, as they listen with serious faces, now and then one of them grunting under his breath.

"Was there any ID of yours on your bike? Your wallet or phone or anything?" asks a man with the same shiny blond hair as Leif.

"I have my phone, but the bike has a plate on it for insurance. I guess they could figure out my name from that."

They all start grumbling. My stressed out, maxed out mind thinks it sounds like motorbikes revving, and I cover my mouth so I don't laugh. Leif taps the nearest guy on the shoulder and points to me, and he gets out of his chair.

"You better sit down," he says. "Before you fall down." Leif steers me into the chair. As I lean against the back I feel how tense I am, like my spine's made of steel, my body rigid with the effort of not freaking out because where is River?

People come and go. I barely see them. Someone puts a hot cup in my hand and I drink what's in it without tasting it. I should call my parents, or text, or tag my mom in on a photo of me with Hollowood Falls VIP, but I'm scared that if I touch my phone, I'll see a message from River as they're being eaten alive. No, I'll never hear from them again because their phone is in the pocket of this stupid hoodie that doesn't have them in it and is all I'll have to remember them by, and the stress and panic and sickening heartbreak of the day all hit at once and I put my head on my arms and give up pretending that I don't feel like I'm dying.

No one tells me to stop crying, these monstrous men who might actually be monsters. They let me feel it all, the only interruption when someone tugs the map out from under my arms so I don't melt it with my tears. A strong hand grips my shoulder and I grab hold, even though I can't raise my head. It's all my fault, for being too smart for my own good. For breaking my own rules. For keeping a secret that didn't need to be kept, because if I'd told River my plan they would have stopped me.

That's how it works in a teenage love story. The townie knows the rules, the new kid breaks them. I wasn't strong enough for River, not brave enough, not Hollowood. Too caught up in my own ideas, because I should have known better. I should have told River that I love them.

My body aches, from the tension and from running for my life, and as the fathers mumble over my head I feel myself slipping into sleep. I stir at the raise in their voices. Chair legs scrape as they start towards the door in a huddle. I stumble after them and outside where people are crowding around a naked person crouching on the lawn. Dawn cries out then runs towards them, because it's River, and they get to their feet and they see me, standing on the lawn still holding their hoodie. With a desperate sob River shoves past their helpers, dodges their mother of all people, and hurls themselves into my arms.

That's about it for a while, as we cling to each other and the crowd disperses. Lots of me wants to put my hands all over naked River and my tongue in their mouth, but the better part of me simply holds them close and feels their heart beat against mine.

"I found your hoodie," I say when I can breathe again. It's pinned between us, and they let go of me to squirm into it then throw their arms around me and keep crying.

"I thought you were going to die and then that I was going to die, and—"

"No one's dead," I murmur, stroking their tangled hair. "It's ok, Riv. I'm here. It's over."

Except it isn't. I'll never forget what I saw. Never stop wondering what it all means, whether I want to or not. River joins the fathers in the kitchen and tells their story, while I sit on the couch trying to ignore the few phrases I can hear: *I saw the security camera in the tree and...never been that aggressive...I thought they'd stop at the fence but this time...*

The couch sags as Dawn sits beside me. "You look exhausted, Marcus. Why not go wait for River downstairs?"

"In their room?"

"I don't expect they'll mind," she says with a wink. The idea of hiding from the day is tempting, and I let her persuade me. Downstairs, I wander around the room, soaking in the details, getting to know River through their possessions. The paintings on the walls and ceiling add another layer to them as a person, as I realize how intricate they are, tiny drawings hiding inside everything, like the castle with a tower and a rampaging dragon in the reflections in the fox's eyes, or the parade of smiling amoebas marching along the edge of this long red streak.

I'm so lost in the world of their art that I don't notice them come in the room until they shut the door behind them. We meet in the middle and all the sweet and tender things I planned to say get blown away by the force of River's kiss.

Fifteen

Bound

They want to drink me. I want to be their water. I want to lie down before this kiss knocks me unconscious, River biting at my lips, sucking my tongue deep into their mouth. We stagger together to the bed, where River pushes me down and then throws themselves on me again. A bad landing, crushing my erection, and with a hiss of pain I roll them off me.

"Sorry."

"It's cool," I say through my teeth, though if anyone but River had done it I might have punched them. "But maybe chill a bit. We did just almost die."

"I know," River says, cuddling up to me with their head on my shoulder. "But I want to get as much of you as I can in case it doesn't work out so well next time."

"There's not going to be a next time," I say as I pull them closer. "I'm never going to ride anywhere without you ever again."

"Good. I don't want you to die. I mean, I just found you." Their voice breaks and I squeeze them tighter.

"I know how you feel. That was killing me, that I wasn't going to get to say goodbye. But there's something I want to say even more important." They whimper, hiding their mouth with their sleeve as I roll to face them. "I keep thinking, maybe this is fate like they said. But maybe it doesn't matter what caused it. Because I want this. I want *us*. I want to know everything about you and I want you to know me, not because of who the world says we are but because of you."

I stop to kiss them—I can't help myself, they're gorgeous, their eyes bright with emotion, their lips kissed pink and trembling under mine. That curl is sneaking across their cheek and I wind it around my finger then kiss it too. I have to say them, the words that make all my other words real, that turn them from a bunch of lines from a romance book into the living truth. I have to say them before I scare myself with what they mean. What they mean is that I'm willing to try. "River Croft, I think...I think I love you."

"Do you mean it?" they say in that soft, wondering voice.

"I think so."

"Good, because I love the shit out of you, and I didn't want to say it in case it was weird, but—"

"It's not weird," I say, pulling them close. "I feel it too."

"Fuck, Marcus, I love you so much."

"I love you too. I'm sorry for today."

They make a little angry noise, screwing their face into my shoulder. "Fuck today. It's over. You're here, you're mine, and I love you."

"I love you too, River. I don't ever want to leave you."

"Then don't."

"I won't. I'm yours for good."

"For real?" they say brightly, lifting their head. "Then you should get undressed."

"Are you sure?" I glance upwards towards River's parents.

"We don't have to fuck. Let's call it third base and a half."

"How does that—"

"Shush and get naked."

Why am I arguing? I've wanted this all day. All week, longer, from the first moment I saw them. Not to fuck them but to be with them, know them, feel safe with them. I would feel safer without their parents one floor above, but River's mom sent me down here with a wink and a nudge, so fuck it. River is mine and I don't care if the whole world knows it.

I'm stale with sweat and so is River, a stray leaf clinging to their wild hair here and there. Neither of us care as River strips me bare. They sit back, gazing at me like they're making up their mind, then pull off their hoodie and stretch themselves over me once more. I groan as I feel them all over again, the rub and pull of their thin t-shirt between our bodies almost hotter than if they were naked.

Below, they're wearing very small boxer briefs that I want to take off with my teeth. Later, whenever, this contact enough as River rolls so they're beneath me then wraps their legs around my waist, my bare cock pushing between their ass cheeks. This can't be what they mean by third base and a half, but before I figure out how to ask, River unhooks their ankles then drops their legs and presses them together, pinning my cock.

"Fuck…"

"Is that good?" they ask, squirming as they work their thighs around me. I can only nod, lost in the sensation. I'm scared to move, to wreck this moment, but when River grabs my hips I know it's what they want.

Their thighs are slippery with my precome, their nails biting into my skin, their body moving to meet me as I thrust. I've heard it said that sex is more than penetration, and this is what that means, that what matters most is sharing yourself, giving yourself, letting all these wants express themselves in you and in the other. A wave of pleasure flows up my spine and I groan, my hips moving on their own.

"Are you gonna come?" River whispers. My eyes closed, I nod, words not worth the effort. "Okay, one sec," they say, reaching for something. I hear the rattle of the shiny lunch box then feel River's hand sneak between our bodies. "Okay. Go for it."

As I start to thrust again, something buzzes against my stomach. River is holding one of their toys against themselves, their eyes crossing from the urgent vibrations. They're so fucking hot I forget what I'm doing, until they moan and rub their gorgeous thighs together around my shaft. They want this, we want this, and I stop holding back, let the hot, wet pressure drive me to the edge and over.

"Holy shit..." River gasps as my cum coats their thighs. "Fuck, I love you so much." And with that they come, their body arching off the bed, their other hand over their mouth, because if we were truly alone they'd be howling. I want to hear them howl, want this wildness in them to live forever. I want to belong in this place, with this magical person. I want this to be my fate.

Sixteen

Welcome Home

Cuddled in bed, I'm nearly asleep when River boops my nose. "You should maybe call your parents if you're staying the night," they murmur.

"Do you want me to stay?"

"If that's what you want."

"But is that what *you* want?"

"Ugh, we suck. Marcus, if you want to stay, I'm happy to have you. Oh god, I mean you can stay if you want and I'll like that. A lot. Fuck." Blushing, they butt their face into my shoulder.

"We might go that far, if I stay."

"What?" They jerk their head up, then see my smirk. "Oh. Wow. Ha, ha. Go. Go call your mommy and ask if you can sleep over."

"Is there a bed for me?"

"Duh…"

Now I blush, because why am I asking? "Right."

"And you'll have to go upstairs, there's like no signal down here."

"That means I gotta get dressed."

"You could wear that." They look towards a pastel rainbow tiger onesie hanging on the corner of the closet door.

"I'll just find my shorts, how about?"

I have to go all the way up to the coat room before I can get a bar on my phone signal. Seconds after I send the text my phone rings.

"So...that was sudden," my mom says in that sugary voice, which I'm probably going to hear a lot if I keep seeing River as much as I plan to.

"Today was brutal. It's too far to ask you for a ride. And they have plenty of room for me. But you should, uh, come and meet the Crofts sometime soon."

She pauses and I hear her whisper to my dad. "Do you think we should?" she asks me.

"I'll explain when I see you tomorrow. I gotta go. Love you, bye."

"Marcus, don't you think—"

I end the call. I don't need to justify myself. Not only because I'm old enough but because they're complicit in this whole mess, and I don't see how I owe them anything. The ends don't always justify the means, and even if I'm happy to have found River, I'm still a pawn in this hidden game. Here comes another player, as Robin appears in the doorway.

"I'm not interrupting, am I?"

"No, I was done."

"I'm happy you're here, Marcus. It's good you found your way back to Hollowood."

Except I had nothing to do with it. "Can I ask you something?" I wait for him to nod, and for my heart to stop smashing itself against my lungs so I can breathe, because this question could change everything. "If I'm from here, if I'm part of all this...how come I'm just me? I mean, I've been out in the moonlight, you'd think something would have happened. Or is that not how it works?"

His huge arms crossed, he leans against the doorframe. "That is part of it. The trait doesn't always express. Sometimes a child is born without the gene splice, even if both parents had it."

"So were my folks, my birth parents, I mean...were they..."

"Just your mother."

"Huh."

"I only knew her a little while but she was a good person. She loved you to bits."

At the thought of my mother tears sting my eyes but I don't mind Robin seeing my pain. The things I'm afraid of aren't the same as they were this morning.

"That place I was today," I say, though it seems so distant now. "You knew about it?"

"We've been watching them for a long time," he says, his easy smile fading. "You gained us some critical information, Marcus."

"I didn't mean to end up there."

"I know. I'm just glad you're safe."

Downstairs, a pile of dirty laundry lies beside River's door. In the room they've switched the lights to the pink and purple I know from their photos, a galaxy-print cover on the bed. River is wearing the pastel tiger onesie and is dusting around the stuff all over their dresser with what looks like a sock. They startle when I close the door.

"Oh. Hey. So." They glance at the sock in their hand like they don't know how it got there, then toss it into the corner. "So I didn't know if you sleep naked or not, or if you meant what you said, or if you were done, and if you just want to go to sleep that's cool, and even if you want to sleep by yourself I have a couch and you can have the bed and I won't think it's weird at all and—"

While they talk I've crossed the room and I now pull them close and answer all those questions with a kiss. I could go on kissing them forever, our mouths made to fit each other, the tease of their tongue over mine sending sparks down my spine and setting off a train of unholy thoughts about what that tongue might do. Later, whenever, because this is only the first night of the rest of our lives.

"I've never fallen in love before," I say. "That's what this is, isn't it?"

"I hope so because this is amazing."

"Right? I could go on like this forever. Just look at you forever."

"Just look?" they say with a grin, rubbing against me.

"I want everything. I wish I could live ten lifetimes and spend each of them with you."

"Dude…" Their grin fades to a look of wonder that matches my strange sense of purpose.

"I don't know where that came from," I say.

"Neither do I but I think we're meant to kiss now."

And we do, and it's everything. Everything I've ever been promised about love, and it's all coming true. All because I met River Croft.

NEXT

LEAVING HOLLOWOOD
(HOLLOWOOD FALLS BOOK 3)

Book 3

Leaving Hollowood

Stone Roth is Hollowood's last bear shifter, but is he more man (and beast) than even I can take?

Being the spare heir of one of Hollowood Falls' first families is about as fun as it sounds. No wonder I'm known as the town's favorite disaster gay werewolf, always on the hunt for a big strong man to bang my brains out.

When I accidentally meet the papa bear of my dreams, can I unravel his tangled thoughts and teach him how to trust me? Or will the chaos that tails me wherever I go ruin the best mistake I've ever made?

One

The Mountain

It was too much to hope for, that Pierce Platter would settle for me. He's been fated to mate my older brother Evan since forever. For even longer than I've had a crush on him.

Let's face it, there's not a guy in Hollowood Falls I haven't crushed on at some time or another. Young, old, doesn't matter, I can find something in any man that'll make me want to worship him. No, it's not healthy, and no, I don't care. I've never gotten anywhere by caring.

Not true. It's just that there's not much else worth caring about. I care about Pierce, and I know we'll always be friends, but seeing him with Evan still burns me up. No, it's more of a singe. Like burnt toast. My feelings about Pierce Platter are burnt toast.

They didn't have a wedding. Mainly because Evan's already married. The whole family treats his human husband Graeme like he's made of glass, as if any second now his personality is going to shatter and he'll reveal how much he hates us.

I don't know why they'd think that. Him and Pierce get along great. You can tell the two of them are hooking up by the way they touch each other. Not sexy touching but the way a couple moves in a small space: a hand on the hip to tell him you're behind him, or that little dance you both do when you're trying to get past each other. Then they'll smirk at each other, then one of them will glance in my direction. Subtle, guys. No one knows a thing.

Why have I been watching my old crush and my brother-in-law flirt? Because I've been sleeping on their couch for the last week and a half. The reason why I'm doing that is a real long story. Are you ready for it?

The joke is, I was being so good. I uninstalled Grindr and quit taking PrEP. I stopped swearing in the house. I quit vaping *and* biting my nails. And I stopped running away to Denver to get railed and hurt and heartbroken and then come home again with my tail between my legs because...well, because I have nowhere else to go and my folks keep letting me. Isn't that the line, that home is the place where they always have to take you in?

Home: it's everything and nothing. It's whatever you make it, I guess. What I know for sure is that a sweeping mountain valley beneath a sky of infinite blue can still feel like the smallest place in the world. When you know everyone in town, they know you too, and most everyone in Hollowood knows me as a fuck-up. Evan Culver's little brother, the bad one, the spare. We all jumped on Prince Harry for complaining about being second in line, but he's right. It sucks to be the late baby your parents had to keep their legacy alive because they freaked out when someone else lost a child.

What a mess it must have been for the Platters when Pierce's little brother died, though Pierce and Ev were too young to remember much about it. Me? I was born nine and a half months later. A couple old cranks in town used to tell me I had the dead kid's soul, until my dad told them to stop. Creepy as fuck, but that's Hollowood all over. That's what you get when every other person in town is a werewolf.

When we were kids it was easier. I'm only a few years older than my cousins, and we would go mess around in the forest, in either form. Somehow Ash and Sunny and River got their shit together, got their GED and got jobs, except for Sunny who's doing occupational therapy by remote learning. The pandemic sucked but at least Hollowood now has the best internet it's ever going to get, and most of the people who stay in town can find work of some kind. Except me.

What's my problem? Maybe it's the years I've spent telling myself and everyone else that I'm too cool for Hollowood. That I'm gonna be one of the few who get out, which is something that takes more brains and focus than I'll ever have.

That's just how it is. That's who I am. One good thing about living in the statistical middle of nowhere is not having to go to regular school. My neurospicy ass doesn't do regular. Sitting still, paying attention, keeping my mouth shut? Maybe if you pay me, but even then you better keep an eye on me because one day I'll go off. Wreck shit, flip tables, real or metaphorical or both. Sooner or later, I always do.

Too smart to conform, too lazy to mask, woke and broke and probably depressed, and right in the middle of all that is when Granny died. Whether she was really my blood kin or not, she'd always treated me better than most people did. Let me sleep on her porch in summer, and a few times on her couch in bad weather. Always had a hot meal for me, a kind word, a safe place for me to hide, lick my wounds, avoid other people's expectations for a while. Losing her was like having the ground ripped out from under my feet, and I don't know if I've stopped falling since.

I wrote to Evan for the first time in two years. He came to Hollowood for her funeral. Saw Pierce for the first time in ten years. Two days later (after I caused a bunch of bullshit) Pierce went home with Evan, and he's only been back twice since. My best friend, my forever crush, and the closest thing the US lycan community has to a crown prince: basically married to my brother.

What's a trauma twink in the middle of nowhere gonna do other than get really into his body? Ask me anything about high-altitude running, because if I'm not in the weight room or asleep, I'm probably on the trails. As tempting as it is to shift, I try to stay human as much as possible. I'm too happy being the beast: alone in the forest, loose and free, no one giving me shit for the way I act or the things I want.

There's always a chance I won't shift back. That I'll let the beast have me, stop fighting against these waves and sink into namelessness. Except it would break my parents, and really piss off my brother, and Pierce...I couldn't do that to him, or myself. I can't have him, but I'd still miss him.

I'm in the kitchen poaching chicken for the week's meal prep when the phone by the fridge rings. "Can someone else get that?" I call. "My hands are all chickeny."

Mom comes in from the dining room to answer it. Hollowood might have decent internet but its cellular reception is a joke. Something about the rare metals in the hills, people say, but it means that we all still have landlines.

"Hello? Oh, Pierce, how are you?" she says, her eyes lighting up. She loves the shit out of her second son-in-law. I meanwhile put down the knife so I don't chop off a finger.

"That's wonderful, dear," she says to Pierce in that sugary voice she saves for him. "And how are the boys? Oh, of course they did, those goofs. Yes, Leif and I are just fine, thanks for asking. Oh, you did? Tell me all about it."

It doesn't matter. I don't care. I don't care that Pierce didn't ask how I was, except of course I do. Until he moved away from Hollowood, he was my best friend, and I thought he felt the same about me. I turn off the stove and put away the raw meat and get out of the kitchen as fast as I can, because even though I shouldn't care, I do, so much I feel dizzy. I have no one but myself to blame. I had so many chances, so many times I could have told him how I feel. Sorry, how I *felt*, because I have to burn these feelings out of me. If I can't have him, I have to stop wanting him.

The only way I know to stop feeling a feeling, or at least the only way I have left, is running. I catch my mom's eye and make my fingers 'run' up my other arm. She smiles and nods, then goes back to her call. "Sorry, what was that, dear? I heard something in the other room."

I love you too, Mom.

I keep my gear in the mudroom that connects to the side door, and in two minutes I'm outside. This late in spring most of the snow is off the lawns but the hillsides are still white in patches. I say hills: I mean mountains, though technically these are only foothills of the main peak fifty miles south of here. If you're not from Colorado, these are mountains.

I start slow, climbing a steep trail that I blazed myself from the backyard. After a few brutal minutes I meet the main Hollowood trail. Most of this forest is state land, but only locals know about this route, a way to cross the valley without going through town. A year ago, I'd have turned left, towards the next valley over. Private land belonging to a numbered company based out of Sacramento, which I know because I tracked them online. Everyone's told me to leave it alone, but I know there's something fucked up going on over there. Still, I've already caused enough trouble, and I won't go over again. That leaves me the whole of the Hollowood valley and that's enough for anyone.

The trail runs levelly across the hillside for about a mile and I feel good and loose by the time I hit the switchbacks. Dirty patches of snow still lie here and there, but my own feet cleared the trail weeks ago. This is the warmest day so far this year and I'm dripping sweat before I'm halfway up this section. When the trail levels out again I walk for a little to catch my breath. The higher I go the harder the wind blows, and with the sweat cooling my back I pick up my pace again.

The trail leads me out of the cedars and across a section where there was a rockfall last year that knocked down the trees and left a big gravelly scar on the hillside. We (me and Ash and River's boyfriend Marcus) cleared the scree off the trail once the rangers said the slope was stable, but it looks ugly, like someone tore off a strip of the mountain's skin and this is the scar. I guess that's kind of how it is, if you think of the soil as skin. Which would mean the trees are fur. Is that why they call those evergreens 'fir' trees? Probably not, it's probably some weird German word that English stole eight hundred years ago and now uses all wrong. There's meant to be a German family who live up here. The great-grandad or someone emigrated around the same time as my own family, and I've heard they're weres too, but I've never met any of the Roths. Not as people or as wolves.

Lost in my head, I don't notice how far I've run until I come out of a patch of trees and see the next valley opening before me. Damn, it's cold, but it's so fucking beautiful that I stand and look for as long as I can. Trees for miles, filling the bowl of the valley without interruption. No smoke, no chimneys, no roofs, no one at all. Just air and sky and stone and leaf and the red ragged trunks of cedars and the whistle of the wind. I could fall into it, drown in the green, never come up for air. Live on what I caught, never speak my name. A craving so strong I turn my back on the temptation and start back the way I came.

Just before I reach the landfall scar, the trail splits. I didn't notice it heading out, but now I see the narrow thread of a path rising from the main trail. It's heading the same way I am, and even though I don't know where it leads, I take it.

Higher and higher I climb until I realize I'm looking down on the forest I was running through earlier. It's windy as fuck and so cold it's sucking up my energy. I dare to stop running so I can check my GPS, but I'm good. I can come down this slope just ahead, where an old creek used to run.

Except the trail keeps going up. Leaving the trail and crossing unknown ground is out of the question, unless I shift. Which means leaving behind all my gear, and these shoes are only three weeks old and cost more than my last phone did. So I keep going up. At least I'm heading east, but the pretty little clouds have asked their big ugly friends to come over and the sky is turning the color of the mountain.

Up this high, where it's too cold and windy for trees or even grass to grow, the landscape gets weird. Like sci-fi movie set weird. Huge slabs of rock rear up from the gritty soil, the only signs of life a thin smear of lichen on the boulders. Nothing to eat or drink, nowhere to hide from the weather, and I'm seriously thinking about turning around and finding the proper trail when I cross a ridge and begin going down. I'd pick up my pace but the trail is barely there, covered in loose gravel and patches of ice, sometimes disappearing as it zigzags down the steep slope.

When I reach the base I look back. Did I seriously just come down that? It looks vertical, the trail nothing but a few thin streaks of paler soil across the surface. Directly in front of me the land drops away, leaving a cliff too high to jump from and too steep to climb down. The trail leads away to the right, slightly uphill. Still, it's getting me where I need to be, and after another quick check of my GPS I keep going.

The trail hugs the base of the big slope for about a mile, curving gradually eastward as it circles a thicket of cedars, their branches formed into a weird frozen wave from the constant wind. Past this, the trail veers off to the left, into the thick of the forest. The hillside to my right dips in, forming a shallow canyon. At the heart of the canyon is a cave. And in the cave, a light.

I've spent my whole life running these trails. I've never come across this place, and like the reckless idiot everyone says I am, I give into my curiosity, moving quietly, like I have something to hide. The light in the cave flickers like a fire, painting the walls at the mouth gold. The opening is wide enough I could walk right in, but when a shadow passes in front of the fire I pause. Am I trespassing? Or are they? Do the rangers know about this cave?

The entrance to the canyon looks really far behind me. I should go away and leave whoever it is alone. Send the rangers to investigate. They have guns. I have a second hand iPhone with a cracked screen and a broken camera, and I need to get out of here before the moonshiners or murderers or whoever is hiding in a cave halfway up a mountain comes out and finds me sneaking up on them. I need to get out but that means turning my back on the whoever and that feels fucking impossible right now. That's how the scary shit starts in a horror movie, when someone turns their back.

Carefully, stupidly, I start backing away from the cave. I'm making way too much noise, the grit under my feet scraping against the rock, my panting echoing off the canyon walls, my heartbeat louder than all of it. The shadows in the cave are moving, growing. They know I'm here. Stepping faster, I glance back to be sure I'm not going to fall over a big rock. I should turn, run, get gone now, but it's already too late.

Someone is standing in the mouth of the cave. A tiny figure, shoulders rounded, back bent. Wrapped in a pale cloak painted with red symbols, they lean on a tall, heavy stick carved all over with swirling lines, with a loop at the top. Their face is hidden by a mask, a fucked up remix of wolf and human features: short muzzle, wide forehead, tall ears almost like a coyote, but no fur. Like the skull of a were in mid-shift.

This is some goddamn Studio Ghibli shit, where it's not that scary except somehow it fucking is. Like the smooth, pale face isn't a mask at all but bone, bare bone.

Then its ears pivot toward me. Something goes off inside me and I bolt. Out of the canyon, running blind, not back the way I came but straight into the woods, dodging trees and leaping over rocks like I have any idea where I'm going. As if that thing is snapping at my heels, all of hell one step behind it.

There's another of those little cliffs ahead and if I was in wolf form I'd leap right over it and keep running. As I am, I'd break my leg or something, so I skid to a stop. I'm completely alone in the middle of a part of the forest I don't recognize. It's dark as fuck this deep in the trees, and when I check the time it's nearly six. Night's coming and so is the cold and I'm not going to be okay out here overnight.

Fuck. I check the GPS again quickly but my battery is dropping. And I can't call home and ask Dad to come find me because the mountains fuck the signal, and I don't want to shift because it feels like defeat. I'm always getting bailed out by my family and I can't keep it up. I made this mess, so it's up to me to clean it up.

Following something that might be the start of a trail or might be wishful thinking, I keep heading east. The vague trail becomes more obvious, tracking downhill as it weaves between the trees. When I come to a little creek I follow it as best I can for another mile and a half before it ends in a rocky pool that must empty into a crevice underneath. Then it's just me and the GPS, which tells me I'm right over the town. As the crow flies, and I wish one of those weird ass Hollowood crows was here. They always seem to know where to go, like they want to help us big wingless idiots.

I'm getting no help from the birds today, and as I finally get out of the trees I can guess why. The clouds have dropped, erasing the peak of the mountain and blanking out the sun. The wind chasing me along the trail bites like it has snow in its jaws. Snow that's going to start falling any minute now.

Fucking fuckity fuck.

In other words, I'm screwed. As usual, I did it to myself.

I have no choice. No options. No way out of this except to keep going. I start to jog along the trail, which keeps heading east but doesn't descend at all. Am I gonna end up running all the way around the stupid peak? No, because I'll freeze to death in my stupid running tights and three hundred dollar shoes that I should just give up on. Strip, shift, get home. Stop trying to be the hero of my own pointless life. But I can't: can't give up, can't admit that I'm beat. The forest is my home, more than that house in the valley will ever be. This mountain is *mine* and it's not going to take me down without a fight.

Two

The Cabin

The sky gets darker and darker and the wind gets colder and I'm still running, trying to let the wolf in me guide my human self. But the cold is intense, my sweat like ice, my feet growing heavier with every step. My lungs ache from the cold air, my stomach clenching with hunger and fear. All my systems are struggling to keep up with my demands to keep moving, but to stop is to die.

Maybe. It's late spring, so it won't be so bad, but that thought is still echoing in my head when the first flake of snow stings my face. In less than a minute it's fully snowing, the hard flakes pelting my cheeks, the path disappearing from beneath my feet like a terrible dream. My mom is going to be losing her shit. If she remembers where I went. If she wasn't too distracted by her darling spare son-in-law. The one who was always meant to be hers. Graeme was the real spare, the betrayal, Evan throwing away his future and everyone else's past to fuck a human. And now Ev and Graeme both get to fuck Pierce and why the fuck am I crying while I run for my life from a cloud? Because even if I have nothing to live for, I'm not nearly ready to quit living.

I'm not going to have much say in that if I don't find shelter. Another prophetic thought I shouldn't let myself have, as my next step lands on a loose rock that squirts out from under my foot. Arms wheeling, heart racing, I manage to keep my balance, but now I can't see the trail at all, the snow already an inch deep and rising. I take a step, but the ground is soft and crumbly, not like the hard packed trail.

Ok, asshole, it's your fancy shoes or your life. I have to do it, have to shift, make myself strong enough to get out of this situation. I can deal with the shame later, when I'm not on top of a fucking mountain freezing to death. The wind whirls around me, pushing at me from all sides. It drops and I smell smoke. Good smoke, not from live trees but from a well-cured log in a clean fireplace.

Staring about, half-blinded by snow, I spot a building. I hope. But it's all I have, and moving as quickly as I dare down the slippery, fractured hillside, I head towards the squared-off shape lurking at the at the base of the slope. If I can't get inside, maybe there's a shed, or a porch I can hide under. Maybe it'll block the wind. Anything to increase my chances of living through the night.

I don't realize how tense I am until I reach the cabin and fall against it like I'm going to hug it. Weird desperate sounds are coming from my throat, halfway between a whine and a sob, as I tack along the wall towards the door. It's too much to ask for it to be unlocked but when I try the old latch it opens.

"H-hh-hhh-hello?" No one answers so I go in, pulling out my phone for a light. With the door shut I notice the dull red glow of the banked fire. I should look around, make sure I haven't walked in on someone sleeping, but all I can think about is getting warm. I find the pile of logs and another smaller stack of kindling on the floor beside the fireplace, and carefully, so fucking carefully, I feed small twigs and slivers to the coals, building up heat so that when I put on a log it catches.

Slowly my muscles begin to unknot. Still I sit on the floor in front of the fire, my hands and feet and thighs tingling painfully as the feeling returns. Now that I'm sure that I'll be okay, I start to notice what's around me. It's pretty small, about the size of a double car garage. There's an old wood stove in the corner and a heavy wooden table with one chair near the window. Under the window there's a big wooden box like a free-standing kitchen cabinet with a white enamel washbasin on top. An iron framed double bed stands against the opposite wall, a bashed up army foot locker at, well, the foot of it. No pictures on the wall, no books, no lamp. Does this place even have electricity? Or a toilet?

The weirdest thing is, it smells like home. Not like my parents' house but like a place I want to be. A place that feels natural, like it wants me to be here too. Like I belong. A fraying plaid jacket hangs on one of the bedposts and even though this isn't my house I put it on, the smell surrounding me like a hug. It's just relief, it's just me being glad that I'm not outside, but as soon as I think this I start to worry.

Someone is still out in the storm. The person who lives here. The person whose clothes I'm wearing like they're mine. I hunt around for a flashlight or Coleman lantern, something to help me look for them. Or just to signal from the front door, in case they weren't sure where the cottage was. Yeah, because nothing made a guy feel better than knowing someone had broken into his house. Except I hadn't broken in, I'd just opened the door. And anyone living up here would know that I hadn't a choice, that it was either invade their house or freeze to death. I'm thinking through how I'm going to apologize when the door opens and the biggest guy I've ever seen walks in, snow clinging to his long hair.

"Hi," I blurt. "Sorry. I was cold. Like really cold. I'm sorry." *Fuck*. Were any of those even words?

He doesn't move from the doorway. He's even taller than my dad and built like a beast, with shaggy hair and a messy beard and a look of total confusion on his broad face. He blinks a few times, then feels behind him to swing the door shut. He crosses the room and drops a sack beside the woodstove, then eases off his heavy wool coat and hangs it on a nail.

Fuck, he's huge. Six foot four, I want to guess, with a massive chest and arms like tree trunks. A bit of a gut but it fits his build. Pale eyes under a serious forehead, the kind that makes people think you're angry all the time. I am definitely staring at him, but really there's nothing else to look at.

"You from the valley?" His voice is low, nearly lost in the roar of the wind.

"From Hollowood, yeah. I didn't think I'd make it all the way home."

He sits down, the chair creaking under his weight. I stay where I am, standing by his bed, wearing his shirt. I can feel words filling my mouth, but I don't want to say them. Don't want to babble, annoy him, fuck this up. And I already apologized. Any more and I'd just be filling the air with sound to keep from hearing my own thoughts.

"Culver?" he says.

"Yeah, but how did you know?"

He shrugs one massive shoulder. "You look like one."

"You know my parents?"

"I met your grandpa once."

"Do my folks know you live here?"

"Don't expect so."

"Does anyone?"

"You do, now."

I'm waiting for him to tell me to take off his shirt. Really I'm waiting for him to tell me to go to hell. Or that I'm welcome to stay. Or anything, but he just looks at me like I'm something he ordered online while he was drunk and then forgot about until the package arrived.

"I really am sorry to just come in like I did," I say after what feels like a really long silence. "I didn't know what else to do. I don't usually get lost."

"I know."

"What? I mean, why? No, actually, how?"

"I've seen you before. I see your tracks."

"I guess not many people come up here. Is that why you don't lock your door?"

"Got nothing to steal."

"What do you do up here anyway? Like, for fun."

"Fun?" he says, like he's never heard the word.

"Yeah. Like, to put in time. Or whatever."

"Never had to think about it."

He falls silent again, leaving me to wonder if I'm pissing him off or if he doesn't care at all. I'm kind of sweating under his shirt, but I don't want to start stripping while he's looking at me like that. Like the thing he ordered without wanting it, like a pointless mystery, his eyes boring straight through to my bones.

"Anyway, I don't want to be in your way. I'll just...be quiet and stuff, and I'll go when it's light."

"Don't expect you'll be going anywhere in a hurry."

"Is it snowing that bad?"

He nods with just a lift of his head, then gets to his feet. I'm holding my breath, waiting for...anything. Waiting like I know what happens next. Somehow I'm surprised when he goes to the fire and puts on another log.

He stays there for a bit, pushing the coals and unburnt wood around with a stick charred at one end from being used like this. While his back is turned I take off his shirt and hang it on the bedpost again. If he notices or even cares, he doesn't mention it, as he opens the sack and pulls out a pair of dead rabbits. And I know some of you are going to get upset by that but if you've never met a cow (spoiler: they're the sweetest, gentlest things on dry land) then you don't understand that being cute isn't enough to keep you from being eaten.

In a couple of minutes, he's skinned and gutted both animals and hung them over the fire to roast. He wraps the innards in the skins and wraps this all in a piece of canvas then puts it outside.

"I thought we weren't meant to feed the wildlife," I say when he comes back in.

"I'm not. But I don't feel like stretching the skins now. They'll keep in the cold."

"You don't have power at all?"

"From where?"

"I don't know, solar panels? Though a mini turbine would work better around here."

He shrugs with one shoulder again. "I don't need electricity."

"What do you do in winter?"

"Sleep."

"Me too, but...seriously? Sorry. It's not even my business. You do you."

He frowns like he's never heard the phrase before. Have I gone back in time or some shit? Was that weird mask-person real or all in my head? Is any of this real or a hallucination I'm having as I freeze to death? I pinch my leg through my tights and it hurts but I'm still not totally convinced. Not until I smell the meat cooking.

Suddenly I am painfully aware of my body. I'm still wearing my wet shoes and tights, my back aches from being tense, I need to pee, and I'm starving. I was planning to eat a couple of those chicken breasts before I left the house. I've just run up and halfway down a mountain on three eggs and a protein bar, and I'm feeling it hard.

I grab onto the bed stand as a wave of dizziness washes over me. I can't sit on this man's bed—not just because my clothes are wet but because...because there's rude and presumptuous, and then there's fucking arrogant. I might have broken into his house, but I'm going to be the best uninvited guest I can be.

The big guy, whose name I need to ask before much more time passes, is squatting by the fire, the hot light carving his still face into beastly shadows. He looks at me out of the side of his eye but otherwise doesn't react as I sit in his chair to take off my shoes and socks. My feet are disgusting, wrinkled like I've been swimming and so damp I leave footprints on the floorboards. I put my shoes beside the fire, my socks draped over them. He doesn't move, except for his eyes, which follow me as I sit down again.

"My name's Chase," I say. "And I really am sorry to do this to you."

"Happens now and then. Hikers. One time a government man."

"Really? Like what kind of g-man?"

"Wouldn't say. Had a lot of tactical gear. He left quick."

"I'll leave too, as soon as I can. Even if there's snow. I'm not far from town. Am I?"

"No. But you won't be leaving tomorrow." He sounds totally sure. Like it's even up to him. As long as it's not a white-out, I'll be fine for the hour or so it'll take to get home.

The rabbits are done cooking and he grabs them off the iron swing-arm without oven mitts or anything and lays them on the hearth to settle. He leaves the cottage and comes back in with a massive log, carrying it under one arm like it's nothing. He stands it on its end beside the table then sits on it.

"You can have your chair," I say. Another shrug. This is going to be a long night. I'm edgy at the best of times, but something about his indifference is freaking me out. He should be angry. Or surprised. Or something. He should care that I broke into his house. He shouldn't be okay with me sitting in his chair, about to eat part of his dinner.

"What's your name?" I ask.

"Stone."

"Really?" He frowns while I think about shoving my head in the fire. Who the fuck doubts someone's name? "I mean, cool. Thanks. I'm Chase. I already told you that. Fuck. Sorry, I shouldn't swear so much."

His lips pull to one side, like he's thinking about laughing at me but is too polite to go for it. "I don't care," he says. "Do what you want."

"That is a recipe for disaster, dude. Not that I want to do anything crazy. That's just usually how it turns out."

"You doing what you want is a disaster?"

"Or like a minor accident. Not usually a raging success, is what I'm saying. Like this run. I could have just gone for my usual run but instead I took this trail I never saw before and ended up...well, here." I don't want to mention the cave and the thing in the mask. That's only going to make me seem even crazier.

He doesn't reply, just gets up and goes to the wood stove and comes back with the skillet. He lays the cooked rabbits in it and puts it on the table between us. Then takes out this scary little knife from I don't even know where, to cut the meat into pieces we can pick up.

"You should eat first," I say as he pushes the skillet towards me.

"You're not hungry?"

"I don't need it."

"Yes, you do."

"It's your dinner."

"You're my guest."

"No, I'm not. I broke into your house."

"I didn't lock the door."

"Yeah, but you didn't invite me or anything. And why weren't you freaked out when you saw me? I broke into your fucking house. I was wearing your clothes."

"You looked cold."

"But..." Why am I trying to make him angry? Why don't I just shut up and eat and be glad I'm not freezing to death on the side of a mountain? Why does this feel so familiar? Not just this cabin but this stupid conversation, this back and forth of him offering what I need but don't think I deserve?

If it was anyone else offering, I'd take it. But I don't want to take anything else away from this strange, quiet man. I invaded his house. I've taken his solitude, permanently, because no one used to know where he lived. I was probably going to sleep in his bed if he hadn't shown up when he did, so I sit with my arms crossed and my head down and wait for him to finish eating. I really am hungry, but I don't want him to suffer when I brought the trouble on myself.

He eats almost delicately, his big hands making soft movements. Leaving a couple of pieces, he tosses the bones into the fire then goes outside. I guess the rest is for me, but I still feel weird about eating it. Instead I try to drag the log he was sitting on closer to the chair so I have something to put my feet on when I'm sleeping. Not that I really expect to sleep, no matter that my head is thumping and my arms too floppy to budge the thick log more than a few inches.

I text my mom, then my cousin River, to let someone know that I'm safe. The messages might not pop up until tomorrow but it's the best I can do. River won't freak out the way Sunny might, and Ash would want to come looking for me. My mom? Who knows? Maybe she'll call her sweet little son-in-law to complain about me. Fuck, thinking that makes me an even bigger asshole than usual.

When Stone comes back in with more wood, he's covered in snow, flakes clinging to his beard like glitter. He sticks another log on and as the room brightens I realize how late it is, and how dark. He stays crouched by the fire, his eyes drilling into me, seeing past my bullshit, right into my soul. A thought so drama that I nearly laugh at myself, if it wasn't for the way he frowns suddenly and turns away.

"Look, I'm sorry to be in your way. I promise, I'll be gone first thing in the morning."

He frowns even harder. "If you think that, you don't know this mountain."

"But I do. I'm up here all the time. That's why I can't believe I've never met you, or at least seen your house. I thought this was state land."

"Maybe it is."

"Do the rangers know you're here?"

"I don't know."

"Why are you here? I mean obviously it's your home and stuff but, like, why hide away like this? Hollowood isn't that nosy, is it?"

"Got no reason to go anywhere."

"You don't ever come into town? I guess not, or I would have seen you before."

"Maybe I did and you missed me."

"If I'd been around, we would have met."

"Would we?"

"I would have gone out of my way for it."

"Why?"

"Because... Well, because you're interesting."

"Interesting?"

"At least to me you are. Nothing ever happens in Hollowood so seeing you would have been *something*."

Poking the fire with the charred stick, he doesn't answer. Maybe I went too far, saying that. Who wants to be a *something*? Who cares if some dumb-ass mountain boy is interested in them? So little happens around here, you could entertain me with dirt, if it was a weird enough color (why else do you think I know stuff about lichen?)

I sit with my feet tucked under me and try not to watch him move around the cabin. If there was only something else to look at besides him and the fire. I guess that this was all we had for centuries and centuries. Shelter and fire and food and each other, and all the other stuff was a bonus, culture a thing we invented only when we'd learned how not to die.

He's clearly not going to eat any more, so I eat the weird little chunks of bony, chickeny meat, picking off as much as I can with my teeth. Wolf-me would eat them whole, which is always a bad idea because I forget that my guts are full of things that my human digestion can't manage (and you thought *your* body was a mysterious shit-show.) I throw the bones into the fire like he did. That's how I'll get through this. Do like he does and otherwise stay out of the way. Except he's standing by the door pulling on his coat.

"I'll be back in the morning," he says.

"You're going out in weather like that? Where? Why?"

"It's not far."

"But why go at all? This your home. Don't leave. Not that I'm telling you what to do. But it's awful out there. Please don't go."

He says nothing, his eyes shadowed, his hand on the latch. "I'll come back. I promise." Before I can answer he opens the door. Wind rips through the cabin, nearly flattening the fire and bringing in a swirl of angry snow that makes me duck. When I look up again he's gone.

Three

Snowbound

Of course I can't sleep. I struggle with insomnia on the best of nights. This is so completely out of the ordinary that even if Stone was here I'd be awake. The lumpy mattress and creaky bedframe are making sure of that. Nope, it's just me and my thoughts, freaking out because why did he leave? That he has shelter I don't doubt. But I can't figure out why he didn't want to stay. I was going to give him the bed. I wasn't going to ask for a thing.

I pass out eventually. I don't know the time, the battery on my phone so close to dead I don't even know if it's worth leaving it on. I wake what feels like seconds later as the door scrapes open. I cover my eyes and groan as the light slaps me in the face.

"Next time, maybe knock first. I don't mean that, I don't mean that. Do whatever." He doesn't answer (not like he needs to) as he goes to the fireplace and starts working the coals. By the time I crawl out of his bed he has a few logs on and the room is starting to warm up.

"So if I had to pee," I ask, feeling both stupid and quietly desperate to know the answer, "is there an outhouse?"

"Nope. Sorry."

"Right. That's fine."

"You can wear my boots," he says as I pull on my socks. "Snow's pretty deep."

He's not kidding. The drift against the front step is nearly knee deep. I feel like a little kid wading through it in his giant Kodiaks. As I step out of the lea of the cabin, the wind slices through my running clothes, hurling snow in my eyes. I step back, then shuffle towards the other corner, but the wind is whirling round me like crazy, and I end up huddled against the wall, praying I don't soak myself. Why would anyone live like this?

Inside, I go straight to the fire. He's at the stove, and as I'm rubbing the feeling back into my hands I smell coffee. Too much to hope for, so I don't ask. If he made some for himself, he made some for me. I hope, because I would fight someone right now for a cup of coffee, if only to dull my hunger. I sit at the table and he sets a dented camping mug before me, steam rising from the holy elixir. It's not, it's just coffee, but yet again he's giving me something I don't deserve, and I'm getting ready to refuse when he sits down on the log with his own cup.

"So," I say instead. "Snowstorm. How long do you think it'll last?

"Should quit today."

"Is that you guessing or..."

"That's what I was told."

"By the people you stayed with?"

He glares at me from under that solid forehead, but I don't flinch. I've had way dirtier looks thrown at me, usually by people who claim to love me. "You don't have to tell me. And don't worry that I'll tell on you. That you live here, I mean. You must want to be here or you wouldn't be, right?"

He grunts in reply, the cup disappearing between his huge hands. Strong hands, made for working, pale scars streaking the backs of his fingers like he once punched a window. A man's hands, and with a guilty heat rising up the back of my neck I take too big a gulp of the bitter coffee and start to cough. *Smooth, Chasey. Real mature, to cough up a lung on this guy's floor because you suddenly wanted his hands on you.*

"Sorry," I wheeze. "It's not covid, I swear."

He frowns, not in anger but in confusion. "Covid?"

"Seriously, dude? The pandemic? The society-is-closed, no-one-left-the-house-for-a-year pandemic? The million people dead, essential workers, Fauci, masks, horse pills... Nothing?"

"I told you I don't see many people."

"Yeah, but dude..." As much as I want to keep arguing, I can't help but believe him from the look of sheer incomprehension on his face. "Let's just say you're goddamn lucky you don't know what I'm talking about. The rest of the world just went through hell. Jeez, you aren't even vaccinated!"

"I don't get sick," he says simply.

"Is that really up to you?"

He shrugs and sips his coffee. I copy him because my brain doesn't know what else to do. Any minute now I'm going to wake up, because this just gets weirder and weirder. The window beside me shows nothing but white. The only other light is the fire, and though I'm not cold, I shiver. I look out the window again, and for a second, just a second, I swear I see the person in the mask. I blink and it's nothing but snow.

We sit and drink our coffee and the wind blows and the fire burns and my brain wrestles with the fucked up reality of this man's life. Seeing no one, going nowhere. "This is the weirdest question I've ever asked, but why do you have two cups if you only have one of everything else?"

"I told you. People get lost up here sometimes. Thought I should be able to give them something to drink."

"Lucky me."

He grunts, pushing out his lips. His mouth is worse than his hands. And by worse I mean even better: broad and firm, his lips sweetly pink in their frame of dark hair. Fuck, I'm such a slut. This guy is saving my life and hasn't asked for a thing in return, so why do I wish this was porn so I could 'thank' him carnally? Maybe see above, under being a slut. It's not my fault that my body's the only thing I have to offer the world. Or maybe it is, but that doesn't change the fact that my dick is poking a hole in my running leggings over the thought of Stone treating me like trash.

Stone, who doesn't talk to people much, who missed three solid years of the most important event in a century. Who still might be all in my head.

Time passes. We finish the coffee then take turns with his boots to go outside. When I come back in, he's setting up a chessboard. A beautiful set made of wood, the edge of the board inlaid with little chips of shiny stone, the pieces intricately carved.

"Do you know how to play?" he asks as I sit down across from him.

"I do, actually. I dated, or sort of dated, this guy from UC Boulder." Justin, an English major with melting hazel eyes, who never smiled except when he was winning, or coming. "I think he taught me so he'd have someone to beat. You?"

"Used to play with my mom. Sometimes I play against myself."

"How does that work?"

"You just turn the board around, and–"

"No, I mean, how do you not just...I don't know, cheat? Wouldn't you know all the moves you were going to make?"

He shrugs. "It works for me."

"I guess that's what counts."

Slowly, so slowly, he lifts his hand and picks up a pawn and moves it one square. I copy his move, then we both sit back. I know how to play, but not how to win. Not against someone who knows what they're doing. Winning was never the point with Justin. Like so many games, I usually played to lose.

Stone is methodical but he isn't much better than me. About six moves in, he fucks up, leaving his left bishop exposed, but I don't take it. I should but I don't, because I want him to win. "So do you really never come to town?" I say as I move a pawn instead of my knight.

"I stop at Sutherland's now and then. He gets my mail."

"You get mail?"

"I buy things sometimes. Had to order that coat."

"I guess they don't exactly grow on trees."

He grunts again, hunching his shoulders briefly, and maybe I'm wrong but I think it's how he laughs. We each make a few more moves, me trying my best not to take his stupid bishop, wishing he'd notice he's in danger.

His hand hovers over the bishop again. I hold my breath, willing him to slide it two squares to the northeast. He makes a fist, then moves his king's castle instead. Right into my knight's line of fire.

He wants me to win.

So I start trying to lose. Fuck him if he thinks I need his help. I'm here by accident, and I don't need him kissing my ass. Picking the wrong move on purpose is harder than I expect, so I play blind, barely looking at the board, waiting for him to either call me on it or win the game. He glances up from the board as I set down my wasted knight near his stupid bishop. I glare back at him, wondering why I'm ruining a good thing. If he kicks me out, I'm screwed. Stuck on a mountainside in snow up to my knees, with no idea where I am or where to go because my phone's officially dead. Still, I can't hold back my groan as he moves his bishop away from my knight.

"I know what you're doing," I say. "You don't need to let me win."

He frowns but doesn't answer as I pick off the bishop with a pawn. It takes me six more moves to trash the board, taking both knights, two pawns, and his queen and backing his king into a corner. "Are we going for the TKO?" I ask.

"The what?"

"The knockout. I can take you if you want me to, but...ah. Your piece, I mean. Your king piece. That one. Fuck. Sorry." Despite the gloom of the cabin and the cloudy day, I can tell he's blushing behind his beard. A bubble of sap bursts from a log and breaks the silence weighing on us. The silence that until an hour ago had been full of the sound of the wind. "Hey, I think the storm is over."

I go to the window but the glass is frosted over, so I open the door. Blinded by the sunlight reflecting off the snow, I cover my eyes and step back, straight into...into Stone, standing behind me, so close his scent surrounds me. A strange, springtime smell of raw earth and crushed leaves and some animal wildness that makes all my hair stand on end.

He doesn't move or say a word. His breath is hot on my scalp, his smell all over me, and I lean back against his massive body and breathe him in. There's something so right about this moment, a sense of perfect comfort. He still doesn't move, not even when I turn my head to press my cheek against his chest. I never want to move again, except maybe back inside the cabin so we can shut the door and I can bury myself in him and him in me and never come up for air. Forget it, I'd let him have me right here in the open doorway, in the sight of God and the crows and anyone who wants to watch. I want this man, with a fierceness I've never felt before, but as I turn around to tell him a low, hungry growl stops us both dead. I look around for another wolf when Stone's stomach rumbles again. His face turns bright red.

"Guess there's no delivery up here," I say, like a jackass. As if, when there's not even signal, or a working phone.

He frowns, I think, because he always seems to be frowning a little bit. "I'll get us some food," he says, stepping away from the door.

"From where."

"Gotta dig it out."

"Of the ground?"

He laughs, I think, with a little huff of breath and that shrug like he doesn't want to admit it was funny. "From the cellar. Papa didn't think to build a door from inside the house."

"Let me help. I'm really good at digging."

"Only got one shovel,"

"That doesn't matt—you're right. I'll wait." He might know I'm a Culver but that doesn't mean I'm ready to let him know the rest. I'm only a good digger as my other self.

Pulling on his coat, he pauses in the doorway. "You know much about woodstoves?"

"Yep. Want me to get it up? I mean the fire. In the stove."

He nods then clumps down the stairs, swinging the door shut behind him with a thud. Thank fuck, because I can only keep holding my hands in front of my crotch for so long. My leggings already show enough when I'm not rock hard. And all I did was smell him. And feel his heat against my back, and watch his strong fingers select chess pieces with delicate precision while I wondered how they felt to suck...

"You *do* suck, Chase Culver, you slut," I mutter as I jam kindling into the wood stove's chamber. "He's not interested in you, he's probably not even gay, he's a stranger whose house you broke into because you're an idiot. Keep your shit together, alright?"

A bad habit, but I talk to myself. Not because it helps me think (nothing helps that) but because there's hardly anyone else to talk to. Everyone else has a life: Evan, Pierce, my folks, my cousins, the friends I made in Denver who barely even like my posts anymore. Me, all I have is an amazing ass and really stable blood sugar and time, endless, useless time. Time to regret all my choices, as a whole and in specific detail. Time to wonder why I bother taking such good care of myself, when I'm the only one who appreciates it.

Lost in my bullshit, I catch the side of my hand on the edge of the stove. "Shit! Ow! Goddamn it, Chase, what the fuck?" I dash outside to shove my hand into the snow. The smooth white surface deceives me and my feet sink deep, slush filling my shoes and soaking them all over again. I'm still swearing when Stone comes around the corner carrying a wooden crate.

"Don't worry about me," I say as he stops to stare. "Just a little burn."

"You burned your feet?"

"What? No. My hand. But seriously, what do you do up here if you get really hurt? Like if you broke your leg or something."

"Rangers gave me a flare gun," he says as he trudges past me. "Suppose I ought to carry it with me."

"Doesn't do you much good if you don't."

Climbing the stairs, he shrugs. "I don't always have a way to carry—I can't rely on it, is all."

"You ought to know I'm going to worry about you from now on," I say, following him inside.

"Why?"

"Why? Because you're up here all alone with a flare gun as your 9-1-1. Come summertime when it gets dry, you're as likely to burn the forest down as get anyone's attention."

"One more reason not to carry it."

"No, that's a reason to get a phone."

"How would I keep it charged?"

"Solar panels. Seriously, I planned it all out one time when I got sick of living with my folks. I was going to buy a tiny home kit and a parcel of land and set myself up with everything I needed. I can email you...okay, maybe I can bring my laptop next time."

"Next time?"

"Sure. Unless you don't want me. To come back, I mean. Because I would. If you wanted." Motor-mouth strikes again, and I bite my lips shut as he slides the pans around on the stovetop. Steam rises from my socks where they lay on the stone hearth, and I move my shoes back from the fire so they don't melt. "Don't leave, okay? Later, I mean. Tonight. This is your home. You can even have the bed."

He doesn't answer. Again. No big deal, that's his thing, not saying much, and here I am running my mouth all over. I tuck my feet under me to stay out of the way and try not to watch him too closely but there's nothing else to look at. I have a bunch of questions but like hell I'm going to ask them. I've bugged him enough already.

We eat baked beans and he eats some weird smelling smoked fish that makes me wonder how I can think he's hot if he's willing to put that in his mouth. And yet I'd eat his ass right here and now if he asked, so who am I to judge? He looks up at me with curiosity in his piercing blue eyes and my doubt disintegrates. He can put whatever he likes in his mouth.

"You hot?" he says.

"Why, is my face red? Maybe I am. I don't know. Are you? It doesn't matter." *Fuck my life, Culver, stop talking.* Frowning, Stone gets up from the table and comes back with an honest-to-god brown jug and a pair of mostly clean shot glasses. He sits down then pours two shots of clear, colorless liquor.

"You make this yourself?" I ask as he pushes a glass towards me.

"Pure as it comes."

"You know moonshining's illegal, right?"

"I know."

"Just so we're clear." The booze smells sweet and a bit like licorice, and tastes like the clay jug. I'm about to congratulate him on his distilling skills when the back end catches up. "Dude...that's some firewater," I wheeze, fanning myself because now I am definitely hot. "You trying to get me drunk or something?"

"No."

"I mean, cause it's totally unnecessary. I don't need to be drunk to want to—never mind."

His hand dwarfs the shot glass as he takes a sip. "Why are you here?" he asks.

"Because I've already been everywhere else? For real," I say as he frowns. "I took that trail only because I didn't know where it went. Which sounds really dumb when I say it out loud. I was going to turn around, then I saw—" I still don't know how to mention the cave without sounding weird. "This other path that was going downhill, and the weather was bad and I didn't want to die, so when I saw your cabin I thought that'd be the best I was going to get. So I'm here by accident. I never even knew anyone lived up here. Except that I heard about a family who moved out of town, up the mountain. Before I was born. Is your last name Roth?"

His forehead lowers, his eyes thinning. "What do you know about the Roths?"

"Nothing. Just that they used to live in Hollowood Falls proper, but now they don't. I've never met any of them."

"Most of them are dead and buried."

"That would explain why I've never met them. But you have, right?"

He doesn't answer, which is getting kind of old. I don't do strong and silent types who won't let me in, won't show me their real selves. Not after all the guys I've known who were happy to use me as a fuck-toy but wouldn't look me in the eye whenever we ran into each other in the daytime.

"Where are you going?" I ask as he gets up and starts for the door.

"Out."

"I said you could stay."

"It's not your choice to make."

"Wait!" I blurt as he opens the door. "You're just leaving like that? I said wait!" But as I grab for his arm he pivots away from me with his teeth bared in a snarl. As I jump back he steps outside then slams the door. For the first time since I got here, he locks it.

Fuck. I'm impossible. They're right, *I'm* the problem. Can't keep my mouth shut, don't know when I'm pissing people off, don't know when to quit. I snatch my phone off the table and nearly throw it in the fire when I remember the battery is dead.

Why won't he let me leave?

At this time of year the sky stays bright forever. I can't be that far from a trail I know. If I shifted, I'd be able to move faster, skip the trails and just go by instinct. But I'd have to climb out the window, which means I'd have to break it as it doesn't seem to open. What does this guy do if a fire starts? Throws a chair through the window and deals with it later. I am not a fire. I am a hot mess and a waster and too nice to break anything of Stone's. So I wait. Badly, pacing the cabin in a circuit from the bed to the window to the fire. I eat what's left of the beans. I don't drink the moonshine. I want him to trust me. I want him to come back and see that I'm not a problem.

There's a tin washbasin on top of the beat-up old food safe, and I use water from the big kettle on the back of the stove and my bare hands to wash the dishes. Then I sweep the floor with a broom that looks like he made it himself out of meadow grass and a stick. Which he probably did, but it works well enough. Now that the floor is clean, I strip down to my shirt and jocks and do a few sets of every bodyweight exercise I can think of.

Sitting with my back to the fire to dry my sweat (because I don't have a shower or even a towel) I wonder if this is what it's like in prison. Eat, clean, sweat, sleep, repeat, repeat, repeat. Or a sailor's wife two hundred years ago, standing at the window wondering if he'll ever return. Fuck, I'm losing my shit and I've only been stuck in here a few hours.

At last the light fades, the red smear of clouds staining the sky an echo of the low-burning embers in the fireplace. I settle the cinders in the ash so they stay hot for the night then lie down fully dressed on Stone's big bed to wait. He'll come back. I know he will. He has to.

Four

The Bear

It's the smell that wakes me. Not a bad smell, but there's a lot of it, a heavy, musky aroma with a hint of crushed cedar. A familiar, animal smell, but it isn't me. I can't see anything in the dark cabin, not even the glow of the sleeping fire. I'm about to sit up when I realize why.

A bear is sleeping in front of the fire, its enormous shaggy bulk blocking the weak light from the fire. The door is closed, and so is the window. So either this bear manifested itself inside this cabin, or...

Quietly, very quietly and very carefully, I undress. I don't want to explain. I don't need to explain. He knows I'm a Culver. He knows Hollowood.

Shifting hurts. It's always an effort but I'm tired and hungry and worried and weak and it feels like someone is pulling out my bones then shoving them back in. I can smell better now, the undertones of Stone's hot skin and damp fur, the smoke that my human nose had stopped noticing hours ago. He breathes slowly, his massive shoulder rising and falling. I want to curl up beside him, feel his warmth surround me as our hearts beat in time.

Outside, the snow glows coldly in the thin moonlight. I stay by the window, the residual heat from the stove heating my flank, the sounds of the night filtering through the glass: the wind shaking the branches, the drip of water from melting icicles, the whoosh of an owl's wings as it takes flight. Slowly the sky turns from black to navy to pearly blue. Just above the trees, a small cloud reflects the first pink rays of the sun, and I feel a tugging in my chest, a wordless pang of wonder that so much beauty exists and that I'm the only one in the world who's seeing it.

Or am I? I feel his gaze on my back. Then a wave of his scent rolls over me as he rises. I turn to face him and even though I know it's Stone beneath that brown pelt, the animal that I am shrinks from him as he raises his head to sniff the air. I drop to the floor, my hindquarters in the air, wagging my tail like a pet dog. He shuffles nearer and I roll to my back, whining with the effort to not pull away from his massive jaws as he touches his nose to mine, then sniffs his way down to my belly.

One bite and I'm done. Or a smack from one of his heavy paws. A fully grown bear can knock over a tree if he's in the mood. Shit, all he'd have to do to kill me is sit on my head. Things my body knows even better than my brain, but I lie there and let him smell me all over, his breath tickling my tender skin. He noses his way up again and then sits back on his haunches. I roll to my belly and edge nearer to lay my paw over his.

I can't tell you what it is exactly that goes when we talk to others of our kind. With my cousins and other kin it's somewhere between seeing and hearing their words. Somehow I just *know* what the other wolf is saying. Stone's bear-brain and my wolf-brain must not match up the same way, his thoughts a morphing field of blurry images, memory forms melting and reforming, communicating more with feeling than anything concrete. I see my own face—my human face—in the mash of visuals.

Yes! It's me, I think-say as clearly as I can. *Wow! It really is you. Wow!*

Hate to break it to you but I'm an even bigger dumb-ass as a wolf than as a human. The black sheep in wolf's clothing, Evan called me once, and though he's never said it again I never forgot. Stone blinks, his adorable fuzzy ears perking up. His thoughts accelerate, a flickering blur of brown and green, trees whipping past like one of Marcus and River's mountain biking POV videos.

You want that? I say. *You want to run? With me?*

He tosses his head with a happy little grunt and I spring to my feet to get out of his way. I want it too, want to stretch my limbs and feel the wind in my face and the stony, cruel, beautiful, mountain soil beneath the pads of my feet. Want to know the wildness in him. He opens the latch with his chin and nudges the door open. His shaggy shoulders fill the doorway as he hops off the steps, the crusted snow crunching under his paws. I follow, catching up with him at the edge of the trees.

I trot at his heels for half a mile, absorbing the details of the land, the air, through my altered point of view. The forest might seem quiet to a human, but to me it's an unending song of fluttering leaves and sawing branches, the thunk and scrape of an animal digging its burrow in the hillside, the distant chatter of a creek swollen with snowmelt. My nose almost hurts from the assault of fascinating smells: raw earth and rot and animal scat, sap and ice and Stone, always Stone.

He dominates my senses, his scent and the shaggy bulk of him ahead of me, the scrape of his claws over the stones as we climb higher and higher across the slope of the mountain. As the trees thin we come out onto a barren plateau. Untouched snow spreads from here to the base of a cliff, shimmering in the spring sunshine. I shiver, not from cold but from anticipation. I've been trying so hard to be normal I haven't gone wolf in weeks. The whole winter passed me by without a chance like this, but I stay where I am. I want so badly to show him I'm not a fuck-up. This place feels special. Not quite sacred but special to Stone, who went out of his way to bring me here.

He takes a few steps then looks back at me. He makes that little happy grunt again, and then he's off, plowing through the snow, running faster than I expect for his size. But under that fur and chub are a ton of muscles. He makes a u-turn then stops. His tongue hanging, he flops into the snow then rolls onto his back, kicking at the snow like a little kid.

Fuck it. Game on.

The snow nearly reaches my chest, and what looks like a smooth surface has been whipped into crests and banks that collapse around my legs and make it hard to run. I've almost caught up when he rolls to his feet and takes off running again. I spring after him, following the path he's carved. Suddenly he stops and rears up on his hind legs and every animal sense in me screams *run away*, because he is fucking humongous. Like a bear ought to be, but logic means nothing to me as my body takes over. I skid to a stop, spin about, and bolt back the way I came. I'm nearly at the tree line before my human brain takes the wheel again and brings me to a stop.

As I trot back to him he drops to all fours, then stands still and lets me sniff him over. The sweet musky scent of him calms me, and I rub against his sides like I'm a cat, hoping the smell will stick. *I'm sorry,* I tell him. *You scared me. You're big.*

He replies with the clearest vision he's shared yet. His memory of me cringing in terror then running away.

I'm not really scared of you, I tell him, nudging my nose softly under his chin, hoping he can understand me. *See? I'm here. I'm here for you.*

The vision fades, replaced by a red-gold haze that spreads from my mind to my body, threading through my veins and muscles until I'm sure that I'm glowing under this fur. Is this what love feels like? I fucking hope so.

With a deep purring growl Stone rolls onto his back again. The scent of his glands sweeps over me, making my mouth water as he stretches out one huge furry forelimb towards me. I nuzzle into the soft skin of his throat, my whole body shaking with excitement. I've never felt anything like this, never been so helplessly aroused, my balls aching, every nerve in my body tightening as Stone holds me against him, stretching his head to bare his neck to me, growling with pleasure as I lick and nuzzle and now and then press my teeth against his pelt.

Eager, desperate even, I climb on top of him, but his belly skin is as slack as his throat and my hind feet slide off to either side so that I end up straddling him. A sweet thrill of pleasure races up my spine as my glans presses against his soft front. He lets his forelimb drop, turning his head to expose unexplored territory. He wants this, I know he does, from the way he's giving in, from the rising red-gold heat of his wordless feelings drowning out my last human thoughts, my last scrap of self-control.

Shaking, whimpering, driven by animal instinct, I thrust against him, wanting to bury myself inside him, to mark him as my mate and make it stick. Make him mine—my pack, my home, my one and only, forever and ever, again and again. Suddenly he sits up, spilling me off him. I scramble to my feet and shake off the snow as he heaves himself up more slowly. With that same grumbling purr he smells me from my ruff to my haunches, his breath tickling as he noses under my tail. I stand still and let him smell me, despite that limbic terror of leaving myself exposed and the competing fear that he hated every minute of—

Fuck! Something hot and wet and firm glides over my balls and bare glans. Stone's tongue, rough and pink and massive. Ecstatic pleasure surges through me, building with every stroke. I arch my back, my tail bent high as I tilt my pelvis to give him more. It's beyond anything I've known, the last sin on the list, the slut and the beast—my two selves—united in one gorgeous moment as I come, spurting onto the churned up snow as Stone's tongue bathes my ass.

My whole groin buzzing, I scramble away from him. I can't believe I let that happen, but as he sniffs at my cum, stiffening on the snow, I know I'd do it again. He lifts his head, white stuff clinging to his chin. I want to ask him a million questions, and none. With a little grunt he turns and starts towards the trees, making my choice for me.

The walk home seems to take no time at all. The only man-made thing for miles, the cabin stands out sharply against the trees. Stone stops at the bottom of the steps and nods towards the open door. I press my nose under his jaw and catch a blur of images: wolves, humans, a fire, a child, all mashed together like a bunch of videos playing on top of each other.

Slow down! Man, I thought my brain went fast. One of his images resolves from the flicker of colored light: a wolf looking back at him from the top of the steps.

You want me to go first? He nods towards the door again with a huff. *Okay but this better not be a trap. Just kidding,* I add as he growls softly.

After a quick sniff to be sure nothing got inside, I scamper up the steps. I pause in the doorway, wondering if what he sees matches what he imagined, but when I look back he's already lumbering around the corner of the cabin.

Inside, de-wolfed, I pull on my dirty leggings and start working on the fire. Stone comes in a few minutes later, wearing his big brown coat but nothing else. Barely looking my way, he pours himself a shot and one for me. Drinks his then pours another.

"You want to, I don't know, talk about it?" I say, folding myself into the chair.

"What's to talk about?"

"Um, I just rode you like a theme park ride. Not that I wish I hadn't, but I've never done that before. Like that, I mean. Only ever as a human. I don't think I've even told anyone I was fu—uh, dating."

"Everyone in town knows the Culvers."

"Which is why I don't stick my di—uh, fool around with Hollowood folk, I mean. Hell, I'm blood kin with half of them. I only hook up with people out of town. You get a pass. You're Hollowood but you're not, you know?"

"Sure do." He downs the rest of his shot. I nearly offer him mine, which I kind of don't want, but I don't want him to be drinking alone. As he steps away from the table his coat swings open, revealing his body in one startling flash of chest hair and belly and the fat head of his cock.

"Holy fuck." The words pop out of my mouth before I can stop them, because if that glimpse is any sign, he's packing insane heat.

"What is it?" he says.

"You and that serious piece of man meat. I meant it as a compliment!" I say as his face turns red. "Honest. You're hot."

"I'm what?"

"Hot. You know, good looking, sexy, that kind of thing. I'm serious," I say as he laughs with that single chesty grunt. "The way you live, you could be the hottest guy on earth and you wouldn't know. What if you're cheating the world by keeping it to yourself, hiding up here? Me, I'd take a piece of that all day long. I kind of sort of thought you maybe wanted that too...shit. You're straight, aren't you?"

"I doubt it."

"What do you mean, you doubt it?"

"Never really think about women that way. Like someone I wanted to...you know."

"But you'd want to...you know, with men?"

"Dunno. Maybe."

"You've never tried?"

"Nope."

"You're not a virgin, are you? Not that it matters," I blurt as his expression crumbles. "You do you. For me, that ship sailed long ago. Right off the edge of the map." With my hand I mime a little ship dropping into the abyss. He grunts, sort of a laugh but also like he's annoyed, or maybe just embarrassed for me. I'm embarrassed for myself and want to crawl into the fireplace and go up in smoke so I don't have to think about him thinking about me being Colorado's cum dumpster. Which I kind of was for a few months. A few times.

Yet somehow I don't have a clue what to do next. How to turn this weird, uncomfortable conversation into the seduction I was really hoping he'd take care of. I've never had to chase (ha!) anyone to get them into bed. I usually just show up and stick out my lips and my ass and play dumb. I want to climb over the table then beg him to fuck me on it, but I don't want to scare him off. Like he's still a beast, wondering how this skinny pink weirdo ended up in his cozy little den.

For courage, for warmth, for the hell of it, I drink the shot, then squeeze my lips together so I don't cough out the biting liquor all over him. As I stand up he backs away, his eyes tracking down my bare chest to the shape of my dick pushing at the front of my running tights. I have so many questions: why he shifted in the night, why he licked me in the meadow, what he wants from me now that we're men. I don't want to ask, don't want to ruin this chance by making him think I don't want it.

I approach him slowly, this rough, raw man who blushes like a baby gay at a circuit party at the first dirty word. A mountain of a man, his hair spilling over his shoulders which rise and fall with his hard breath as I grip the front of his coat and look into his eyes.

"What are you thinking about?" I ask.

"You," he murmurs, low and quietly.

"What about me?"

"I want to touch you."

"What else?" As he struggles to answer I take that last step and close the distance between us. Hard and heavy and dripping precum, his bare cock pushes between my slippery thighs. "Fuck, I want that in me," I whisper despite myself.

"What d'you say?"

"I said, I want to climb onto that log of yours and have it split me open like a...ugh, a log splitter. Forget it, just..." Going up on my toes I press my legs together, catching as much of his dick as I can between my lycra-covered thighs. He moans, his head falling back as his hips move by instinct. His shaft presses hard against my balls but it's worth it to see him like this. "Goddamn, you are fucking ridiculous. In a good way, I mean."

Stone doesn't reply, too far gone, his eyes closed, his mouth hanging open, his tongue flickering over his lips as I squeeze his shaft between my thighs. And then the beast in me takes over. My mouth flooding with spit, I climb off him and kneel at his feet.

His eyes crack open. "What are you doing?"

"Seriously? You're the one who walked in here naked."

His face goes red, the blush creeping down his chest. "I forgot about needing clothes," he mumbles.

"You forgot? Sorry, but that is the weakest excuse possible."

"I don't ever have someone else to think about," he says, sniffing. Fuck, is he crying? Did I break him by trying too hard? I can't get anything right, but maybe I can fix this.

"I'm sorry," I say as I get to my feet. "I didn't mean it. I just...I've heard a lot of bullshit from people. I kind of assume everyone's lying to me." His head hanging, he doesn't reply, sniffling and blinking, this beautiful mountain of a man wounded by pathetic little me. "Hey, it's okay," I say as I gently grasp the front of his coat again. "We're good. We don't have to do anything. Let's just go to bed. To sleep," I add as he his head jerks up, his eyes wide with fear.

"Are we going to both fit?"

"It's big enough. Honest. I've put up with way worse."

He puts on a pair of old cotton pants that might have been blue or black at one time and have been washed to that buttery gray, the knees patched, the hems frayed. Though it won't be dark for a few more hours, the clouds have turned the sky the same shade of faded grey, and I quickly bank the fire as he puts away a few things in the kitchen. I'm hungry and he must be too, but I'm not going to interrupt this sweet little moment of home-making.

Crouched in front of the big stone fireplace, I let the feeling sink in. At the last of those meetings I had with Dr. Lowenstein, she told me I never let myself feel anything deeply. I told her she was full of shit. Wasn't that why I was in therapy, because I felt too deeply? Later I understood what she meant, that I don't let myself feel my feelings all the way, that I'm always on the hunt for a distraction from the difficult shit that needs to be done if you want to (ugh) grow as a person. Not just feeling bad when you've fucked up, but feeling good. That goblin in my brain always tells me *you could feel better*, never letting me enjoy what's right in front of me, always daring me to go harder.

This...I don't know how I could feel better than this. We're warm and safe, and even though we didn't fuck (furry ball-licking doesn't count, shut up) I feel close to him. We shared something unique, crossed a boundary I didn't know existed. I don't care if he never wants to fuck me as a man if we can have the other.

After a few tries we figure out a position in bed, him spooning me though at a distance, his arm tucked between us. The blanket barely reaches the edge of the mattress, but his warmth makes up for the little breaths of cold air that tickle my knees. My stomach hurts and the bed sags under Stone's weight but I don't ever want to move. Want to stay here forever, away from all the bullshit: my family, the future, the world.

Five

A Taste of Honey

I wake up with my nose against the log wall of the cabin. Somehow we switched places in the night. Stone lies flat on his back, softly snoring, and I take the chance to check him out in the quiet light of morning.

His soft body hair lies sleekly over his pale skin. His stomach sags like he's lost a bunch of weight. The low-angled light filtering through his untrimmed beard reveals the blunt shape of his face, but I can't tell if he's handsome or not. It's too late to wonder about that, I'm fixed on him. For now, because god knows you can't trust me to see anything through. I might wake up tomorrow and decide I want to be anywhere but here. Or not. Maybe I'll never feel like that.

I've been with enough guys I've figured out what I don't want. Stone has none of what I don't want. What he has is solitude and safety, two things I desperately need. Plus that dick. Like the incurable slut that I am, I lift the blanket carefully to take a peek, but the cool air wakes him and he rolls towards me.

"Mornin', darling," I say as he lies there blinking. A million feelings parade across his face: confusion, shame, hope, fear, his eyebrows crawling over his forehead and each other before settling in a kind of puzzled scowl.

"I didn't crush you?" he asks.

"Do I look crushed?"

He glances down with a smirk, his thick lashes dark against his cheeks. Yep, it's not just me: he is fucking fine. A beautiful bruiser, and if I'm careful he's going to be mine.

"Can I make you breakfast?" I ask, hoping he says yes because my head aches with hunger. "Don't worry, I cook all the time at home. Just point me at the food."

There's not much in the old food safe under the window except the end of some dry-cured sausage, so I put on my fleece and follow him outside and around the corner of the house to the hatch that leads to the cold cellar. Snow has fallen from the roof, half burying the left-hand door, and Stone clears it with another of his home-made brooms and a whole lot of grumbling to himself.

"Is everything okay?"

"I can't believe how many winters I've put up with this," he says, hanging the broom on a peg that must be there just for this.

"We can build an awning in the spring. I don't mean we, but I could help. If you wanted help. I know some people like to work alone." *Shut up, Culver, can't you see he's embarrassed?*

I step back as he opens the heavy doors. Stone steps lead down into a little room with low ceilings and crumbling brick walls. The rough wooden shelves are empty except for a few dented metal canisters and a couple of half empty burlap sacks.

"Bad time of year," he says as I pick through the sprouting onions in one of the sacks.

"It's cool. I lived on food stamps once. I'll figure out something. You go and light the stove."

When he's gone I look through the sacks again. I can roast this pumpkin and maybe one of the better onions, but that could take hours. I settle for carbs, taking the onion, a chunk of lard in cooking paper, a can of cornmeal, and a smaller jar of what might be cranberries. There's a jar of honey too, but I'm running out of hands, and I wedge it in the front of my leggings. "Okay, you paleo motherfucker, let's see what we can do."

Without eggs, my vision of some kind of pancake goes in the trash. But the scraped up bits of honey and lard and cornmeal batter taste good with fried onions and the salami. While we eat the mess, Stone makes coffee lumberjack style, hucking the grounds in the pot and boiling it all together. I try to drink some but the smell is enough to make my heart race and I leave the cup steaming on the table and start cleaning up.

"Why are you doing this?" Stone asks as I pour water into the basin to wash the dishes.

"You're letting me stay here for nothing. I gotta pay you back somehow. Plus I like doing things for people I like."

He doesn't reply, watching me over the rim of his mug as I clean our plates and forks with my fingers because I still haven't found any soap. I pour some water in the skillet and put it back on the stove to boil off the burnt stuff. I'm not this well behaved at home, but I don't want him to regret letting me stay.

When the pan's clean and dry I rub it with some of the lard. "You've had this thing forever, haven't you?"

"My mother's mother brought it from her home country," he replies, the first time he's mentioned his family.

"Then it's like a hundred years old. That's wild." I hang the pan beside the stove on the nail where he keeps it. He's finished his coffee but when I come to get the cup he grabs my arm roughly. I wince and he lets go with a gasp.

"It's okay," I say. "You just startled me."

"I hurt you."

"Not really. I'm tougher than I look." I step closer so I'm standing between his spread legs. "I had fun yesterday," I say, ignoring his dick in those soft old chinos that cling like gray sweatpants. "That was a lot of firsts for me."

"It was?"

"I've never met a were-bear. Never mind done something like that when I wasn't, you know, like this."

"Like what?"

"A man. Talking to another man. Who has a blob of honey right there." Taking my chances, I wipe away the shiny smear on his lip with my thumb. He inhales hard, his teeth chattering. His hair has fallen over his right eye and I brush it back from his face.

Purring like a giant cat, he closes his eyes as I keep stroking his hair. I want to kiss him. Want to bite his lips, suck his tongue deep into my mouth, lick him everywhere. I can't, I won't act like a horny dickhead, because I want this to be good for him. I want him to feel safe. This huge guy who could break my neck with his bare hands: I want him to feel safe from me. From the chaos that follows me wherever I go. The problems I cause for myself and everyone around me. I want to be his safe place.

I weave my fingers through his surprisingly silky beard to find the hot pulse of his throat. I stroke my thumb over his lips again and when he moans I lean in and kiss him. Softly, asking nothing even though I want everything. He tastes like honey and hot coffee, his gorgeous lashes fluttering against his pink cheeks. He's rough and sweet and hard and tender and I want him to eat me alive.

As I lean into him, his dick in those damn chinos bumps against my thighs. I lean closer, bending my knees to rub myself against him, but he sits back with a tense expression. "Too soon?"

"Maybe."

"Whatever you need, honey."

He smiles quickly, his cheeks turning red. Has no one ever been nice to this guy? As I go back to combing my fingers through his hair the tension drains out of him. Slowly, like he's choosing a chess piece, he lifts his hand and sets it on my waist. Spanning the waistband of my leggings so his thumb and two fingers and half his palm are against my bare skin.

"I've been thinking about you," he says, his voice purring in his chest.

"J-just now?"

"For a while. I watch for you when're you're running."

"Wow, stalker vibes. What do you think about?"

"How pretty you are. Is it wrong to call you that?" he asks as I giggle, because that word shouldn't hit like it does.

"Honey bear, you can call me anything you like."

As he drops his eyes he smiles again with a brief, shy flash of his teeth and I'm slayed. How am I the one in charge here? Or are we both in too deep, making it up as we go because we don't know where we're going. I know where I want to be. Thinking it, I can't think of anything else, and without asking or explaining I sink onto my knees.

"What are you doing?" he stammers as I slide my hands up his thighs towards that goddamn tentpole poking through his chinos.

"What does it look like I'm doing?"

"Chase...I'm too big."

"How do you know? You don't know a thing about it. Sorry, that was rude," I say as his face falls. "But seriously, you are exactly the right size. Every bit of you."

"I don't want to hurt you," he mumbles as I stroke his shaft through the taut fabric.

"You won't. Trust me."

Drooling, shaking a little, I gently unzip his pants and take out his goddamn ridiculous dick. Nearly as thick as my wrist, darker than his skin, veined like it came from a fetish website, and belonging to a trembling virgin were-bear who smells like honey and cum. Licking my lips, I look up and the sight nearly kills me. His eyes are closed, his long lashes dark against his cheek, his hips tilting forward, asking for me to keep going.

I think. I hope. I should really ask him. If he really is a virgin (a question he never answered properly) then I don't want fuck this up for him. I want to take my time. Not just for his sake but for mine, because Stone has literally the biggest dick I've ever seen, which is saying something because I've been to some wild parties.

Crushed against me by my leggings, my own hard-on throbs jealously as I lean in and swirl my tongue around the end of his cock, gathering the bead of precome. I stroke my tongue up and down his shaft, not caring that he tastes like sweat and dirt because under that he tastes like a man.

I smear the thick head of his cock across my wet lips then lick them clean, moaning as I taste him. I need him inside me, want to drink every drop of his cum, want to let him tear me apart and then fuck me back together.

I close my lips and press them against the dripping head of his cock, then start to bob my head forward, opening my mouth more each time, taking him a little deeper. Like he's pushing into the other part of me. The thought of this monster cock splitting my asshole makes me groan. Stone's eyes flutter open. As he gazes down at me, I open wide and take him into in my mouth. He gasps, his eyes rolling closed again as I hollow my cheeks, sucking him deep

His hands drift about, plucking at the blanket and distracting me until I grab one and stick it on the back of my head. The weight of it unlocks something in me, a physical limit that no longer exists, his cock filling my throat, tears blurring my eyes, my own heartbeat roaring in my ears and my cock throbbing in time.

He's not going to care what I do to myself. He's not even going to know. He's going to love everything I do because he doesn't have a comparison. I wriggle my leggings down my hips to get a hand on my dick. I want to come when he does, want his pleasure to be something we share. As I start to thrust into my hand his eyes roll open. Good, I want him to see this, see me choking myself on his gorgeous cock, watch me drink him down like honey. He's close, his heavy balls tensing, his hips jerking, not quite fucking my mouth but almost. We can do that next time, because this is just the first time. This is the start of the rest of my life, I'm sure of it, like

I'm sure that I love this, love being so totally used by some gorgeous man who's too good for me.

Not just some man but this man. I look up and our eyes meet and that's the end of both of us. His whole body tenses, his butt nearly lifting off the chair as he blows. His cum leaking around the seal of my lips and dripping down my chin, I follow, fucking into my hand like I want him to fuck me as I spill onto the floor at his feet. The start of the rest of my life.

I don't try for more. I'd do anything he asked but that was slutty enough for his first time. Instead we shift and head into the woods again. I want to ask about the cave, maybe even try to find it, but I don't know how to bring it up. Stone hasn't said much of anything since I sucked him off, which could be a bad sign or no sign at all, seeing as he wasn't much of a talker to begin with. He leads me in the opposite direction from the cave so I leave it be for now, following at his heels like the good boy I'm trying to be.

The snow has melted everywhere the sun hits, baring soggy brown grass and gravelly patches. Leaf buds sprout from every little shrub like pale green stubble, literally when it comes to the tender needles of the evergreens. Coming over a little rise we both stop. Columbines are flowering in the sheltered valley below us, their fluttering purple flowers bright against their clover-green leaves, the cloudless sky above us so blue it hurts to look at, and even my inhuman senses recognize the beauty. I lean against his bulky shoulder, wanting to share the feather-light joy flooding my heart, but Stone starts down the slope without me catching more than a glimpse of his thoughts.

And they're dark, leaving me with a coldness in my belly and a headful of questions. Like where we're going and why, and why he's ignoring me, and what I can do to make him feel better. All I can do is follow him along the pretty valley as he plods along, crushing the flowers beneath his heavy paws.

The valley opens up at the lower end. Below us, rooftops poke out of the tree cover. An asphalt road snakes away into the hazy distance. Hollowood Falls, and there's no way I would have made it home that night. Not without sacrificing my shoes and phone and stuff. Even like this I might not have made it, not knowing where I was going. It's all good having a hugely magnified sense of smell until your nose freezes solid.

I lean my shoulder against his but he pulls away. I don't want to annoy him but I need to know what he's thinking, why he's brought me here. I put my head between my forepaws and creep towards him with my tail high, ready to apologize for whatever I did that turned him cold, but he pivots towards me with his teeth bared.

He growls low in his chest and I whimper, pressing my belly to the prickling ground. If I only knew what I'd done, I'd undo it. Except maybe I can't. Maybe letting him fuck my mouth was too much for him. Too much touching, too much closeness, too many firsts, and all of them with someone who's no better than a stranger. I want to shift and talk it out, but maybe that's the problem, the talking, when we were getting along so well without it.

I'd do it again, let him lick me from nose to tail, let him mount me or at least try really hard. I'll do anything he wants if it means I can stay, but I can't even tell him, my animal body frozen in fear of his jaws and claws and the bitter rage in his eyes.

Shaking, whining, nearly pissing myself with fear, I force myself to crawl nearer. I don't know what's happening but I hate it, hate that he's so angry when I've done nothing except try to make him happy. I'll do anything to make this stop, make him like me again, make him even happier, but what I want doesn't mean a damn thing as he rears up on his hind legs with a furious roar to split the mountain and send me pelting down the valley, running for my life.

Back home to Hollowood Falls with my tail between my legs. Again.

Six

Spoons

My brain starts working again after a couple of miles. I lie down right where I am and pant for a minute to cool off while I get my bearings. I'm close to Hollowood, the air full of human smells, wood smoke and tires and fabric softener and the hamburgers someone is grilling for dinner. Amongst all the sounds that go with the smells, I hear the whizz of bicycle chains and the hard breathing of the riders. As I get to my feet I see them, my cousin River and their boyfriend Marcus, ripping along the trail downhill from me.

When I bark River's head whips around. They wave then they and Marcus stop as I trot to meet them. "Haven't seen you in a few days," River says as they scratch behind my ears (they're the only one I'll take it from so don't even try.) "You doing okay?"

I lick River under their chin and they laugh and push my head away. "That tickles, you dick. But what's going on? You need somewhere to crash tonight?"

I shake my head, glad I can't blush. Is there anyone in Hollowood who doesn't see me as a charity case? The worst thing is, I do need their help. I sniff the hem of their hoodie, then take it carefully in my teeth and tug.

"You can't have this one but we have loads of stuff at home I can loan you," River says, pulling on their bike gloves. "You can come with or just meet us at the house, okay?"

"Is everything alright?" Marcus asks. A full-time human, he got cool about a whole lot of stuff when he got together with River last year.

"I guess we'll find out in a bit," River says, turning their bike.

"It was getting late anyway," Marcus says, doing the same.

"But you're staying over tonight, right? You don't have to go home."

"Yeah, I'm staying over."

They chat back and forth as they ride and I run along obediently behind them. At River's place, I wait in the garage while they find me another hoodie and a pair of my uncle's sweatpants. Shifted, dressed, I join them in the basement, which is mostly River's bedroom. They've painted the walls with this endless fantasy mural and under the glow-in-the-dark gaze of a Pride flag-themed Cheshire cat in a neon purple tree we tear through a shameless quantity of snacks as I give Marcus and River the least amount of info I can about my last few days.

"Do you think you'll ever see this guy again?" River asks as I scrape the last smears out of my third pudding cup.

"I have to. The fucker has my phone. And my Merrells."

"Shit! Well let me know if you want us to come with. You know, for back-up."

"Thanks, but I don't think there'll be a problem."

I borrow a pair of flip-flops and shuffle down the road to my parents' place. I don't know if River texted my mom or something, but both my parents are waiting on the porch. My mom comes to meet me halfway up the walk.

"You couldn't have called?"

"My phone died. Then I kind of left it behind."

"Where did you leave it?" my dad says, joining us.

"At the place I was staying. I thought I'd be going back. I didn't know he was kicking me out."

"What did you do?"

"No idea."

"You must have done something."

"Yep, because it's always my fault."

"I didn't say that."

Not out loud. But he doesn't need to, when I know that's what he's thinking. "You don't even know where I've been."

"Then tell me."

"Let's talk inside," Mom says firmly, and I forget my shitty comeback and follow her into the house, my dad breathing down my neck like he thinks I'm going to make a break for it.

"So?" he says as soon as the door is closed.

"So I went for a run and got lost. It started to snow and I had to take shelter in this guy's cabin for a couple days."

"This *guy*?" I can hear everything he's not saying in that one word, picture the man he's thinking of: some smooth VC shit-head with an unbuttoned shirt and bottle service. Which was absolutely my type a year ago, which makes me even angrier because how dare my dad know the sort of guys I used to like to fuck.

"His name's Stone," I say, my voice barely shaking. "I think he's a Roth. His place is uphill, sort of southwest of here."

"You don't know?"

"It's just a cabin in the middle of nowhere. It's not like there was a street sign or anything."

"Your GPS—"

"Worked until my battery went flat."

"Did you say he's a Roth?" Mom says in that low, firm voice she uses to be heard when the menfolk are bickering.

"He never said for sure. But when I said the name he freaked out."

"And that's when he kicked you out," Dad says, shaking his head like he's the one losing.

"No! That came after."

"After what?"

"You know what, I don't like you interrogating me, okay? I've had a really fu—messed up few days, I'm tired and I'm cold and I have a lot on my mind that I have to think about before I start talking about it, okay?"

"You can't avoid me, Chase," he says as I start backing towards the stairs.

"I'm not avoiding you, but can you give me a break? I need a shower, and dinner, and I'm super tired and I know this is important," I say, raising my voice to talk over his interruption, "but nothing's going to change in the next hour, so let's not pretend this is an emergency. I'm home safe, and that's what matters. Right?"

"It's fine, honey," Mom says to me, putting her hand on Dad's arm. "We can talk about it later. We can wait," she says firmly to him as he tries to butt in again. "He's your son. Be a little nicer."

"Like that's ever worked," he mutters as I turn to go upstairs.

Maybe try harder. I've been home for ninety seconds and I'm ready to punch a hole in the wall and or my dad's face and then walk right back out the door and never come back. Even if I have to crawl to Stone on hands and knees like the miserable dog I am and beg him to take me in.

As my parents carry on their never-ending discussion of yours truly, I escape to the bathroom where I stand under the shower until I stop crying. I shouldn't have sucked him off. I shouldn't have ever touched him. I should have left the first chance I had. Or just done everything differently. Nothing hits like the shame of discovering what it is you want out of life then ruining your chance of ever getting it.

I sleep through dinner. Not on purpose, but the last few days kicked my ass, and without my phone I have no idea of the time. I come upstairs to find the house dark and quiet, because it's twelve thirty at night. The fridge shelves are stacked so high with leftovers that at first I think the lightbulb burned out. My servings of the meals they made while I was gone. Fuck, I'm costing them a fortune just by existing, and giving nothing back.

My stomach now knotted with guilt and not just hunger, I load a plate with a random bunch of food, pork chops and spaghetti and roasted squash and a chicken Kiev that I nearly can't eat even though it's one of the best I've had. That was my special dinner as a kid, the meal he'd only make for my birthday, which means the big asshole missed me while I was gone, then treated me like shit as soon as he had me back.

Every two minutes I reach for my phone, realize it's gone, then hate myself for needing it so badly. Needing that pale flicker, that tiny thread of other people's attention. People out there in the world, living their best lives. People who wish they had my life: living in a beautiful place, devoted to my health, happy with my solitude. A nice little story I tell the world in the hope I'll start to believe it too.

Instead of going back to bed, where I'm either going to cry or jerk off or both but definitely not fall asleep, I put on season two of *Steven Universe* with the sound really low then stretch out on the couch and let my brain soothe itself with the movement and color. Drifting in and out of sleep, I finally nod off, and wake up to the smell of fresh coffee. Really good coffee from Mom's super expensive machine Ev and the boys got her for Christmas.

I turn off the tv and join her in the kitchen where she's already prepping a second shot for me. She watches a lot of barista videos and I watch her as she packs and loads the filter then steams the milk in the little metal jug with quick, fluid movements. She pours the milk with a flourish, drawing a cat's face in the froth.

"That's so cute! I should…I would take a picture *if* I had my phone."

"I can't get the mouth right," she says with a sigh.

"For teaching yourself I think it's great."

"I missed having you around," she says as I sip the cat's ears away. "I know sometimes it seems you're underfoot but it's really nice having you here."

"I didn't mean to be gone so long."

"I'm just glad you're okay."

"Me too."

We take our coffees into the living room where I flop down on the couch again. She wanders to the window, which looks over the front lawn and the road. "Chase," she says, pointing with her cup. "Are those your shoes at the bottom of the driveway?"

I join her at the window. A pile of clothes sit at the end of the driveway, my bright green and orange shoes beside them.

"That chickenshit! Sorry."

"Do you mean that man Stone?"

"I was going to go up there today."

"That was nice of him to save you the trip."

"He couldn't have said hi or something?"

"He probably thought you'd be asleep."

"I was but... Fine. Whatever." It makes sense, but I hate it. Hate that he was so near and I didn't know. Hate that he knows where I live, while all I have to go on is memory and instinct. Not that it makes a difference now that I don't have any reason to go back.

Asshole. Can't even leave me that, can't stand the thought of having to see me again. I leave my coffee on the bench by the front door and cross the gravel driveway barefoot, hoping that hairy motherfucker up the hill feels every pointy rock. I hope it fucking broke him, doing this to me.

My clothes are folded neatly, my phone sitting in one of my shoes. There's a piece of wood in my other shoe. A spoon, carved like Stone's chess pieces, with a shallow, heart-shaped scoop and a handle shaped like...

"Fuck! What the fuck, you fucking..." I want to break the spoon in half then set it on fire then jam the burnt bits up his hairy ass. The handle is carved like the heads of two animals. A wolf and a bear, facing each other, their noses touching. Like they're kissing.

Why they fuck did he make this? Why did he give it to me? Why did he kick me out without a word then give one of these spoons? Every house in Hollowood has one. Some people keep them packed away. Others frame them and hang them up over the front door. There's a case of them up at the lodge with the other town records, dating back a hundred and fifty years. None of them have a bear. Just wolves.

My hands shaking like that coffee was a triple, I scoop up my stuff and hobble back to the house. As I'm plugging in my phone in the kitchen, Mom comes in with the spoon.

"He left this for you?"

"I guess. I don't know why."

"No?"

"No, I don't know why he kicked me out then made me a spoon."

"He might not have made it," she says carefully, setting it on the table.

"Then who?"

"No one knows."

I whirl around to face her. "What do you mean no one knows?"

"It's true. Whenever anyone from a founding family finds their mate, they receive a spoon just like that. Carved just for them.. No one has ever seen who brings them."

"That's fucked up."

Tilting her head, she gives me a funny little smile I've never seen. "That's fate."

"Whatever. It's a piece of wood."

Her smile fades, leaving me with a rotten taste in my mouth, and I duck out of the room. Downstairs, I pack a portable battery charger, half a gallon of water and a few energy bars in a light backpack. I don't need to find him, but I want to. I want to give back that stupid spoon. Like I want another souvenir of getting hurt. It'd just end up in that box with all the other crap I've kept from guys who screwed me then screwed me over. Eric's fountain pen. Luis' copy of *Dorian Grey*, a first edition he threw at my head, which I thought I would sell but haven't. A fuckton of business cards from when I was tricking out of that Uber.

I wrap the spoon in a spare beanie and tuck it in my backpack. When my phone reaches fifty percent I duck upstairs to Mom's office where she's scrolling through the news. "I'm going for a run. Might be gone all day. But don't worry, I'm not going to take any trails I don't recognize."

She takes a deep breath like she has a lot to say, then exhales slowly with that same funny smile. "Be careful."

A last guilty urge makes me go and kiss her on the cheek. "I'm good. I'll be home for dinner."

"Have fun."

I assume she's being sarcastic. At least a little.

The first leg is easy as I jog to the gravel scar then find the trail leading uphill. It's when I reach the cave in the cliff that I lose my way. I was running for my life the last time, and I can't remember if I even took the trail on the left or just ran through the forest blindly. It's past noon so I get out an energy bar then start down the trail.

What else can I do? Before leaving the house I thought about shifting then hunting him by scent. But I can't talk to him that way, unless I shift back. Seeing as I'm coming up here to tell him what a colossal jerk he is, I don't really want to do it while I'm naked. The trail leads me gradually downhill, curving back and forth as it follows the contours. The spring growth has recovered from the brief blast of winter and everything smells alive. Birds swoop overhead or hop along the forest floor pecking at whatever birds peck at.

One of those crows lands on the trail ahead of me. They're easy to recognize, with those yellow rings around their eyes and the white feathers on the top of their head. As I get near, the bird takes off and flies a bit further. Then does it again, landing on a branch sticking out over a little creek. I remember this creek so I follow it until it disappears underground.

I check the map and my little blue dot is on top of Hollowood, right where it should be. As I scan the forest hoping for a landmark, another crow, or the same one, flies past me and lands on a stub of a branch a few hundred yards ahead. Good enough.

The birds (there's five of them by the end) lead me out of the trees. I still don't recognize the land so well, but last time I was here it was white with snow and I could barely see. We (me and the birds) cross a little valley and climb the next rise. Hollowood Falls lays below me to my left, its roofs floating in a sea of trees. To my right is the peak, snow-covered year round. Ahead of me, the silver thread of a stream winds through the shallow valley, the last trickle of what used to be a glacier ten thousand years ago. On the far side of the valley is the cabin.

Part of me wants to turn around and go back the way I came. I know where he lives. I don't want to bother him. Except I came up here to tell him what a jackass he is. I'm halfway down the slope when he appears at the edge of the trees. I nearly run away, but he's not dangerous when he's a man. Unless I really piss him off, which is almost guaranteed. It's too late to worry about any of that that as I pass the cabin and start up the other short slope. He takes a step back into the trees. Then another.

"Hey!" I shout as he fades into the shadows. "Don't you walk away from me, you chickenshit." He's out of sight by the time I reach the edge of the forest. I find him behind a clump of cedars with his coat half off. "You ass. You were going to shift, weren't you?"

He jerks the smelly old coat on again as I start hunting through my backpack. "What do you want from me?" he grunts.

"I don't want anything from you. I especially don't want this." I hold out the weird spoon. He stares at it but doesn't take it. "Why did you even make it?"

"I didn't make it."

"Then where did it come from?"

"Grandmother."

Something in the way he says it makes my skin prickle. No, it's just the sweat cooling on my back and scalp, and that hint of fear in the air is just my hunger and anger. "Why did you give me your grandmother's spoon?"

"Not *my* grandmother," he mumbles into his beard. "Everyone's."

"You're not making any sense. And you know what, I don't even care. I don't want it. I don't want to be reminded of this. If I could, I'd forget it ever happened." He still won't take it so I pull his arm up by his sleeve and slap the spoon down on his open palm.

He curls his fingers closed it. "Didn't know you hated being around me."

"Ugh, don't you get it? I *didn't* hate it. I'm pissed off because it was good. It was really good and I fucked it up somehow and now it's over." I step back, needing distance so I don't punch him. Or kiss him. Or smell him any more than I do already, his earthy scent of musk and icy rock. "I guess I'll just go back to fucking strangers and save myself the trouble of getting to know people."

He looks up from the spoon in his hand "What do you mean by strangers?"

"What do you think I mean? Sorry, I forgot, you live in the middle of nowhere and have no idea how easy it is to get good dick if you don't care who's giving it to you. Didn't you know I'm trash?" I say as his mouth falls open. "Couldn't you tell when you were stalking me?"

"Is that why you're angry with me?

"I'm angry because I was happy, you jackass! Like really, actually happy, for the first time in forever. But I don't get to be happy, do I? I just get used and then dumped and that's how it's always going to be. The worst thing is, you didn't even have the guts to tell me what I did wrong. I got dumped by a fucking bear." He doesn't say a word, just stares at me with those pretty eyes, and if I don't leave right away I really will kiss him. "Whatever. You have nothing to say, I guess. I don't know why I fell for your shit. Hiding out up here like the unibomber, playing chess against yourself because you're scared to look other people in the eye. Have a nice life."

Wishing I had a door to slam in his face, I sling my backpack over my shoulder and walk away. Yesterday we crossed this woodland then met a trail that took us east. Yesterday, when I thought we were coming out to play. When I thought I'd found my safe place. My person. My home. Instead all I have are these shoes, this phone, this pointless life. This habit of ruining everything I touch. I don't know what else could have turned him so cold.

I reach the valley of columbines, their purple flowers dancing above the brilliant green of their leaves. I can't take a step without crushing them, and then I don't care. Fuck the flowers, fuck Stone and his mountain and everything on it. I kick at a clump of blossoms and they shred into purple confetti. I do it again and again, a frenzy of destruction, mashing their pointless beauty into the dirt. I'm about to bring my foot down again when I see the bird.

A little brown speckled bird pressed against the ground, quivering in fear of my big stupid feet. Hundred bucks says she's nesting, like I've seen them do before. And I just about stepped on her and killed her and her babies.

It's me. I'm the problem. A monster through and through. And I always will be.

Seven

The Getaway

I don't remember the descent. It's dark by the time Mom finds me on the porch swing, rocking myself into a trance. She makes me come inside where I go straight to my room and don't come out again that night.

I don't want to tell you what went on, but it's ugly as fuck and doesn't make me feel much better. I wake up on the carpet, my drawers emptied around me and half of my closet after I decided around two in the morning to remake my whole life, starting with my aesthetic. I pee then go to bed properly.

Where I lie awake for the next three hours trying to make up my mind. I can't stay here. He's too close, and I'm too weak. I'll be up there every other day, nosing around and hoping for a chance to lure him back to me. Which is bullshit because he doesn't deserve me. Yeah right, he doesn't deserve an unemployed, uneducated, cock-sucking backcountry werewolf with ADHD and no future.

No one needs me here. No one wants me here. No one wants me at all, except as something to shove their dick into then throw back in the gutter. I should play to my strengths. Go back to Denver and find someone dangerous and let him wreck me permanently. Quit pretending I'm a good boy and let my slut self off the leash, confirm everyone's worst expectations of me. Go out in a blaze of bad choices. Make him hate himself for letting me go.

When I hear my dad go downstairs, I wait another twenty minutes for him to eat breakfast then leave. He's a foreman for the state's contracted highway maintenance company, which is partly why he thinks I'm such a waster. I tried temping for the forestry road crew a few summers ago, but I couldn't handle the smell of tar, the boredom, or the casual homophobia, and quit three weeks into the season. I've had a few jobs since, but with nowhere to go and nothing to do, I've never needed much money.

That's a change I could make. Get a job. Save up until I can afford to move out and don't have to lean on anyone. Succeed so well that my dad's embarrassed about the way he's treated me. I can ask Ash and River today how they found jobs. Even Sutherland needs help at the store now and then. I have to grow up, stop depending on people for things I could do for myself.

After breakfast I go for a run in town. I nod at a few people who wave but everyone's used to seeing me and they mainly ignore me. As I'm starting up the hill the last time, a shiny blue VW zips past. I keep expecting to see it again, heading downhill. No one in town has that model of car, but I can't remember why I recognize it. Not until I get home and it's parked in the driveway. My mom's at the front door talking to the driver, who turns as my steps crunch on the gravel, then comes to meet me.

Pierce Platter. My prince. Who hugs me even though I'm gross with sweat. I wait for the jolt, the rush, the melancholy thrill I always feel when Pierce touches me.

And it doesn't come. He lets me go and I step back and try to see what about him has changed. But it's me who's changed. Stone changed me. Asshole.

"Where's Ev?" I ask Pierce as we start towards the house.

"Aspen. It's their anniversary. I dropped them off at the hotel then didn't feel like going home."

I'd have chosen being alone, but I say nothing as we go inside. In the shower I hum song lyrics the whole time to keep my brain from sinking its teeth into my response to Pierce. My lack of response, like my crush has been overwritten by my feelings for Stone. I don't have feelings for Stone. I have memories, and unanswered questions, and a fuckton of self-loathing that bubbles along under everything else, but that feeling is about me, not him.

Pierce is in the kitchen with Mom. I stop on the bottom stair where I can just see him through the doorway. He's still so good-looking, with those smoky eyes and perfect profile and a really expensive sweater that clings to his chest. And he might as well be a picture in a magazine. I'm not panting or shaking, my stomach isn't in a knot and neither is my dick. I'm cured. No, I have a new disease.

I walk into the kitchen and his smile fades. Is it that fucking obvious? I pour myself a glass of water, focusing on the running tap to ignore their murmured conversation. I'm pouring a second glass when he joins me at the sink. "You doing okay?" he says gently under the sound of the water.

"Define okay," I reply, and I must sound bleak as hell as his face pales.

"You want to talk about it?"

Our eyes flick towards my mom in unison. He chuckles softly and squeezes my upper arm. A touch that would have made my heart melt (and something else harden) as recently as a week ago. Today, it's just his hand and my arm. Just a touch.

"Thanks for the coffee, Dawn," he says to my mom.

"Are you boys going for a walk?" she asks.

"I miss the trees," he says with a sideways smile. "I didn't think I would."

"Leave that," I say as he reaches for his gorgeous leather jacket hanging off the back of his chair. "The sap's up, you'll get hit for sure."

He laughs easily. "That's something I don't miss. Are you ready to go?"

We walk for a bit without talking. That used to make me nervous, and now it's just nice. Pierce is still my friend, someone I can be myself with and not worry that I'm making him nuts, partly because he has a lot of the same problems.

"How are your folks?" I ask him as we pass Sutherland's.

"I don't know. I haven't seen them yet."

"You came to see my mom before yours?"

"I like your mom. Did you know she called us to ask if we'd seen you?"

"No. That's…nice."

"She was worried. That's really why I came. I wanted to see how you were doing."

"Really?"

"Of course. I worry about you, little brother." Evan has never called me that. Only Pierce. Fuck, I never had a chance with him, did I? He must have decided years ago that I was off limits. What have I put him through these last ten years? Following him around with my puppy dog eyes and accidental touches and moody bullshit, projecting all my romantic wishes onto a man who loves me like a brother.

So full of thoughts that I can't say another word, I follow him past the lodge to the main Hollowood trail. He heads east, towards a place I never thought he'd want to see again, but I follow because it's Pierce and I love him. Like a brother.

"You ever get anywhere with that detective you were talking to last year?" he asks as we're dragging a fallen branch off the trail.

"About Granny's passing, you mean? Not really. There's so much weird shit in the soil here, the lab guy said it could have been a reaction between a bunch of elements that poisoned her."

"Hmm. Sounds shady."

"I don't know. He was from U of C Denver, they know some stuff about the soil here."

"I guess I just wanted someone to blame," Pierce says, as we start down the trail again.

"Me too. But it was nothing but bad luck. Everyone in town's on filtered water now, just in case."

We don't speak again until we reach the rockfall where I got trapped last year. The night Pierce and Evan came to rescue me. The night Pierce let fate take over, which is why I blamed myself for their mating for so long. As if Evan had come to town specifically to drag me out of a hole in the ground.

The other valley starts on the far side of this ridge. The private land held by faceless owners out of state. I used to cross the property line all the time to snoop around, but after the sick shit Marcus saw last summer I don't dare.

"We up here for any reason?" I ask, my voice thin against the rustling aspen leaves.

"Not really," he says absently, picking his way around the boulders that clog the trail. "What's been going on next door?"

"In the other valley? I don't know. I don't come this way anymore."

He stops and turns around. "Probably a good idea."

"I'm trying to keep my shit together these days."

"Got any pro-tips?" he says as he comes back to where I'm standing.

"Hell no. I was going to ask you." We both laugh, and then keep on laughing until my stomach hurts and I can't breathe and I don't remember why we started.

"Your fucking brother," Pierce wheezes, rubbing his eyes.

"You don't need to tell me."

"I'm sure you've seen some shit."

"Different shit than you, though."

"And that husband of his." He shakes his head. "The filth that comes out of Graeme's mouth, my god."

"What, in bed?" I ask before I realize I don't actually want to know.

"Everywhere! He swears like a pirate."

"You get along with him?" I ask as we start back along the trail towards town.

"Now that I know he's taking the piss ninety percent of the time. Ugh, I mean he's joking," he says as he reads my confusion. "Shit, he's even got me talking like him."

"How's Evan dealing with it?"

"Fine. Everything's good."

"Cool." *Ask him ask him ask him ask him...* "Can I ask you something?"

"Of course you can," he says with that friendly insistence that used to get my hopes up.

"What was it like, seeing him? My brother, I mean. When you knew."

"That he was my mate? I might not be the best person for you to ask, little brother."

"I don't have anyone else."

"But I fucked it up. I felt it but I fought it. Ran off to Denver to fuck the pain away, then held a grudge for the next ten years."

"Yeah, but when he came back."

"I think I told him to go fuck himself."

"What?"

"At Granny's funeral, even."

"Wow."

"Yeah." He rubs the back of his neck. "It was bad."

"What about now? How does he make you feel?"

Watching the trail, Pierce smiles, a soft little smile that damn near breaks my heart. "Safe."

"And when he's not around?" My voice cracks and Pierce stops me with that touch on my arm.

"Chase, what's happened?"

"I fucked up," I gulp, rubbing my eyes, tired of tears. "Like really, really bad. Like ruined my life bad."

"No," he says gently. "We'll figure it out." He hugs me, and though it doesn't make me tremble it feels good in a whole new way. Pierce was my crush but he's also my friend, and he says nothing as I sniffle into his shoulder.

"That's why I was gone," I tell him when I can talk again. "I was with him."

"Your mate?"

"I thought."

"If you're hurting this bad from missing him—"

"I miss him because he made me leave him." I can't keep it together. Pierce doesn't care, keeps holding me, supporting me as I sob like my soul's trying to leave my body. I should have kept the spoon. I should have told Stone how I felt. I should have begged. I never should have left.

On the way home Pierce distracts me by telling me about his new hobby slash fitness kick, dancing west coast swing with Graeme. "He needed someone to block out part of a routine, and then I kind of liked it. We were meant to go to a meet in Reno this weekend but it was going to overlap with their anniversary."

"Probably better he picked his husband over you."

"Yeah, right," he says with a guilty laugh. "That would have been bad."

We take the branch of the trail that brings you down to the lot behind Sutherland's General. My dad's out front talking with a couple of the Hollowood elders, River's grandparents Gunnar and Patience Croft, who are both in their seventies at least. Patience lost an eye years ago, the socket covered with a brown leather patch tooled with flowers, and Gunnar is so bald his head shines in the sun. They stop talking as we get close, which means they were talking about us. Or maybe just me

"The Crofts were hoping to see that spoon of yours," Dad says instead of *hello*.

"I gave it back."

"You what?" he said in his start-explaining voice as the seniors swap glances.

"You heard me."

Dad looks at Pierce who doesn't flinch. I try not to as he looks me up and down like he wishes I'd disappear. "You're coming to the Lodge. There are things you need to know."

"No, there aren't. Or if there are, I don't want to know them." I start for home before I offend the Crofts, who might think I'm a fuck-up but have always been too nice to tell me to my face. Pierce catches up with me when I'm nearly at our road.

"You might want to hear this," he says. "It might explain a few things."

"You're in on this too?"

"I'll come with you."

"Okay. But that's the only reason I'm doing it."

Built a hundred years before I was born, the Lodge isn't just where people throw parties and weddings and stuff. It's the closest thing Hollowood has to a museum. Photos line the walls, group shots of New Year's Eve and May Day (which is its own thing around here.) Banners for old social clubs and parades hang from the mezzanine that looks over the ballroom slash dining hall, along with the town flag of a crescent moon rising behind a zigzag line representing the mountains.

The back rooms are full of artefacts from when the town was founded. We follow my dad through to the room where they keep the town records. Everyone who's lived in Hollowood is mentioned in these books. Along with a bunch of other stuff no one understands, about where we all come from and why we are the way we are. When you turn sixteen, they bring you here and show you your own name, but I could never make sense of the rest.

Dad pulls down one of the big leather covered books from the antique cabinet where they're stored. He lays it on the special reading platform that keeps the spines from cracking, and carefully thumbs through the yellowed pages to our branch of the family tree, our names written medieval style in ink that sometimes looks green, sometimes blue depending on the time of day. Pierce's name is written in a circle that connects to Evan's.

"Is it really true that no one sees who writes the names?" Pierce asks my dad.

"I never heard that," I say as Dad nods. "Then it's like the spoons. A mystery."

"That's weird," Pierce says, following the lines on the page with his eyes.

"That's Hollowood," I mutter, making him snort as the tries not to laugh.

"Then this shouldn't surprise you," my dad says way too nicely. He points to my name, and the circle beside it that wasn't there last time I saw it. The one that reads *Stone Roth* in gothy letters.

"Why did you do that?" I say, my voice sticking in my throat, my heart beating so hard I feel it in the palms of my hands.

I've never had a choice. If I hadn't found him on my own, they would have dragged me up there by the scruff of my neck and made me want him, sooner or later. Made sure their second son, their spare, did right by his bloodline and obeyed the pack's made-up mythology. "Why did you write his name there."

"I didn't," Dad says simply, and for once he's not glaring at me.

"Then who the fuck did?

He blinks at the swear word but stays chill. "As I told you, we don't know."

"I hate this fucking town! No one knows anything."

"Chase—" he warns, but I don't care.

"Don't bother. And you can forget about it me going through with it. Any of it. I don't want to see that hairy sonofabitch ever again."

"Son, in our world you have to be prepared to make sacrifices for the good of the—"

"If you say pack, I swear to god I'll scream. If he doesn't want me, what am I supposed to do?"

"If you bothered to put forth a little effort—"

"Do you even hear yourself?" I'm shouting but I don't give a fuck. I'm done being used by this man and this town. "You have no idea how goddamn hard I tried. I would have given him everything, and he pushed me away. You always complain that I can't take care of myself. Then when I finally do, you tell me that's wrong too, that I'm supposed to crawl back to him and kiss his ass because someone pranked the town records? Fuck him, fuck Hollowood and the fucking legacy. I'm wasting my life on this superstitious garbage. Just like him," I say, pointing at Pierce.

"And look what happened," Dad says.

"He married my perfect fucking brother." Pierce gasps like it's him I'm shouting at, and the fact that I've hurt him hurts worse than anything my dad could say. "You know what, I don't care. I told you I didn't want to know any of this. I'm out."

I'm almost running by the time I get outside. Pierce catches up with me and matches my angry pace down the hill. "Sorry to throw you under the bus," I say, slowing down.

"It's okay," he says with half a smile. "That was brutal."

"I can't stay here. I can't stay in that goddamn house with him."

"I get it. Do you need to grab anything or do you just want to get out of here?"

"What do you mean?" I say, my steps slowing.

"Come with me," he says. "Back to Evan's. A couple of days away from all of this will do you good."

"Hell, yeah. Let me grab a couple things and we can go."

"I'll say bye to your mom."

A toothbrush and a few changes of clothes, my headphones, my chargers, my wallet that would be empty if Mom hadn't given me a hundred bucks from her mysterious stash none of us have ever seen (I have theories, but even I'm not a big enough asshole to have actually looked for it.) My life in a backpack and it's never seemed so small.

We make it out of the house before my dad gets back, which makes me think he's avoiding me. I don't like going off at him like that, but I can only take so much of his pack legacy BS. That might have worked a couple generations ago, back when people everywhere married because they had to and never divorced. When keeping the family together was the only way to get ahead. Humans aren't like that anymore, so I don't know why we should be. Maybe it really would be better if our kind died out. No more hiding, no more lying, no more myths and caves and mysteries.

I gnaw on my thoughts for a while but once we're out of the mountains the long straight highway puts me to sleep. I wake up as we're pulling into a gas station with a fast food joint across the parking lot. "Is this okay?" Pierce asks as he waits for someone to pull out of their spot.

"I'm good with whatever."

Inside, we order together and he waves me off when I reach for my wallet. "Thanks for that," I say as we fill our cups at the pop machine.

"I'm the one with a job," he says, smiling. "They haven't even asked me to pay rent, just chip in on groceries and the bills."

"What's the job?"

He chuckles. "I work for your brother."

"Doing what? Or do I want to know?"

He laughs again. "It's just proofreading."

"That makes sense. You always liked reading."

"Technical writing isn't the most exciting thing, but editing it is something AI can't do well."

"Yet."

"Right? Hopefully I'll figure something better out before then. What about you?"

I shrug, because I really don't know. "I should probably get my GED before I start making plans."

"That might help."

Pierce has been on the road since six this morning so I drive for the next hour or so while he dozes against the window. I give him back the wheel when we get close to the city. Soon we're driving through a quiet neighborhood full of trees and nice old houses set back from the street. They live at the top of a court in a slightly newer house, a split-level like the Crofts' but built of grey bricks and siding. A fluffy white cat comes to meet Pierce, winding around his legs while he makes kissy noises at it. He holds out his arm and the cat springs up to climb onto his shoulder then curl around the back of Pierce's neck.

"Ms. Dolly Parton, may I present Mr. Chase Culver. He'll be staying with us for a few days." The cat's blue eyes widen as it peers at me from Pierce's shoulder.

"That's not a—"

"No, Dolly is just a cat." He scoops it off his shoulder and holds it over his head. "What am I saying, just a cat? She's the bestest kitty in the world." Its legs dangling, the plume of its tail twitching, the cat makes a weird sound, a robotic sort of chirp. Pierce gives it a last cuddle then lets it jump from his arms, leaving white hairs all over his blue sweater.

"Didn't think you liked cats."

"Neither did I," he says with a smile, brushing uselessly at the hair. "Come upstairs and I'll show you where you can put your stuff."

The room is halfway between an office and a guest room, with a messy computer desk and wood-framed futon made up like a bed. I stretch out on the futon just to test it...

...and wake up around midnight. The house is dark and quiet. When I come back from brushing my teeth Dolly is curled up in the dead center of the futon. I peel back the blankets and slip under without waking her. Now I know why the room feels so comfortable even though I've never been here, because the pillow smells like Pierce. And I lie there and think about what that might have meant a year or even a week ago. How hard it would have been to be in the same house with him with no one around, no one to see what we do. How did I hold out for so long?

I've been such a slut around other men. Never thought twice about it. I spent ten years convinced that Pierce was my soul mate, that our friendship was only the start. Now it's all that I need from him. Friendship is enough. It's the reason I'm here, because it meant I had somewhere to go.

Eight

Full Moon

I wake up with Dolly Parton's ass in my face. The cat gets up as I roll away, stretches its back and tail, then hops off the bed and starts pawing at the door, making that little chirp. "You've got Platter pussy-whipped, don't you?" I say as I pull on my shirt. "Well, don't go thinking it's gonna work on me. I'm immune to pussy."

They have the kind of coffee maker that would have my mom in tears, with two steam spouts and bronze everywhere. While the pressure builds I find ground coffee and a cup then start looking for something quick to eat. Skipping dinner last night was a bad move, and if I don't have breakfast with this coffee I'll be coked out for hours. Except there's nothing to eat. There's loads of food, and fancy stuff too like chia seed pancake mix and coconut flakes and an entire produce section in the fridge, but no eggs or meat. Not even milk for the coffee, unless you count oat milk, which I try because what the fuck else can I do?

I'm munching walnuts as I hunt through the walk-in pantry for something that goes with couscous but that doesn't need an hour of prep when Pierce comes downstairs. "Finding everything okay?" he says through a yawn.

"Not really. And since when are you vegan?"

"I'm not. I'm just going with the flow."

"And Evan's cool with this?"

"We eat out a lot, just me and him. We'll go for lunch, drill a big steak when it's cheap, then have whatever Graeme makes for dinner. If you want we can do that."

"I have to be careful with that money Mom gave me."

"Keep your money. This one's on me."

I eat some more nuts and a couple apples then go for an easy run while Pierce does some work stuff. At the steakhouse, the hostess greets him by name. The waitress too, and he introduces me to both of them.

"If he hadn't told me, I'd still guess you were Ev's brother," the waitress says to me, though this isn't the first time I've heard it. "Do you fellas need to see a menu or can I just bring you the usual?"

"Why mess with success?" Pierce says, winking at her. She blushes then hurries away.

"Isn't that like a major red flag," I say, "when a guy orders for you?"

"If he does it to show off and never lets you choose for yourself, yes," Pierce says, pulling the paper off his straw. "But trust me, this is the most pure protein you can get for the money around here. You will regret ordering anything else."

"You didn't even ask how I like my steak."

"Medium rare?"

"Show-off."

The restaurant isn't busy and our meals arrive quickly, the steak so big there's barely room for the tiny green salad on the side of the plate. "You weren't kidding," I say. "How often do you come here?"

"Once a week. Graeme doesn't like the smell of meat cooking."

"He's not around, though."

"It lingers. And he's putting up with enough as it is."

"I guess." I have more questions (I always have more questions) but I don't want to bug him. Not while he's eating. And then all the questions disappear as I take my first bite of what turns out to be one of the best steaks of my life. It's an effort to not inhale it, every mouthful tender and lush and perfectly seasoned. Even the salad's great, the bitter leaves cutting through the fatty feeling in my mouth. Pierce Platter took me out for a steak at a nice restaurant, and I keep forgetting he's there.

I catch a glimpse of the bill when she brings it, and my heart almost stops. "You'd think for coming here once a week they'd give you a deal," I mutter when she's gone.

"Tell me that wasn't worth it," he says as he puts his credit card back in his wallet.

"Yeah but... Is that what it's like, being a grown-up? I mean having a job and stuff? Like obviously it is, but...forget it."

It seems so far beyond my reach. I can't imagine having so much money that I can tip not just the waitress but the hostess. At the house, I shut myself in the guest room and switch back and forth between doom-scrolling and sort of sleeping. Tonight's the full moon, and I can feel the pull, my senses dialed way up, my skin prickling like the hairs are already growing.

I come back from the toilet to find Dolly curled up on the futon, where she stays for the rest of the afternoon while I lie around her. Pierce makes a chopped salad with chickpeas for dinner and we sit out on the back deck to eat it. I don't have much to say so I watch the clouds and think about Stone. What he eats in summer, what he does for money, whether he meant 'hibernate' when he said sleep and if there's any way I could do it too. Sleeping for a month means not thinking for a month, which sounds like the greatest thing ever.

After cleaning up from dinner, we come back outside and Pierce gets out his vape and we smoke some weed that tastes like vanilla ice cream and makes me melt into the deckchair. At this time of year the sky stays light forever, the clouds glowing rose gold in the hazy light. Everywhere you look in their yard, flowers are blooming. My brother's house is a kind of paradise, but it will never be my home.

"Did you know the Roths at all?" I ask.

Pierce opens his eyes and breathes out a sigh. "I've heard of them."

"Stone's the last one, you know? Shit, imagine that. Being the only one." I bite the insides of my cheeks, not wanting to surrender to my feelings. "That's the saddest thing ever. But why do I still care?"

"Because you're a good person?" Pierce says.

"I'm not. I'm a disaster. I can't keep a job, can't make anyone happy."

"You're young. And none of those things make you a bad person."

"I am. I said some brutal shit to him."

"You were probably upset."

"You're not going to quit, are you?"

"Trying to make you feel better? Nope."

"See? I am a bad person. I should be letting you make me feel better. I don't know what I'm saying. I'm sorry. I give up."

"Give it another day or two," he says through a cloud of sweet smoke. "Think about it when you're not so emotional."

"Yeah right, that never happens."

"It will."

I want him to be right. I want time to change everything, so I don't have to change it myself. I want to start over again, do it right. Go slow, let Stone learn how to give before I start asking for more. I want the last week (just a week, holy shit) to have never happened, so I can try again and get it right.

I don't want to say any of these things out loud, so I ask the other question that won't go away. "What are we doing about tonight?"

"Up to you. We usually go out to the reservoir."

"You are not driving, Mr Cabbage Head." He laughs in that sloppy stoned way that tells me I'm right.

"It's probably too late anyway," he says, glancing towards the east, where the near full moon is approaching the horizon. Or our part of the earth is turning to face it, if you think about the universe. Either way, I can feel like a trembling in the ground and a humming in the air.

Shifting on purpose is different. The call of the moon is an itch under the skin, a boiling in the blood, the body trying to make the change whether you want it to or not. Hollowood gets both quiet and loud the night of a full moon. Some people stay in, keep to themselves. Other people roll with it, and I've had some crazy nights on Cuttler's Green, wolves by the dozen romping and fighting and play-mating and anything else we wanted until moonset, when the change was taken back and we'd all sneak home naked and feeling high as fuck. With Stone it was different. It felt special, so special I don't want to overwrite the memories by fooling around with Pierce. I've done that plenty, but it belongs in the past.

"It's fine if we stay here," he says after a little. "We've got the neighbors thinking we dog sit for someone with huskies."

"Dude, we don't look like huskies."

"Apparently they don't know that."

"And what about Graeme?"

"He's never here. Spends the night at a hotel, gets a massage and whatever. Me-time, he says."

"That's nice of him to give you guys space."

"They've always been doing it, even before he knew."

"Huh. Imagine if he was a were too?"

"Dude..."

"Just saying, it's real convenient that he's never around."

"You are one sick little puppy, you know?"

"What else is new?"

When the moon is so near I can smell it we undress in the house. Leaving the lights off, we step out on the deck as the humming in the air reaches that certain frequency. Pierce turns to me like he wants to say one last thing and then it's too late as the change takes me, the sounds smearing into nothing as the cells of my body rearrange themselves into their other state. I saw a video of plastic that can be trained to change shape and I wonder all the time if that's what we're like. Plastic with memory that bends into something unlikely then returns to its original state. A very human thought that sinks beneath the waves of pure animal feeling.

I want to run. I wish we weren't here, in this little box of a yard. It's too late to ask, because the last thing we need is to get picked up by Animal Control. Pierce's wolfness has dark fur and a slim snout and a flicking tail that lifts as he sees me. We scent each other, but when he butts me with his head to get me to play-fight I sit down with my nose on my paws. Whining, he circles around me a few times then sits beside me and leans against my flank.

You miss him, he thinks as his soft red warmth seeps out of him and into me.

It's that obvious?

It's sweet.

But why do I still care?

Fate. One word, a thousand images: Evan as a child and the man he is now, all of our kin whose matings were made under the same conditions, ordained by some mysterious force that came in the night like a thief and changed your life whether you wanted it or not.

Fuck.

I know. Brother, I know.

It's too much for my wild heart and I throw back my head and let go with a howl full of longing and shame and devotion, a prayer to whatever cruel god created us and a cry against all that we've suffered since. Pierce joins me, along with every dog in the neighborhood, a choir of yapping and barking and yes, proper howls, as the wolves they once were call out to the wolf that is me.

The next day we both sleep late, though I'm not half so tired as if we'd spent the night running wild. Just before noon we're chilling in the living room, Pierce scrolling socials while I quietly look up how to enroll in the state Department of Ed high school completion program. Like any other dogs we both perk up as a car door slams. The front door opens and a melodious Scottish voice calls out "daddy's home!"

Pierce almost somersaults over the back of the couch he's in such a hurry to get to the front door. "I would have come to get you," he says in a cute little voice.

"It's no bother."

"But where's Ev?"

"Gone to see someone in the Falls."

"Oh? Ohhh…"

They murmur back and forth over the sound of suitcase zippers, then Pierce comes back to the living room blushing, followed by the most beautiful human being I've ever seen in real life, with softly wavy hair falling around his angular face and eyes the color of a sandstorm and skin that would make a Korean girl die from jealousy. I don't want to fuck him, I just want to look at him, like he's a statue in the world's gayest art gallery.

"You must be Chase," he says. "A pleasure to meet you."

"Same." We shake hands across the back of the couch then he leaves the room. I grab Pierce's sleeve as he tries to follow. "Dude, are you fucking kidding me? How did my brother hook up with *that*?"

"Ooh, my ears are burning," Graeme calls from the foyer.

Pierce rolls his eyes. "He's also the biggest smartass I've ever met."

"Which is saying something coming from you, isn't it, love?" he says, patting Pierce on the ass as he passes on his way to the kitchen. "By the by, the new bed is meant to come today."

"Awesome. That futon's brutal."

"It's not that bad," I say vaguely as Graeme bends over to get something from a low cupboard.

"It is after six months," Pierce says dryly.

"It's not that I'm not glad to have you here," Graeme says to me as he starts pulling vegetables out of the fridge, "but how long will you be staying?"

"Just a couple days. I had to get away from my dad for a bit."

"Yes, your father has a rather large personality."

"Oh my god, nailed it. Huge personality."

For lunch Graeme makes a big stir fry that's actually really good, with cashews and weird mushrooms that look like crumpled pieces of paper, and some stuff called tempeh that's like flat tofu but sort of better. Him and Pierce do work things in the afternoon while I stay out of their way. There's a few books stacked under the tv and instead of picking the manga I make myself flip through a non-fic by some Doctor Octopus-looking guy about making your weirdness your strength. Sounds more like fiction considering how people usually react to my weirdness. Is there a market for disaster gay werewolves?

Around four I go for a run in their neighborhood, if only to burn up the energy that lingers after a full moon. When I get back, Evan is getting out of a rental car. He greets me with a grunt and a nod.

"I thought you'd stay the night," I say.

"It wasn't them I went to see."

"Wait, why would you go all that way...you asshole!" He went to see Stone, I'll bet anything. "Tell me you didn't."

"What? I can't look out for my little brother?" he says as he opens the trunk to get his bag.

"It'd be a first. Why are you even getting involved?"

"He treated you like shit. I wanted to know why."

"You did? What did he say?"

"Can I at least get inside my house and have a piss and maybe have something to eat?"

"Sorry, sorry, go ahead."

The foyer is full of big pieces of cardboard and plastic wrap. I'm about to tell Evan about the bed when we hear grunting coming from upstairs.

"Push, you slut," Graeme hisses.

"Gray," Pierce moans tensely. "It's not going to fit! Oh wait...yeah, baby!"

"What the fuck?" Evan shouts, dropping his bag.

"I bloody told you we should have started sooner, didn't I?" Graeme says as Evan shoots me a filthy look.

"We goddamn talked about this," he yells as he stomps up the stairs. "And the minute I'm not around you assholes go right ahead and—" He pulls up short at the door to Pierce's room. "Right," he mumbles, shoving his hands in his pockets as he backs up. "The bed. Looks good."

"You thought we were fucking, didn't you?" Pierce says sharply as he comes out onto the landing.

"It's fine," Evan says.

"It's not fine. You don't trust us at all."

"I do!"

"It's no problem," says Graeme, following Pierce out of the bedroom.

"It is so a problem," Pierce says. "He still doesn't trust us not to fool around when he's not here."

"It's not like we've him much reason to trust," Graeme says with a guilty grimace.

"Yeah, well..." Pierce deflates, leaning back against the doorframe with a groan. "Ah, shit."

I creep through to the living room and put on my headphones so they can argue in peace. Or fuck it out. Or whatever three guys do when their lives are all jumbled together by marriage and fate. Pierce comes downstairs sooner than I expect and flops onto the couch beside me.

"Sorry you had to see that," he mutters.

"I've seen worse."

He leans his head on the back of the couch "Sometimes I ask myself if it's even worth it."

"Sticking around? I don't know. But how would you feel if they told you to never come back?"

A tremor passes over him. "Probably like I wanted to die."

"Then it must be worth it."

He turns his head towards me. "How'd you get so smart, little brother?"

"Hung around some smart people, big brother."

I don't get a chance to talk to Evan about him meeting Stone until we're unloading the dishwasher after dinner.

"He's fast," he says, passing me the next plate.

"He ran away from you?"

"You sure do know how to pick guys," Ev says with a frown and a smirk, Mom and Dad's faces blended into one.

"I didn't pick him. I just showed up. Did he tell you he'd been stalking me?"

"Eventually. Why'd you give back the spoon?"

"Why would I keep it?"

"One fight doesn't end a relationship."

"I hope you told *him* that," I say as I nearly shut the cupboard on my thumb. "Not that we really even had a fight. He just...changed his mind."

"Not exactly. If you'd stayed in town another night—"

"You can thank Dad for fucking that up."

Sorting the cutlery, Evan laughs quietly. "He told me you cussed him out."

"Did he tell you why?"

"Didn't have to."

"What did Stone say? Why did he kick me out?"

"I don't think he expected it to work. He thought you'd come right back."

"He almost bit my head off. Like, literally. Why would I go back?"

"You tell me, guy who went back."

"It was to give him the spoon," I say in a small voice.

"You could have just thrown it out. Or given it to Mom or something. No one made you climb that mountain twice."

He's right again, like a big brother is supposed to be. And I'm not okay with it, like any little brother. "You still haven't really answered the question," I say as we start on the cups. "What made him want me gone?"

"He didn't say much about that. He looked pretty depressed about it, really. Like he hadn't thought it through."

"So he just freaked out?"

"You know he hadn't spoken to anyone in months, right?"

"Then I show up like fucking Goldilocks, sit in his chair, eat his food, sleep in his bed, suck his... Damn it. You know what actually sucks?"

"That even though you hate the fact that your life is out of your hands, you want go through with it anyway?"

"Dude..."

"How did I know?" he says as I gape at him, but the answer pops into my mind before he explains.

"Shit. Because it was the same for you. Right."

He closes the dishwasher then leans against it. "Our parents don't set it up, Chase. That's never been the way. And there's never been a mating where it didn't work out in the end."

"You're sure some don't stick together just so they don't get called out?"

"I guess that could happen. Do you know the divorce rate in Hollowood Falls?"

"You're going to say zero, aren't you?"

He smirks. "Numbers don't lie."

"Did you guys get a spoon?"

"We did."

"And Graeme's really okay with it?"

He laughs, rubbing his neck. "He's dealing with it better than I might have."

"Yeah, you never were much good at sharing."

"It's selfish, though. If I get two, why don't they?"

"Good thing they get along."

"Right?"

Both our heads snap around as someone whistles from upstairs. "Better see what they want," I say, but he's already on his way, nearly breaking into a jog as he leaves the room. He knows what they want, and so do I, from the whistle, and Ev's dirty laugh as he shuts the door behind him.

It opens again and I hear someone's bare feet on the hardwood. "House-guest!" Pierce says, and the feet stop.

"Bugger," says Graeme. "Ah well, we'll make do." As his footsteps retreat I settle into the corner of the couch and put on my headphones. It's going to be a long night. For all of us.

Nine

"Hollowood on Line One"

S o that's where we're at. I don't know if I'll ever see Stone again, or if I'll even go back to Hollowood Falls. But one thing everyone says about Hollowood is even if you leave, it never really leaves you.

One morning about a week later, I wake up to the sound of them making breakfast. The microwave dings, and Pierce's next words fall into a sudden silence. "...nothing wrong with being vegan. I just think that for the amount of cum you swallow, you might as well eat eggs too."

"Fuck me blind," Graeme moans as Evan sputters through a mouthful of coffee or something. "You did not just say that out loud."

"I'm going to leave the room and pretend I didn't hear any of that," Evan says.

"What?" Pierce calls after him. "They're both zygotes. It's biology."

"Ach, what does it matter?" Graeme says, his spoon tinging off the side of his cup as he stirs. "I'm getting plenty of protein."

"For fuck's sake, Gray…" Evan groans from the foyer as the other two crack up.

I roll to face the back of the couch as Graeme wanders to the patio door. He usually has breakfast on the back deck, and he puts his bowl of bircher muesli on the wide arm of the couch to open the blinds. Then freezes, his hand on the chain of the blinds.

"Lads…" he calls with a funny wobble in his voice. "Lads, would you come here for a tic?"

"What is it?" asks Pierce over the sound of the blender.

"Hollowood on line one."

They both join him at the window in a flash. "Jesus…" Pierce breathes. "Are you sure?"

"That's not a wolf," Evan says, shaking his head. "That is not a wolf."

"No shit it's not a wolf," Graeme hisses. "But if a giant wild animal shows up in our back yard, odds are it's something to do with you lot."

I can't see past them so I get up and join them at the patio door. A shaggy brown bear is sitting on the lawn. His adorable ears twitch as he sees me. "Fuck."

"Is that him?" Pierce asks me with a grin.

"Yep."

"You Culvers, I swear to…" Graeme breaks off, then picks up his cereal bowl. "I'll take my breakfast on the front porch, how about?"

"You know, you two are perfect for each other," Evan says to me as Graeme leaves. "Neither of you do what you're told."

"What you tell him?"

"To get mom and dad to bring him down."

"Are you new? He'd never want to do that. He's even weirder than me."

"He didn't seem that weird."

"That's cause you're used to me."

Stone scratches behind one ear then lumbers to his feet and starts to nose around the yard. The neighbours might be cool with giant huskies but he is so completely a bear that we'll have Animal Control, the Parks department, and the local news here in no time.

"You're completely sure it's him," Pierce says as I go to open the patio door.

"Maybe have your phone out if it's not."

"To video?"

"To call 9-1-1, dickhead."

"Hey, I'm not the enemy."

"Sorry. Just...don't go anywhere." I know it's him but do I know him? He's making it hard to get to know him, but this tugging in my chest won't stop. "Why is he making me do this?" I ask as I start undressing.

"Are you seriously asking?" Pierce says.

"It's hard to know what he means. It's not like when you and me talk. It's all blurry, just feelings and memories and stuff."

"Interesting."

"It's annoying as fuck." Hopefully I can convince him to shift so we can talk with words. Not that he's awesome at that either. Why has fate thrown me together with this puzzle of a man then made me want to solve him?

I shift in the living room, less worried about Pierce seeing me than his neighbors. Stone is sitting at the back of the yard beneath a tree all covered in hazy white flowers. More flowers speckle his fur and the bright grass around him like flakes of snow. My puzzle, my prize, as stubborn and strange as I am, as lonely and hurting and hungry for solitude. My mountain, unmovable, dangerous. Mine.

I hope. I can't allow my human heart to forget how he drove me away. If I knew what to do, I would do it, if he'll promise to meet me halfway. As I step onto the deck he stretches out on his belly and lays his big head on his paws, his sweet little ears perked towards me.

We touch noses, then he rolls heavily onto his back, his hindquarters flattening a bed of snapdragons. An animal's apology, all groveling and sad eyes, but I've played that card so many times he can't play it on me. I sit and wait until he's on four legs again then approach him and butt my nose against his neck.

Why did you come?

He tosses his head with an angry grunt. This is going badly and we just got started, but he lowers his head and presses his jowls against mine, flooding my senses with the glimmering red gold warmth of his need. I answer with the black murk of heartache and self-doubt that I've been swimming against ever since.

Did you ever trust me?

Whining like a puppy, he drops his head to my shoulder, the flurry of images accelerating, too fast for even my jumpy brain: the sun and the moon, the stars and the snow; the forest and two people who must be his parents, their faces morphing back and forth between their two states of being; heat and light and a thrumming buzz like the cicadas in L.A. and what might be the sound of my neurons exploding.

I pull away from him, panting out the boiling energy as I pace the yard. He waits with his head on his paws, until I nudge him behind his ear. I picture his human face, his big brown coat, his massive hands. *We need to talk. With words. Or this won't work.*

He groans like I'm wounding him, but when I get up and start for the house he hoists himself to his feet and follows me. Pierce is at the patio door with his phone pressed against the glass. Videoing the whole damn thing, but if he sends it to my parents I will end him. As I raise a paw against the glass he puts his phone away then lets me in, politely turning his back as I shift.

"Everything going alright?" he asks.

"Can't you tell from the footage?"

As the back of his neck goes pink I yank on my sweatpants, then grab the throw blanket on the back of the couch. Stone shifted too and is huddled naked on a deck chair.

"You're a piece of work, aren't you?" I say as I drape the blanket around him.

"What does that mean?"

"You know what, I have no idea. My grandpa used to say it. I think it means whoever loves you needs to be strong."

His head drops, then he takes a breath and sits up. "Come home."

Something no one has ever said to me. Not even my parents. Not even Mom, because I never called to ask, I always just showed up. I want to say yes, for the sadness in his eyes, and the hope, and all the things I've ever seen in him. But I can't give in. Not yet.

"Is that all?" I say, hating the sharpness in my voice, clinging to its edge as he shakes his shaggy head.

"It was wrong to make you leave," he says, his voice growing stronger with each word. "I wanted you there, wanted to know you, but that meant you knowing me. I didn't want that. Didn't want you tied to someone like me. I wanted you to be free. I thought I could make it so. That we could go back to how it was."

"You mean when you used to watch me running? Honey, I was never free."

"I'm sorry I hurt you. I'll do my best not to do it again."

"I believe you." I don't know if that's what I'm supposed to say, but it works for us.

"I missed you, Chase. I forgot what it was like to have something to live for."

"Wow." I press my hands against my thighs to keep from grabbing him and kissing his brains out. "Got any more?"

"I need you, Chase," he says, reaching for my hand. "I can't keep going like I was. Waiting for time to catch me. I want to live for something. For you."

"Fuck!"

"Did I say something wrong?"

"No, that was perfect," I breathe. Maybe the last breath I'll ever take because he really is perfect and this is too good to be real. Except it is. He's real and he's mine and he's here for me. He's here to take me home. I throw my arms around him and kiss his face until I find his mouth and then I kiss that until he kisses me back. Sweetly at first, then with hunger. Then like he's starving, his tongue tasting me deeply when his teeth aren't nipping at my lips.

The chair creaks beneath our weight as he pulls me hard against him. I pull back, because wrecking my brother's lawn furniture isn't going to win us any points, which matters because I'm about to get railed in his guest room. I fucking hope, but Stone's dick is hard against my thighs, telling me all I need to know.

"I missed you so much," I say roughly, my mouth watering from the scent of his bare skin. "Don't ever do that again."

"I won't," he says, nuzzling at my neck, the head of his dick catching on the waist of my track pants and smearing his precum on my bare stomach.

"Can we go inside before we get arrested?"

"Why would we get arrested?" he says as he lets me go.

"Um, try indecent exposure?" I say as he stands up, because the blanket barely covers his ass. "And I don't know what we're going to do with you. It's not like you're going to fit in anyone's clothes."

"I kind of didn't think about this part," he grunts as he follows me into the house. "I just wanted to find you."

With his wild hair and the hairy trunks of his legs sticking out from under the fluffy green blanket, he looks like a tree that sprouted indoors against the backdrop of Graeme and Evan (and Pierce's) modernist crib. My mountain, my man, and I can't keep from kissing him.

"Take me home," I hum, resting my head against his furred chest.

"Can I really?"

"Honey bear, you can do anything you want with me." I reach up to kiss him again. He holds me tighter to him, lifting me clear off my feet. A perfect kiss, overwhelming, possessive, and all mine. Always and forever, a promise I'm ready to make as soon as he takes his tongue out of my mouth.

"For fuck's sake!" Graeme exclaims from the doorway. Stone sets me down, grunting as his dick hooks on my sweatpants again. He's dropped the blanket and is standing naked, in all his uncut glory, in my brother-in-law's living room.

"Dude, seriously?" Evan says over Graeme's shoulder as Pierce stares over his other with his mouth hanging open.

"Sorry," I blurt as I snatch up the blanket and shove it at Stone, who holds it awkwardly in front of his groin. "He doesn't have anything to wear, and—"

"It's fine," Graeme says with a wobbly smile as he begins to shoo the others back towards the front of the house. "We all get a bit carried away now and then."

I help Stone wrap the blanket around his waist like a sarong. "How did you even get here?" I ask with a yawn as I switch on the coffee machine.

"I walked."

"You what? How long did that take?

"Couple days," he says with that one-sided shrug.

"Wow. Okay, you're staying the night."

"Why?"

"Um, because you just went on a two hundred and fifty mile hike for no good reason?"

"I had a reason. I came to see you."

"After my brother told you to ask my folks for a ride."

He shrugs again, "Didn't want to bother them."

"Dude. They'd sit up and beg at this point if they thought I was going to settle down. But you should totally stay, just to get to know my brother more."

"Why?"

"Because if we're mated he's now your kin. Don't worry, he's way less of a pain in the ass than I am."

"Who were those other men?"

"His husbands."

"Both of them?"

"Where have you been? No, don't answer that. It's a long story. Stay the night and I'm sure they'll tell you all about it."

It's all of nine in the morning and everyone else has a job. Stone spends most of the day asleep on Pierce's old futon in the empty garage. The quick shift back and forth knocked the wind out of me too, but after a nap on the couch I walk the two miles to and from the shopping center to pick up a t-shirt and sweats so Stone doesn't have to wear that blanket from now until we get back to Hollowood. I'm impressed, and really very flattered, that he walked all that way for me, but I'm hoping we can get a ride home.

Home: he wants to take me home. Maybe it won't be forever—maybe we'll hate each other by the end, break Hollowood's streak of happy marriages. I don't know of anyone who's mated across species lines, but if there's proof, it's in those old books in the Lodge.

Dinner is weird but good with Stone sitting beside me, answering the others' questions but otherwise staying quiet. Every now and then he looks at me, and it's like a hug, such warmth in his clear eyes, such peaceful joy in his soft little smile. Every time he does, it makes me blush and bite my lip and wonder how I pulled off that hard-as-candy slut act for so many years. Not that I don't want this man to do borderline criminal things to my body. But only him, from now until forever. He feels me looking at him and gives me another sweet look and I have to cover my mouth so I don't sigh out loud.

With a scraping of chair feet the others get up from the table. "Come on, lads," Graeme says to them. "Quick smart if we're going to catch that film."

"What's he talking about?" Evan says to Pierce as Graeme hurries from the room. Pierce tilts his head towards me and Stone, and Evan startles like he's waking up. "Right. The movie. Sure."

"Don't wait up," Pierce says with a wink as he follows Ev. The front door closes and then it's just me and Stone alone.

"That was weird," he says.

"I think they did that on purpose."

"Why?"

"So they don't have to listen to us kiss and make up."

"But we already—oh," he says with a grin as I put my hand not on his leg but on his dick, which instantly hardens. "Right."

"So."

"So."

"Upstairs? Don't worry, I asked if we could stay there. Graeme and Ev have a king-size. They said it's fine."

"Okay."

"But just so you know," I say as we get up. "They've only had the new bed for a week, so let's try not to wreck it."

"How would we...oh. Right." He ducks his head shyly and it's like fireworks go off inside me, lighting me up everywhere.

"Did anyone ever tell you you're gorgeous when you blush?" I say, wrapping my arms around his neck.

"No," he murmurs, a little smile coming and going from his sweet mouth.

"Come on, papa bear. Let's go see if the bed's just right."

Ten

United

There is no way in hell we'll break the bed. For one thing, it's gigantic, taking up most of the room, which might have been a mistake if it wasn't so obviously designed for fucking, with eye bolts sticking out of the heavy wood frame in strategic places and cushy leather covering the high foot board.

"Why is it built like that?" Stone asks from the doorway.

"Because my brother's a freak," I mutter as I covertly kick a coil of rope under the bed. "Or somebody is."

"Do they use those to...do things to each other?" he says uncertainly, his forehead creased with worry.

"I guess."

"Do you want to...do things?"

"*Some* things, maybe. But forget about that. This here is all about you and me."

With him sitting on the bed I can kiss him more easily so I do. I wish we had all night instead of a couple of hours, because I could do this for a real long time, stroking my fingers through his wild hair as his hand creeps up the back of my shirt and his other hand grips my ass. His dick rubs my thighs, promising, promising, and when he squeezes me harder I gasp against his mouth.

"Was that okay?" he says.

"Super okay. Do it some more."

I expect another kiss but instead he pulls up my shirt and starts to lick my chest, grazing my nipples with his fat tongue. I want this all over, my knees going soft as he closes his mouth over my right nipple and sucks.

"You're going to wreck me," I groan, grabbing his shoulders.

"I'm sorry," he murmurs against my skin.

"Don't be. I want to get wrecked."

He raises his head to look in my eyes. "I don't want to hurt you."

"But what if I want you to? I mean it," I say as he frowns. "I want you inside me, papa bear. I want you to break me apart. Fuck me so hard I don't know right from wrong. Ruin me for every other dick on earth."

"You're crazy," he says, but he's smiling and it's gorgeous.

"Maybe. But what if I'm just crazy for you. Can we at least try? Please?" I wind my hips, my hard-on rubbing against his. He nods as his eyes flutter closed.

"Though if you wanted to help..."

He meets my gaze again, his grip on me tightening. "Yes?"

"I'm just saying, it'd be a lot more fun if you did."

"Tell me what to do."

"It's easy, honey." Laying my hand against his cheek, I run my thumb across his sweet lips which open like he's trying to breathe me in. "I remember what that big bear's tongue felt like down there. I want to feel *this* one. I want you to make me wet, make me ready for you."

He groans deep in his throat, a rumbling like an avalanche. He's my mountain, my beast, and I want him to eat me alive. As soon as possible. I pull off my shirt, but when I grab for his he shrinks away from me. "You want to keep it on?" I ask.

"I don't look so good under here right now," he rumbles.

"I liked it before."

"I haven't felt like eating much since you've been gone. I'm all soft."

"That's okay. You can wear your shirt if you like. Whatever makes this good for you."

"You're what's making it good."

"So good." I never want to stop kissing him. He's so strong and smells like the sky and the earth. His soft untrimmed beard strokes my bare chest, his rough hands spreading my ass cheeks like he almost knows what he's doing. Or is it just that I like this so much, the instinctive way he touches me, the strength I can't ignore?

I want to make it easy for him so I climb on the bed, planning to ask him to lie down so I can get on top. But he grabs my hips and keeps me there, at the edge of the mattress.

"You're so pretty," he says, running his hands over my ass. "So smooth. And I love your smell."

"Go on."

"I love your shapes. Your smile. Your laugh."

"I love that you came here to find me," I say over my shoulder. Maybe I love him, but that's something to think about later. Right now all I want is to feel. Feel his hands on my ass then the heat of his breath. Feel the red glow of love that's pouring from my heart, because it's his breath, my mountain, my man. My papa bear, the only one that feels just right, as he strokes his thick tongue over my hole.

Is he really a virgin? Or just a natural? I stop trying to think as his tongue spirals into me, his drool dripping down my balls, his coarse hands gripping me like I'm going to try to escape. Never, ever, ever. Always this, forever and again. As he bathes my hole with his tongue his beard tickles my thighs and I shiver, my arms nearly giving way.

"Is it good?"

"Holy fuck, is it ever. You're doing great, honey bear. You might make me come just from that."

"Do you want me to?"

"Yes. No. Make me wait. I want to want it more." I want it to be the best ever. I want this night to change me. Too much to expect of a fuck, unless it's the first of the rest of my life.

"What do I do now?" he asks through wet lips.

"Finger me open."

"Like this?"

"Mmmfp..." He pushes in deep but too quickly and I tense at the stab of sensation. "Maybe a bit slower next time," I grunt. I swear I've had smaller dicks in me. Am I out of my mind trying to take this beast? I don't need to prove anything to him.

Just to myself. Because if we can't fuck, then fate can fuck off. I can't live without sex, but I don't want to live without Stone. I need this to be good for both of us.

That means taking our time. Time that I'm not sure we have. We could have been in here for hours, though when I think a bit harder it can't be more than twenty minutes. And with the filthy shit I've heard coming out of my brother's bedroom in the last week (and this room, with this bed) the rest of the household can deal with it if we're still going when they get back from their movie. My brain's about to dive down the rabbit hole of what they're seeing or if they faked us out and are chilling in the backyard when my body's reminded of what it's doing by Stone pulling out his finger just as suddenly.

"Did I hurt you?" he says nervously.

"Not really. More surprised me."

"What should I do?"

"That but slower."

"Like this?"

"Fuck...yes. That. Like that." As he pushes into me slowly I quit talking. Moving against the pressure of his touch, I roll my hips, moving his finger in and out, feeling him everywhere, wanting him deeper.

But I'm going to have to ask for it, guide him through step by step. Something I've never had to do. The men I've fucked have always just taken whatever they wanted, made me the means to their end, a toy they put their dick in then left on the shelf. I thought that was all I needed, or did I think it was all I deserved?

That's all behind me now, and screw you if you laugh at the metaphor. I deserve this man's love, as much as anyone deserves love. I want to give him everything, not just all I am but everything in the world. He deserves to have someone to love.

"Is it okay?" he asks, feeling me shaking from the weight of my emotions.

"Yeah, but can I kiss you again?"

"Always."

I kneel at the edge of the bed, my arms around his neck, my dick against his soft, furry belly and his hands on my ass. He's so sweet to kiss, so gentle and then so ferocious, and I grind against him he slides his fingers inward until he reaches my hole. My dick snared in the fabric of his shirt, I'm pinned between his body and his touch, his face inches from mine so he sees every gasp, every crease of my forehead, every helpless reaction as I tilt my hips to give him more of me.

"Should I—"

"Yes." I know what he's going to ask and the answer is yes, as he works his finger into me again, his long arms cradling me, crushing me against his soft belly like he did when we played in the snow.

Just as helpless as I was that day, I thrust against him, driven by blood-thirsty instinct. My man, my mountain, letting me ride him as his thick fingers fill me. It's like nothing before, a holy kind of fucking, and before I can stop it I come, wrecking the front of his shirt and cursing like the devil.

A shudder rips through me as he pulls out. "Was I supposed to do that?" he murmurs.

"Doesn't matter," I pant, resting my head on his shoulder. "It was awesome."

"But—"

"Don't worry, papa bear. I got more in me. But first I want to get *you* in me."

"Are you sure?"

"You just got my engine warmed up. Don't you want to take me for a ride?"

"You really want to do this?"

I almost crack another joke, tell him it's all a scam, but I'll break this precious man if I don't handle him with care. "I do. I've wanted this for so long. Maybe even before we met. Wanted someone sweet like you. Someone I cared about. I want to make this good for you. I want to make you happy."

"You do. Like I never knew I could be."

As we kiss again I slide my hand inside his waistband. He goes still and so do I, but then he twists his hips toward me and I feel him. "Your dick is ridiculous," I say as I wrap my fingers around his thick shaft. "In a good way. Like too good to be true."

"It's all for you."

"I want it. I want to see it," I say as I squeeze him. "Please?"

He nods and I carefully ease him out of his baggy sweats. "Fuck. I think I ought to ride you. Not like that," I add as his eyes fly open. "Just lie down, okay? Oh, and maybe lose these."

As he pulls off his sweatpants and gets on the bed I help myself to a few pumps from the bottle of industrial strength lube on the built-in side table. I'm never going to be able to look at my brother the same again.

Shoving that thought aside, I straddle Stone, his dick riding between my slippery cheeks. He can't speak, his mouth open, eyes half closed, those pretty lashes trembling against his cheek, and I stretch over him to kiss him once more. He's a beast and a beauty in one and I can't wait any longer.

"Now look, you," I say as I sit back again. "Don't go asking every other minute if it hurts. Don't worry about me. I know what I'm doing. You just let me do it, alright?"

If I can, because oh my God, just the tip of him is splitting my ass in two. If he wasn't a virgin I'd raid the side table for a popper, but that's more gay than he's ready to be. We're doing this the old fashioned way, with faith and time and gravity as I rock back onto him, my body shaking in disbelief of what I'm asking it to do. No, demanding, because this is what I wanted, this strange mash up of pleasure and pain, the stinging and stretch, the sense of being so totally possessed. In this endless moment I belong to him completely.

And there's still more of him to take. I didn't come all this way to quit now. I want to know everything about Stone, not just what he feels like in me but what he craves, what he fears, why he started watching me and what he planned to do about it. I want to know him inside and out and I want him to know me. I want to give him the parts of me I've never shown to anyone, all the sad and ragged edges, the loneliness I've tried to kill with sex and booze and screwing up.

I don't want to run anymore. I want to live.

Like telling a secret that was making me lose my mind, to think this unlocks something deep inside of me. Not my body but my soul. But is there any difference? Aren't we all our bodies? Shameless, overflowing with love for this sweet, strange man, I thrust down on his perfect dick at the same time as he thrusts up, filling me completely and making my teeth rattle.

"Chase..." he whispers, his eyelids trembling, his hands tight on my thighs.

"It's good, papa bear," I murmur, my voice catching in my throat. Good isn't even the word. More like world-ending, heart-stopping, undeniable. I want to move but my arms won't support me, my whole body shaking from the sweet ache of his incredible dick filling me like no one ever has.

"Chase. I want...I want to fuck you."

"Yes. Please. Now." *Please wreck me. Possess me. Make me want no one else ever again.* He doesn't have to do a thing and it'll still be true. Not because of how this feels but because of who he is. Because he's so sweet and gentle in every other way.

He looks me in the eyes as he starts to rock, not thrusting but just moving in me. I want to look away, escape into the hugeness of the sensations, but he deserves more. He deserves all of me, and I stop trying to ride him and let myself soften. He moans as he feels me surrender, his grip crushing my hips as he fucks up into me. It's all I wanted and a million times more, and it's all mine forever from this moment on.

Fate can take me and do what it wants. Fate in the form of this man, my mountain, my miracle. I'm shouting his name and the good lord's too, and if this isn't love then I don't fucking care. I'll take it again and again, for as long as Stone is strong enough to give it to me.

He doesn't last long after that. Fine with me, the spicy tingle of my ass stretched around him starting to feel a lot more like pain as the adrenaline wears off. I cleared it with Pierce to have the room for the night, and as soon as we're under the covers Stone wraps himself around me, my back to his chest. Usually when a guy comes in me, I want to get it out right away. Tonight I don't want to even move, want to hold onto the proof of Stone as long as possible, to feel this safe and wanted every day and night.

"You are a piece of work, Chase Culver," he murmurs into my hair.

"Am I?"

"A little masterpiece. Was that the wrong thing to say?" he asks as I shiver, struck by how much he can say with so few words.

"You can stop asking that," I say, snuggling deeper into his arms. "To me, everything you do is right."

"Except that one thing," he says so softly I almost don't hear him.

"And didn't we decide not to let that get between us? Because if you think one little fuck up—"

"That wasn't little, what I did."

"Point is, you can't fuck up any worse than I have. I don't just mean sleeping with the wrong people. I mean real dumb shit. Stuff that could have got me killed. What did you do? Got freaked out by your feelings. That's all. If I had a dollar for every time I made the wrong choice because of my emotions, let's just say Ev would be crashing on my couch and not the other way around."

"So we're good?"

"Honey bear, we are so good."

"I like when you call me that."

"What about papa bear?"

He purrs as his dick thickens against my backside. "That's good too."

"I won't use that around company, how about? Them included," I say as the front door opens and the others' voices echo up from the foyer. They're talking super loud and all at once, which means they either went to the pub or are putting on a show so we know they're home. Either way, I don't think I can look any of them in the eye right now.

"We don't have to get up, do we?" he asks.

"Nope. This is us all night."

He relaxes again. "I like your brother. And his husband. And the other one too."

"I think they like you. But next time my brother tries to hook you up with a ride, take it, will you? Even if it is with my folks. And don't worry about them. They have to like you." Even if they didn't, it's not up to them. This isn't chance or accident, not the fallout from one of my fuck ups. This is my fate. This.

No one says a word the next morning at breakfast about whether they heard us or not. I don't really care, not after we listened to them bang Pierce on the dining table not long after they got home. I just hope they shut the blinds. Nobody says anything either about the fact that Evan is leaving Graeme and Pierce alone together all day by driving me and Stone back to Hollowood.

I especially don't say it. I say some other words though, because he's my brother and it might be nice for me to worry about him for a change. "I hope I wasn't too big a pain in the ass the last few days," I say as we inch forward in the coffee-shop drive thru.

"It was fine," he says absently, slumped against the car door.

"They seem like really great guys. Both of them."

He raises an eyebrow. "You've known Pierce forever."

"Yeah, but I've never seen him be in a relationship. I think it'll work out fine."

"You do, do you?"

"I know I'm just your dumb-ass little brother but—"

He sits upright to nudge me with his elbow. "Don't say that. You're not dumb."

"I know."

"Maybe a bit irresponsible."

"I was a hot mess. The fact that any of you still put up with me—"

"Stop with that self-hating bullshit. You're worth more than that. Even if I don't always show it, I know you are."

"Thanks."

"I know it looks messy," he says, reclining again. "It's been kind of intense, getting to the point where we all get along most of the time."

"You'll get there."

Instead of our parents' place we get Evan to drop us off at Sutherland's store. I'll see my folks tomorrow. For now, all I want is to get through Hollowood Falls and out the other side, up to our nest in the sky, our den for two. There's only one man I want, for the rest of my life. For the first time, that man wants me too.

So that's how it all happened. Come on, you didn't think I'd tell you that long ass story and not give you the happy ending, did you? While I'm saying goodbye to my brother, Stone goes into Sutherland's to pick up his mail. Along with a couple of seed catalogs and a thick envelope covered in foreign stamps, he has a big black messenger bag over his shoulder.

"I wondered how you got things up and down the hill," I say as I follow him between the buildings to the big lot out back of the store.

"This is new. Had Mrs. Bentwick make it for me. Should fit one or the other of us no matter what."

"What do you mean, no matter what?"

"So we can take our clothes with us."

"We can wear it shifted?"

He shows me the adjustable straps, the way they'd fit around an animal's torso so a big dog—or a smallish bear—could carry it on their back or chest, depending on their size and build. "She's a genius," I say. "We're going to try it out, right?"

In answer he pulls off his shirt, and though I want to drop the bag and throw myself at him to prove that he's gorgeous to me whatever shape he's in, I don't. Not until he tugs the bag from my hand then pulls me into his arms. Something's changed, some shyness in him fading as he learns to trust me. I hope, I fucking hope, as he rests his forehead against mine with a sigh of relief. I feel it too, the unwinding of some deadly spring that's been coiling inside me for years.

"Thank you," he whispers hoarsely, such a hollow ache in his voice that it takes my breath away too. So I hold him tighter and will my love into him, try to send the same energy he gives to me when we're shifted, that red gold majesty that makes my heart hum. Maybe he feels it as he cuddles me closer, his stiff spine relaxing as I stroke his back. We kiss, and it's as natural as breathing, as being alive. It's everything a kiss should be and it's mine forever.

"Will you make me a promise?" I say, because if it really is forever then we gotta get it right from the start. I love him (holy shit, I absolutely do) but I won't put up with him sulking and growling and being scared of using words. "If you have feelings about me you need to sort through, don't lie. Don't tell me you're fine if you aren't. And don't hide it by shifting when what you know we ought to do is talk it out."

He nods, so I kiss him, to show him I mean it, to show him he's loved. "I'm sorry I did that to you," he says. "I promise, I won't do it again."

"I know you won't. And I promise the same to you."

"I just thought you needed to know what I'm really like."

"But you're not like that. Not through and through. That big, lonely, frightened animal is just one part of you. And I've done too much scary shit to myself to be scared off that easy. Sorry, honey bear, but you're going to have to deal with me from now on. I'm not going anywhere."

The truest thing I've ever said. Right now, I'd be happy if we never left the mountain again. Never gave up a minute of this magical serenity, this safety. Stone is my safety, my one and only. Wherever he goes, that's where I'll be, from this moment until forever.

NEXT

THE TRUTH ABOUT HOLLOWOOD
(HOLLOWOOD FALLS BOOK 4)

Book 4

The Truth About Hollowood

Between my rough childhood, my bad attitude, and the fact that I'm a monster, my life hasn't been easy. All I have left is my job, and this case might be my last. It's hard enough staying shifted twenty hours a day, watching other monsters get taken to pieces in the name of military science. It's ten times worse when my enemy hires the last man on earth I should be anywhere near.

The same man I keep meeting in that cheap motel, our meaningless encounters launching a full blown obsession. The same man who now means more to me than anything on earth. The man I'm willing to die for, if it means I can save his life.

But my instincts and Ronan's skills aren't enough to stop Hyperion's dangerous activities from spilling over into the valley next door. A little mountain town called Hollowood Falls. One of the strangest little towns in America, where mates are made by a powerful magic that reaches back into the depths of time. A place I've never been that somehow feels like home. A place worth fighting for.

No one comes out of Hollowood Falls unchanged. It's where we'll have to turn for help, to save them and to save ourselves.

PART ONE

BLAKE

One

The New Hire

I'm used to faking it. Pretending to be what I'm not. Pretending not to be what I am. Pretending that I'm not losing my shit when inside my head there's a five-alarm fire and no one at the wheel of the fire truck. Pretending to be normal when I'm actually a monster.

That's not a metaphor.

In fact, it's my job. Nothing makes people let down their guard like a dog. At least, that's the theory, and so far it's been pretty much true. That Romanian mob boss used to talk to me like I was a priest he was confessing to, which made busting him real easy. We're not going to have the same luck with Tanya Grange. I wonder if that's because she thinks she's doing the right thing.

I'm lying on my square of carpet in the corner of her office chewing on this thought when she snaps her fingers. I jump up like the well-trained security asset I pretend to be and go to her desk. She points to a place just beside it where I'm meant to wait until she gives the next command. She's been under a lot of stress lately and it shows, in her smell, in the tension around her eyes. Security has been a real issue this year, and I've heard her taking major heat from the people funding this fucking nightmare.

Because it is a nightmare. The kind that makes you hope there's a God so you can pray to Him to wake you up. There's no waking up from this hell. From watching monsters just like me get imprisoned, tormented, tortured, killed. Knowing that if she ever found out what I am, that I'd be the next one thrown into the fighting pit, or strapped down to the operating table, or... I can't think about any of that. Not if I want to be able to do my job. Not if I want to stop this.

So I sit and wait for her visitor to arrive. Another 'scientist' maybe, or one of the Belarusians in their expensive, badly fitted suits and brand new shoes, here to be misogynist while Grange grits her teeth and prepares her precisely targeted clap-back. They always crack, because she's always right. If they have second thoughts, I'm there to make sure they take their medicine.

She snaps her fingers again then gestures, flattening her hand and holding it palm down, the sign for me to lie down. I'm just settling with my head between my paws when the door opens and the guy I railed through the hotel mattress last weekend walks in.

Not while I was a dog, before you get all worked up. As far as I know, he doesn't know a thing about this side of me. I sure didn't suspect that the smooth-talking Irishman I picked up in the gas station parking lot a few weeks ago had anything to do with the Facility. I probably wouldn't have fucked him if I did. Probably, because he was without a doubt the hottest hookup of my life, with molten eyes and a gym-hard body and no hesitation in bed. Such a good lay that I asked for his number.

Grange looks at me sharply. Fuck, was I growling? My whole body is tense, the fur raised on my neck, my lips curling back over my teeth, my heart racing as the man (whose name I never learned on purpose) closes the door behind him.

"Please stay where you are, Mr. Wednesday," Grange says, getting to her feet. "My bodyguard gets a bit edgy around strangers."

"That's a fine looking animal," he replies in that peat-soaked brogue that makes my human brain sizzle as Grange leads me towards him. "Do you know the breed?"

"It's mixed. Too many pedigree dogs are inbred idiots."

Laughing softly, he puts out his hand and I sniff it, though I already know how he smells. Know that he likes to be held down and fucked hard until he begs for mercy, and I'm only too glad when Grange leads me back to my place beside her desk. Wednesday sits down across from her, plucking the knee of his tailored slacks as he crosses his legs.

"I've had a good look at your security systems, Ms. Grange."

"Tanya will do, Mr. Wednesday."

"Then please, call me Ronan. As I was saying, I can't see any obvious problems, but then the attackers wouldn't have been looking for an obvious failure to exploit. They'd be looking for something obscure, some glitch or loophole they could keep using."

"What's your next action?"

He exhales hard. "I need more information. I'd like to do a more concrete analysis. Look into every part of your security. For all you know, they've got a drone in a tree picking up your every transmission—"

"Impossible. The sensors on that perimeter fence pick up everything within three hundred yards."

"Underground as well?"

Her eyes widen briefly. "You think they tunneled under?"

"I'm not ruling it out," Wednesday replies with a shrug. "Somewhere there's a leak. My job is to find it and stop it. I'm not ruling out anything. That's the easiest way to miss an answer that's staring you in the face. At any rate, that's where I'd like to start. A full sweep of the perimeter, then work my way inwards."

"We can do that," Grange says, tapping her watch to bring up the calendar. "But you'll have to wait until tomorrow. There's a lot of difficult terrain to cover and it's too late in the day. I'll have the team log your physical signature now so you won't set off the sensors."

They leave the office, me at Grange's heels. "Can I ask why you've a dog for a bodyguard?" he asks as they walk, their footsteps ringing off the hard tiles. "Seems you'd do better with, you know, a human."

"This is a male-dominated industry," Grange says. "I don't want to waste time wondering if I'm safe around my own staff."

"Even dressed like that?" He gestures to her typical daily outfit of black cap, black fatigues, and zip-front jacket in mil-grade microfiber.

"How I dress has nothing to do with it," she replies without missing a beat. "Some men will do anything to gain an advantage. Of course, some men are just assholes."

Two
Security

P eople look at history and wonder how good people can tolerate doing bad things. I know how: by keeping their mouths shut and their heads down and hoping like hell that they live to see the next day. I've been on this job for six months, and it feels like I've never known anything beyond life at the Facility.

It has a name, some made up title about biological research. My crew thinks the less I know about a job, the better I'll be able to put up with it, and in the past that's been true. There's no easy way to put up with what goes on at the Facility, where people like me get taken to pieces to see what makes them tick. As if the truth about shifting is written in our flesh and bones, there for anyone to read if they look hard enough. Truth is, I don't know a damn thing about what made me who I am. If I did, I sure wouldn't tell these psychos.

In the security suite Ronan gives a sample of epithelial cells, then gets his body scanned in the pod. The team will build a signature to feed into the AI that monitors the system so it doesn't read him as an intruder. The Facility maintains a strict 'shoot first, questions later' policy, though thankfully the ordinance is just a dart filled with a drug to knock people out and scramble their memories. Hikers wake up in the state forest next door, at the bottom of a hill they don't remember falling down but close enough to the ranger station that they can find their way easily. Our first line of security is convincing people this place doesn't exist.

Grange snaps her fingers so I follow her and Ronan out of the security suite with its banks of monitors. This section of the Facility looks like any other industrial or medical site, with polished floors and pale beige modular walls, the nervous system of electrical and comm cables hidden by a drop ceiling. It smells like it too, a constant haze of ozone, chemical disinfectants, human sweat, and feces. The scent of Ronan's cologne and his salty skin sticks in my nose like a splinter, making my groin ache and my mouth water, distracting me from my real job of eavesdropping on his conversation. Thankfully the implanted microchip can pick up audio and my team aren't depending on me to remember.

"Do you have much turnover on your staff?" he's asking.

"Everyone knows they won't get a better deal elsewhere," Grange says. "I think we only lost two people last year, and none so far this year. We don't give them any reason to want to move on."

"Can't argue with job security. Still, this kind of work isn't for everyone."

"Our psychological profiling weeds out ninety-nine percent of unsuitable candidates."

"And that one percent?"

"I know what you're suggesting, Ronan, but there's no chance one of our team is the leak."

"That you know of."

"Mr. Wednesday—" she starts, in that icy tone that gets under every man's skin, but he holds up his hand to stop her before she gets going.

"You're paying me to find the hole in your security net, Ms. Grange. I'm not ignoring any possibility until I can rule it out conclusively. If Jews could hide themselves among the SS, don't tell me it's impossible that you've got a traitor in your midst."

He knows. He knows this is terrible and fucked up. And he knows there's a leak, a whistleblower, somewhere in the Facility. He's just as smart as I suspected, which means I can't meet up with him later this evening. We've all worked too long and hard to embed me, and I can't risk blowing my cover.

"Point taken," Grange says to him with a steely glance. "In fact, you should consider me your number one suspect."

"You say that as if I don't already."

They stop at the exit, where he and Grange both have to swipe their pass-cards to open the two sets of sliding doors. My dog body is registered system wide as the only thing on four legs that doesn't need to be locked up, and I follow them out to the foyer and then outside. Ronan's shoulders straighten as he takes a deep breath, freed from the claustrophobic atmosphere, the smell of chemicals. Out here, it's all cedar and soil, rotting wood and sprouting leaves and a hint of something from the next valley over. Some animal scent that doesn't match anything I know. I can't always smell it, just when the wind changes direction.

Today it's blowing in my face like the heat from an oven. Sensing my tension, Grange sets her hand on the back of my neck, a touch meant to remind me of my commands, her control. Grange's last bodyguard died when his collar caught on something and he choked, so I'm never leashed, being trained too well to disobey. At least, as far as she knows.

A big engine growls as a heavy vehicle crawls up the graveled driveway. Beneath the scent of diesel and grease I catch a big whiff of the other-valley smell. Grange's hand stiffens, her other hand going for the pocket where she keeps the whistle. She doesn't trust my training. Clever bitch.

The truck clears the ridge and rumbles past, on its way to the holding pens. They've caught something, and my stomach clenches in sympathy for what the poor beast is about to endure.

Grange lifts her hand as someone hails her on her cranial mic. Everyone in the Facility has an implant, and getting staff to consent to it is one of the reasons the job pays so well. "Send her in," she says.

Nala. My trainer. My last link with the real world. As I start trembling Grange makes soothing noises and strokes the back of my neck.

"What does your bodyguard know that we don't?" Ronan asks.

"Nothing important. He just knows it's time for his run."

"A big dog like that needs plenty of exercise, I expect."

"It's important to keep your assets in working order." An asset. An object. A weapon she keeps by her side. But even weapons need maintenance, and as Nala's white van pulls to a stop I can't hold back my whine of desperation.

"I'll be back at first light," Ronan says, one eye on me. "You have a good night." For whatever reason, he winks at me. Like he thinks I'll understand. Like he knows...but he can't. No way. Not a chance. If he was on our side, they would have told me. Wouldn't they?

As Nala gets out of the van, the animal part of me takes over, whining and shaking, craving the sense of safety I feel when I'm around her. Grange lifts her hand from my neck and when Nala whistles I trot to her. As she scratches behind my ears I rub my jowls against her legs like a cat.

"Miss me?" she says with a grin and not a hint of irony.

Like a drowning man misses dry land.

"I thought I'd take him over the state park and let him have a swim," she says. "I'll dry him off before I bring him back, don't worry."

"Not a fan of the smell of wet dog?" Ronan asks Grange as he fishes his car keys out of his pocket.

"Not exactly."

In the back of the van Nala clips me into a harness, the way all dogs should be in a moving vehicle. After all, I'm a valuable asset, and even a fender bender could send me through the windshield. As she gets behind the wheel I lie down and try to remember everything that's happened in the last few days, so I can file my next report.

Three

R & R

The state park trail is a hard run, mostly uphill. By the time we reach the point on the ridge where the fence has been flattened by a falling tree, I'm ready for a nap. But I know what's waiting for me, so we cross the property line then return downhill to the identical white van parked behind the old Sinclair gas station, on the road that leads to Hollowood Falls.

A place I've never been, though I've been living next door to it for months. Nala's told me it's a nice town, with lots of historic buildings and cute little stores, solar panels on every roof and smiles on every face. It's named for, you guessed it, a waterfall, audible to my dog's hearing as a distant hissing thunder. The weird smell comes from this valley as well, rolling down the hillside like mist and making my skin prickle even before I shift.

The van is stocked with whatever I need to rehumanize myself: sweats, jocks and socks, a pair of running shoes, deodorant and toothpaste, and a thermos of hot coffee, which is what I go for first. Dog food sucks, or at least it does when you know what you're missing.

'Speaking' in ASL and counting on the RFID lining of the van to hide Nala's keystrokes as she transcribes, I go over the events of the past few days, adding my observations to the audio that's been stored on the chip our team put into me to replace my Facility chip. All this gets added to a micro-SD card that Nala will send back to base by whatever means she has. I've never been told how, so that I can't ever tell. A layer of security that can't be broken, and I have a few fake answers ready if it ever comes to torture.

Like every minute in that hell-hole isn't torture.

When Nala gives the all-clear that we haven't been picked up by a drone or other surveillance, she gets back behind the wheel. She drives right out of the valley, down to the weird little subdivision called Cattail Crossing that some genius developer plopped down on the side of the highway. Technically it's part of Greater Municipal Hollowood Falls, leading to the unkind nickname of Coattail Crossing, because none of this would be here if not for that tourist hot spot in the hills. They know it too, because everything is named after it, from Hollowood Pest Control to the Fallsview Mall.

Rather than a big chain restaurant, Nala takes me to the same diner we always use. Built to look like a genuine train dining car, the place was here long before the suburb. The owners are hard-left off-gridders who don't even have basic cable, never mind wi-fi. When we walk in, the waitress is just hitting play on a VHS of the original 'Twin Peaks.' Total mood, and the waitress chuckles when I order coffee, black.

Is that all you're getting? Nala signs.

Not hungry.

You're seeing that guy again?

I need it.

She rolls her eyes. *You can't keep doing this.*

It's the only way I can keep going.

Blake...it's so dangerous.

You think I don't know that?

The waitress sets down Nala's plate of beans and cornbread, and though my stomach growls at the smell of normal food, beans are the last thing I want to eat before I get my ass blown out by Ronan Wednesday. Because I do need it. Worse than ever, my hand shaking as I pick up my coffee. Need him to make me feel like a man and not a wordless, helpless animal.

On the way down I took a blood sample and a swab, and as Nala starts the van I text the all-clear result to the number Ronan gave me. His test comes back a few minutes later. I don't know if he's fucking other people (I'm sure not) so we made a deal to check in. I don't have a problem with condoms, but I'm glad we can go without. I don't want anything getting between me and him. I want it all.

I have another couple hours before I'm expected back at the Facility. More than enough time to get to the cheesy old motel where we've been meeting, not far from the cheesy old diner. There's no tracker on the van but Nala's driving away almost before I have the door shut.

Though the building is old, the equally elderly owners put in a self-check-in kiosk last year, which means I only have to swipe my burner credit card to get a key. I choose the same room we had last weekend at the far end of the building, then regret it, then realize it doesn't make a difference. If I'm being watched, it's too late to do shit about it.

I text the room number to Ronan then take a shower, using up all of one of those little bars of soap. I miss showers, miss the feel of my own skin, the way the suds slide down my thighs. I trim my shaggy beard, then go for it and shave, half hard from the slick, deadly glide of the razor across my cheeks.

I wedge the door open then sit on the bed to wait, hoping like hell that I'm wrong. That the smells at the Facility confused me, that my dog eyes saw wrong. That I'm not involved with the one person in the world who could ruin not just my life but this whole operation.

Except I am. One look at him as he walks in and my doubt disintegrates. This is the very same man who looked me in the eye two hours ago and called me a *fine looking animal*.

Dropping his black duffel bag beside the door, he takes in my nudity in a glance as my dick hardens against my thigh. He approaches carefully, his nostrils flaring as his breath quickens. Both times we've met, it's been a silent battle of wills to see who kneels. Something in his slow movements, the way he's biting his lip, tells me what he wants.

"I don't have all day, you know," I say in a hard voice.

He takes a quick breath then starts getting undressed. Faster, fumbling with the fly of his expensive slacks. Damn right he couldn't have walked the perimeter today in those and that fitted turtleneck.

I'm sitting on the edge of the bed and as soon as he's naked I slide forward and slap my knee, like he's the dog. He stares at me a few seconds, his lips twitching, hands curling and uncurling at his sides. Then he steps forward and straddles my thighs. He's built but smaller than me, shorter and slimmer, his stomach almost hairless. Gripping his hips, I stroke my tongue up from his navel to the center of his chest. As he sucks in a breath I turn my head and scrape my teeth across his nipple. He responds with an open-mouthed grunt and a jerk of his hips, his dick slapping against my stomach. He grabs hold of my shoulders as I do it again.

"Just get on with it," he grunts.

"What if I don't want to?" I say, my lips moving against his skin. "What if I've changed my mind and I want to make you suffer for it? Make you wait all night."

His hands tense but he doesn't answer. If only I could take all night. If only I could play with him until he's out of his mind, then push him over the edge. I have something like ninety-five minutes, so I slide my hands down to grab his ass.

"Who am I kidding?" I say, leaning back to see his face. "I've been thinking about this all day."

"All fucking week, try."

I squeeze harder and he grunts, pushing back against my grip. If only he knew what this meant to me. Those first months on the case were brutal, until I said I'd quit if they didn't let me have some down time. Time I've filled with bad sex with men whose names I never wanted to know. I didn't want to know Ronan's name either, and now that I do, it's holding me back. Last weekend he was just a body. Now he's a whole person, the worst person I could possibly choose to distract me from the horror that surrounds me every day.

"I'm going to hurt you," I said, spreading his ass cheeks, spreading him open. "I'm going to fuck you so hard you'll never want to see me again."

"Good luck," he says in the same dry tone. "You'll only make me want it more."

Like we were meant for each other. Damn this life of mine, but if it's mine to live I'm going to do it on my terms, even if that means I have to lie to this man, hide who I am and what I know. I pull him closer, tilting my hips so my dick rides under his balls, the head stroking over his hole. He groans again and thrusts against me, his nails biting into my skin.

So much wanting, so little time.

I wet my fingers by shoving them in his mouth. He gets it, knows to work his tongue against the intrusion, let me gather up his spit. As I smear my fingers over his hole he arches back, asking for more. Last time we fucked like animals, kneeling on all fours. Tonight we're playing by my rules. He hisses, humping as I push a finger past the tight rim of his ass, again as I wrap my other hand around his dick.

"Fuck!" he says through clenched teeth as I add a second finger. "Later."

He barks a bitter laugh that turns into a deep, ragged sigh as I start to stroke him inside and out. Pinned between my two hands, his body moves instinctively, giving more, taking more. My wrist aches from being bent, but it's worth it for the look on his face, part pleasure, part pain as I shove in deeper.

When his face tenses like he's going to come I let go of his dick. "Don't even think about it," I say, twisting my fingers inside him. "That cum is mine."

He nods with a jerk of his head, his eyes tightly closed. Like he's not really into this and is just making himself do it. I know that feeling. Right now I don't care. He can stop me any time. He's smaller than me but he's built like a mercenary, and I bet he's got weapons. He could stop me if he wanted to but he doesn't as I add a third finger, twisting into his throbbing ass, his muscles sucking me even deeper.

Between the ticking clock and the heat of my need I can't wait much longer. He's gorgeous right now, his chest and face pink and dabbed with sweat, his fingers weaving through my hair, his dick sliding against my front, slick with precum.

"Are you going to be good?" I say through clenched teeth. He nods, winding his hips. "I'm going to fuck you hard. I'm going to cum in you. And you're not going to spill a fucking drop, are you? You're going to hold onto my cum until I say. Aren't you?"

He nods again, his mouth hanging open, eyes rolled back. He wants me as badly as I want him, and when I pull out he gasps.

"Get up." He climbs off my lap and I stand up, then walk him backwards until he hits the wall. He's even shorter than I remember, gazing up at me with something like surprise as I wrap my hand around the back of his neck.

"Turn around." He doesn't want to, his lips thin, his brow dropping. But he does it, lets me turn him and push him face first against the wall. "Stay."

I leave him long enough to grab the lube from the bathroom. Breathing hard, he flinches as I smear it over his hole and inside him. I wanted to fuck him like this but I'm too tall. There has to be some way to make this brutal, make him hurt. Make him think twice about seeing me again. He's not the last lonely man alive. I'll find someone else. Someone who isn't a threat.

Because I'm the security leak. I'm who he's been hired to find and stop. I'm his enemy, and all I can think of is how to get inside him. Not wanting to let him relax, I slide my hand around and take hold of his shaft. He hisses and goes up on his toes, his muscled ass cheeks clenching like he wants something between them. Good enough. So what if I have to crouch. I should suffer too, should want to never do this again.

One hand on him and one on me, I bend my knees and lean into him, pushing against his hole. He rises higher on his toes, his hands braced on the wall, his ass all mine. I take it, take him, pushing into him slow and unstoppable, letting go of his dick to get my hand under his chin, make him feel how totally I own him in this moment.

"Don't you dare come," I breathe as I start to move in him. "Not until I say. Not until I'm done with you." He nods as best he can, digging his nails into the wallpaper, twitching his hips in time with mine. He wants this, wants me to push him hard, make him work. Make him earn it, and does he ever, his legs, his whole body shaking from the strain as I slam into him. Suddenly he stiffens, grabbing at my arm, and I hold still.

"Good boy," I murmur, though I might be talking to myself, because every part of me wants me to go, go, fuck harder, get off. I want to want it more, want to come in him so hard he tastes it. He's breathing fast, and when I reach for his dick he's half soft. Not for long as I work him back to full hardness, his soft moan tugging at my soul. "Such a good boy, taking my dick just like I told you."

I thrust, shoving his shaft through my tight grip. Again, again, as he whimpers then hollers, stiffening his legs and pushing back against me, giving more than I knew he could give me. His ass fits me perfectly, the way his dick fits my hand, like this was meant to happen, like this is fate and all we did was show up and let it happen. Just when I think I'm going to blow my load, he cries out in something like fear. Then comes, thrashing back and forth, shoving himself onto my dick, his cum coating my hand and the wall.

"S-s-s...sorry," he gulps. "I'm sorry."

"Don't worry, baby," I murmur, clenching my teeth against my own climax. "I'll let you off with a warning. But next time, don't fucking count on it."

If Ronan thought that him coming would stop me, he's going to be disappointed. I want more of him, want to brand myself on him body and soul, make him give me everything. Want to make him come again, and again, and again, until he can't see, can't think, can't do anything but get fucked by me. I wanted to fuck him till he hates me but it's never going to work. So I'll make him want me more than ever, and then I'll break his heart.

Four

Come Down

I fuck him how he likes it: face down on the bed, his legs splayed, all my weight on him. His hands lie slack on the bedcovers, so I grip his wrists and stretch his arms wider, moving only my hips. I can't get as deep but it's worth it to feel his whole body surrender, to know that at last he feels helpless.

As his voice rises I stop moving, fighting my own battle. But he's too far gone, and he takes me down with him, the rhythmic clench of his ass around me breaking through my self-control as I come, biting his shoulder so I don't raise the dead with my shouting. It's everything I wanted and it's still not enough. Nothing will ever be enough to save me from the hell inside my head.

"Don't you let that go," I murmur. "You hold that cum in you, Ronan, like a good boy."

Fuck. I don't know his name. Except I do. Thankfully he's still high on his orgasm, and as I climb off him he groans, shuddering as he clenches his ass cheeks together.

"Don't make me fuck you again," I say, even though it's exactly what we both want. He shudders again, his hands knotted in the bedcover, and something twists inside me. Some ugly fist crushing out the last of the good. I fucked him like I hated him. I'm becoming the monster I feared. I shiver as the sweat cools on my back. "Time for a shower."

Facedown on the bed, he nods, then carefully rolls to his side and sits up. Physically pushing his ass cheeks together to hold my cum in him, he follows me into the bathroom. I didn't mean he had to obey, but now that he has, I'll get what I can from him before I have to go back to living the lie.

In the shower I make him kneel, then I back up onto his face. I can take it either way, and Ronan knows a few things about eating ass, his long tongue teasing me open, making me groan and arch my back to give him more of me as the water hammers on my head and chest, my dick so hard it casts a shadow. All the while I watch the water running down the drain for a smear of cum. I hope he doesn't spill it, I don't have time or energy to punish him for it.

I'm suddenly struck by thoughts of taking him over my knee and spanking him, turning his fair skinned ass bright red while he shimmies and wails. It pushes me to the edge and I turn around, leaving him with his tongue sticking out, but when I grab him by the hair he understands and opens his mouth to take me deep. Deeper, the water washing away his tears as I fuck into his throat, his whole body tensing as his ass threatens to open. But that's what I want, for him to let go, give in, give up. Be mine completely.

"Open up, you slut," I grunt through my teeth, and he does it, loosens his jaw and lets me all the way in, my cum shooting down his throat as he lets the rest of it go in a dirty trickle that disappears between my feet then spirals down the drain.

And then it's weird. I leave him in the shower to clean himself up, drying off quickly and getting dressed while he's still in the bathroom. He comes out with a towel around his hips to find me at the door.

"When can I see you again?" he asks.

"I'll let you know."

"Can't you give me something to hang on to?" The ache in his voice matches the ache in my soul. Is this mission killing him too?

"Next weekend," I blurt before I can think better of it. "But I'm not promising anything."

He doesn't quite smile but his shoulders drop as he relaxes. "I'll wait to hear from you."

I want to say a thousand other things, but it wouldn't make a difference, would only make this worse. So I say nothing at all.

As I start walking I ping Nala to come and pick me up. I don't know what we'll do when the bad weather returns. Hopefully we'll have busted this shit-show by then, but our team leader Curtis doesn't seem to be in a hurry. I don't even know what counts as enough information for them to make a bust. Curtis barely acknowledges me as it is, even though I'm the only reason we've gotten this far on the case.

As we drive I finish off the coffee and eat the sandwich Nala bought without me asking. I could eat two more. Or a steak dinner. No, what I'm craving is a double order of kung pow chicken from House of Jade, that Chinese joint in that skanky strip mall on the outskirts of D.C..

What I'm really craving is Ronan Wednesday.

That night, Grange watches Ronan through the surveillance array they embedded in the house they rented for him in Cattail Crossing. I don't know if she's looking for something in particular, or if she just wants to get a read on him. On the wraparound monitors in a room off the security suite, we watch him step around the unopened boxes of stereo equipment and other household stuff that litters the foyer and living room. The proof of a normal life, and I wonder if he ordered it as cover, or if Grange's company set it up.

He then takes a really long shower, standing under the stream of water as it cascades over his face. Trying to blank out his mind. I hope. I shouldn't even care how he feels. I shouldn't but I do, because I want to know if he's coping better than I am. I want to know if I'm enough for him. I can never be enough.

He puts on sweatpants then goes downstairs, where he drinks a meal replacement shake standing over the sink. That explains his ripped torso, but how can he not be starving? He downs a bunch of pills then goes back upstairs and flips open his laptop. To watch porn. This I don't have to guess at, the security camera over his bed picking up the screen so clearly I can see the expressions on the actors' faces. See him stroke himself vaguely through his sweats as he scrolls the page, clicking on videos then switching them off seconds later, until he abruptly slaps the laptop closed and shoves it under the bed, then goes into the bathroom to take a sleeping pill.

"Pathetic," Grange murmurs as he turns off the light and the feed dims. Fuck her.

Five

Observations

They call it puppy love and it's the fucking truth. It takes me over every time I see him. Every time I smell him, and I can smell him from two rooms away. Every ghost of his voice on the wind, every mention of his name makes my ears prick up and my mouth water and my heart accelerate. If I had to do this as a man, I'd never be able to pull it off. It's hard enough to not act friendly, to do what I've been supposedly trained to do and treat him like a potential threat.

He took five days to complete his survey of the perimeter. Now he's reviewing the infrastructure at Ground Zero, physically checking in on every sensor, camera, drone nest, and other security device around the Facility buildings, from the non-descript one story block that houses Grange's office and the security suite to the incinerator. Grange isn't meant to have anything to do with the 'research' side of things, just with managing the workforce, and I often wonder how much she knows about what goes on. If her bosses are anything like mine, she knows as little as possible. I'm still going to take her down.

The only place on site where Grange doesn't keep me beside her is in the gym. I don't think the little windowless room was meant for that but she insisted, so while she puts in her five miles on the treadmill and does her kettlebells I wait in her office. My team have talked about me shifting and using this time to raid her files, but thankfully they haven't insisted. I'm in enough danger as it is. And I don't want to think about how they'd treat Nala if I was caught.

I'm dozing on my carpet in the corner of Grange's office when the door opens. "As long as she won't mind," Ronan says over his shoulder as he walks in.

"Ms. Grange gave you top tier clearance, Mr. Wednesday," says Grange's PA Manfred, a weasely tech head from Heidelberg.

"Isn't that nice of her," Ronan says with a grin as he helps himself to a seat.

Manfred's pale eyebrows do their own workout as he decides how to deal with this mercenary. "She considers you a highly valuable asset," he says in his pinched voice. "Do you wish for a coffee while you wait?"

"No, but I'll go a tea if you have it."

"I will find out if such a thing is possible," Manfred replies. "Ms. Grange will be with you shortly."

As the door clicks shut Ronan's grin switches off. Sliding down in his seat, he covers his eyes, rubbing his temple with his thumb. I've been trained to stay put unless she commands me, but as he sucks in a hard breath and exhales shakily I get to my feet. He's in pain, mentally if nothing else, and before I can think better of it I go to him and nudge his knee with my nose. He looks up from under his hand and manages a thin smile.

"Fuck, what a day," he sighs. "No, what a week. I wish I'd known going in what I was up against."

He leans forward and rests his elbows on his knees, and just like any other dog I put myself under his hand. Like any other human, he starts to pet me, ruffling his fingers through the thick fur at my neck.

"You know what happens next, don't you?" he says softly. "Of course you don't, you dumb fuck. Shit, I'm sorry," he says as I tense. "I take it back. Though I know you don't understand a word I'm saying."

Except I do, my heart aching even as his touch sends shivers down my spine. I want to tell him everything. Tell him to get out before it's too late.

Tell him that I'm a danger to him, that the feds will take him down with the rest of the Facility. I want to hold him, tell him that it doesn't matter, that none of this matters. I want to fast forward to tomorrow night so I can fuck him until he forgets.

A soft whine escapes my throat. Gazing into my eyes, he frowns, tipping his head like he's studying me, but before he says anything more the door opens and Grange comes in.

"You know that's not a pet, right?" she says as she sits down at her desk.

"I thought it no harm if he's off duty."

"He's never off duty." She snaps and I go to her, lie down as she gestures.

"Awfully well behaved, isn't he?"

"Well trained," she insists.

"Either way. Usually dogs avoid me. This one acts like he knows me, the way he looks at me."

"All part of the training," Grange says in the same flat tone. "Trust me, he'd rip out your throat where you stand if I gave the command."

You go on thinking that, bitch.

"A proper judge of souls, is he?" Ronan says, back to his sharp self.

"I'm afraid I don't follow," Grange says with a hint of irritation.

"Anubis. The dog-headed Egyptian deity who weighed your heart after you died. Gatekeeper of heaven. Fed the sinful to the monstrous goddess Ammit. Like St. Peter but with sharper teeth."

Before she can reply, a message pops up on her watch. She frowns at it, then flips the switch under the top of her desk that makes the left-hand wall of her office slide open to reveal the bank of security monitors. Ronan whistles in admiration.

"Not my idea," she says dryly as the monitors come to life. "The last director of operations had a James Bond fetish." Most of the monitors show things Ronan would have already seen: hallways, exterior doors, the three main holding pens. One monitor on the far right shows an animal transport vehicle backing up to the open access hatch of one of the quarantine pens. Two handlers appear and open the van's double doors then skip out of the camera's line of sight. After a minute, a long snout appears, followed by the heavy head and shoulders of a full-grown black bear.

"Fuck me sideways," Ronan breathes. "Sorry, turn of phrase but is that..."

"There are plenty of bears around here," Grange says as the beast gingerly steps out of the van.

"And you've permission to hunt them?"

"We have the right to cull wild animals that damage our property."

"Doesn't seem fair, though, the poor bugger. How would a bear know when he's crossed a property line?"

"Immaterial," Grange says, watching intently as the bear begins to nose around the enclosure. "We have too much at stake here. If something puts our work at risk, I'm not going to think twice about stopping it."

"Shoot first, ask questions later?"

"Who said anything about asking questions?"

She's watched him every night this week and tonight is no different. That means I've watched him every night as he eats take-out or MREs then brushes his teeth and watches porn with the lights out, though he never seems to find anything that turns him on. I did that to him, or maybe that's just my arrogance talking, me thinking that I'm such a good fuck that he can't think of anyone else.

Tonight is different. Maybe he ate on the way, because he's been on the phone since he got home. "Where does he keep that fucking thing?" Grange mutters under her breath. Instead of watching in the security suite, she's kept the bank of monitors open in her office. My bed is in the corner of the same wall, so I have to watch from the corner of my half-open eye as Ronan paces his empty house. "That asshole, he's not even speaking English."

"We think it's Gaelic," Manfred says. He's standing at Grange's elbow, the flickering grey of the CCTV feed washing out his features so he looks like a skull.

"I don't like it. I don't like *him*. Why did they send me this asshole? Manny, I need answers."

"Jawohl." He just about salutes but catches himself. Grange isn't paying attention, her eyes following Ronan from screen to screen.

Answers. Grange is a woman who gets answers. And something tells me she's not going to like what she hears. Ronan meanwhile has put down his phone and is booting up his laptop. Not to watch porn but to write, though he tilts the screen down as much as he can so the camera over his bed can't see what he's typing. A few minutes later he stops to answer the phone though he doesn't say anything. He hangs up after a few seconds, then taps a few keys on the laptop. He closes it and puts it on the ground, then pulls a silenced hand gun out from between the mattress and box spring, presses the muzzle against the laptop and unloads three bullets into it.

"Wednesday, you son of a bitch," Grange hisses through her teeth as Ronan retrieves a different phone from between the mattresses. Holding the phone's screen an inch away from the wall, he begins to scan the room, starting with the baseboards then working his way around the window frame.

Grange taps on her watch then raises it to speak into the mic. "Are you seeing this shit? No, don't bother. I'll sort it out...You know what, fuck HQ. They dumped this asshole on me, they can deal with the clean-up."

Ronan has climbed onto the bed to scan around the light fixture. The monitor flickers darkly as he passes the phone's blank screen across the camera that feeds it. It darkens again then flares, a startling flash like lighting a strip of magnesium that washes the whole room, turning Grange's face stark white before the monitor fades to gray snow.

"That asshole! I'm going to fucking—" She chokes back whatever she was going to say, but her meaning is clear, her hands balling into fists on the arm of her chair, her jaw rigid with rage.

She's going to kill Ronan Wednesday. And I can't do a damn thing about it.

Six

Escape

I don't sleep that night. I can't, I'm too busy trying to think of a plan to save Ronan's life. Not because I've caught feelings, but because he's Grange's enemy. That puts him on our side, which makes him *our* asset. And I'm not going to let that bitch keep us from gaining an advantage.

"Run him hard," Grange says when Nala comes to pick me up the next day.

"Sure thing," Nala says as she palms a bit of jerky to feed me. She goes down on one knee and holds out her hand, but I don't move until Grange snaps her fingers. I try not to seem too eager, but Nala's my only hope of saving Ronan's life.

Instead of the diner she takes me to a chain restaurant on the far side of Cattail Crossing. The place is full of retirees there for the early bird dinner special, making us the youngest people here. Perfect cover for a deaf guy and his social worker, which is how we play this if anyone asks, and the hostess barely glances at us as she leads us to a two-seater booth near the bathrooms.

How much longer do they need me to keep doing this? I sign once she's gone. *Because it's getting really hard.*

No one said this would be easy, Nala replies.

You don't know what I'm going through. If they find out about me—

They won't kill you.

That's what scares me.

When the waitress shows up with our water, Nala orders a chicken salad. I point to the steak dinner, then watch Nala as she translates the choice of sides that the waitress recites, putting up my hand for the baked potato and steamed veg.

What's going on? she asks when we're alone again.

That guy. The new guy. Wednesday. They want to...Grange is going take him out.

Why do you care?

I look away, unsure how much I can tell her without her hating me. Nala touches my arm and I turn back to her.

Is that who you've been hooking up with at that motel? she asks. I nod once and she groans. *Are you crazy?*

I didn't know it was him!

And you didn't break it off?

I can't.

Does he know about you?

I don't think so.

Blake...you can't worry about him.

They're going to kill him.

That's why you can't get involved.

That's why we have to.

We?

He could be really good asset. He knows things I don't.

You think you can turn him?

He's a mercenary. Gun for hire. Not part of their world.

I don't know.

Please.

This time she's the one who looks away, shaking her head. *Curtis is going to freak out,* she signs.

I don't care. We can't let him die for nothing.

You don't know that's their plan.

Am I ever wrong? She doesn't answer. She doesn't have to, because I've never guessed wrong. *Nala, please. Let me do one good thing.*

Damn it…I suppose you want his address.

It'll save me some time. And it might be what saves his life.

We eat in silence, not because we're faking hearing loss but because she's furious. I don't care, or at least not enough to change my mind. Back in the van she pulls up the intel on Ronan's house, which the team has been monitoring from the outside thanks to a drone hidden in the tree in a neighbor's yard. *I'll find out from Curtis when we're planning to make a move,* she says as I study a map of the subdivision.

Thanks. What are you going to tell Grange?

I don't know.

Be safe.

Fuck you.

I'm sorry.

Save it, she says, her sharp motions putting the mood into her words. *I hope he's worth it. I hope he's worth what you're sacrificing.*

His subdivision is across town, but when she slows to turn onto his street I wave her on. She sucks her teeth but doesn't say anything until we're parked behind a strip mall a quarter mile down the road. Newly built, the houses back onto undeveloped land, a high chain-link fence dividing the overwatered lawns from the arid, rocky scrubland that stretches all the way to the foothills.

What are you doing? she asks as I kick my shoes off in preparation for shifting.

I can't just walk up to his door. He'll shoot me. Or pretend he doesn't know what I'm talking about. And what if we're wrong?

What if you're wrong?

I'll stake out his house for an hour, tops. Make sure nothing's wrong, then come right back. I wait for her to say more, but instead she chokes back a sob and puts her arms around my neck.

"Be careful," she breathes in my ear. "Please."

I nod, because I don't know what to say. Don't know if I have the strength to speak without breaking down. I need to keep my shit together or we're all going to die. If I know Grange, she'll make it hurt.

Sniffling, Nala climbs into the front of the van and shuts the curtain between us. I strip quickly, stuffing my clothes in the storage compartment where they belong. I have no plan. No idea how I'm going to approach Ronan. No idea how I'm going to get home.

I have no home. I have the Facility, and Nala's van, and whatever bone the bureau decides to throw me when this is all over. If I live.

I don't have a choice. I do, but I refuse to make it, refuse to give Ronan up. Grange will torture him, or worse, have someone else do it for her while she watches through her fucking monitors. And he'll either blab and ruin whatever scheme he's running, or hold out and...I can't think about that, not if I want to see this through. I don't mean the bureau's mission, I mean tonight.

Shifting hurts, the food churning in my stomach, the fear tensing my every muscle. I've never felt the pull of the full moon, and I wonder as I often do if that's just me or if the lunar cycle is a myth. I'm a fucking myth, a fantastical beast, an impossibility in the flesh. I'm not the only one.

I'm still settling into my dog-form when Nala gasps. "Shit..." She yanks the curtain aside and signs the one word I hoped wouldn't come up on this doomed adventure.

Wolves.

Seven

Cattail Crossing

No, no, no. Not possible. Not possible that Grange's slave army is operational. We'd have seen it coming. The whole point of the mission is to see it coming, and we fucking missed it. Nala has more to say but there's no time to say it, so I press my paw on the door release they installed so I'd never be trapped. Unfortunately, the door opens.

I don't want to do this. I don't want to find out the hard way what Grange's mercenaries are capable of. I've seen enough evidence in the shredded, bloody remains that get scraped off the floor of the fighting pits and shoveled into the incinerator. That's going to be Ronan in about five minutes if I don't get my furry ass moving.

Nala's talking, not with her hands but her voice, but I can't hear a word she says over the thunder of my heart. Trusting that she gave me the right intel, I hop down from the van. The smell of the asphalt is nauseating, but that could just be fear, because threading through the heavy scent of tar and rock dust is the trace of Grange's wolves, a raw, musky smell with a metallic tang of blood.

The sun is dropping behind the ridge to the west, drenching the clouds in brilliant gold as I scramble up the short rise behind the strip mall without looking back. The wolves' trail leads directly to Ronan's house across the stony ground, though the animals themselves have disappeared into the gloom of dusk. Keeping my nose down I move slowly, not wanting to seem a threat. Just a stray dog looking for a hollow to lie in.

Then I see them. Two long shadows stretched in the dirt a hundred yards away from the fence. Waiting for it to get dark, for the families to finish their backyard barbeques, for their kids to go to bed. I backtrack to that mound of boulders I just passed and lie down to wait. We worked so hard to get me embedded that I don't want to blow my cover until I can't avoid it. Maybe they're just wolves, bored of the state park and drawn to the smell of cooking meat.

As the sky fades to velvet blue the stars come out. The moon is past full and won't be up for hours yet, and despite my tension or maybe because of it, I'm halfway asleep when I sense motion in the black shadow where the wolves are hiding. Moving as quickly as I dare and staying well away from the fences so I don't set off someone's motion detector, I slink towards them, fighting against my every instinct to run away. Save myself. Save Nala, who's going to catch six kinds of hell from Grange for losing me, but the bureau wouldn't have assigned her to the case if they didn't trust her to know what to do in a bad situation.

Me, I have no idea what to do. Despite all the planning, the strategy meetings, the mentoring by those Pentagon spooks, we never accounted for me having to fight Grange's wolves in a public place. Because it's going to be a fight, I can trust my instincts on that.

I'm probably going to die.

Yet I keep going, creeping with my belly nearly on the ground, willing those beasts to keep their minds on the job. Ronan's house is a newish two story with a paved patio and sweet fuck all in the yard for cover. I halt, pressing myself to the ground, as the two shadows leap over the five-foot fence like it's nothing.

Damn, they're huge. I'm a big dog but they're full grown wolves, the biggest wolves I've ever seen, and this is the worst idea I've ever had. I should have walked up to his front door and confessed. Instead I'm going to try to stop six hundred pounds of teeth and fury from ripping him to shreds. I am definitely going to die, but somehow that's not enough to stop me from dashing at the fence and hoping like fuck that I can jump that high.

It's a near miss, my hind feet nearly catching on the top of the chain-link. I land hard, sinking into a crouch and wishing there was a shrub or a tree or anything at all between me and Grange's pet mercenaries as they whirl around, lips pulled back from their enormous teeth.

I might have just pissed myself. I don't have a fuck to spare as the wolf on the right launches itself at me, its jaws snapping. I fling myself out of the way and bolt for the front of the yard, which is not nearly far enough away. Without stopping to think I leap towards the house as the second wolf (or the first, who cares?) comes hurtling towards me. And then it's on, the worst game of tag ever, as I dash back and forth in his narrow back yard, barely dodging the wolves time and again, so close that I feel their breath on my heels.

Triggered by our movement, the lights flick on in the neighbour's yard, blinding me so that I run head first into the fence. The next second I'm breathless as one of the brutes slams into me, mashing me painfully against the mesh. The other wolf skids into us both and the two square off, snarling and snapping at each other as I fall gasping to the ground. Please, please let Ronan have heard us, let him be smart enough to know what it means, to know that his life is in danger.

The wolves have sorted out their scuffle. Something's wrong with my right ear, and with my ribs, a wicked pain stabbing my side with every breath as the killers advance on me, taking their time, licking their lips, all too aware that I'm beat.

If only I'd thought harder about this.

We could be at that lousy motel right now.

We could be together...

Something strikes the ground between me and my death. Again, a small, hard object that embeds itself in the turf, raising a puff of dust. By the time

I figure out that they're bullets, the wolves have vanished. A van door slams, then a vehicle peels away from the front of the house.

I should get up, run away, keep it simple. I did what I came here for, but the pain in my side makes it hard to even catch my breath.

"Hang on," Ronan says softly into his phone. "There's a third."

He thinks I'm a wolf. He thinks I'm his enemy. This morning, I was. Now I've changed the game, shown my hand. Blown the mission in the name of maintaining my access to casual sex. Or something. Nothing makes sense any more. Not the mission or my role or the world. As Ronan slips the safety on his handgun, I summon my last strength and shift.

It hurts like fuck, like I'm being sawn in two as my injured ribs try to reassemble themselves. Ronan gasps, a choked, horrified sound. "Jesus, Mary, and...you are shitting me."

My right ear has started to throb. My hand comes away sticky when I touch my face. I crack open one eye to find him squatting by my head staring at me, his gun hanging limply.

"I'll call you back," he says then tosses his phone aside. Sighing, he runs his hand across his face, then returns his gun to his shoulder holster and starts to feel me over.

"Only lost a bit of your ear, it looks like, you lucky bugger," he mutters as he feels down my legs. "A cracked rib or two. Could be worse."

Easy for him to say. Getting shot didn't hurt this much. I try to speak but can't manage more than a hoarse moan.

"Stay here. I said stay," he whispers intently when I try to sit up. "I'll get you something to wear."

He must have been ready for this sort of thing because he's back seconds later with a black gym bag. He uses wet wipes to clean the blood off my face, then sticks a dermal analgesic patch over the ache in my ribs.

"I haven't any shoes that will fit you," he says as I struggle into a sweatshirt.

"Doesn't matter," I mumble. "Let's just get out of here." Before someone comes to finish the job.

While I put on the sweatpants he gets out a brown bag that looks like a MRE package. He slips his phone into the pack then carefully seals it, but not before I get a whiff of the contents.

"Acid?" I croak. He flashes me a tight grin, then puts out his hand to help me to my feet.

"Hope you don't mind walking," he says. "There's no chance of me risking starting that car."

"I'll manage."

Once we're a few houses away, he pulls out yet another phone, which takes a thumbprint, a retina scan and a voice command in what must be Gaelic to activate.

"Pinball?" he says to whoever answers. "Yeah. You'd not believe me if I told you. No, there's no going back. Doesn't fecking matter, does it? I got you some take-away, though. Yes, very tasty." He glances at me from the corner of his eye. "You want me to drop it off? No, it'll keep until tomorrow."

The house we're passing has a landscaped front yard full of rocks. Ronan hangs up then sets the phone on the sidewalk, picks up a fist-sized stone and smashes the phone. Hard fragments of plastic spray across the concrete.

"You go through many of those?" I ask as he drops the remains into a pouch like the first.

He snorts a laugh. "I should have bought stock."

I'm about to ping Nala when something stops me. Some cold prickle of intuition creeping up from my tailbone that suggests we're both safer if I don't activate the connection. The same feeling that told me to get the fuck out of Kiev in '21, or that night in Damascus when I stole a jeep and started driving south without knowing why.

As we pass through the gates of Ronan's subdivision onto the main road, a fire truck screams past, headed towards the column of smoke rising from the general area of the strip mall where I left the van.

"Is that your doing?" Ronan asks.

"Not on purpose."

I can just manage to walk, thanks to the dermal patch and my weirdly fast healing. I want to run, because that feeling that's saved my ass in the past is screaming at me to make sure Nala's not—

Of course she isn't. She's totally fine. It's the grease traps in the donut shop that are on fire, not the white van, but as we get closer to the mall it's obvious that the smoke is coming from behind the building. The whole parking lot has been cordoned off by yellow police tape. Three cruisers, a fire truck, and an ambulance block the road, their lights reflecting off the billowing smoke. A cop with a glow stick is directing traffic around the obstruction. Other officers are in the donut shop interviewing the workers and the clerk from the convenience store, so we join the locals loitering around the news van pulled up to the curb.

Putting on a drop dead perfect Midwest drawl, Ronan falls into conversation with the camera man. Thank God he's functional, because it's all I can do to stay upright. I've fucked up everything. Did exactly the wrong thing and got someone killed. Not just a team member but Nala, my best friend, at times only friend in the bureau. Feeling sick, I retreat to the edge of the crowd.

"Well, could be worse," Ronan says as he joins me. "Apparently there are no casualties."

"That almost *is* worse," I mutter.

"Maybe she got out in time."

"Or maybe she's in E Block right now."

His face hardens. "Grange wouldn't do that."

"Like hell she wouldn't. Nala's not my first handler."

"That's murder," he says softly.

"No shit."
He flashes me a dirty look "Don't go being smart with me."
"Sorry. You're right. I just hate this. I hate it so fucking much."
"Forget about it. Let's get away while we can."

Eight

Hollowood Falls

The night slips away from me, turning into an endless waking dream as I follow Ronan around town. I know I need to snap out of it but between the pain in my ribs and the horror it's all I can do to put one foot in front of the other. He finds us a car, and coffee and a pack of THC gummies that I'm tempted to eat all at once but don't because I need to keep my shit together. Don't I? Or am I allowed to let him take care of me? I don't deserve it. I'm putting his life in danger every second we're together.

Leaning my head against the car window, I watch the highway markers flick past and try to think of the next step, but all I can think of is Nala in the pit. Grange watching on her fucking monitors as the holding bay doors grind open and—

He corners hard, and I clamp my hand over my mouth as my stomach threatens to eject the remains of the steak dinner.

"Do I need to stop?" he asks. I shake my head, terrified beyond words of the darkness outside this little bubble of steel and glass. I don't want him to stop the car, I want him to drive it to the edge of the world and then over into oblivion.

Instead he takes us to a little motel that could have fallen out of a time warp, all white stucco and streamlined corners, the flickering neon cocktail glass on the sign painting the mist in trembling red and blue. Or maybe it's my eyes, because every bit of me aches as he heaves me out of the car.

The motel room matches the vintage exterior, with avocado green carpet and a secret fortune in teak furniture. He sits me on the bed and pokes and prods my ribs until I push him away.

"A shame we couldn't have taken you to emergency," he says as I swallow the pain meds he gives me. And then it hits me: I don't know what those pills were. I don't know shit about him. I've been telling myself he's on the good side, but what does that even mean? I've thrown away the rulebook because of one mistake.

I've never been the right fit for this life. Took the bureau's offer because I didn't have a choice. Didn't know what else to do other than accept this violence and fear and a sudden, ugly death. I'm no better than those mindless killers in Grange's stinking pits, an animal being used for a job that humans aren't brave enough to do themselves.

"Do you feel alright?" Ronan asks as the bile rises to my throat again.

"What did you just give me?"

"Tylenol."

"Show me the bottle."

He passes me a silvery blister-pack with two pills missing. "Are you not feeling well?" he asks.

"Where are we?"

"Hollowood Falls."

"That's the next valley over!" I yelp, springing to my feet, my heart ready to run. "Are you trying to get us killed?"

"You don't know Hollowood," he says in a smart-assed voice like we're in a James Bond movie.

"Like hell I don't," I spit, wanting to slap that smirk off his pretty face. "Why do you think I'm here?"

"I don't know," he says, getting up slowly. "Why are you here?" He takes a step towards me, the cold tension in the movement making me take a step back, then another. "What are you up to, living under Grange's nose like that? Who ordered you to get me into bed?" This last he says through his bared teeth, but I'd hate me too if I was him.

"I didn't mean to," I blurt as my heels hit the wall. If he's armed, I'm dead. Unless I shift and rip his throat out. Throw away my last shred of humanity, and God knows I'd deserve it. "I mean, that wasn't part of my mandate. That just kind of happened. You don't believe me, do you?"

I'm the taller of us but he somehow looms over me as he presses me against the wall, his hands braced on either side of my head.

"Why were you in my back garden?" he asks in the soft voice of a lover even as his ice-cold eyes are tearing me apart.

"I was trying to save your life."

He goes completely still, then with a sigh he closes his eyes. Frightened by his quiet as much as by his rage, torn between these relentless feelings of fear and longing, shame and hopelessness, rage for the suffering I've witnessed and endured, I reach for him, putting my hands on his waist.

He sucks in a breath. "Bad idea."

"I don't care." I grab his shirt so he can't pull away. "I want to forget what just happened. I need you to make me forget."

"You've a broken rib. You're in no shape—"

"Please," I say, pushing my hips forward to rub against him. "I need it. I need you. I need you to fuck me like you own me."

Another conversation we've never had, always going with our instincts. From the first time I saw him, I trusted him, without knowing why. Put my job on the line and my brain on hold, trusted him with my life. Now I'm here in the most dangerous place in the world for me to be, about to let this man do terrible things to me, but I can't help but want it. Want him to take away the horror and the shame, burn it out of my mind with the heat of his desire, make me want to stay alive.

"Can I at least know your name?" he asks, studying my face.

"It's Blake. Is your last name really Wednesday?"

"On my mother's grave. Now get on your knees, Blake."

He puts his hand on the back of my neck but I'm already dropping to the floor. Handling himself through his black sweats, he pulls me nearer, shoving my face against his front, but when I put my hands on his thighs he pushes me away. "I'll tell you when you can touch me."

He strips off his sweats and boxers without breaking our gaze. I want to look away, but something tells me that's exactly what he hopes, that I'll break the rules as fast as he sets them. Another silent negotiation, the way it's always been.

Holding me by the hair, he strokes himself over my face, smearing my cheeks with precum. I want to grab him by the hips and take him deep but I'm not ready to find out what his punishments are like. This is punishment enough, to make myself so vulnerable, to let myself be used like this when all reason and logic should stop me. I won't stop, can't stop wanting this, as I open my mouth and let him have me.

Deeper, making me flinch as his dick strikes the back of my throat. "Is this what you wanted?" he purrs as the tears spring to my eyes. I nod, or try to, my moans stifled by his thick shaft, my body trembling with breathless tension.

"Just as I thought. Now suck."

I do it, my hands knotted in the fabric of my sweatpants to keep from touching him. I want to please him, prove myself to him, be worth his time and trust. I want this to be what he wants too, to forever play this game, this back and forth, this dance of violent intimacy. He starts to move, pulling out to give me just enough air then winding back in, clutching my head in both hands as he fucks my mouth.

More than once he stops and pulls out completely, stroking, sometimes slapping his dick against my face but not letting me suck. My hands are locked behind my back because I can't stop wanting to touch him. It's everything I wanted and I still want more, want him to own me forever.

Forever's too much to ask for as he tenses with his oncoming climax then pulls me away, holding me by the hair in a wrenching one-handed grip as he milks himself off onto my face. Still panting, not letting go of me, he crouches down to lick his cum off my face in long, wet strokes, then feed it to me straight from his tongue.

"Swallow it."

Of course I do. This is what I wanted. All of this and more but I know better than to ask for it. I'm his to command, so as he gets up I stay where I am, kneeling on the floor, my dick throbbing, my lips bruised, my tongue swollen, my brain turning inside out as Ronan Wednesday pulls a gun out of his bag and points it at me.

"Now. Start talking."

PART TWO

GRAEME

Nine

An Uninvited Guest

Hollowood Falls: the place is magnetic, I swear to fuck. My husband Evan spent ten years barely speaking to his parents, yet we never once moved further than a six hour drive away from his hometown. I didn't even notice, I'm so in love with the bastard. And I always will be.

You've got to excuse me in advance. I'm a mouthy fucker. But I speak from a loving heart, I swear. It's only that growing up with a malignant sack of shite for a father then spending six years in the SAS has left its stamp on me. You've been warned.

There's a lot about Evan's hometown that makes me want to curse. The way Evan's father puts the wind up him every time they're together. The shocking absence of vegan food to be had in a town that's a leftist enclave running on green power. The fact that I used to think I'd left strange things behind. Turns out I went and married one.

Don't get me wrong: I love that man, with all my heart (the bits Pierce hasn't infiltrated, mind) but when I said for better and for worse I didn't know that his worse involved being a werewolf.

That morning I wake up alone, which is strange because I have two husbands. Alright, technically I only have the one, but ever since his fated mate moved in... That was a difficult weekend, I won't lie. Learning the truth, meeting Evan's family, meeting Pierce, the man he ought to have married instead of me. Who's ended up with him regardless, thanks to me being broad-minded and Pierce being really quite a dish and helpful as anything around the house, and…

Look, we're making it up as we go, the three of us. Whatever we're calling this, it's unusual for there not to be at least one or the other with me come morning. Most nights are a game of musical beds, depending on who feels like having Evan wrapped around them like an octopus.

No matter how happy he seems in the day, he's been coming apart at night, unable to game or sit through a movie but too agitated to sleep, no matter how hard we fuck him. When he does sleep, he wakes in terror from nightmares he refuses to tell us about. It's breaking my heart but he's a grown man and I can only be so big an arsehole to him. I love him too much.

They're not in Pierce's room either. I've got to give that man credit, because we more or less turned his bedroom, which was our old spare room, into a fuck-den, complete with restrains built into the bed and a great big mirror at the foot. He's never once complained, bless him.

I find him downstairs making one of his herb teas in the clear teapot we got him for his birthday. Evan is slumped on the couch swaddled in a blanket, poking at his phone, the screen's light flickering over his face.

"Did he have another of those dreams?" I ask Pierce under the hissing of the kettle.

Pierce tips his head toward the patio door. Cracks spider-web across the glass from an impact point about the height of a wolf's shoulder.

"He didn't. In the house?"

"Check out the floorboards." Long claw-marks score the hardwood from the foyer right through to where Evan leapt. Head first into a double glazed patio door.

He's burrowed deeper into the blanket and doesn't move when I sit by his feet. "How's your head?" I ask.

"Fine," he mutters.

"Bullshit."

"I said it's fine," he says more sharply, swatting at my hand as I tug the blanket.

"Gray, give him a break," Pierce says, swirling the teapot. "It's just a few bruises."

"Could be a concussion. You know those don't always show up right away." But I'll say no more about it. I'll just be sure Ev stays awake for a few hours. Something rank is in the water, as my mammy would say. I can't let my guard down.

"What the fuck does he want?" Evan mumbles.

"Who?"

"My dad. He just texted. I do not have the energy for his shit right now."

"We should all take a day off," Pierce says as he steps over the back of the l-shaped couch with a trio of mugs. "Put your phone on mute, drink this, and ignore him for an hour."

"No, because then he'll call," Evan says, struggling upright as Pierce hands round the tea. It tastes like hot peppermint sangria but is apparently a sterling liver tonic, and I sip it and think of other worse tea I've drunk. Like that jail in Syria where it tasted like the camel dung fire it was brewed on.

"Ugh..." Evan sets his tea on the coffee table then slumps into the corner of the sofa again, one arm over his face. "No, Dad, I don't know where the fuck my brother is," he groans. "Why does he ask me this shit?"

"Maybe because last time Chase went missing, he ended up here?" Pierce says from behind his up-bent knees. As Evan grunts a reply, a flicker of movement draws my eye to the rangy werewolf who has just leapt over the back fence and is approaching the broken patio door. Fucking Hollowood Falls. That place never lets you go.

Evan meets his brother at the door in the back of the garage. Chase Culver is the twink version of his elder brother, with a tumult of messy curls and a taste for big hairy men. A bit of a tosser but he's got a good heart and has been doing better now that the Culvers aren't estranged.

He comes in dressed in a pair of Pierce's old jeans and a t-shirt, looking around like he's never seen the place, though he spent two weeks last year sleeping on our sofa. He has a nylon dog harness and gets his phone out of the pouch attached to it.

"None of you guys have seen Stone?" he says as he perches on a kitchen stool.

"He's not off hibernating somewhere, is he?" I ask.

"It's too early for that," Evan answers curtly. "Chase, what's going on?"

"I don't know. But he's been gone all week. That's a long time for him. I'm worried that he went, you know, over there."

"He didn't go down the other valley, did he?" Pierce asks, his face paling.

"I asked him not to, I swear," Chase replies as Evan drops onto the couch with a groan.

"So he's finally been arrested for trespassing? Serves you both right. Come on, Chase, I thought you'd settled down. Now you've got him imagining all sorts of bullshit too—"

"It's not bullshit!" Chase says sharply.

"Prove it."

"Okay, I will. How's this?" He climbs over the couch and shoves his phone at Evan, who takes it and starts to scroll through the article.

"This isn't for real," he mutters as a video starts. "This isn't...fuck!" He drops the phone on the coffee table like it's on fire. The video keeps playing, the output of some medical imaging device, a full body scan of a werewolf in the midst of shifting, gray and ghostly but so viscerally real I swear I can hear the cells of its body slipping and sliding over one another.

"We gotta go," Pierce says in a wavering voice as he backs away from the couch. "We gotta get out of here."

"They're not coming here," Chase says, retrieving his phone.

"Doesn't matter," Evan says in a matching shaky tone. "We gotta get back to the Falls. Now." He throws off the blanket revealing a wicked bruise on his shoulder and another on his cheek.

"I fucking knew you'd hurt yourself," I say, as he jumps up from the couch and follows Pierce out of the room. "And would someone mind telling me what the fuck is going on?"

They explain on the way to Hollowood Falls. The more I hear, the more I understand their urgency. Why Pierce didn't pack any nice clothes. Why Evan asked if I had any small arms hidden about the house. Bloody good thing I did, because we are up against an army.

Ten

Special Ops

In a way it explains everything. The strange sounds from that valley. The medical-green buildings scattered here and there with no other sign of life. The tragedies that dog this little village in the Colorado foothills, the accidental poisonings and odd disappearance of entire families.

"The state forestry department was already planning to shutter the wildlife research center when that fire happened and all the records were lost," Chase says as I thumb through screenshots of classified documents. "It was the '70s so the government hadn't gone all in on computers yet."

"And when did the Hyperion Group buy the land?" I ask.

"It would have been in '94, if they were part of that first numbered company."

Hyperion, those filthy buggers. I'd left the armed forces half because of their rotten opportunism, only to find them popping up again to ruin everything I've made for myself. Not if I ruin them first.

It's their sort of scheme, too: vilely capitalist, driven by dark money and appealing to the world's worst aggressors, people who trade weapons and drugs and human lives to the highest bidder. If they'll sell mine workers and women, why not brainwashed, blackmailed, medically traumatized werewolf mercenaries?

Pierce is driving because it's the only way all four of us fit in the VW. Wincing, Evan twists in the passenger seat to glare at his brother sitting beside me. "Chase, how did you pay for all those FOI claims and lawyers and shit?"

"I've got money," Chase says with a one sided shrug.

"Since when? You haven't had a job in...ever."

"Started a small business," he mumbles, looking out the window.

"Doing what?"

Chase glances around the car, his cheeks hot. "Can we not talk about this right now?"

"No, actually I want to know. You're not dealing drugs, are you?"

"No," Chase retorts. "Jeez, no. I started an OnlyFans."

Pierce bursts out laughing. Evan's glaring at Chase with a look borrowed straight from their father.

"And what does Stone think about that?" I ask.

"That we should be charging more," Chase replies with a cheeky grin.

Evan gasps, shocked beyond necessity. "You're kidding. The both of you?"

"Turns out a lot of people like to watch guys banging in a forest."

"You do it outdoors?" he yelps. "But hikers... forestry workers... your cousins..." He wrenches around to point at me. "If I ever, *ever* find out you watched—"

"Ugh, please!"

He rounds on Pierce, who's snickering to himself. "And you—"

"What did I do?" he says innocently.

Evan sinks in his seat. "Chase, if I find out you're lying to me—"

"Not about this," Chase replies, more serious than I've ever seen him. "Not about Stone."

"Is he really, you know, down there in the valley? With them?" Pierce asks, and the weight of each word lays heavier on my conscience. I could have stopped Hyperion ten years ago. I should have, and then this might not be happening.

"I don't know where else he could be," Chase says, and there's no mistaking the tense emotion in his voice. "I've been up and down that mountain fifty times. They're just gone. Him and Grandmother."

The Hollowood boys startle, the car weaving as Pierce's head jerks around, Evan staring at his brother in horror. "Did you say—"

"Yep. This is it, bro. They crossed the fucking line."

I've seen that fixed expression before, on soldiers faced with the moral necessity of their duty. Chase is a twit, but he's family. He matters to Evan, so he matters to me. Hyperion doesn't know what it's messing with.

No one knows. Not Pierce or Evan, not a one among them knows the truth about me. I didn't want to reveal it to anyone ever again. But when you're born like me, you've a sense for when the truth can no longer be hidden. A truth that keeps me silent as our car leaves the highway and begins to climb the switchback county road that leads to Hollowood Falls.

As we near town, I mentally review it not as a quaintly underserviced tourist village but as our field of operations. Situated high amid the foothills, the town has only one road in and no roads out unless you count the rugged trails through the state park. The rare metals in the soil and the rocky landscape itself make cell phone service patchy at best, texts often arriving days late, calls disconnecting without warning. The worse sort of place for a modern conflict.

"Pull off at that petrol station ahead," I say to Pierce as we pass the turn off for the state park.

"We've still got half a tank."

"Just do it. We'll get water and such, treat this as the emergency it is."

"Right. Sure."

I send Pierce into the little shop to stock up on basics and an emergency kit or two if they have them. The town is hidden by the bends in the road, the quiet forest stretching off in all directions, and as I top up the petrol I try to savor the calm before the storm, this moment of uncomplicated peace.

Until my military-grade paranoia reminds me of the ever present danger of fire with this much standing timber, these many wooden homes. Wells are uncommon in Hollowood as the local water is highly alkaline and unpleasant to drink. Most households get by on rainwater, stored in great steel tanks on the high side of their properties. No fire engines, no ambulances, no permanent staff at the ranger station. The Dew Drop Inn however pumps well water for its pool and gardens. Sutherland's Dry Goods also has a well, and I keep up my cataloging of our assets and weaknesses as we roll through town, until we pull into the busy parking lot of the building known as the Lodge.

A century and a half old, the Lodge is yet another log building, with a wide sweeping roof and a main room that seats two hundred and fifty people. Behind in the poky little offices, the elders maintain the village archives, among them ancient books that now and then exhibit odd behaviour. My name is written in one such book, though everyone I've asked claims that they don't know who added it. I'm outlined with an octagon, to show I'm Evan's spare, and not 'fated' to mate him like our Pierce. A gambit I've accepted at face value, as they've taken our marriage. God knows I'm proof that anything is possible.

One of the Culvers' younger cousins Raven is out on the deep veranda that wraps around the building, loitering with their boyfriend Marcus at the top of the wide wooden stairs. A distant relation of Della and Reid Osier and their son Baz, Marcus is another oddity, fully human though his history belongs to the town. His parents once lived here, but disappeared while on route to the east coast to visit family. Barely an infant, Marcus was rescued from the site of the crash then lost to the adoption system for most of his life. Until Hollowood drew him home, by luck, coincidence, or by the unprovable but inescapable fate that rules this valley and its ancient bloodlines.

His wee enby-friend River belongs to a separate branch of the wildly tangled tree. The pair wave to us as we get out of the car. Chase takes the stairs two at a time to join them and they fall into quiet conversation.

"I really hoped Stone would calm my brother down, not pick up his bad habits," Evan says to me as we unload the boot of the car.

"They're good for each other," I say. "And he loves that big man of his. You Culvers don't like to let go."

"Nope, we sure don't," he replies with the first smile he's had for hours. I lean over and kiss him on the unbruised side of his forehead.

"Be careful, love. I don't want to see you get hurt."

"Fingers crossed, right?"

It's going to take more than luck, but I let it go as I follow him inside. I've been here for weddings, Thanksgiving, Halloween, and May Day, which is quite the do for the townsfolk. I've never seen the Lodge like this, with the main hall dark and quiet, no bunting or flags hanging from the mezzanine, no long tables groaning under the bounty of homemade foods, the casseroles and meatball stews and venison, with a token salad for me off to the side.

We carry on to the offices, where a dozen or more people have gathered in a long boardroom whose windows look out at ground level. Evan's father comes to hug Pierce, shake my hand, and ignore his son.

"Sorry if this is taking you away from something important," Mr. Culver says to me.

"This *is* important. My brother-in-law is missing."

Mr. Culver's chest swells, his shoulders rising as he glares at Evan. "He's what?"

"Isn't that why we're here?" Pierce asks. "Because of Stone?"

"Yeah, what's going on, Dad?" Evan asks.

"Where's your brother?" Mr. Culver asks him as if he hadn't spoken.

"I don't know, outside somewhere." Mr. Culver's eyes harden, then he shoulders roughly past Evan and marches out the door. "Nice to see you too, Dad," Evan says in a small voice.

"Fuck him," I murmur. "Let's find someone who knows what's going on."

"You mean like those guys?" Pierce asks, nodding to the two men at the front of the room presiding over an assembly of Hollowood's first families. The pale, dark-haired fellow in tactical black is sketching the valley system on a portable whiteboard. The other man wearing prison-grey sweats sits in a folding chair to the side, his broad head hanging between his shoulders, his grey-blue eyes tracking mournfully across the room.

"Do you know them?" I ask Pierce quietly.

"Nope."

I do, and I'm still considering whether to make it known when Blake Nyland's gaze meets mine. "Don't worry," I say in a carrying voice that has all eyes on me as he sits upright. "I haven't the authority to arrest you anymore."

The other man jams the cap back on his marker and turns to him. "Is there anything else you'd like to tell me?" he says in a quiet Galway lilt. "Starting with who the fuck he is?"

"You want to tell him?" Blake says to me with a false little grin. "I'd hate to misrepresent you."

I ought to mind my own tongue, but fuck Blake Nyland, that disobedient cur. "This is why you got taken off that case, you know? For holding grudges."

He glances at the ring of silent faces. "You can tell Wednesday everything," he says with another false smile. "Yours is the only opinion that ever matters, right?"

"Sit your arse down, Nyland," the other man says sharply as he goes to get up. Blake freezes, then sinks back down with a whipped expression. Good.

As the other man turns to the board again the door opens behind us and Chase and his father come in, followed by Marcus and River. They take seats around us as the Irishman draws a blue x on the upper hillside near Chase and Stone's cottage.

"As I was saying, our agent Icarus—"

"Hey, that's me!" Chase says. "Oh shit! I wasn't supposed to tell them, was I?"

"Tell them what, Chase?" his father asks as everyone turns in their seat to look at him.

"I've kind of been...I mean, can I tell them?" he says to the man at the front. "You know, that I'm working for you?"

"*Are* you working for me?" he asks with a quick frown.

"Yeah, I'm Icarus."

"For fuck's sake, Chase," Evan groans.

"I'm not lying."

"Then why doesn't he recognize you?" Mr Culver asks.

"Because we've never met face to face. I just transfer data."

"Can you prove it?" the man says evenly.

"Everyone's on my ass today, aren't they?" Chase mutters as he gets to his feet. He goes to the front of room and whispers in his ear.

"You're shitting me." The man tosses the marker aside. "Is there anyone here that isn't in this mess up to their blessed eyeballs?"

"Depends who's asking." I say as the others begin to whisper among themselves. This meeting is getting out of hand. If Blake Nyland is involved, I need assurances that he's not going to fuck it up. I need to know who I'm being asked to trust.

"I can't expose these people to that information," Irish says with a funny little smirk that must get him slapped quite often. "But I can't avoid telling *you*. Can I?"

"Not a chance."

"Alright, let's take twenty minutes' break," he says to the others. "We'll reconvene at fourteen forty."

With Blake at his heels, he follows me and the Culvers out of the board room and into what resembles a schoolroom from a museum, with a chalkboard and a roll-down map of the world and a row of green-legged desks up the far side. I was hoping Mr Culver wouldn't tag along but I can't say no to my father-in-law. Particularly not when he's built like a superhero with the ability to turn into an apex predator.

We help ourselves to the hard chairs scattered in the center of the room. "Alright then," I say to the stranger before everyone has properly settled. "Who the fuck are you and who put you in charge?"

Eleven

Hyperion

"My name is Ronan Wednesday. I'm on loan from MI5, trying to soak up the flood of oligarch money that got yanked out of the UK. Top brass didn't think to let me know there was another man in the field," he adds tersely, glancing at Blake slumped in the next chair.

"And you?" I ask him.

"FBI, but same. I've been at the Facility for months trying to set up a sting."

"Months?"

"Undercover."

"Do you mean as a guard?" asks Evan.

"You could say that."

"He's a dog," I say, already bored of his head games.

"Look, it doesn't matter what the history is between the two of you, we don't need to resort to insults," Mr. Culver says as the others start to mutter.

"It's not an insult," Blake says tiredly. "It's true. I'm only half human."

"You're that big black dog, aren't you? The one that's always with Mockingbird," Chase says, bouncing out of his seat like a schoolkid with an answer at the ready.

"That's me."

"Oh my god, it's so nice to finally meet you! I mean, not really because..." He gestures at our grim expressions. "Is she okay?"

"We don't know," Wednesday says when Blake doesn't answer. "Her vehicle was destroyed but it might have been by her."

"Oh my god. And what about Stone?"

"Stone?" Wednesday asks.

"My mate. Big guy, big beard, sometimes he's a bear."

"They brought a bear in a few days ago," Blake says.

"I knew it! Dad, what are we going to do? We're gonna get him back, right?"

"You don't know that's where he is," Evan says.

Chase whips around to glare at his brother. "Unless you know more about this than me, which you fucking don't, you can shut your—"

"Boys, give it up," Mr. Culver says sharply. Chase checks himself, then bolts from the room.

"I bet you expect me to go get him," Evan says to his dad.

"He's your brother."

"Yeah, and I'm his keeper. What an honor."

"Evan, this is not the time—"

"Of course it isn't." They hurry from the room still griping at each other, leaving me with Wednesday and Blake.

"Now that we have that nonsense out of the way," I say, "I'd like to have a wee chat with the two of you military men about our mutual enemy, the Hyperion Group."

Wednesday's eyes widen briefly, the only sign he recognizes the name. "Mutual enemy? Isn't that a coincidence. Too bad I don't believe in coincidences. Who are you and who are you working for?"

I relax, putting my foot up on the nearest chair to break the interrogative mood. "At the moment I'm not working for anyone but myself. My brother-in-law has been kidnapped by thugs I spent the better part of a decade trying to destroy. I walked away before the fight destroyed me, and now I wish I hadn't. Wish I'd died on that hill, you ken? Because then I might have stopped this from happening to the people I love."

"And where do you know this arsehole from?" Wednesday asks with a nod towards Blake.

"From when he fucked my commanding officer then stole my fucking jeep."

Jerking upright, Blake throws up his hands. "Those two events were totally unrelated," he blurts.

"That's not how it looked from the wrong end of a court martial."

He swallows his comeback, slumping down again as the fight drains out of him. "I'm done," he says dryly.

"You the fuck are not—" I start, doing my damnedest not to jump out of my seat and choke him into obedience.

"I don't mean with this case. I'll see it through, whatever it takes. But I'm done getting used like this."

"You volunteered."

"Not for this case," he says wryly. "In Syria, yeah, and I thought I could handle it. One way or another, they've been holding that over my head ever since."

"Ask for a discharge."

He laughs hollowly. "And deny them of one of their greatest assets? I would if I thought they'd let me go."

"They can't keep you against your will."

"They already do."

Wednesday is silently inspecting his shoes, sneaking glances at Blake now and then. God help us, am I the only man on earth who doesn't feel the lure of Blake Nyland? And is it so wrong of me to wonder how I can use their push-pull attraction to our advantage?

"Look, my history is just as sorry a tale," I say, "and telling it is a waste of time while my brother-in-law and your partner might be going through

God knows what. I'm prepared to trust the both of you. Even you, Nyland. But if you cross me again, I won't mess around. I'll just shoot you dead."

I believe everything they tell me. Mainly because it's too wild for anyone to invent, from the pharmaceutical cocktail that prevents the kidnapped werewolves from reverting to their human form to the girlboss supervillain and her hide-out on an artificial island in a manmade lake. The months of undercover work as Tanya Grange's bodyguard have done a proper number on Blake, who only speaks when Ronan prods him and otherwise glares at the floor like he wants to burn a hole in it to jump through. I almost feel bad for the bugger. I feel worse for Ronan, who's had to put up with him in this mood.

I know how my boys get if they go feral for too long. Once or twice Evan's nearly reverted during sex, on heavy nights in Pierce's room, and forgive me but I slapped it out of him. A little impact play finds its way into our sex life often enough he didn't take it personally, and as for me, I won't take any chances. I put up with enough as it is.

Not put up with, that's the wrong way to think of it. I fully accept who Evan is, and Pierce as well, and you can't help but feel sorry for anyone who goes through what they do, who lives with such a weighty secret. The fact that I fell for Evan, out of all the men in the world, says a lot more about Hollowood's so-called fate than I'm ready to admit.

"So you really didn't know that he was embedded there?" I ask Ronan as we erase his chalk diagrams of the Facility buildings from the blackboard.

"The last prez broke a lot of interdepartmental links," he replies. "I bet you anything there's a paper dossier in my temporary mail-slot back in DC with full intel. It's funny that you know him too."

"Mil Sec seems to pass him around like a useful bit of gear. When I met him, he'd already been on five continents."

Ronan glances at Blake who's waiting by the door, prodding at the bandage wadded over his right ear. "I don't think they know what it does to him," he murmurs.

There it is again, that softening of Ronan's tense alertness when thinking about Blake. A gain or a liability? A question for later as we return to the ballroom where preparations are going full tilt. Hester and Rayne, two of Hollowood's eldest citizens, sit at one end of a long table cleaning hunting rifles, while Mr. Culver explains a nylon dog harness like Chase's to a group of volunteers. At the back of the hall, the kitchen blazes with light and noise as the usual crew of retirees gets to work on their standard fare of beefy casseroles and barely drinkable coffee that I will inevitably have three cups of in the next two hours for some masochistic reason.

Pierce breaks away from Mr. Culver's audience and hurries to meet me. "Thank fuck you're back. Ev's losing his shit."

"Now? Of fucking course. It's fine, I'm not mad," I say as Pierce frowns. "Tell me what happened."

He exhales slowly, preparing himself. "Has he ever told you about the time he and I went down that valley?" he says, quietly moving us further from the others.

"Sort of."

"Right, because you only found out he's a shifter a year ago."

"He said you two got into some trouble when you were kids. He got stuck somewhere and you had to help him out."

"Me and a small army." He glances around at the Hollowood folk in hunting flak, the table loaded with weapons. "We used to dare each other, right? Who would go farthest, who would touch that tree or whatever. One day, when we were really deep, we saw a building. Just a shed, and I dared him to touch the wall. Something spooked him and he fell into... I don't know what it was. Like a building with the roof cut off. A huge round pit too deep for him to jump out of, with reinforced edges and these big steel doors like in a mine or something."

"Were you wolves?" When he doesn't answer I take his hand. I hate when this effervescent man is so still and stuck for words.

"I had to leave him there," he says in a panicked whisper of confession. "I had to go get help. There was nothing I could do on my own. But I couldn't get to him or talk to him, and I wasn't sure he knew what I was up to. I had to leave him in that pit, and I don't think he's ever forgiven me."

"Don't be daft. What else were you to do? He can't hold that against you."

"We've never talked about it, but that's when I decided I had to get out of the Falls. Get away from everything to do with this place. I had to leave him in that death trap, Gray. I..." He trails off, his face ashen, his hand sweating in mine.

"It's alright, love. Where is he?"

He leads me past the kitchen to the cozy little study where outsiders are shown the less occult artefacts of Hollowood's history. Evan is curled up in the musty armchair, his knees around his ears, his hands inside his sleeves, but when he sees me he struggles to his feet and gives me a hug.

"Did you call Dr. V?" I ask as he plops down again.

"Can't get a signal," he rasps. His eyes are red, and his lips from chewing on them. This is hitting him harder than I expected. But I didn't know then what I know now. Fucking secrets, standing between us, making us believe what can never be true.

"Perhaps you ought to stay here," I say, pulling up one of the light chairs. "If you're feeling poorly you'll only make bad decisions."

"They need me."

"We'll be fine."

"What do you mean, *we*?"

"Did you think I was going to sit this out?"

"You don't need to get involved."

"What I do is not for you to say, love. And did you forget what I was doing before we got together?"

He sits forward so our knees intersect. "I just don't want to see you get hurt," he says in a sad voice that reminds me of his chaos muppet of a little brother.

"You never mind me. I can take care of myself."

"Well, now I kind of have to come. Don't I?"

"Don't ask more of yourself than you're able to give. Pierce told me what happened when you were young."

"You told him?" he hisses at Pierce lurking by the door.

"Someone had to," Pierce replies. "At least now he understands why you're messed up."

"You're not messed up," I say firmly, taking Evan's hands. "It's called trauma. Don't blame yourself."

"I have to help my brother."

"You won't be much help if you have a panic attack out there," Pierce says, and I wish I could tell him to hold his tongue. This is no time for realism, not when we're trying to bring Evan back from the brink.

"I'm good," Ev says, giving me a weak smile. "If you're with me, I'll be good."

"As you like."

He slides forward and leans in for a kiss. The last kiss we might get for hours. The last kiss we might ever have, because confidence and hunting rifles aren't much of a match for Hyperion. Yet I can't stop the Culvers and their kin from carrying out their extrajudicial raid. I can only go along to make sure it doesn't go to shit.

"I'll catch you guys out there," Pierce says. He has a sense of when to leave us to ourselves, and as the door swings closed behind him Evan's hands tighten on my shoulders. As he arches against me I lean into him, my knee resting on the seat between his legs. I love this man more than I knew

I could love anyone, and the thought of losing him to Hyperion sparks a wildfire in me.

I need to fuck him. Or suck him or have him take me. Mark this last moment of safety, go into battle knowing what we're both fighting for. He wants the same, grinding his cock against my thigh, sucking at my tongue, clawing at my clothing. We have only a moment, but before I decide how to use it he pushes me back then slips off the chair to kneel in front of me.

"Please, Gray. I need this. I need you."

"Your family—"

"Then say no. If you don't want to, say no."

All that protects us is a dusty lace curtain covering the window in the door. But I can't refuse him, can't leave him this distracted wreck, jumping at shadows and mournful with longing. I know him too well, know how my refusal at a time like this can wound him worse than anything.

And forgive me but I want it too, want to let go of this wearying tension, this terror seeping into my bones at the thought of the dangers ahead. Want to feel wildly alive one last time, in case this really is the last time. He clings to my waist, his face pressed against my front, his breath seeping through my clothes. When I touch his head he looks up expectantly.

"You're a filthy fucker, Evan Culver. Don't ever change." As he groans in relief I turn my body so my back is to the door, then let him inch my pants down my hips to get at my cock.

I've never known a man so obsessed with my cock, though let's not pretend it isn't an impressive sight. He tongues me slowly, wetting me all over with a soft, tickling stroke as I resist the temptation to grab him by the hair and bury myself in his hot mouth. I'd likely kill him, or at least knock him out cold, but time is not on our side.

"Come on, love, I thought you needed your mouth full of my cock. So get to it."

He answers by opening his mouth and taking me deep. Such a sweet mouth, and I let myself go with the feeling, the heat and the slippery tension and the way my toes curl when he sucks me hard. I want it to last forever. I have maybe five minutes before someone comes knocking, and no matter what other kinks I cultivate, exhibitionism isn't on the list. Filthy talk, on the other hand...

"Are you going to swallow all my cum like a good boy?" I say. Nodding, Evan moans around me, the vibration and movement sending shivers down my thighs. "You'd better work harder than that for it. I want you choking on me. Totally mine. All day and all night." If he lets me, I'll go on all night. Call him my slut, my fuck-toy, my pretty little hole. I don't know where it comes from or why, but it drives us both wild. "Fuck, yes. Like that. Show me you want it."

His eyes rolling closed, he sucks me deeper, his cheeks red from his breathless effort, his free hand straying to his own cock shoving at the front of his pants. I'm tempted to deny him but he needs the release, the full-body tonic of endorphins and dopamine to bring him back from the edge of terror.

"Go on, then," I grunt. "I want you stroking yourself when I come. I want you to come with my cock in you." He's already yanking down his sweats, and as he takes hold of himself I start to move again. He moves in time, rising up on his knees to give me more. Suddenly he stiffens, his hand working furiously, his climax catching him without warning.

That does it for me, and choking back a shout I come, holding him by the hair as I spill into his mouth. I let him go and he sinks back on his heels with a drunken smile. My devoted husband: happiest when he's full of me.

Twelve

The Mission

As we're about to leave the room, I hear voices from deeper in the building, Mr. Culver's baritone and Ronan's lilt. I shoo Evan further from the door as they pass.

We catch up with them as they survey the great hall, where the citizens of Hollowood have split into teams, with two humans in hunting flak for every wolf, who'll be equipped with a harness and a tracker.

"This is all very impressive," Ronan is saying to Mr. Culver as we edge around them.

"It's something we've had to think about all our lives," he replies. "So what kind of support can we count on from your side?"

Ronan frowns. "Support? For an unlawful raid on private property? Never mind that it's a military grade facility."

"So are we."

"You can't think I'm going to let this go ahead in good conscience," Ronan says, incredulous. "People could get killed."

"We're well aware of that."

"That's not the point. Are they prepared to do time for armed assault? And don't you dare call this self-defense."

"What would you call it?"

"How about trespassing, forced entry...hey, I'm not done talking to you!" he says, dashing after Mr. Culver as he heads for the doors. "I am authorized to use force, you know."

Mr. Culver turns so suddenly Ronan nearly collides with him. "Do you think that's a good idea?" he grates, his chest swelling.

The room falls silent. Ronan takes a healthy step back as everyone turns towards the little drama. "Fine. I can't stop you," he says, "but you can't stop me from calling this in. What my team does with the information is out of my hands."

"So you're a snitch?" Chase says sharply.

Ronan licks his lips, his eyes slowly tracking around the room. "I'm an officer of the law," he replies in a thin voice.

"Do you think what they're doing is lawful?" Chase replies. "Kidnapping? Torture? All the shit you were sent here to stop, in other words. So why haven't you done anything about it yet? How long do we have to keep living like this? If you're an officer of the law, enforce the fucking law."

"That's not how it works, Chase," Mr. Culver says quietly, taking his son's arm as the others' attention wane. "He needs warrants, due cause."

"Exactly," Ronan says more steadily. "To go charging in like this violates the whole principle of the law."

"But if you happened to see illegal activities somewhere, even if you didn't lawfully enter, you could obtain a warrant, right?" Evan asks him.

He looks about the room again, stopping on Blake, who Pierce is showing how to wear the nylon dog harness so it stays on while you shift. The bugger's going back in.

"You're set on doing this?" Ronan asks the Culvers.

"The wheels are in motion," Mr. Culver says grimly, gesturing around them. "It'll take more than you to stop us now."

Ronan stiffens, his hands curling at his sides, then relents. "So be it," he says, his shoulders sagging. "But the minute I think you've crossed a line or lives are in danger, I'm hailing HQ and calling in the big guns."

"Good to have you on the team," Mr. Culver says, clapping him hard on the back. "Now what about your friend?" He nods towards Blake.

"He stays with me."

After much back and forth, the canteen manager Ginger has accepted my natural authority on the matter and started buying proper tea, and I request a last cup before we deploy. Evan's too edgy for coffee so we head outside to the veranda to get away from the ominous mood.

The Lodge sits at the top of the road, the little town of Hollowood Falls stretching down the mountainside, its houses tucked amid the fringes of the forest that blankets the valley. Sutherlands' Dry Goods and the few smaller shops to either side of it have stood on that lot since the town was founded, their wooden siding bleached silver by fifteen decades of weather.

As the clouds split, sunshine floods the valley, the pollen in the air glittering like a million tiny stars. Standing behind me at the railing, Evan puts his arms around me, resting his chin on my shoulder.

"It's such a pretty place" I say.

"It's stuck in a time warp," he says, his chin poking my shoulder. "Plus you'd starve to death if we lived here."

"Aye. We'd be growing our own produce."

"Everything else we'd have to order from that Whole Foods on the other side of Cattail."

"And the winters are shocking."

"And my dad lives here."

"So once again, that's a no to ever moving here."

"You said it." He kisses the side of my neck and I set down my tea on the broad railing to turn around and kiss him properly. He tastes of our sex, my skin ground into his very pores. I don't want to lose him to those demons next door and it makes me kiss him desperately, as if my kiss is his protection, as if I'm saving his life.

This is what ruined Blake. This desperation, this unswerving devotion to one singular person that makes you abandon common sense and integrity, loving someone with so much feeling that you put duty second. I can't let my heart cost us everything.

"I wish we didn't have to do this," Evan murmurs as the sunlight fades.

"Amen."

We head back inside to retrieve my bag from the boardroom. Mr Culver is at the whiteboard with Blake and a few others, and excuses himself to join us.

"You don't look very good," he says to his son by way of a greeting.

"Gee, nice to see you too, pops."

"I don't expect you to get involved in all this."

"Why wouldn't I?"

"I know you don't get along with your brother."

"But he's still my brother. I don't get along with you. Do you think I'd leave you to rot in that hellhole?"

Mr. Culver runs his tongue over his teeth, weighing his words for a change. Mrs. Culver has schooled them both soundly for being the cause of most of their own problems by speaking without thinking. "That is not what I'm implying," he says, his voice tense as he reins in his emotions.

"I know you don't give me a lot of credit, but I'm doing my best. I love my brother. I'm not going to abandon him."

"Alright, but I want you near me at all times."

"No way," Evan says with a laugh. "We'll kill each other. I can't take orders from you. We can barely be in the same room together."

"I'll mind him," I say before Mr. Culver unloads on his son, who's only speaking the truth. This won't be the first time I've inserted myself in their pointless bickering, and right now we don't have time.

"You just be careful out there," he says to Evan. "I want you back in one piece."

"I'll do my best."

"That's all I've ever wanted." Blake calls to him and he strides away without another word.

His face taut, Evan watches him go. "For a minute I thought he was about to break his streak and tell me he loves me," he mutters.

"Let's save our miracles for when we really need them."

Thirteen

Reunion

No hunting party would set out this late in the day, but Blake has been AWOL from the Facility for nearly twenty-four hours. We need to assume that time is running out between now and whenever this Tanya Grange makes her move.

While Ev disappears to try calling his therapist once more, I make myself useful, loading comm gear and first aid kits and thankfully very little ammunition into the jeeps parked out front. Despite the prevalence of guns in Hollowood households, the residents steer away from making them a fetish as I've seen in other small US towns.

I half expect Mr. Culver to make some grand speech from the Lodge veranda, but he simply goes from team to team, speaking quietly to each. Once the jeeps have gone, our three teams head down the road to Sutherlands' Dry Goods, to take the little known trail that leads from its back lot.

Myself and Evan are paired with Evan's aunt Honey, whom I've never met in her wolf form. Blake and Ronan are accompanied by Mr. Culver, with Blake as the four-legged team member. Pierce will track for Truegood Sutherland's daughter Joy, who's as accomplished a hunter as a human as when she's a wolf. She's paired with Baz Osier. Not quite nineteen, he's promised his parents not to shift.

"They get shitty about it because I lose my locs," he says in the gravelly voice of a young man new to adulthood. He runs his hand over the faint nap of hair on his brown scalp. "Got to start all over every time."

"Is that the same for your father?" I ask.

"Yup. Going on six years for him."

"Is that so? I've been meaning to ask, is your name short for Basil?"

"Nah. Basquiat."

"As in the artist? I've never met so many people with peculiar names as before coming here."

He frowns. "What's so weird about being named after an artist?"

"Nothing, nothing, only doesn't your last name Osier mean Willow?"

"Yeah, so?"

"Basquiat Osier...willow basket... Sorry! I couldn't help myself," I say as Evan groans.

Baz eyes me coolly. "No problem, Graham Cracker."

"Oooh!" I press my hand to my heart. "That hurt but I'll take it. How about we call it even?"

"I'm sorry about him," Evan says as Baz shakes my hand.

"S'cool," the young fellow replies, showing his teeth. "You can't help the hand fate dealt you."

As Pierce starts laughing, Evan shoves me aside. "Can you dial it back, you Lothian shitbag? You too, Platter," he says, rounding on Pierce snickering behind him.

"Hey, don't look at me. I'm named after dishware."

"That's something else I've always wondered." I say, mainly to keep from laughing as we start down the road again. "Of all the names you could have been given, why Evan?"

He pulls up, perplexed. "I don't know. You'd have to ask my folks."

"I'm going to because honestly, what have we got?" I count them off on my fingers. "There's Pierce, Chase, Stone, Leif and Dawn, River, Honey, Basquiat and Truegood, which I admit aren't things but are unlikely names. And then there's Evan. I mean it suits you, but *Evan*?"

"I said I don't know! I didn't pick it, did I?"

Mr. Culver has stopped to watch us so we hurry to rejoin them. By the time we reach the group I'm sweating under the close-fitting Kevlar, my shoulder holster seeming heavier with each step, but half of that is from fear. No matter how well you train, no matter how many clever scenarios you've devised to get in and out of trouble, the field of battle can burn all those assumptions to the ground. These people aren't soldiers, they're hopeful volunteers in a half-formed militia that never truly expected to be called up. Some of them might well die in the next few hours. Hyperion don't fuck around. People I love might die, and there's not a fucking thing I can do to stop it.

As we near the old general store Blake's head snaps up. He presses his fingers to a point behind his ear. "It's Nala," he says to Ronan in a stunned voice. "How did I not pick up her signal until now?"

"Probably because the service here is brutal," Chase says. "Who's Nala?"

Blake glances at Ronan for permission then signs a word. Chase gasps, his eyes lighting up, and the pair of them start a rapid fire conversation in ASL.

"No shit," Chase says as Blake wraps up a long description. "That explains a lot."

"Not to us," Evan says with a pout. "Let's start with when you learned to—"

Chase cuts him off with a pointed look and a sharp gesture. "No one needs to know that."

"Forget it, Ev," I say as he goes to argue. "The less said the better."

"But—"

"The less said the better. Are you daft?" I mouth the word *surveillance* and Ev's eyes fly open.

"Really?"

"From here on you'd best assume the worst."

Blake is listening intently to the signal from his transdermal implant, signing as he goes.

"Do you know where that is?" Ronan asks Chase.

"Sure do."

"Where are we going?" Evan asks as Chase starts down the alley between Sutherlands' and the neighboring store.

"Nowhere special," Chase replies over his shoulder. "Just a hole in the ground."

In single file we follow Chase along the trail up through the woods, the humid air thick with tree sap, the birdsong muted as if before a heavy rain. When the trail branches north I recognize our destination but say nothing. Everyone in Hollowood knows about the rockfall, where time and erosion caused a rift in the mountainside, a deep crevice one barely sees until one's about to fall into it. Chase himself had to be rescued from it after Granny's funeral last year, a messy business I begged out of, only having found out that I'd married a werewolf the day before and not feeling up for a challenge. What I wouldn't do to go back to those easy days before I knew, when I thought I was the only one keeping an impossible secret.

As we near the great standing boulders that mark the crevice, Chase whistles, a perfect imitation of a bird we hear in Hollowood every day. The same bird answers back but in a higher register. Chase wolf-whistles then dashes up the last hundred yards of the trail, Blake on his heels. As they reach the cleft in the rocks a Black woman in close-fitting tactical gear steps out from behind the bigger boulder on the left. Pushing past Chase, Blake pulls her into a tight hug.

"I'm so sorry," he gulps.

"Don't say another word about it," she urges. God help us, it's another dislocated Brit, her accent that of the child of ex-pat Jamaicans who'd brought her up in the East End.

"How'd you get away from them?" he asks as she steps back. She signs to him, Blake nodding along with a shocked expression.

"So now what?" she asks. "Are these his people?" She points her thumb at Ronan.

"Nope. Local folks."

Her mouth falls open. "What the hell? Why would you involve them?"

"It's complicated."

"Never mind complicated. I'm gonna call Curtis."

"We can't call it in," he blurts as Nala grabs her phone from inside her vest. "Don't you remember? Facility protocol states if someone shows up with a warrant all the animals are to be euthanized."

"Fuck!" Chase blurts. "Why did he have to go down there? I told him he was being dumb. Big dumb show off. It's all my fault." He scrubs the looming tears away with the back of his hand as a grumble passes through the teams.

"It's no one's fault," Mr. Culver says, putting his arm around Chase's shaking shoulders. "But we we're not going to take any chances. We'll get him back as soon as we can. Him and anyone else in there. Blake, you said there's a few pens attached to the main lab?"

"Plus the ones on the island. High profile cases they've been working on for a while."

"What's a while?" I ask.

"Longer than I've been there. But I don't know a lot about them. She leaves me in a quarantine room whenever she goes in. Can't risk them picking up any diseases."

As Mr. Culver begins to question him, Chase beckons his brother aside.

"I was going to come along to be useful and stuff," he says, twisting the straps of his harness like he's wringing its neck, "but I don't think I should."

"What do you mean?" Evan says, frowning. "Are you backing out?"

"It's just that I'd do anything to get Stone back."

"Isn't that a good thing?"

"You don't get it," Chase says through his clenched teeth. "I'd do *any-thing*. Me." He taps himself on the chest. "Think about what I'm like on a good day. Right now I'm desperate. I have exactly zero brain. I will fuck this up, I just know it. So don't make me go."

"It's alright, Chase," I say before Evan starts to argue with his brother. I'm in no mood for a Culver brother showdown, not with their pushy father in arm's reach. "If you're this wound up you'll only be in the way."

"Yes. Exactly. Thank you for saying that. See? I can't go."

"Fine," Evan says tiredly. "You're right, you do just get in the way."

"You could wait here," I add brightly as the tension between them ratchets up again. "If we need help, you'll be able to pick up our signal from this location better than they can at the Lodge."

"Cool, I'll do that. And I promise not to fall in the hole, bro." He gives Evan a brotherly punch on the shoulder. The same shoulder that met the patio door this morning. With a hiss of pain Evan doubles over, clutching the bruise. He straightens then punches his bewildered brother on the same spot.

"What the fuck?" Chase whines, rubbing his arm.

"Just get the hell away from me," Evan growls.

Those fucking Culvers. This fucking town. One way or another, Hollowood's going to be the death of me.

PART THREE

BLAKE

Fourteen

Down in the Valley

Graeme Harkness, of all the luck. He's even better looking with a few years on him, with that sprinkle of grey hair and without that Freddy Mercury moustache. Even with the moustache, I wanted to fuck him so badly in Syria I let his CO rail me instead. Stupid, stupid, stupid, and I should have gone to jail for what happened after. The relief I felt when I got shipped home and not locked up is nothing compared to my gratitude to the universe that Nala is alive. It nearly makes up for knowing that Ronan Wednesday wants me dead.

Every time close my eyes I see that gun pointed at me, and his cold, blank expression as dizzy, fuck-drunk, unarmed and humiliated, I told him everything. Not knowing if he was my ally or my killer. Every deplorable detail of the debt I owe the State Department, every horrific thing I'd seen on the Facility's monitors and operating tables. That shook him a bit, but he didn't lower the weapon until I was hoarse from repeating myself. And from sucking him off, which was everything I wanted and the worst thing in the world. Back and forth, up and down, heaven and hell, and me in the middle again.

Meeting the Hollowood folk softened him up a bit. And Nala, who's pretty strong proof that I'm not full of shit. She and Ronan have mapped out the Facility well. As Grange's security czar, Ronan even did us the favour during his survey of sabotaging several cameras and other sensors, providing us a blind corridor,

Used to navigating these arid woodlands, the Hollowood folks move quietly down the hillside. Evan Culver chews his lip and now and then grunts in pain but otherwise keeps pace, at least as well as I do. Apparently he threw himself at a patio door this morning. The bruise on his face confirms it. The walking wounded against a global network of criminals with the combined budget of several small nations, and if only this was a movie and not my life. I don't have the strength to battle dragons.

When we reach the valley floor we take cover in a hollow ringed by shaggy old cedars whose fallen leaves soften the stony ground. As people break out canteens and energy bars I sit beside Nala.

"Was that your plan all along?" I ask. "To go up in smoke?"

Grinning, she waggles her head. "One of my plans. I just had that old feeling, you know?"

"Yep. Like the way I'm feeling like this is the end for me. Not that something's going to happen today but that this is the last job I'll take."

"What are you going to do instead?"

"I don't know. I'll figure something out. If I have to do time for what happened in Syria, I will."

"That has to be cleared from your record by now."

"We'll see. We have to live through this first."

Nala hisses, shaking her head. "Child, why did you have to remind me?" She takes a long drink from her slim canteen.

Ronan stands on the far side of the hollow, talking to Mr. Culver and now and then glancing my way. "I'm glad he's wasn't killed," I say as he laughs behind his hand at something Mr. Culver said.

"Do you think he would have been?" Nala asks, offering me her canteen.

"Would you survive getting jumped by a pair of those jacked-up werewolves? You know they can't feel pain, right? They fight until they die."

She swallows hard, and I look away, force myself to drink more water and not to think about Ronan's bloodied corpse. I think instead of the Facility as I know it, from charts and maps and security monitors, and from my explorations with Nala while Hyperion still allowed it.

They're the puppet-masters, pulling Grange's strings, running their dirty money through an even dirtier enterprise that will either net them millions or be a profitable write-off if the research fails. We can free every victim and burn this place to the ground and it won't be more than a blip on their radar. And yet it's everything to us. Our lives, our freedom. Our rights, because I've seen the future of my kind of people, and it looks like Hollowood Falls.

I can't think of a time when me being a shifter was no big deal. Most people in the bureau either don't know I exist or think it's some kind of smokescreen, a rumor that dogs me, all puns intended. To Hollowood folk, I'm only strange because my shifted self isn't a wolf. But Chase Culver mated a bear, and his father showed me a taxonomy of the variants in a crumbling book in the town's archives. To them, the fact that I have this ability means nothing at all.

The afternoon is passing quickly and we soon set off again. Before long I recognize our surroundings. As we approach the fighting grounds I realize I'm holding my breath. I let it out slowly as I follow Honey up a little rise. She stops abruptly then retreats a few steps.

"Green buildings," she whispers. "Three small sheds."

We return downhill where the others have gathered around Ronan. "I've not been able to do much here," he says. "The animals move around enough in their pens and such that a static image would get noticed."

Heads turn as a pair of black birds go swooping past. They alight on a branch at the top of the rise, preening and snapping their beaks, the yellow bands around their eyes and the cap of white feathers marking them as the endemic variety of crow, called 'preacher birds' by the older folk in the district. Cawing noisily, they take off towards the pits.

Motioning us to stay put and stay quiet, Mr. Culver gets out his binoculars then creeps up the slope. After a minute he scrambles down again, laughing under his breath.

"They're putting on quite a show for the cameras," he murmurs.

"The birds?"

"Hollowood's crows are...unusual. Sometimes you'd think they're on our side."

"I did see a few cameras yanked from trees on my survey."

"That's exactly the sort of thing they'd do."

As another trio of crows pass overhead he takes Ronan up the slope. They lie side by side, swapping the binoculars back and forth, Ronan shaking his head in disbelief. They scramble back down to brief us.

"There's about a dozen or more birds," he says, dusting twigs from his clothes. "The ones that aren't attacking the cameras are diving in and out of one of the pits. I reckon that's the first we ought to check."

"What if I try to smell him out?" Honey says.

"That's a good idea for a few reasons," Mr. Culver says as she kneels to untie her boots. "If he's in rough shape the last thing he'll want to see is another bunch of humans with guns. Joy, can you give us a hand with these cameras?"

She's already stringing her bow. "You can hear a gun retort for miles," she says to my questioning look. "This barely makes a sound."

"And she never misses," Evan says.

"Not never," she says, blushing a little. "But I sure wouldn't bet against me."

It takes her five shots to take out the four cameras. As she sets out to retrieve the three arrows that didn't get stuck in trees, Honey slips up the bank and around the nearest pit to the next one. The few crows sitting on the reinforced steel edge take flight as she approaches.

Then Stone growls. Even knowing the source, the sound makes us all stop what we're doing. Choosing speed over caution, we join Honey at the edge of the circular pit. Nine or ten feet deep by about fifty feet across, its concrete base is stained with old blood in rusty smears and spatters. The wall of unfinished rock is punctuated by four heavy steel doors which open onto underground pens.

At first I don't see Stone, but he's directly below us. Whimpering, he goes up on his hind legs, the tips of his claws just reaching the top of the wall. He drops onto all fours again and begins to nose around the pit. His belly hangs slack, like he hasn't been fed in a while, dangerous for a bear this late in the summer when he ought to be packing on weight for the winter.

He returns to us and stands up again. "If he'd shift we could just drop the ladder," Evan says.

"He might not be able to," Nala says. "The animals—I mean inmates are dosed with a chemical that interferes with the neural signal." She fetches what looks like an epi-pen from her waist pack. "I don't know if this will work on someone his size, but we've used it before," she says, handing it to Mr. Culver, who squints to read the microscopic text on the label.

"You did clinical trials?" I ask.

"Hmm," she murmurs, zipping her pack closed.

"On who?

"On you."

"Excuse me? You did what?"

She looks at me a moment then exhales hard. "Before Igor, do you remember where you were embedded?"

"I was in Dubai." I can feel the tiles under my paws, hear the wash of waves, though as I probe the memories they crumble like sand. "Wasn't I?"

"You were in Dubai *four* years ago. *Two* years ago you were in Nigeria and we almost didn't get you back."

"I don't remember that." Except maybe I do, as a vison flits past of dry soil and blue sky and a thousand yellow taxis, pursued by the sound of drums and a blare of reggaeton.

"I know you don't," she says kindly. "But we found you and set you right again, so this is likely to work on our mate in the pit. He's only been dosed for a week. You'd been missing for eight months."

She pats me on the arm but I don't feel it. As she rejoins the others I let my knees soften and sink into a crouch right where I am. Eight months I can barely remember, though bits are coming back as I probe the memories. A diamond smuggling ring with complicated ties to the national oil industry. I remember their shoes, the loafers of black velvet or poached leopard skin. One of the buyers had had his own face embroidered in what looked like cheap crystals but was probably a hundred grand in gemstones.

Something makes me look up to see Graeme wandering towards me. I'm not in the mood to get hassled, but he says nothing as he hunkers down beside me. He offers me his canteen and I gulp the water gratefully, my throat loosening.

"Six months you've been in here, right?" he says softly. "Fucking arseholes. Have they not got evidence enough? What are they trying to prove?"

"That these aren't just animals. They need proof that they're human too."

"You're not enough to convince them?"

"Not outside my department. You know, sometimes I think the bureau's funding—"

"The fuck they are. Don't fall for that sort of delusion. You know what Hyperion's like. This has them written all over it."

"What if Hyperion isn't the top?" A suspicion I've never told any-one, and his disgusted expression is why.

"If you go looking for the men behind the curtain you're likely to find them, even if you have to invent them yourself. Hyperion are only doing what their financial backers ask of them, no?"

"So when does it stop? When do *we* stop?"

"When we're doing more harm than good."

"Then I should have quit years ago." Graeme's compassion hits harder than if he was giving me shit for falling apart, and I rest my head on my folded arms, not wanting to weigh him down with my emotions. No one deserves to have to deal with me.

"I've got to say, I'm a touch embarrassed that this was going on next door and I never cottoned on," Graeme says when I've stopped sniffling. "I should have put the clues together."

"Clues?"

"Little things here and there. The buildings, the fences. Young Marcus got lost over here once and came across pits just like this. Was nearly mauled by a pair of wolves. He said that there were monsters too, and that threw me off. I thought he was high. But d'you recall those fighters in Damascus with the sand-proof hoods?"

"With the augmented reality lenses?"

"Hmm, and I thought, what if..." He trails off, raising a finger for me to keep quiet as his eyes track across the trees. He looks about then picks up a stone the size of a golf ball. Amid the sigh of the wind and the others' quiet murmurs I hear the buzz of small propellers. Graeme has risen into a crouch and suddenly winds up and flings the rock. It strikes the drone which collides with a nearby tree and falls clattering to the ground.

"Nice shot," I murmur as he helps me to my feet.

"Hopefully I got it before it got us."

Still, they have to know we're here. Five cameras down in half an hour? Grange's mercenaries could be waiting for us over the next rise. But I shove all that out of the way and rejoin the team at the edge of the pit. Wolf-Honey is down in the pit and has made friends with Stone. They stand cheek to jowl as Nala approaches them in full dog-soothing mode, cooing to him in her childhood patois.

"Does he know what I'm about to do?" she says warily as she retrieves the syringe from her belt. Honey nods with two tosses of her lean head. She steps back another few feet from Stone's weighty claws as Nala crosses herself then uncaps the syringe.

"He won't feel a thing," Evan calls. "Bears have tough skin."

"That's what I'm afraid of," Nala replies. "That I won't even break his skin. I've only got one more of these." But as she gets nearer Stone sits down with a huff then rolls to his back, exposing his softer underbelly. Crouching by his left flank, Nala feels around, choosing a spot just inside his hip. She crosses herself once more, then raises the syringe high and slams it down, holding it firmly against his skin to give the drug time to penetrate. As she backs away Stone lets his head drop, then rolls onto his side with a groan.

"How long will it take to work?" I ask Nala as she scrambles up the rescue ladder.

"Five, ten minutes at least to get into his bloodstream."

"I don't know that we have ten minutes," Graeme says. He has Mr. Culver's binoculars trained on the woods to the northwest. "Blake, remember those AR hoods?"

"Shit! Incoming hostiles, sir, I mean Mr. Culver."

"Is anyone else penned up in here?" he asks Nala.

"There's a few. The panel on the lock lights up if someone's inside. These clones should get us into most places." She hands him one of a pair of blank white key cards.

"What about the island?" I say.

"We'll split up," Mr Culver says. "Joy, your team will stay here with Nala and Stone and open as many pens as you can, then get the hell out. We're going to the island."

Fifteen

Panic

It's a gorgeous afternoon to be walking in the woods. The cloudless sky seems so close you could touch it, the mountain peaks standing out crisp as cut paper, the rocks seeming to glow in the bounty of sunshine. I'd ask to stop and take some pictures if we weren't walking to our deaths.

The others aren't bothered, or are way better actors than I am, or perhaps underestimate how much danger we're in, chatting easily, their weapons holstered or slung on their backs, Honey carrying a deer's shinbone she nosed out along the way. After an hour we halt in the shade of an outcropping of rock. The others sit down at once and break out the canteens, but I can barely swallow for the fear.

But I keep my mouth shut and my eyes open, hoping that my paranoia will come in handy, be what keeps us alive instead of the thing that pushes me over the edge of panic and into the realm of bad decisions. If I have a keen sense for when everything is about to go wrong, I earned it from a lifetime of things going wrong.

Graeme and Ronan have hit it off, like military types often do, and are sitting together with their backs against the rock.

"That's quite the career you had for such a short time in service," Ronan says. "What made you enlist in the first place?"

"It was the only way I could get away from my family," Graeme replies. "I wasn't about to follow my shit of a father into the roofing trade, but

I was nothing special at school. It was either the army or the priesthood. Given that I like to fuck men and not little boys, it wasn't a hard choice."

"For fuck's sake, Gray," Evan groans from the other side of the hollow.

"Though I do make you sing like a choir boy on occasion." He starts giggling as Evan makes a sick face.

"My dad's right here, you know."

"Sorry, sorry. You know I'm worse when I'm nervy."

"We should get moving," Mr. Culver says, his expression unchanged. "I'd like to be out of here before nightfall."

Amen.

After climbing steadily for another half hour we cross a ridgeback and start down towards the lake, just visible through the trees as a twinkle of reflected light. Every second I expect an ambush, from above or below, and by the time we reach the base of the ridge I'm trembling with anxiety. Or is it the knowledge that beyond the water lies the beating heart of Hyperion's monstrous project, a building so secure even I've never gone past the front entrance.

We pause at the edge of the tree cover. A few hundred yards away, a green access hut stands alone on the pebbled shore of the small lake. The smooth water reflects the lowering sun in broad strokes of glittering gold. Grange's artificial island is constructed from half a dozen shipping containers on pontoons and is moored in the middle of the lake, surrounded by a flotilla of what looks like hundreds of black basketballs.

"What are those balls for?" Graeme asks as he hands the binoculars to Mr. Culver.

"Normally you see them in reservoirs to cut down on evaporation but I expect they're sensors," Ronan says. "Touching one would move them all."

"And what's with the Tardis?" Graeme nods at the green hut on the shore. "Is that an access door like the others?"

"It leads to the tunnel under the lake," I say.

"Is that the only way in?"

"That I know of."

"Then let's hope this works," Ronan says, holding up one of Nala's key cards. With Honey trotting ahead to smell out any trouble, we leave the trees and start for the hut.

"Let's go," Mr. Culver says to Evan as he stalls at the edge of the slatey shore. "Come on, son, we've got to get a move on." He reaches for Evan, who sidles away from him.

"I'm not going down there," he says dully, gazing at the hut with the glassy eyes of one of Grange's doped up slaves.

"You don't really have a choice. Now snap out of it and get your ass moving."

"I'm not going down there," he repeats, shaking his head violently. "That's how they get you."

His lips thin, Mr. Culver exhales through his nose. "You know you're being ridiculous, don't you?"

"Mr. Culver," Graeme warns as Evan twists away from his father's reach once more. "Sir, talking to him like that won't help—ah, fuck!"

As Mr. Culver makes a last grab, Evan wrenches himself away from his father then bolts, disappearing into the woods. Graeme dashes after him, but as a wolf bursts from the ground cover and takes off like a shot he pulls up short. He returns to us, anger distorting his face as he pushes past everyone and stops in front of me.

"Did you see what I did?" he snarls. "That right there is what you've never had the fucking guts to do."

"You mean give up on someone I love?"

His teeth bared, he grabs the front of my jacket in both hands. "Fuck you, Nyland, you fucking coward," he spits. "You traitorous, maladjusted, sack of—"

"Graeme," warns Evan's father in a tired voice. "We have to keep moving."

With a last furious grunt he shoves me away, so hard I fall on my ass in the dirt. It's the least a coward like me deserves. He's right, I don't have the guts for this. Can't handle the cost, the fact that people die in the line of duty. Couldn't live with losing Ronan, and I've only made things worse, put all our lives in danger because I'm too weak to let go of someone that was never mine to begin with. Just some guy I fucked in a cheap motel to get over my shitty life.

I stay down, not wanting to draw any more of Graeme's anger, not having the energy either. As the others fall into conversation, Honey trots over to me, then lies down beside me, her haunch against my hip. She yawns with a great stretch of her long pink tongue then lays her head between her paws. Automatically, I start to pet her. Softly at first, then rifling my fingers through her thick fur. A touch I wouldn't dare if she wasn't a wolf, seeing as I barely know her. This is the kindness an animal gives, wordless acceptance and a soft, warm presence. Tolerance for our wretched humanity that makes us think we're so smart yet keeps us blind to so much.

And that's what I keep clinging to. My humanness, as if it's superior, as if I'm not better off as my other self. I wouldn't keep making the same mistakes if I was a dog all the time. Wouldn't keep letting my human emotions get in the way of doing the right thing. I'd be warm and dependable. Love unconditionally. Wordless, goalless, free.

As the others' tempers rise, so have their voices. "We're taking a real chance on this tunnel," Graeme's saying. "With this much security about the place there's sure to be cameras and all. Will we even be able to get out the other end?"

"You don't have to come with us," Ronan says evenly.

Graeme purses his lips, shooting a cold glance in my direction. "That doesnae answer my question."

"Alright, then I don't know," Ronan replies with one of his false smiles. "And swimming's not really an option."

"You've got that right, who knows what's in that fucking water?" Graeme glances over his shoulder in the direction Evan went, then looks again. At the same moment, Honey growls.

An enormous wolf is watching us from the edge of the forest. Not Evan but a bigger wolf with paler fur and fury in its amber eyes. Honey lifts her head, her lip curling back as she growls again. As she rises to her feet I crabwalk backwards, away from the wolves and the fight that's seconds from starting.

The fight I ought to join. Grange's wolf outweighs Honey by at least a hundred pounds. If there were two of us we could take him. Maybe. Before I make up my mind either way, Mr. Culver grabs me by my shirt collar and hauls me to my feet. The others are halfway to the hut, and shaking off Culver's hand I start after them. What I ought to do is do what I'm told. Stop trusting my gut, stop pretending I belong in this lethal trade.

At growling I look back. Teeth bared, hackles raises, the wolves face off. Honey stands her ground, her body coiled to attack, but as Grange's wolf suddenly hurls himself at her she bolts, straight along the shoreline away from us. In a single motion the bigger wolf skids to a halt, pivots, and takes off in pursuit.

"Godspeed, lass," Graeme mutters as he watches them disappear around the bend. "I hope this is worth what we're all paying."

"We have to bring an end to Hyperion's work here," Mr. Culver says.

"Oh aye, but I'd much rather be doing it in a courtroom than mucking about like this."

"Believe me, we've tried. I was this close to remortgaging the house to cover a retainer but my wife talked me out of it."

"Next time, call me. I'll throw in on that."

"That was before I'd met you."

"I just hope he's alright," Graeme says, and it's clear who he means from the catch in his voice. His husband is out there somewhere, panicked and frightened and in every sort of danger, and I have no one to blame but myself. Conveniently enough, my punishment is waiting for me behind the heavy steel door Ronan has just opened with Nala's key-card.

"Ever get the feeling you're walking into a trap?" Graeme asks, his voice echoing down the stairwell as he peers over Ronan's shoulder.

"Why do you think I'm still alive?" Ronan replies.

"Fair enough. Let's go."

They start down, the metal stairs ringing with their every step. Mr. Culver lingers, scanning the forest for Honey or maybe his son. He sighs, a heavy sound of remorse, but as he steps through the door I see a blur of movement: Honey, running for her life, the other wolf three strides behind. I flatten myself against the door as she hurtles past, then I shove the door closed. Not quite in time as Grange's wolf slams into it, nearly throwing me down the stairs.

Ignoring the beast's slavering jaws I fling myself at the door again, my feet slipping on the smooth concrete as I fight to keep it from opening further. A fight I'm going to lose, the pain in my side building like a landslide about to spill, the fatigue of too many hard days and nights sucking the strength from my limbs. I don't even have breath to tell the rest of them to run, complete the mission, leave me to my ugly fate. Ugly but useful, if letting this monster rip me to shreds is enough to save their lives.

Then the door shifts. Not open but closed, as Mr. Culver throws his shoulder at it. Further, as Graeme adds his weight. Together we force the wolf back as it tries to bite the door, foam flying from its jaws, its claws scraping metal.

"Fuck this for a joke," Graeme rasps. One hand braced on the door, he pulls his sidearm from his shoulder holster, turns it about, and brings the handle down on the wolf's nose with all his strength. Again, and I swear I hear bone breaking. He raises his hand a third time but the wolf has had enough and pulls its head back and we slam the door shut.

"You okay?" Mr Culver asks as I slither to the ground.

"Doesn't matter if he is or not," Graeme says as he steps over me to descend the stairs. "There'll be time for coming apart later."

If we live. And it's starting to look like a pretty big *if*.

Sixteen

The Tunnel

The tunnel is built from concrete sewer tubes laid across the lake bottom. I've been down here plenty but never as a human, and the roof seems too close to my head. The other set of stairs is a blurry smudge at the far end and I can barely hold to the others' careful pace. We should be running full speed, getting the fuck out of here before something happens. Before we're screwed. Before Grange flips a switch somewhere and floods the tunnel, with water or poison gas. Maybe she'll knock us out and we'll wake up in the pits or on the operating table. Everything feels like a threat, every step takes us closer to death, and when Ronan touches my shoulder I nearly elbow him in the face.

"You're not well," he says.

"No shit, Sherlock. Sorry, that was rude."

"Forget about it. We're all stressing a bit. But will you be alright?"

"Hard to say when I don't know what we're going to find. Like I told you, I've only ever been as far as the entrance."

"Right, right." We walk another twenty paces in silence before he clears his throat. "Well if you're feeling a bit off, tell me. You won't make good decisions if you're overwhelmed."

"Oh, so you've met me."

He laughs quietly. "It's true for anyone, isn't it?"

"You seem to be doing okay."

"Trust me, on the inside I'm absolutely shitting myself."

"Like a duck. Gliding smoothly, but under the surface you're paddling like crazy?"

"Something like that."

We walk further, our footsteps and breath rattling off the roof, Honey's claws clicking on the concrete. Security camera hoods bulge from the sidewall every twenty yards, gleaming like the eggs of whatever freaky bug dug this oppressive nest.

"She knows we're here," I say as we pass another.

"I know."

"She'll kill you on sight."

"I know, but I'm not worried about that. I'm worried about what she might do to you."

"Don't. Don't worry about me."

"Purely out of my general good nature," he says with a quick grin. "No one should suffer like that."

Not because I'm important. Just because I'm someone. He cares because I'm a living thing. It's enough for now, because this morning he could barely look at me.

We walk for what feels like an hour without the end of the tunnel seeming to get any nearer. It's probably five minutes, but I'm slipping over the edge of normal function and into pure survival mode, every step an effort, every breath a stab of agony. I won't stop, won't give up, won't disappoint these people. Not again.

At last we reach the exit. The door at the top of the stairs opens easily, letting us into the entryway where Grange used to make me wait. The walls are covered in the same click-together plastic modules as the other Facility buildings. White sterile-room suits hang from a row of pegs. A box on the wall holds blue shoe covers. After a quick debate, we put on the suits, though there's nothing to protect Honey. But who needs protecting, us or the inmates? Questions I can't answer, but she follows us without balking as we pass through the double sliding door at the other end of the room and enter one of the most secret places on Earth.

It resembles every other part of the Facility: modular walls, a drop ceiling, and the smell of disinfectant. The hallway runs for thirty feet then turns. Doors line the right-hand wall, but after a quick sniff Honey leads us past them to the corner, where Ronan gets out his phone and pulls up a rough schematic of the building.

"We'll split up," he says, barely voicing the words as he highlights the two routes. "Leif and Graeme, and the three of us."

With weapons drawn, our feet thankfully muffled by the slippery shoe covers, we slink around the corner and along the hall. Every second I expect a guard or a goon or another giant wolf to appear and arrest or attack us, and by the time we reach the point where the hallways intersect I'm so tense I can barely breathe. Good thing I'm unarmed or I'd probably take out one of our own team members.

Graeme and Mr. Culver take the left branch while Ronan, Honey, and I carry on straight ahead. We pass a window that looks in on a sort of garden, a square of artificially green lawn with a single wilting tree and a few scrawny bushes in the middle. Across the square, another much larger window looks inward, covered by sheer beige curtains. Beige on beige, the palette of sedation, reminding me of my stays in hospital after the last few jobs. I never used to need so much help. Those first few years felt like living in a video game, where the danger never touched me and no one really died. A story about someone else.

Hazy memories of Nigeria float past: the heat, the dust, the pattering sound of small gemstones being poured onto velvet. I'm losing my grip on the present, nearly colliding with Ronan when he stops. He flashes me a tense look but says nothing, only points with a jerk of his chin at the bend in the hallway. Honey's ears prick as sound filters back to us, the beep and jingle of some game the guard must be playing on his phone.

So much for high security, I mouth, wishing Ronan knew ASL. Pressing his lips together, he tenses against the urge to laugh. Her tongue hanging, Honey shakes herself then trots innocently around the corner.

"What the fuck? How'd you get out?" The guard opens a drawer and gets out some heavy metallic object. Tail wagging vaguely, Honey waits as the guard approaches, his boots clumping heavily. Her ears lowered, she leaps to the side as an orange dart flies past and bounces off the plastic wall.

"Jeez...I don't got all day, you know."

"In that case," Ronan says as he steps around the corner with his gun levelled, "let me save you some time."

What a show-off, but I keep my thoughts to myself as I join him and Honey. Like so much of the Facility's security staff, the guard is a white guy in his mid-forties with a Marines tattoo on one forearm and a snake on the other and about fifty extra pounds around his middle. Here for the pay packet, and just amoral enough to not care what it takes to earn it. He blinks at us a few times then reaches for his belt.

"Don't fucking bother," Ronan says, raising his gun so the red tracer dances around the middle of the guard's forehead. "I don't need information from you so I'm quite happy to shoot you dead where you stand if you try anything. Now put down your weapon. Slowly."

The guard blinks a few more times, then with a grunt of disgust tosses the dart gun aside. As Ronan approaches he puts his hands behind his head.

"Buddy, you can take whatever you want. I got a family, you know?"

"No problem," Ronan says with a businesslike smile. "I'd prefer not to have to shoot anyone. You don't mind if my friend frisks you, do you?"

"Like I said, take what you want."

I feel him over, taking his phone, a Luger from his hip holster, and a six inch blade from his belt, as well as black key-card like Nala's and a small black box with a single button in the center.

"Panic button?" Ronan asks as I zip-tie the man's wrists together behind his back. "Does this go straight to Grange?"

He nods again. "Meant to get someone here in ninety seconds."

"That quickly? Impressive," he says as he clips it to his own belt. "Now, if you'd like to stay on my good side by saving *us* some time, tell me which rooms are occupied."

He doesn't just tell us, he leads us. Maybe he's looking for a career upgrade because despite Ronan not asking him questions he tells us everything he knows. Which turns out to be virtually nothing.

"They just pay me to stop people going through, you know?" he says, elbowing me as he twists to talk to Ronan on his other side. "I don't know jack about the patient."

"Yes, thank you. I'll be sure to remember."

He stops at the farthest door. As Honey lowers her head for a sniff she stiffens, then jumps up on her hind legs to scratch at the door like any other dog.

"Jeez, what's got into him?" the guard asks as Honey drops to all fours again, whining and wagging her tail.

"*She's* obviously interested in what's behind the door," Ronan says with that glassy smile as I pull out the key-card and swipe it across the panel beside the door. The door unseals, releasing a heady waft of antiseptic that makes Honey snort and shake her head. The room itself is set up like a hospital, the figure in the bed half buried by the mass of tubes and wires connecting them to the machines standing to either side, their face covered with a respirator mask.

"God above, is it a child?" Ronan says in horror, for the person's legs barely reach to the middle of the bed.

"It's Grandmother."

"What?"

"What?"

"I meant, why did you say that?" Ronan asks me. "How do you know?"

"I don't know." I mean it, as I don't remember speaking, yet nothing could convince me that this is anyone else. "Whoever it is, she's clearly really old." I point to the wrinkled hand laying on the pale green blanket.

He gives me another strange look then approaches the bed. The guard does too, until Honey's growl of warning stops him. He steps aside and lets her pass. Whining, she goes to the bedside and puts a paw on the blanket beside the person's wizened hand. Which stirs, the clawed fingers uncurling, spreading, then lifting to cover Honey's paw. Whimpering, Honey licks the frail fingers.

"Fuck me," Ronan whispers. I look up and meet the person's gaze. One eye is the bright blue of a husky, the other an uncanny red with no white and a pinprick of a pupil. One tiny fleck in an ocean of blood, and all of a sudden I'm falling, falling into a warm and salted sea, the water closing over my head as I sink into nothingness. Then the person shuts their eyes and world around me springs back into focus.

"I said, are you alright?" Ronan says, gripping my arm, his face pale.

"I don't know."

He studies me briefly, expressions flashing across his face. He settles on grimly determined. "We've got to get moving."

"We're not leaving her here."

"I never said that. But I don't know what we'll do about all..." He gestures at the winking, flashing machines tethered to the tiny body. "We're as likely to kill her as save her."

The choice is being made for us as the person begins to feel themselves over, plucking at the wires and tubes running every way. Ronan might doubt but I don't. I smell no sickness, no imminent death. I smell chemical cleaners, and the guard's oniony sweat, and something else. The same strange scent I used to catch drifting over from the valley next door. The smell of Hollowood, a woodsy, earthen aroma touched with a hot peppery tang, a wild, hungry smell that makes my mouth water and my palms itch, makes me want to leap and yell and fuck. I start unplugging wires from the sensors on her arm and chest. Red lights begin to flash on the consoles of the various machines as we disconnect them. Unimportant, when all that matters is our freedom.

"I wonder what sort of help gets here in less than two minutes," Ronan says as I tug the saline tube out of the cannula on the back of her hand.

"I wondered that too."

"We should ask—oh fuck!"

I look around and the guard is gone. "When the hell did—"

"Doesn't matter. We need to leave. Now." From a sheath up his sleeve Ronan produces a carbon blade knife that slashes through the last tubes like an axe through butter. I bundle the tiny person into my arms, blankets and all, expecting them to weigh next to nothing, but they're surprisingly heavy. And strong, wrapping their thin arms tightly around my neck as I lift them.

Ronan's at the door and signals me to wait, so set them down on the bed again. They start clawing at the respirator mask so I take it off, and the bottom drops out of my world.

Not human. Even less so than me, the face narrow and elongated, not wholly wolf-like but not unlike. Not human but living and real. Grandmother stretches out a long arm and lays her hand on the top of my head and all of my memories come surging to the surface. All of them, all at once, every eye blink, every sigh, every shame and glory since I was born up until five minutes ago. All of them happening all at once and on top of each other yet all of it making perfect sense without making any sense at all.

Welcome home, says a soundless voice the color of moonlight. *We've been waiting.*

Seventeen

The Island

I might have stayed like that forever, falling deeper into Grandmother's uncanny gaze, lost in the storm of emotion and memory. What happens is that Ronan grabs me by the belt and yanks me away from the bed. I throw up my hands as he pulls back to slap my face.

"I'm fine, I'm awake. What happened?"

"You tell me. But later. We've far bigger problems." He glances at the door and the red light blinking above it. "I reckon there's no sound so as to not frighten the animals, but that's definitely an alarm."

Honey yips and we turn to see Grandmother settling herself on the wolf's broad back, high up near her shoulders, her gnarled hands knotted in Honey's ruff.

"Good enough," Ronan says. "Let's move out."

The hall is as deserted as before. We walk fast, then start to jog when it's clear Grandmother isn't going to get jostled off her mount. Pain stabs through my ribs with every footfall but I grit my teeth and keep running. When two gunshots echo down the hall, Ronan stops to yank off the slippery foot covers then bolts, weapon in hand. We follow more slowly but as we round the next corner I stop. Someone in black fatigues is slumped on the floor, their back against the wall, but when they don't move I get closer. It's our guard, unconscious or dead, but I assume it's the first as there's no blood anywhere. Honey trots past, her nose in the air, and leads me around the next corner.

"Took you long enough," Graeme says with a dazzling smile. Armed with a semi-automatic he must have liberated from the security station, he's standing overtop of three people in white lab coats lying on the floor with their wrists zip-tied behind their backs. "And you've brought a friend. Who's tha..." he trails off as he takes in the uncanny little person clinging to Honey's back. "I see," he says shakily. "Alright then."

"Where's Mr. Culver?" I ask. He jerks his head to an open door, but before I can move, Ronan and Mr. Culver come scrambling out, along with a middle-aged Black man dressed in hospital scrubs with a shock of snow white hair. They're followed by a loud bang and a trickle of acrid smoke. The man makes to go back in but Mr. Culver puts a hand on his arm.

"She must be spooked, Leif," the man says in a husky New Hampshire accent. "Let me at least talk to her."

Mr. Culver looks at him for a long moment then nods. The man approaches the door then whistles, and a wolf yips in reply. Pushing tears from his reddened eyes, the man gets down on one knee and whistles differently.

"Come on, baby," he murmurs shakily. "Come back to me."

Every nerve in my body is begging me to run. Every second we stay here brings us closer to disaster, but something tells me to keep my damn mouth shut as a wolf steps cautiously through the doorway. The man opens his arms as the wolf takes a few more steps. Then it leaps at him. I nearly scream, and thank God I don't as the wolf starts licking the man's face. Flinging his arms around the wolf's neck, he bursts into tears, burying his face in its fur as it as it tries to climb onto his lap, wagging its tail madly.

"Freeman," Mr. Culver says softly. "We can't stay here." The man nods, then whispers something to the wolf, who calms at once.

"That guard told us ninety seconds from alarm to response," Ronan says as Mr. Culver helps Freeman to his feet.

"It's been going off for a good five minutes," Graeme says, "so we can assume the other teams have done us a favour. Is there any way off this raft that doesn't involve that fucking tunnel?"

"There's a dock on the other side of the island," says Freeman. "We've watched their boats come and go through Hope's cage."

"Don't panic, anyone," Mr. Culver says. "We're going to get through this." But the tension around his eyes and his tight grip on his rifle tell me he's as frightened as the rest of us.

Going by Ronan's sketch, we find the closest door and escape the sickening smell. The sun is setting behind the mountains, lighting the sky in lurid shades of purple and fiery red. The water laps softly at the edge of the modular decking that circles the buildings as we follow Freeman and his wolf-mate Hope around the corner to the dock. Made of the same plastic decking, it extends far into the water. A narrow, low-sided fishing boat is moored just past the flotilla of black balls.

"That will never take us all," Graeme says as the boat dips under Mr. Culver's weight.

"We'll have to take turns," he says. "I'll take the Bonnys and Grandmother across first, and then—hit the deck!"

I don't think, I just obey as Mr. Culver raises his rifle and fires over our heads. A drone falls twitching to the deck, landing near Graeme who kicks it into the water. A second later, the drone's munitions go off, the deck rocking wildly as the water erupts in a huge spout.

"We're sitting ducks out here," Ronan barks, scanning the sky. "You'd best go now if you're going."

As Freeman and the other wolf climb aboard, Mr. Culver fires another round at an incoming drone which explodes mid-air, showering us with hot splinters of plastic. One must have struck Honey, who falls into the water, Grandmother still firmly mounted. Or did she jump? Because she starts to swim, not back to us but towards the shore.

"What's she thinking?" Ronan says.

"Maybe she's not thinking," I reply, remembering how hard that one touch rocked me. "Maybe she's just doing what she's told."

"If so, she ought to have bucked command. She'll never make it." The worst is, he's right, Honey is already struggling, splashing about without making much headway. Mr. Culver and his friend Freeman are trying to start the boat engine, but we're running out of time to save them as Honey's head dips under.

"Fucking hell," Graeme mutters. He shoves his gun into Ronan's hands then unzips his jacket.

"What are you doing?" Ronan asks as Graeme strips off the jacket and then his shirt. "You're not going to go after them are you? If a wolf isn't strong enough how are you going to be? Oh Jesus. You're not...you are, aren't you?"

"I'm what?" Graeme says with venom as he kicks off his shoes.

"One of them."

"Not exactly. And I'll thank you not to stare." He covers his naked groin but not very well, given that there's a hell of a lot to cover. All of which stops being important as his hand begins to elongate, his fingers fusing together as his skin thickens and begins to sprout fine gray hair. In less than a minute he's shifted into an elegant stallion with a silvery mane and a white blaze on his gray forehead.

"Jesus wept," Ronan gasps, halfway to tears himself. "Isn't there anyone besides me in this fucking valley who isn't something else? Dogs and wolves and God only knows, and now you're a fucking horse?"

"Not quite," Graeme replies in a wet, inhuman voice. He pulls back his lips to reveal a mouthful of wickedly sharp teeth.

"You feel like explaining?"

"Not at the moment." Instead he leaps into the water, going right under the surface. He pops up a few seconds later beside Honey, who is barely keeping her head above water. Grandmother reaches up to grasp a handful of his mane, then pulls herself handily onto his back. He snorts, tossing his head, then takes off, swimming with powerful kicks and leaving Honey in his wake. Freed of her load, Honey starts swimming faster and the pair are soon lost in the twilight, leaving behind the five of us, and a boat that can carry four.

I know what I have to do. I know who's least important. If anyone has to take a chance, it's me. "Get in the boat," I say to Ronan. "I'll meet you on the shore."

"But Blake..."

"What?"

He stares at me, his eyes wide, his mouth half open, his words sticking in his throat. He looks like he did last week when we met at that shitty hotel. Shocked, on his way to numb. I can't leave him like this. I have to say something, let him know it's okay, that my life doesn't matter as much as his. Tell him that I'm not afraid even though I am, because I don't want him to worry. Tell him that I wanted so much more for both of us, and I'm sorry that I had so little to give. I want to do all these things but instead I take his face between my shaking hands and kiss him.

Just once, to know how it feels, to know the taste of his lips, but when I go to lift my head he grabs me by the hair and kisses me back. Hard and fierce, a kiss full of longing, an intimacy neither of us wanted until now. Now it's everything, and it's the last I'll ever have of him, as I push him away from me, towards the boat.

"Go. Just go. While you still can."

"Blake—"

"I'll be fine. I'll see you soon." I back away from him, off the dock onto the sturdier deck, then turn around. I don't want to see him walk away. I don't want to know what it looks like to say goodbye to Ronan Wednesday.

Eighteen

The Wolves

You're picturing this night, I know: the dark forest beneath a velvet sky, the soft lap of water against the dock footings, the chill of the air on my skin as I get undressed. What you can't feel is the squeezing, itching discomfort that sweeps across my body, radiating from the mutant organ that makes shifting occur, or the disorienting head-rush as the curvature of my ear reshapes to draw in ten times more sound. My eyes are not much more acute, but now my ears and even my sense of smell draws my attention to the group of lycan and human mercenaries gathering on the shore near the tunnel entrance.

As Mr. Culver pulls away from the dock behind me, rowing to avoid starting the engine, I say goodbye to yet another set of good clothes and slip into the water. I might be a mongrel, but something in me is a born swimmer. Man or dog, I always feel at home in the water, and I've almost caught up to the others when Graeme reaches land.

He clambers onto the shore and stands for a moment, streaming water, his sides heaving, Grandmother still clinging to his back. Tossing his head, he shudders from head to tail, then suddenly bolts, disappearing into the night, though his hoof-beats linger.

Honey shakes off the water, then butts her head against my side. A wave of images sweeps through my brain, swamping my own thoughts in a tide of light and heat and sound, faces emerging then washing away seconds later. The sound shapes itself into a woman's voice: *Shit, you don't know how...*

Honey raises her head and the world re-emerges from the swirling chaos. She looks at me hard, her nostrils flaring as she reads my scent. I've never been so close to a shifted creature before, only seen them through a fence or the bars of a cage. She smells like the valley, like wet fur and lilies, rank and sweet and baffling. I drop my head, whining in confusion, desperate for her to do anything except stare at me in that intent and curious way. No one wants to be stared at by a wolf, the animal part of me cowering as she steps nearer. She pushes her snout against my shoulder and the images rise again, but slower.

She's talking to me.

Trembling, I close my eyes, try to sense her meaning, because there is meaning in there somewhere. I know those faces, the sound of those voices, know that these flickering visions of a path, a mountain, a fence and the freedom beyond it represent us and the way we're going to escape.

When she steps back I rise and follow her, away from the water and into the woods. Graeme's scent is easy to pick out and we lope along in something like pursuit for a few miles, gradually climbing higher up the spur of the mountain. We cross a small creek and pick up the scent again, but when we cross the next rivulet through the rocks Honey leaves Graeme's upward-bound trail and starts moving across the slope.

That's when we smell them. The other wolves. Not our crew but Grange's, and either they're bred for stink or they're closer than we expect because it's all I can smell, that ozone tang of blood and chemicals. Honey changes course, angling upwards, but I can barely keep up with her faster pace between the pain in my ribs and the throbbing of my ear and my general exhaustion. Still we run, and run, and run, higher and higher, until we leave the trees behind, not bothering to conceal ourselves, just running, until I feel like this is all I've ever done, run up this fucking mountain in the dark while my soul is being torn apart.

I left Ronan behind. I left him to die. I sacrificed everything, and then a little bit more, and now all I have left in the world is this hill and my four paws. It's not enough—I'm not enough to save even my own life, as a pair of gigantic werewolves burst snarling from the cover of the rocks ahead.

We leap back but there's nowhere to run as two other pairs converge to surround us. Everywhere I turn is teeth and fur and fury, their tongues dripping froth, their eyes glassy from the chemical cocktail fed into their systems by Grange's collars. Honey's a puppy beside these hulking monsters, meaning I'm dog food. Barely a mouthful, my whole sorry career about to end on this barren mountainside, killed by my own kin, no witness but the waning moon and an infinity of stars.

Wind whistles through the gaps in the rocks, my paws shifting on the loose shale that pricks the pads of my feet like glassy sand. Tiny, meaningless sensations, the kind you're meant to grab hold of when you're on the brink of death. Because that's what this is: the moment we die, as the biggest of the two facing Honey leaps at her, jaws snapping. Honey dodges, colliding with me and throwing me towards the others guarding the ring, who fall back but don't attack me like I expect. The big wolf lunges again, leading with his chest, and Honey slips around him and rips at his ear with her teeth before dancing out of reach.

A growl passes round the ring as the bleeding wolf falls back. Five wolves remain, and now two surge forward, trying to pin Honey between them. One yelps and pulls away with a long gouge across his snout. The three watching me haven't moved. I can't get around them but they won't attack so I go on the offensive, barking and snarling as I leap at them, refusing to give into my gut-clenching terror. If I have to die, let it be like this, not in some dank, forgotten cell but here under the stars, fighting for one more glimpse of the sky, for one more night on earth.

There's a thud and a rattle of shale behind me as a hulking wolf knocks Honey to the ground. Before she can roll to her front he has her throat between his foaming jaws. My heart freezes in my chest as I wait for him to bite, rip, ruin, but as the seconds pass I understand what it is they're trying to do.

They aren't here to kill us.

They're here to arrest us.

I throw myself at the wolf holding Honey, biting at his flank and scoring two ugly gashes in his haunch. He lets go of her to round on me but the scent of blood has started the others howling.

No matter how hard Grange trains them, drugs them, beats them, she can't crush out that last spark of wildness. She's only twisted it, weaponized their carnivorous nature to send them into killing frenzies whenever blood gets spilled. A fact I hate exploiting, but at this point is us or them, and in the end it's for their sake that I've done everything.

Somewhere under the collar and drugs and agony, these werewolves are just like me. Fighting a war they didn't start, risking their lives on someone else's orders. Grange's goals might be mercenary, but her means of achieving it aren't much different than the bureau's.

We're the means, the weapons, the suckers, but I can't spare the sympathy, and as a gap opens up in the circle I bolt, ignoring the sounds of fighting and yelps of agony as Grange's pets turn on each other.

Honey's right behind and soon overtakes me as we tear across the hillside. My lungs burn, every step jarring my injuries and rattling my bones, but if we stop running we're screwed, so I swallow my exhaustion and focus on keeping my legs moving.

A piercing whine splits the air, making Honey stumble. It gets louder and louder, battering my aching head and making my breath stick in my throat. The moon is rising behind the ridge ahead of us but faster than any moon and more full, the trees casting skeletal shadows that reach and grow then shrink away as I realize that deep hammering sound isn't my heartbeat but a helicopter.

It bursts over the ridge, its blazing lights blinding the both of us as it bears down on us faster than any wolf could run. Honey checks in mid stride and takes off in another direction, towards a little clutch of trees hidden in a hollow in the otherwise barren hillside. Just enough cover we can stop to rest, before the wolves or worse catches up with us. Something hits my haunch and sticks there, and though the blow isn't hard I can't resist the spreading numbness of the tranquilizer in the dart, or the black silence that swallows me whole.

Nineteen

The Facility

I wake up in Grange's office. The wall of flickering monitors bathes the front of the desk in blue-gray light, the back of the room lost in the wavering shadows, and at first I wonder if I've died, and this is my punishment, my version of purgatory. Not hell but limbo, because I died for a good cause. Maybe I'm dreaming. Or maybe just now waking up, and all the chaos of the last few days was the dream, but as I lift my head I feel the collar around my neck.

"Wednesday, you fucker…" Grange hisses under her breath from behind the desk as four monitors in a row wink off. As she gets up I lay my head down and close my eyes again but I can't pretend to still be asleep, as the collar transmits my heartrate to her watch.

I haven't worn this collar in weeks. Months even, and I've let myself forget how much I hated it, for what does and for what it represents. Grange should be collared too, because she's not the one in charge. Just another slave to this cruel machine.

As she approaches, my nose paints the picture: she's muddy, and sweaty, and bleeding a little, her teeth grinding as she breathes hard through her nostrils. Any good dog would notice its owner's distress, so I open my eyes. She's standing over me, her executive fatigues streaked with dirt, her hands twitching by her side. Her face a stiff mask, she raises her arm like she's going to perform some function on her watch. I tense, awaiting the convulsive jolt of the electric shock or the prick of a dermal spur.

"I'm coming down," Grange says into her watch. "Tell that bitch it's do or die."

Aching all over, I follow Grange out of the office then outside. I don't know what she can hear but to me the night is alive with sound, the ordinary background noise of insects and wind competing against the distant thudding of the helicopter and the shouting and burst of small arm fire coming from much nearer. Hung up on the noises I don't notice where we're going as I follow her across the unlit compound until we reach the pits.

A guard in dusty fatigues opens the door in the green access hut. The smell of Stone and the other captives hangs in the air as we descend the service stairs to the curving corridor that encircles the pit. Another guard lets us into one of the holding pens, the door locking automatically behind us.

Nala's sitting in a folding chair in the middle of the bare concrete room. Her face is bruised and her lip is cut but I'm surprised that she isn't handcuffed. A miscalculation on Grange's part, because Nala could break her neck in a couple of moves.

"What did you do to him?" Nala asks sharply as Grange pulls a thick nylon leash out of her thigh pocket and clips it to my collar, then hands me off to the guard in the room.

"Nothing. He's just a bit woozy from the tranq. Don't worry, I won't hurt your little dog," Grange replies as she pulls on her Kevlar-backed gloves. "You, on the other hand, I'm going to grind into the fucking dirt. Who's your boss?"

"Mr. Eat Shit," Nala enunciates, showing her teeth. "A real nice guy, he—uhn!" Grange's backhand throws her sideways. She sits upright slowly, probing her cheek with her tongue.

"You realize I have better things to do with my time than squeeze you for answers I could get from someone else?" Grange says as she stalks around the chair.

"Then go do that, why don't you?"

In answer Grange hits her again, a swift jab to the jaw that makes my own teeth rattle. "I don't know, I'm kind of enjoying fucking you over the way you fucked me," she says, flexing her gloved hands as Nala struggles upright again. "Still not going to hit me back?"

Nala wipes her bloody mouth on her shoulder. "Why should I give you an excuse to shoot me dead?" she slurs.

"You think I need an excuse?"

"Then get the fuck on with it, love."

"You think you're so fucking smart. How smart are you going to feel when I cut your little puppy dog to ribbons right here in front of you?"

"You sick bitch! You leave him—agh!" She doubles over as Grange straight-arms her in the gut.

"Mind your manners, Agent Warnock. And you," Grange barks, rounding on the guard. "Keep that animal under control, understand?"

"Yes, Tanya."

I sit up straighter as he tightens his grip on my leash. It's the only thing keeping me from leaping at Grange and biting the life out of her. Not to save myself but to save Nala. I've done everything wrong and now me and my best friend get to watch each other die.

"I fucking hate dogs," Grange says simply as she gazes down at me without a hint of human expression. "For all I know, he's the informer. Imagine that."

A whine escapes my tense throat even though I'm pouring my entire self into not reacting at all. Staying perfectly still. Remaining the dumb, wordless, domesticated animal she believes me to be.

"Imagine that," she repeats, half to herself. "If he was one of..." Frowning, she crouches on one knee to look me in the eyes. Lifting my jaw, she turns my head to and fro, handling me with casual control as she searches for something I can't let her see. Then her pinched expression brightens with a sudden realization. She gets to her feet, brushing my hair off her gloves.

"Don't let either of them leave this room," she says to the guard. "I won't be long. Then we'll see who's full of shit, and who's dead."

Flashing Nola an ugly grin, she swipes her watch over the lock control. "Lab, it's Sparrow," she says into its nano-mic. "Start deicing a shot of serum thirty-eight."

As the echo of her footsteps dies Nala slumps forward. Resting her elbows on her knees, she rubs the back of her neck. The guard has relaxed his death-grip on my leash enough I can obey my shuddering muscles and lie down.

Serum thirty-eight. The missing link, the last component of Hyperion's system, the catalyst they've propagated at the cost of untold lives, weres kidnapped to be used as test subjects for the most horrific of experiments. Some of which I've witnessed, seated at Grange's side behind bulletproof glass while the victim writhed and screamed and died on the operating table. That might be me in a few minutes, the trials showing a one in four chance of hypertropic deformation resulting in an unviable hybrid. Science jargon for being too monstrous to live. Will that be me, with fangs growing so rapidly they pierce my own face, my muscle cells bursting with the speed of change?

Even if I live, I'm going to die.

Nala sits up slowly, sucking blood through her loosened teeth. "She's going to kill that dog, you know," she slurs. "Right here in front of you. She'll probably make you help. Make you hold him down while she skins him alive."

The guard clears his throat, his hand flexing on the leash.

"You got pets?" she says. "Better yet, you got kids? What do you tell them when they ask what daddy does for a living?"

His shoulders drop as he groans under his breath. "Look, lady, I'm just doing my job."

"Lady. Right," she says, nodding as she looks him up and down. "That's the problem, innit? You're just doing your job. That makes you just as much a slave as the animals. Worse, because they don't have a choice. You, you're choosing to be here. Choosing to dance with the devil. The funny thing is, I bet you think you can just quit any time. That she'll let you leave, knowing what you know. You'd be dead in less than a day. You walk into that office to resign, you'll never walk out again. You'll be dragged out in a body bag and fed into the incinerator—"

"Shut up," he hisses through his clenched teeth.

"You know I'm right."

"So? What's your point?"

"No point," she says with a shrug. "But if I'm going to die I'm going to make her work for it. You, you could get out right now. Say the word. You can live through this. I can make that happen. She can't. She won't, because you're a liability. In fact, I'll bet she replaces the entire staff. And by replace I mean murder. Because you're all in on it. Aiding and abetting sedition."

"It's a research facility," he grates, like they tell them in the training videos.

"Sure thing," Nala drawls, kicking out her feet as she settles back in the chair. "Funded by the Russians for the purpose of developing a terrorist cell that can destroy the US from within. Yes, very important research. You speak much Russian, darling?" She repeats her speech in a thick Chechen accent, glancing at me as she calls him *milyy*.

I go off, snarling and lunging at the leash, dragging the stumbling guard as I hurl myself at Nala like I want to eat her alive. Just like I've been trained, the trigger word drilled into my subconscious over weeks of training, augmented by the buzzing of the transdermal chip behind my ear. Which means it's still picking up sound, still keeping track of everything around me. I let that drive me, the knowledge that we're not completely fucked, that even if Nala and I both die, Grange will serve time for her crimes.

Choked by the collar, fighting for my life, I drag the guard closer to Nala, who watches me indifferently. Suddenly she throws herself out of the chair, pivoting on one leg to bring her other foot up and around and into the side of the guard's head with a sickening thwack.

As he falls hard he lets go of my leash. I'm on him before he lands, my teeth skidding on the tactical nylon fabric of his sleeve as I bite at his arm. As Nala steps on his other arm I get a grip on his hand, my teeth pressing into but not breaking his skin.

Stinking of fear and cheap body spray, the guard stops squirming. "Call him off!" he begs in a strangled whisper as Nala frisks him.

"Get fucked," she replies cheerfully.

"Please, lady," he gasps. "They said they'd kill my mom."

She draws back. "Your mum's in here?"

Gulping, he shakes his head. "They have her under surveillance. They show me pictures of her at the grocery store. At her book club. At home."

"Of course they do," Nala says, lifting her foot off his wrist. I release his other hand but as she helps him to his feet the door opens.

"What the fuck is going on?" Grange shouts as she strides into the pen, her voice ringing off the dirty concrete walls. She raises her weapon and fires, not at Nala like I fear but at me.

Twenty

Get Out

Grange has wicked aim and the medicated dart strikes my shoulder, the stiff needle embedding itself deeply in my skin, her next words melting and bending as my head starts to change shape, the catalyst kick-starting my hormones and forcing me to shift. Whining in agony, I flatten myself against the cold floor, my skin feeling like its being torn in a thousand places, my bones seeming to creak as they reform. It's violent and violating and leaves me shuddering in naked, nauseous misery. I force my eyes open to find Grange standing over me, her feet either side of my head.

"Who the fuck is this? Better yet, who's Ronan Wednesday? Hmm?" She taps the side of my head with the toe of her boot. "What does he turn into? A snake? A rat? Or is he a fucking asshole right down to the core?"

I want to punch her. Grab her by the throat and end her. I can barely breathe, exhausted beyond belief by the cruel night and the rapid shifting and the godawful facts of my life. I'm useless after all, a liability when I'm meant to be an asset. A loser.

"Ronan Wednesday, what a fake-ass name," she says under her breath, "And Hyperion's who sent him to me, those Balkan fucks. They can deal with the clean-up, because it's going to be fucking messy. Do you hear me?" she says, knocking my forehead with her boot again. "By the time I'm done with him, Wednesday's going to beg me to let him die."

The door is open, letting in the damp night air and sound of gunfire, the rumble of a big explosion somewhere far away as she removes a syringe with the yellow cap of a sedative from her waist-pack.

"You," she says to the guard. "Make yourself useful and go find me a collar and a body-bag. Go on, get moving," she says as he glances at Nala, poised on the edge of her seat. "I'm not worried about that bitch."

She should be, but I'm the last one who's going to tell her as she stands over me, the syringe held like a dagger. "And to think, she says through her bared teeth, "all this time you've been listening in, watching everything I do. I'm going to find out who you're working for, even if I have to cut it out of you."

Neither of us see it coming, and it's the last thing I expect, as Nala hits Grange full force with the folding chair and sends her sprawling, the syringe flying from her hand and disappearing into the dark corner. Before Nala can help me up Grange is back on her feet, blood leaking from the split in her lip, a wicked concrete burn on her cheek.

They circle each other, Grange swaying like a boxer late in the match. I don't feel much better, my vision clouding as I struggle to my feet. Grange lunges and they grapple briefly before Nala falls back, her hand pressed to her shoulder, blood seeping from between her fingers.

"Piece by piece," Grange hisses, wiping her knife clean on her pants as they resume their deadly dance. "That's how I'm going to take you down. You and all the rest. Everyone who's been fucking with me."

"Who's been fucking with you?" Nala asks, hoarse with pain.

"Everyone. Vladimir, the board of director, the hacks in security. Ronan fucking Wednesday. Sent here to ruin me. To destroy me. Well, they can't have me." Grange's voice cracks. Her eyes are glassy, the knife trembling in her rigid grip as she lunges again, slashing at Nala's stomach.

"They've got you doped up, haven't they?" Nala says. "Just like the animals—"

"I am not an animal!"

With a strangled scream of rage Grange hurls herself at Nala again. Driven by the drugs in her system, she moves with frightening speed and precision, shaking off Nala's kicks and punches as she slashes and stabs, aiming for her eyes, throat, stomach, using her fists where she can.

Dodging a slash that would have spilled her intestines, Nala stumbles over the damn folding chair. Grange tackles her and they hit the concrete hard, grunting and cursing each other as they wrestle on the rotted concrete.

I can't stand by; I have to act, but I can barely lift a corner of the folding chair. The syringe of sedative on the other hand...

As much as I might want to, I don't need to kill Grange. I just have to stop her, stop this fight before I lose Nala for good. I have seconds to act as Grange rolls on top, one hand around Nala's throat. I have nothing to lose, but neither does Grange, and as she draws back the knife I lurch forward and stab the syringe into the side of her neck, the only place I know I won't hit bone or her bulletproof vest.

Grange screams, a demonic howl of interrupted bloodlust, clawing at my hands as I lean into it so the maximum dose will enter her system. The shot is for rabid monsters twice her bodyweight and her eyes roll closed in seconds. As she starts to drool I drag her limp body off Nala, who gets slowly to her feet.

"Damned drama queen," she says as she picks up Grange's fallen knife. "Couldn't have just shot me like a normal—"

"Can we not talk about it?" I say through my chattering teeth.

"Sorry, mate. Let's get you out of here."

The fighting has stopped or moved away and we come out of the access hut to an eerily quiet night. Even the usual twitter and patter of nocturnal birds and small animals is stilled, and our breathing sounds painfully loud as we stumble through the dark woods. I can't stop shivering, my pale skin starkly obvious, my bare feet seeming to find every sharp stick and stone.

We halt in the lee of a big bolder. "I'm going to shift back," I say softly, my hands shaking too hard for me to sign. "If I can't keep up, you keep going."

"No, Blake—"

"Yes. I'll follow your scent. I won't get lost. But I can't do it like this. Go on and I'll catch up."

Her face taut with emotion we don't have time to share, she nods. "Good luck."

"Same to you."

She slips away, her all-black gear quickly fading into the darkness. Grange's drug is still in my system and I struggle to trigger the reaction, the brain signals disrupted by the artificial hormones.

The change leaves me dizzy and painfully hungry. Nala's trail hangs in the air like a flag and I follow her easily, my low, sleek body slipping between the trees, the rough pads of my feet hardly making a sound.

But I'm tired. So unbelievably tired, and the treetops block the stars. The dark land rises and falls, the trail of scent winding around naked spurs of rock and over rifts and little canyons, always tracking downhill. Following the ridge, I come out onto a low peak overlooking a narrow canyon. Someone is moving below, a slim, quiet man whose salty-sweet scent catches in my chest. Ronan, and I nearly bark to get his attention when a thin rustling reaches me from the opposite ridge, followed by the rank smell of a werewolf. I flatten myself against the hard ground as the collared wolf creeps to the edge of the rock. It's followed by two blobby figures with dull red eyes, their heads merging into their shoulders in the silhouette of Hyperion's hooded mercenaries.

Shit. I can't hear what they're saying through those helmets. Double shit, as they split up, the wolf and one of the soldiers disappearing into the dark while the other soldier picks his way down the shadowed side of the slope then hurries after Ronan, who's disappeared down the narrow split at the lower end of the canyon.

The clouds have gathered, swallowing the yellow moon and leaving us in profound darkness as I scramble down the ridge and pick up the two trails. Though the night seems to swarm with enemies I know they're mainly in my mind, as only fourteen werewolves have survived Hyperion's experiments. That one I just saw would be enough to put an end to me, and I'm no safer around Hyperion's human mercenaries, so I stay well back, following the dry scrape of his hard-soled boots on the gritty soil, the smell of his gun oil and the eggs he ate for breakfast. listening all the while for any sign of wolves or other guards on my tail.

When he stops so do I. A surprising truth about combat is how much time you spend waiting. For the artillery to cease firing, for the enemy to come in range or pass you by without engaging. For an order to pass down the line of command. For the end of your tour, for retirement. For a single combatant to finish tying his fucking shoelaces, because I won't attack this man unless he gives me a reason.

We catch up with Ronan at the edge of a band of trees. Open ground stretches below him a good mile, and he lingers behind a spiny shrub considering his next move. Hidden by a heap of boulders and the abnormal shape of his head, Hyperion's man draws his weapon and aims for Ronan's back.

That's reason enough.

Without a sound I leap from the hollow where I've been hiding and dash the last hundred yards. He has just time to turn when I'm on him, snapping at his gun hand, my teeth barely catching on his slippery tactical wear.

Something hits my flank with the force of a lightning bolt, throwing me through the air. I forgot about the gloves with the built-in tasers. Forgot that these suits are built to make the wearer werewolf-proof, to protect Hyperon's human fighters from the lycan ones.

Winded, aching, short on time, I lie where I fell as the horrific headless figure strides towards me, dart gun in hand.

Death, please. Not captivity. Not Grange's pens and the collar and the drugs, the loss of self, the nightmare. Like a nightmare, I want to run but I can't even stand, my hind legs scrabbling uselessly in the dirt.

He raises the dart gun and I close my eyes. Better me than Ronan. With any luck the experiments will kill me sooner rather than later. If I'm really lucky someone will leave me alone with Grange for ten seconds too long and I can pay her back for everything she's put me through.

But instead of the crack of the dart gun and the punch of the drugged needle I hear a handgun's loud retort, feel the vibration as a man falls to the ground. Then footsteps and the steely smell of blood then Ronan's hand on my neck, feeling for my pulse. I open my eyes and lick his hand and he smiles like I just gave him the world.

Twenty-One

Crows

The nightmarish paralysis lifts now that I've been freed from death. At least temporarily, but with Ronan beside me the odds look better for us both. He feels me over for injuries then we slink away, leaving the guard groaning in the dark.

Always tracking downhill, we creep along the edge of the woods for another half a mile. Alone with Ronan in the still of the night, it's easy to forget why we're here as I trot along at his heels, lapping up his mouth-watering smell. Hard to resist the urge to shift and present myself, give in to my hot-blooded need to be touched, held, made real through someone else's desire. Soon, soon, as a prize for surviving. Assuming he still wants me.

It's enough that he's alive. He can hate me for the rest of his life, as long as he gets to live it. I've done enough damage, fucked up his plans and my own so badly that I won't blame him for wanting me gone.

We stop in one of those little hollows that dot the hillsides, where he offers me a few handfuls of water from his nearly empty canteen.

"I don't suppose you know where we are," he says softly. He laughs as I lie down to make clear that I don't. "I didn't think so."

A pair of those beady eyed crows are watching us from a nearby branch. Another couple fly past overhead, so close that I hear the air ripple over their wings.

"Mind your manners, birdies," Ronan says as the birds jostle for space on the thin branch. "Though they were clever before, with the cameras."

The first pair take flight, circling once above us then landing in another tree fifty yards downhill. As a third joins them, I get to my feet. I know this creeping feeling. It's saved my life before, this instinctual discomfort that rises from my toes until it consumes my whole awareness. These birds are allies. They know the truth, in ways they cannot say. But only humans are stupid enough to believe they're the only thinking creature in the world. I take a few steps towards the flock, then look back at Ronan.

"You really think they know?" he says to me as a fourth bird joins the others. I take a few more steps and he sighs then shoves the canteen in his pack. "Well, we've fuck all else. Lead on."

The birds are barely visible in the darkness under the trees, but I can follow their noisy fluttering easily enough. Ronan brings up the rear, muttering now and then about black dogs in the mist and cursing softly whenever he stumbles.

I slow when I smell rusting steel and concrete. The birds keep on, leading us from tree to tree until we come to a clearing with three pits, marked by green access huts like all the others. The air simmers with the scent of old blood and fear, a grinding tension that scrapes at my nerves.

"God damn you, Hyperion," Ronan breathes, clenching his fists. I follow his gaze to the row of bleached skulls staring back at us from across the nearest pit. Wolf and human both, and in between two or three caught in the act of shifting, with elongated jaws and nasal cavities and broad foreheads.

Faced with the final proof of Grange and Hyperion's sadism, I recoil with a snarl, my head singing with rage. Rage and fear and shame that it took us so long to act. That we let so many of my kind die a brutal, ugly death and get mounted up like trophies, all because my superiors couldn't be convinced to act.

Ronan crouches beside me, stroking my back as he hums a soft tune, some sweet little lullaby as soothing as his gentle touch. He knows me, knows what it takes to keep me safe, and I can't stop myself from nuzzling under his chin. Laughing softly, he keeps on petting me. Then pauses, turning his head to and fro. "Do you hear that?"

So it's not my nerves, not my imagination, but a real noise, a repetitive mechanical clunking. It leads us around the edge of the clearing and further downhill. At last we reach a road, overgrown with grass and knee-high tree sprouts. Crows stand in a bluntly obvious line down the middle. Ronan shrugs then starts along it, towards the noise.

The road soon converges with a chain-link fence topped with rusted razor wire. Aspen saplings crowd against the other side of the fence, their thin branches shoving through the chain-link in a rustling green hedge. We travel along the abandoned road as the noise gets louder and louder until we reach a tall chain-link gate.

Like the fence, the gate is grown about with saplings. A scanner for the automatic opener is mounted on a pole nearby. The front panel of the scanner and several wires dangle from the housing, which is frosted white with bird shit. Every few seconds, the opening mechanism kicks in then reverses as it senses the resistance of the branches growing through the mesh, the gate rolling slightly open then shutting again in a repetitive grating rhythm.

"It seems too easy," Ronan whispers, drawing his gun. We approach cautiously, passing behind the scanner in case its camera still functions. But even if we're detected, who could get to us in time?

Another truth of warfare: grand gestures and big battles aren't the only way to win. After everything we've done, everything we've endured, the terror and the violence, we're saved by some birds, some branches, and a broken gate, as first Ronan then I squeeze through the foot-wide gap.

We continue along the old road another half a mile until it ends at a graveled road heading uphill. The scraping of the gate still reaches my ears, but so does another sound, the shuffling mutter of a large group of people trying to stay quiet. Keeping to the shoulder, my nose seeking out any whiff of Grange or her doped-up mercenaries, I lead Ronan up the road towards the sound and the smell of sweat and large vehicles.

Rounding a bend, we duck behind a tree. A shiny black 4x4 is parked diagonally across the road. A man in a black ball cap and a zip-front jacket stands beside it, talking on his phone. He turns, and my heart starts beating again at the sight of the big white letters printed on the back of his jacket.

"Thank fuck. I've never been so glad to see the FBI," Ronan says, grinning as he throws his arm around me. "I hope one of those arseholes has some decent coffee."

Twenty-Two

Grandmother

The stake out is a typical bureau shit-show, where everyone's passing the buck back and forth and no one has time to answer our questions. I don't care, I've already done my part. Gathered the evidence, helped the victims. Whatever justice gets served from here on is out of my hands.

We accept a lift up to Hollowood from a junior aide with carefully sculpted stubble, who spends the drive telling Ronan about his best friend's sister-in-law's puppy adoption saga. Dogs can soften up just about anyone. Grange being the exception, but fuck her. She doesn't deserve dogs.

Everyone in town seems to have gathered at the Lodge, the parking lot full of dusty trucks and 4x4s. Inside, Ronan goes to fetch coffee from the busy kitchen. I follow the gray-haired woman acting as quartermaster to a side room, where I shift and get dressed in yet another pair of donated sweats and a faded hunting jacket.

I feel hungover, my body wrung out like a rag, my stomach both aching with hunger and churning at the thought of food. Barefoot, I come out to the veranda, where Evan and Pierce are sitting on a bench, wrapped in blankets and hugging steaming mugs of what smells like cocoa.

"Is Graeme around?" I asks as they shuffle over to make room for me.

"Not back yet," Pierce mumbles into his mug.

"I'm sure he's fine."

Evan tugs the blanket closer around his neck. Sniffling, he lays his head on Pierce's shoulder, and I bite the inside of my cheeks to keep the sorrow from taking me over too. These guys didn't sign up for any of this. Came for a visit to Evan's hometown and ended up in a war. At least I knew the risks I was taking. Knew there was a chance I wouldn't make it out alive. I want to tell them that Graeme did what he thought was right, that if he died it was for a good cause, but I'm a stranger to them, and part of the reason why he's gone.

Ronan comes outside with Chase, who's clinging to the arm of a huge man with a thick brown beard. The big guy is wearing a wool blanket around his hips and a plaid jacket whose sleeves barely come to his elbows.

"I know it's weird," Chase says to him as he balks, "but do it for me. He saved your fucking life, alright?"

Grumbling in his chest, the man shuffles forward and puts out his hand. We shake, his hand dwarfing mine, and he's about to back away when Chase clears his throat.

The big man frowns, his eyes disappearing beneath his heavy brow. "Thank you," he mumbles.

"No problem."

"Sorry about Stone," Chase says to me as the man scurries down the stairs and disappears around the corner of the building. "He's weird about, you know, people."

He's about to start down the stairs when Stone comes trundling around the corner again, the blanket flapping around his bare knees. Chase meets him at ground level, where Stone bends down to mutter into his ear.

"What are you talking about, you saw a horse?"

Ronan's breath catches as our eyes meet. Evan and Pierce meanwhile haven't moved. They don't know. They're married to him and don't know he's a shifter too.

"I think we'd better see what that's about," Ronan says as I get up from the bench. "You too," he says to Graeme's mates.

"They're both full of shit," Evan grates, hunching the blanket around his ears. "There's no horses around here…" He trails off as a gray horse emerges from the early morning mist, a tiny cloaked figure clinging to its withers.

"That's weird," Pierce says as the horse bends its forelegs and partly kneels to let the little person dismount.

"Not as weird as that," Evan murmurs as the fine-boned horse begins to contort, collapsing into the shape of an athletic, muscular man with an enormous…

"Holy fuck," Pierce breathes, his eyes swelling. "Our husband's a horse?"

"A kelpie, I believe," Ronan says as Evan sets his mug on the bench then dashes down the stairs. "Though fair warning, they've been known to eat men." Pierce gives him a dirty look but says nothing more as he goes down to join his mates.

"Does it start to seem normal after a while?" Ronan says, coming to stand beside me at the railing.

"I wouldn't know normal if I saw it, so…"

Smiling, he slides his arm around my waist. "Maybe that explains what you saw in me."

"Your unnormalness? Wait, is that a word?"

He laughs and pulls me nearer, and I'm about to kiss him when I notice Stone approaching with a glassy expression, Grandmother bundled in his arms like an elderly cat. As they reach the top of the stairs she lifts a bony finger and he halts. She crooks the finger and beckons to me, and it's like there's a hook in my heart as I stumble forward until I'm stepping on Stone's toes. He doesn't flinch or even blink as once again Grandmother stretches out her bony arm to put her hand on my head and reach inside my brain.

Deeper, into my soul, into my history, dragging the both of us backwards through time as I see myself shrink to a spark in my parents' eyes. Their history next, the days and years flicking past in an instant, until I follow my mother alone, through her youth then infancy. Deeper, further, following the thread of my ancestry through the fabric of the past to a windy cliff face overlooking a wine-dark sea, the crash of waves not enough to drown out my kin's wild howling.

You and I, child, a voice says, a voice that comes from everywhere and nowhere, dry as old leaves, as cold as the night. *We know this way. You have not forgotten. You were never alone.*

Twenty-Three

Victory

I wake with a start and a pain in my arm. Grandmother and Stone have gone and Ronan is staring at me, his eyes wide, his hands locked around my upper arm. "Can you hear me?" he says urgently.

"Now I can. What happened?" I ask as he helps me to the bench.

"It was just like in that hospital room on the island, when you went completely blank."

"That not what it feels like on my end."

If he doesn't understand he doesn't judge me either, doesn't doubt me out loud as I try to explain the kaleidoscopic assault of memory and dreams, the light and sound and intangible sensations, and the difference between what I just felt and the less intrusive experience when Honey tried to communicate with me.

"Grandmother said the same thing now as she did on the island. She said *welcome home*. I don't know why, I've never been here in my life. And after all this, I kind of hope I don't ever have to come back."

"It's awful pretty in the daytime, though." Even now it has an eerie charm, with the house lights twinkling among the trees, the mist around the Dew Drop Inn glowing blue and red, the stars filling the wedge of the sky.

"The winters must be brutal," I say, thinking of that ice storm the year I lived in central Pennsylvania.

"There's that. What about you, where did you grow up?"

"All over. We moved a lot. My dad, well, I think he was like me but he was hiding it. Then when I was nine or ten he fucked off for good."

"That's dreadful! What happened?"

"I don't really know. Mom would never say, just that it was best for all of us that he wasn't around anymore. She died when I was seventeen, before I could get her to explain. The army was the only place left for me."

"And now?"

"I've got to get out of the game before I get myself killed. Or someone else. I don't know what I'm going to do, but the bureau can find itself a new sucker."

"We'll figure it out tomorrow," he says, putting his arm around my shoulder. Again, I lean towards him for a kiss, and again pause, as a gleaming black 4x4 pulls up in front of the Lodge. Nala leaps out, nearly bashing the door into the eager young subordinate who was about to open it for her.

"You small-minded bureaucrat!" she shouts at Curtis as he follows more slowly.

"You will watch your tongue, Agent Warnock," says Curtis' PA Reba, a square-shouldered woman with a military haircut and zero imagination, as she gets out of the other side of the truck.

"Don't you *Agent Warnock* me, Reba, you brown-nosing so-and-so. And as for you, Curtis Nixon, I have photos of you."

"That's no way to talk to your superior officer," Ronan murmurs as the three continue to argue.

"You going to tell her that?"

"Not on your life."

"Look, Nala," Curtis says tiredly, taking off his glasses to pinch the bridge of his nose. "I've agreed to not charge them with conspiracy. But you can't argue with the trespassing."

"I can and I will. Sir, you know I respect you but you cannot think that's an appropriate response. These people here are the victims. They're the ones who have lost family and friends. The Bonnys have been held prisoner for nearly two decades. And you want to blame them? For what? For fighting for their freedom?"

"Don't put words in my mouth, agent," he warns Nala, who hisses through her teeth. "I can't be taking sides."

"The state had better take a side," Honey calls out to him, for the yelling has brought a dozen people out onto the veranda. "Leif's mother was poisoned by the leachate in the creek, remember."

"Then there's the cruelty to animals," Nala says, counting on her fingers. "The soil pollution, the human remains, the—"

"Okay, okay, I get it," Curtis says, throwing up his hands. "One way or another, we're shutting them down. It may mean letting the world know your little town exists."

"Many people do know," says Mr. Culver as he descends the stairs. "They just try not to think about it. But you're right, this is something the federal government needs to intervene in immediately."

"Better get going on some NDAs," Curtis says to Reba, who's hovering at his elbow like usual. Her face lights up as she starts flicking through forms on her tablet.

"Easy does it," Mr. Culver says, and if I knew him better I might think he was smirking. "Folks here are more than willing to keep a secret. You might find them not so willing if you try and force it on them."

"We can't leave this unsecured. The place will be a zoo. I mean a media circus. I mean—look, this is a top secret investigation."

Filthy with mud, bleeding from a gash in his forehead, Mr. Culver smiles mildly. "I can't help thinking if you'd done something about Hyperion sooner," he says, "there wouldn't be any secrets to keep."

Curtis whips off his glasses again, clutching them by the arm as he massages the bridge of his nose. The chief is as damaged as I am, which is why he stays out of the field these days. "Alright," he grates. "Let's talk numbers."

"What kind of numbers?"

Curtis exhales hard then jams his glasses back on his face. "Community reparation numbers. Need anything paved? Better goddamn broadband?"

"That's a start," Mr. Culver says, his grin spreading. "And an upgrade to our water system, given that our wells have been affected by Hyperion's actions. Do you know much about geothermal energy?"

"A little."

"Come on, we'll get some coffee," he says, throwing an arm around Curtis' shoulder. "My buddy Robin makes a mean cup of coffee, better even than the stuff at the Lodge." He steers Curtis across the road towards a strip of houses set among the trees.

"What about us, are we free to go?" I ask Reba as she starts after them.

She turns, her face lit from below by the glowing screen of her tablet. "Sure, but don't go too far."

"I am going right over there," Ronan replies with crisp emphasis, stabbing a finger at the Dew Drop Inn, lying quietly below us quiet at the bend in the road. "I am going to sleep, and if anyone wakes me tomorrow before..." He jerks up his arm to consult his watch. "Ten thirty in the a.m., do not count on my cooperation."

As Reba mumbles some reply Ronan flashes me a pointed look then starts down the stairs. I linger on the porch, not sure if he wants me with him until he snaps his fingers. That arrogant...

I still obey, catching up with him as he crosses the road. "Don't do that again, okay?"

"Are you sure?" he asks with a sidelong glance.

"Alright, it worked, but...ah, fuck it. Who cares?" I say as he takes my hand. I lean over to kiss his cheek but he catches my chin and makes me stop to kiss him properly: on the mouth, not holding back, standing in the middle of the road. Unashamed, claiming me in front of anyone and everyone, after everything. The lies we told each other, the trust we nearly broke. If that's not enough to drive him away from me, then nothing in the world can keep us apart.

Except maybe Nala, who stops me with a sharp whistle. "Not so fast, you," she says as she strides towards us.

"It's good to see you, Nala, but—"

"Hush up. I'm speaking to this one." She inserts herself between Ronan and I, prodding him in the shoulder with a sharp finger. "Are you going to be good to my boy?"

He glances towards me. "I'm going to try."

"You had better be good to him. He's not as tough as he makes out. So you best remember this: You hurt my boy, you hurt me." She taps her chest.

His eyes fly open. "I wouldn't dream of doing so."

"We'll let bygones be bygone, no?"

"Yes. Exactly that."

"Good to hear." Before he can step away, she claps her hand on the back of his neck. "And don't forget, Mr. Wednesday," she says with a lethal grin, "if you do fuck with him, we're going to hear every word of it."

My hand goes automatically to the implant scar behind my ear as she pinches his cheek. She lets him go then turns to me, her fierce look fading to that expression of pity I so often see. But she cares about me, so I'll allow it. I couldn't do a thing about it anyway.

"And as for you," she says gently, "you stay out of trouble. I mean all the way out."

"That's the plan. Early retirement. Think I'll take up landscape painting."

"Don't take any shit. From Wednesday, from Curtis, from no one."

"Just from you, Nala. Like always."

"You joker. I'll miss you."

"Stay in touch."

"I expect we'll see plenty of each other before all this gets settled."

"If we're in D.C. at the same time, let's have dinner."

"House of Jade?"

"Where else?"

We hug, then she hugs Ronan, who's still blinking in shock. Then Reba calls to her and with a sigh and a last wave she walks away, melting into the thickening mist as Ronan takes my hand.

Twenty-Four

Fate

"Have you got a fated mate like the rest of them?" Ronan asks as we start walking again.

"No idea. Maybe it's you."

He laughs softly. "Wouldn't that be something?"

"I'd want it to be you."

"You would not. I'd make a terrible husband."

"So would I."

"I snore."

"Dude. I'm literally a dog."

"Only some of the time." His expression sobers. "Does it matter that I'm not? That I'm only this?" He gestures dismissively at himself.

"Not to me it doesn't. And fuck what anyone else thinks."

He grins, and though I'm ready to shove him against the motel wall and kiss that grin off his gorgeous face, I let him unlock the door to our room first. Once inside I give him time to slip the chain bolt, then I push him against the back of the door and kiss him until he's trembling. Or maybe his shaking is only a symptom, as the fear he's lived with all night loosens its tense grip on his somatic system.

"Are you okay?" I ask as he buries his face in the crook of my neck.

"I don't know," he replies, his voice muffled. "Can we talk about it tomorrow?"

"Sure." He stiffens in my arms and I let him go. "I might grab a shower if you don't mind."

He nods absently, looking about like this isn't the room he expected. Something tells me to stay with him in case he needs me or, worse, disappears, but I stink like I was dug out of the ground. In the shower I scrub down quickly, not wanting to get stuck in my fucked up feelings. My own residual fear from the night just passed, the continual fear that I'm not worth what I'll cost him. In time, in emotional labor, in putting up with me on my bad days, when simply being alive seems too much to take. Ronan is so much more to me than just a man. First my sanity, then my enemy, but now what is he? Is this our beginning or our end?

When I come out, the room is cold and dark and he's already in bed, breathing deeply. Shit. But that's better than if he was gone. I hang up the towels then switch off the lights and slip under the covers, trying not to disturb him. Too late, as he stirs then rolls towards me, the light from the bathroom outlining his face and bare shoulder in ice-white.

"Sorry," he mumbles. "Hell of a day."

"Forget about it," I say as I slip my arm under his head. "Sleep is probably better for us than what we were going to do."

"Hmm...but I want to," he says, cuddling closer to me. "I want to be with you."

"You *are* with me."

"Flirt. You know what I mean."

"Do you really need to get laid that badly?"

"Says the guy with two broken ribs who was begging for it last night. Sorry. That's probably the last thing you want to remember."

"Yeah, the interrogation really killed the mood. But it's alright. You did what you had to. I'm surprised you believed me."

"I had three choices. Two made sense, and one was pure selfishness. I could either arrest you, or kill you, or trust you. The first two would have meant giving you up for good. The third...well, here we are."

We kiss again but slowly, tasting each other deeply. I want to know everything about him, every way to please him. but when I put my hand on his hip he pulls away.

"What's wrong? Tell what you need."

He stares at me, then drops his head. "I don't know what I need."

"Do you want me to fuck you?"

"Yes. If you want. If you're not into it, just say."

"I want you to feel good," I say, brushing back the fall of hair from his hot forehead. "I want you to feel safe, to know that someone's looking out for you, and that you can just let go and exist for a while."

He moans, a soft, heartbreaking sound of human loneliness as I go on stroking his face. "You can't imagine how much I needed to hear that," he says.

"I might have some idea."

"How did you do it for all those months? How did you stay sane?"

"By hanging around that gas station looking for Mr Wrong. Instead I found you."

He laughs weakly. "Does that make me Mr. Right?"

"It makes you mine."

He moans again, relaxing against me as I begin to softly stroke his bare skin, down his side and up again, skimming over the puckered scars on his back. As he starts to breathe deeper I slide my hand lower, down his thigh then up over his ass, dipping my fingers into the crack. Biting his lip, he hooks his knee over my hip, rocking back against the pressure as I stroke his hole.

"There's lube in the bathroom," he says. He goes to sit up but I push him down again.

"Stay where you are," I say. "Just like this."

Everything in his carry-all in the bathroom is in blister packs, and it takes me a minute to be sure I have lube and not toothpaste. When I come back Ronan is still lying on his side with his leg bent, facing away from me, his ass a shadowy invitation. I climb onto the bed behind him, stopping to kiss the twisted shrapnel scars peppering his shoulder.

"I didn't do my bloodwork," he murmurs as I tear open one of the packs of lube.

"I'm going to assume you haven't raw-dogged anyone in the last twenty-four hours." He laughs again, ending on a little sigh as I smear my slick fingers around his hole.

"In truth I haven't been with anyone but you in...well, in a long time."

"I kind of wish that was true for me. Not that I've slept with anyone since we got together," I say as he twists to look up at me. "Before that. I didn't used to go to a hotel, right? Just fucked behind the gas station."

"Blake, you didn't."

His look of pity hurts worse than if he called me a slut. "I needed something. Something to make me feel even a little bit human. I don't know...I don't know if I'll ever do it again. Live as a dog, I mean. I don't know if I want to remember."

Twenty-Five

Safety

What's happening to me? Just when he needs me to be strong, I'm breaking apart. Letting my negativity take over, ruin this moment for both of us as a sob threatens to burst from my throat. Ronan sits up and puts his arms around me, and despite the parts of me that want to find the nearest cliff to jump off of, I let him hold me. Let him pull me down to lie beside him, rest my head on his shoulder as he strokes my hair, his lips brushing my forehead as he murmurs that soft melody. Little by little it works, as I will my rigid muscles to relax, my body to accept that for the first time in too long, I'm safe too.

"The shit you must have seen," he says when I'm breathing normally again. "How long were you embedded?"

"Six months."

He flinches, his arm tightening around me. "How did you stomach it?"

I can barely answer, the words sticking on my tongue. "I don't know. I really don't. Just kept telling myself I was doing it for the right reasons."

"You poor bugger," he murmurs.

"It was horrible."

"Tell me."

"No. It's too much to put you through." Too much for me to relive, but he doesn't argue, just keeps petting my hair as I cling to him.

"Then we'll find you a therapist," he says gently. "Someone with combat experience who's not going flinch. We won't let this eat you alive."

We...like he's made some commitment to me, when nothing was ever said. Only felt, with a sureness that frightens me, and I pull back to look him in the eye.

"I'm sorry I fucked up," I say. "My team was so close to bringing an end to Grange's project it and I blew it the fuck up. Because I couldn't handle losing you. I couldn't live with letting you die."

"You're a proper eejit, you are," he says with half a smile. "But thanks."

I want to say more, pour my idiot heart out, beg for a promise, but I don't want to break the spell that's made him think I'm worth his time. I hope the magic never fades, as he kisses my forehead, then my mouth.

This: this is what I fought to protect, not just this man but the feeling of safety I find in his arms. It feels like a miracle, an even more mysterious thing than I am, that he knows me like he does, all the strange, monstrous parts of me, and yet still wants me.

His hands roam over my bare back as he sucks at my lips, his dick riding hard against my stomach. I don't want to let go of him, don't want to ever stop kissing him. Except to maybe do a bunch of other things. Touch him, suck him, fill him, give him everything he wants.

I angle my body to reach between us and run my fingers up his length. He moans into my mouth, thrusting against me, smearing my stomach with precum and stoking my desire even hotter. We have the rest of the night—the rest of our lives—to fuck like howling animals. This is what I want right now, this closeness, this shared sensation as his dick slides against mine.

I wrap my hand around us both and Ronan shivers, thrusting into my grip, the silky press of his skin and the hard flesh beneath nearly pushing me over the brink. Too soon, when I want this to last forever, the sweet succulence of his kiss echoing the hot, sucking pressure below as Ronan wraps his hand over mine.

Too much, but we have forever to do this, as often as we want, and so I surrender to the pleasure of this moment, to the rushing, roaring climax that tears through me like wildfire, burning away my fear. As my cum coats his fingers he groans, tenses, shudders, then follows me over the edge, adding his cream to the slick mess that coats both our stomachs.

I'm still catching my breath when he grabs my hand and begins to lick it clean, thrusting his tongue between my fingers then sucking each of them in turn. It's dizzying and filthy and so fucking hot, and as he glances up at me my dick stiffens as if nothing has happened. As if all he has to do is look at me and I'll be ready for him. As if that wasn't always true.

When he's done with my hand he stops to kiss me, a wet, sticky kiss that tastes like cum and makes my balls throb. I'm happy to wait, as he licks his way down my torso and back up again for another messy kiss.

"Oops," he says as he leans back and reveals the Rorschach of cum he's smeared on my front from his own. "Should I start over?"

"Don't worry about it. We can take a shower in a bit. Right now, I just want to hold you."

Biting his lip, he settles against me, his head on my shoulder. I don't know why I think I can take care of this man, or why he wants to let me try. I only know what my instincts tell me, and for the first time in more years than I want to count, my instincts say this is exactly where I should be. With Ronan.

I roll to my side, pulling him closer. He doesn't question it, nuzzling into my neck with a sigh.

"Why do you make me feel so safe?" he says. Something I should be saying to him, but if that's what we give each other, I'm happy.

"Maybe it's because I'm not afraid of you," I reply.

"You should be," he says softly.

"I have been, a couple times. But I never blamed you."

He sits up with a frown. "I interrogated you at gunpoint for three hours."

"You were only doing your job."

"That's so but I shouldn't have fucked you first. And I could have let you put on clothes. And while we're at it, I must say I'm royally pissed at your bureau. I can't believe they didn't let me know about you."

"Would you have acted differently around me if you knew?"

He studies me briefly. "That might have been a bit of a problem."

"It doesn't matter. It's over, and I don't plan on doing anything like that ever again."

"I'll make sure of it."

"Thanks. So did you still want to fuck?" I ask as he lies down again,

"It'll keep," he says, nestling his head on my shoulder. "As long as you're happy."

"I am."

"Are you sure?"

There's another question that he's not asking. Some inner hesitation that's driven by a life of lying, of doing bad things for a good reason. "What's wrong?"

He exhales slowly, his breath flowing over my bare chest, his fingers twining with mine. "Nothing. Only, I've never let myself get this close to anyone. I don't know how to feel, to be honest. None of this seems quite real. The night, the Facility, the way we met. I don't know how you can still trust me."

"I don't know either. Maybe I've been screwed over so many times I can tell when someone's trying not to."

"I just don't want to start you hoping for too much. Hoping for things I won't be able to do."

"Like what?"

He swallows, clinging to me so tightly I feel the movement of his throat. "Like keep on making you happy."

"My mood is my job. You keep being yourself. We'll figure it out as we go. If we can't, we weren't meant to last."

"But I want to make this last. I want this to mean something."

"It does," I say. "You do. Trust me, Ronan. You matter to me."

"It half killed me, letting you go," he says as I stroke his hot face. "I should have shot the bitch on sight, the minute I walked into her office. We should have moved on her sooner. We could have stopped all of this. I'm so sorry, Blake. I'm sorry we let you all down."

"You didn't," I say as he hides his face against my shoulder again. "You did what you could. You weren't calling the shots."

"I don't know why I'm so shook, after all the shit I've seen. But that was war. This was hell."

"But it's over."

He raises his head, and the sight of his teary eyes catches at my heart. "Is it really over?"

"For you, for now, yes. Right now, all that matters is you and me."

We kiss again, a sloppy, snuffling kiss. I don't care, I want it all, his bad days and his good. Want him to know he can let down his guard with me, be hurt, be afraid. Admit his mistakes, so he'll forgive me for mine. We can be afraid together. Be hurt together. Be wrong and do wrong, but do it for the right reasons and do it together.

"Sorry for that," he says at length, wiping his eyes.

"For what?" I say, my own eyes stinging, my voice rough. "For being human?" He laughs, a soft *ha* that ends on a sigh of contentment.

"Thanks for being *more* than human," he murmurs, relaxing against me.

"Hey, I just woke up like this."

He laughs again, and a little thrill spikes through me. He's gorgeous when he laughs. When he smiles. When he sighs and lays his head on my shoulder again. He's gorgeous and he's mine, and it's everything I've ever wanted.

I've had enough of big plans and big causes, of giving my service to the world as a way of avoiding myself. Avoiding my pain and bad memories, the sort of things you can't ever hide from without hiding from the good as well.

I want the good, the small, ordinary moments I've never had, isolated from the truth of my strange nature, and from the ordinary world because of that strangeness. A secret that's been my shame all my life. An accident of chance that kept me leashed me to other people's needs, never believing my own needs were enough.

I need to be seen, to be held and understood for who I truly am. I need Ronan Wednesday. Need his strong and sensual body, battle scars and all. Need his strength, his devotion, his sincerity, his bravery and even his fears, which are so like my own.

And I think he needs me too. If fate controls my life, then it's fate that brought us together, that makes this feel so right, as Ronan settles beside me again with a contented sigh.

What we've done together—what we all did—will change lives for the better, give Hollowood Falls a future without fear. The kind of future everyone deserves. Even monsters like me.

EPILOGUE

GRAEME

A Hollowood Wedding

You can take a man out of Hollowood Falls, but you'll never take Hollowood out of a man. Something I've come to understand in a whole new way this past year, as Evan and Pierce have grappled with learning the secret I've been hiding about my own uncanny nature. It was easier coming out as gay, as I didn't give a fuck what my family thought of me. This time, I had something to lose.

A year later, things are back to normal. Well, as normal as they were in a house with two werewolves and a kelpie. This weekend in the Falls has been a bit tense, but that's unavoidable when Evan's around his father.

They've been trying, no doubt. Done loads of joint therapy, with Dr. Vanian and with a family therapist who only knows their emotional history and not the lore behind it. It's working in as much as Mr. Culver keeps his thoughts to himself more often, and Evan tries not to assume the worst before it happens. We all give them plenty of grace. One can't undo a lifetime's bad habits overnight.

Otherwise, the weekend has been easy. Perhaps because there's been so much happening. Hollowood Falls loves a party, and from the minute we arrived yesterday we've been swept up in dos for Ronan and Blake's wedding. The ceremony's taking place outside, under a primitive log-built gazebo which Chase and others insist on calling a temple. I won't dispute them. This is not my hallowed ground but theirs, and the people of Hollowood Falls may worship anything they like. I'm glad I was warned so I could dress for the weather, hot sunshine filling the valley as we watch the happy couple muddle their way through their vows then kiss with tears in their eyes. Plenty of wet eyes in the congregation as well, even Pierce blinking and rubbing his nose with the back of his hand.

Or is that due to the smoke trickling from behind the altar? I was warned there'd be some hocus pocus, some Hollowood business that might not make sense but that was perfectly harmless. Having been brought up in a household that mingled ancient folkways with an overbearing Calvinist work ethic, I can't shake my suspicion of most New World spiritual practices, with their appropriation of indigenous rites and active pleas to utopian capitalism. Hollowood Falls has its own native faith, one that lurks on the margins yet controls all their lives. Even mine, if you consider that old book in the town archives linking my name to Evan's and thereby to his family.

The person known as Grandmother has now climbed onto a stool behind the low altar, her face hidden behind a ghostly mask, bone white and smooth as polished stone. I look away, my shoulders tensing as my body dredges up the memory of that night last year, when we rescued her from Hyperion. A strange, hallucinatory night, for the old witch had possessed me, ridden me across the lake then onward for countless miles in a semi-lucid haze. Hours and hours, her will goading me like a whip, until I came to my senses on the lawn by the Lodge.

"Are we meant to do anything?" I whisper to Evan as Sutherland lays an old book from the archives in front of Grandmother.

"I have no idea," Ev replies. "I've never seen this before."

Humming a soft dirge, Grandmother opens the book, thumbing slowly through the crackling vellum pages. She stops at a spread and begins to wave her hand over the book, the herbal smoke billowing thickly around her and the two men before the altar. She runs a crooked fingertip over the page, tracing a family tree that spreads from one margin to the other. Sutherland turns the page so she can follow one of the branches. As I'm wondering how she's going to mark the book, she draws in a huge breath of smoke then blows it out in a steady stream across her open palm and onto the page.

Sutherland gasps, sucking in his own lungful of smoke. He starts to cough, clutching his chest as he wheezes. Facing the altar, Ronan grabs Blake's hand.

"Did you know that's how they do it?" he asks breathily.

"Nope."

"I guess that's it then. No way out."

"Gee, thanks," Blake says with a laughs. He pulls Ronan close and as they kiss again the crowd breaks out in applause, then hoots and hollers as they go on kissing, swaying as they cling to each other, shamelessly in love.

Against all odds, I'm not the only one who brought food I can eat to the reception pot-luck. Wee River has been edging veganism since their boyfriend Marcus gave up meat, and their wonderful spinach rolls are nearly gone before I get to them. It's a casual event, people coming and going, joining conversations then moving on. Nearly everyone here has known each other since birth, and I sit for a while with Marcus and his parents, who are among the exceptions. Though they once lived in Hollowood, the Bonnys are East Coasters, from an enclave of lycan families that includes our Pierce's line. Freeman and Hope are a reserved couple comfortable with silence, and I let Marcus tell me about his new bike while I eat.

Mr. Culver joins us with a plate full of dessert squares and cookies, which he's learned better than to even offer to me. Hollowood has figured out vegetables, but not vegan desserts.

"Any updates from Oregon?" Mr Bonny asks him, referring to the secure and extremely secluded property where the shifter mercenaries are recovering from the months of torture by that nasty piece of work Tanya Grange.

"Not much to tell," Mr. Culver says, picking apart a chocolate chip cookie. "None of them seem ready to move on from rehab."

"That was a terrible place, Leif," Mr. Bonny says, shaking his head. "No one on earth should go through what they did."

"What *you* went through, old friend. Hopefully we've seen the last of this so-called Hyperion Group."

"Let's hope," Freeman says, glancing at me as he and Mr. Culver toast with their paper cups of beer. I don't want to burst their bubble by telling them that Hyperion can't be stopped so easily. That's for the feds to worry about, or me some other day.

If we want to get home tonight, we need to be on our way, and I wander outside in hope of finding my boys. Chase is on the veranda, scrolling through his and Stone's fan mail I expect from his guilty blush as he shoves his phone in his pocket.

"You leaving already?" he asks me.

"It's a long drive."

"Yeah, we're cutting out soon. Stone's done enough peopling for like a month. But can I ask you something?"

"What do you need?"

"Nothing, just I was talking to Pierce earlier. He told me that Ev finally came out to his therapist. Didn't she know he was gay?"

"Yeah, but she didn't know he was a werewolf."

"For real? How'd she take it?"

"Quite well, all things considered. It's really helped them get to the root of his PTSD. Being trapped over there when he was young did a proper number on his wee head."

"I guess so," Chase says in wonder. "And how about you? They still shitty about your little secret?"

"They're fine. I had to ask them to lay off the rude jokes, though." I don't mention how wounded Evan was at first that I'd not told him. How pissed off Pierce was at him for being so upset. How many nights ended with me sleeping alone, on the couch a few times when they were both sulking, though I can't blame them for taking it hard. I had every opportunity to bring it up and somehow convinced myself that my secret wasn't worth sharing, that it would be too big a burden for them. Yet who else could know the truth about me and still care for me so deeply as those who know what it's like to be somewhere between a man and a monster?

"I might take them back home next year on holiday," I say. "Let them finally meet my family."

"Ev's never met your folks?"

"Not face to face. I went non-contact with most of them some years before I met him. But I'd like to see my grandparents again before they kick off, ken?"

"I bet it's really pretty, where you're from."

I smile, thinking of the sooty harbor-side industrial estate that stands on what was once holy ground to my people. "The water's nice."

We return inside, where Mr. Culver is speaking with Pierce and Evan, him and Pierce laughing together as Evan fumes, just like old times.

"I'd better break that up or I'll have to hear about it all the way home."

"Is it hard, keeping two people happy?" Chase asks.

"It's not my job to make them happy. My job is to keep things fair and honest. Their moods are their responsibility."

"I sure couldn't live with that asshole. Ev, I mean. Pierce is cool."

"Pierce is a pain in the arse, the mouthy bugger."

"Oh yeah?" Chase says with a gleeful grin. "Like how?"

"Never you mind. But I'd not give him up."

Pierce shoots me a pleading glance. Time to rescue Evan from his father and leave Hollowood Falls behind once more. We stayed last night at the Culvers as the Dew Drop is booked to capacity. Though we've been invited to stay again, I like my creature comforts, my bed and my backyard. I like my boys to be able to relax, which doesn't happen when Ev's around his parents.

I like Evan to be happy, even if I can't directly make it so. I can only provide the conditions for his happiness to flourish. I think I'm doing alright, his tense shoulders dropping, his eyes brightening as I approach. We say our goodbyes to his father and a few other people nearby, but if we were to do a circuit of all the guests we'd be here until tomorrow.

Though I miss the VW, the Lexus fits the three of us more comfortably. Fuck me, I'm settling down. Getting comfortable. Working on my relationships instead of fucking off on another call of duty. Seeking happiness where I am, not projecting it onto some far off future. I've been changed by love as much as Evan has. He changed me.

As the electric engine coasts silently through the switchbacks, Pierce slides forward to tap my shoulder. "Pull off at the gas station."

"I asked if you had to piss before we got in the car."

"That's not why," he says, grinning as he tugs at the knot of his tie. "I want to enjoy the nice day while we're here. Have some fun before we have to drive all that way."

"What do you mean, fun?"

"Just pull over, would you?" Evan says. He could use some fun, to shake off the dour mood from a day in his father's company. As soon as I stop the car Pierce and Evan get out and start undressing.

"What the hell are you doing?" I ask Evan as he tosses his jacket into the back seat then starts on his shirt. "We're on the side of the road!"

"No one is going to care," Pierce says, hopping on one foot as he tries to take off his shoe without unlacing it.

"Speak for your selves. I fucking care."

"We used to do this all the time when we were kids."

"What, fuck in public?"

"What are you talking about?" Evan says.

"That!" I yelp as he pulls his shirt over his head.

"Cuttler's Green is across the road," Pierce says, hobbling barefoot over the gravel. "We used to come down here on moon nights to run around and burn off some energy."

"You mean to do that now? In the middle of the day?"

"Welcome to Hollowood, baby."

"Don't *baby* me, you... oh fine, I'll come with at least. Someone ought to mind your clothes."

Cuttler's Green is a long, broad field of wispy prairie grasses growing on what was once cultivated land. Standing beneath a tree, I watch my lads in wolf mode race to and fro, leaping over each other and tussling over twigs that snap in their heavy jaws. What would the dentist think?

Pierce trots up to me, shoving his head under my hand. I ruffle his dark mane, marveling at the solid bulk of him, the wiry softness of his fur. Evan barks once from his hiding place among the grass. Pierce darts away, swatting me with his fluffy tail, and I wonder why I'm denying myself, pretending I still have a secret to keep.

Wishing we were a little further from the road, I undress carefully, stacking my clothes on top of Evan's shoes. I may be about to run around in a field, but this linen suit is bespoke and I'd rather not have to have it cleaned. Which should of course be my main concern when I'm standing naked in a field.

I'm making a mountain of this molehill, and before I get any more self-conscious I sink into that quiet place within that allows the change to manifest. No matter how much science you throw at the phenomenon, there's something uncanny at the heart of this intersection of body and will. A gift we never asked for, a truth too strong to tell just anyone, buried in our very cells.

As I trot out into the field my boys come bounding towards me, their red tongues flagging, their tails held high. They circle me, rubbing against my flanks like huge cats, nosing under my chin and my belly. Pierce runs a few steps and I trot after him. Evan bounds past me, and then we're off, all three of us dashing across the sage green sward.

And it's glorious. It's wild and strange and unexpected, that something so natural, so utterly basic as running across a field could make me feel so startlingly alive. And so much more, as if this the final proof that we were destined for this life together, that here at last is how to life this life. I've spent too long regretting this strange body of mine. For the first time I can remember, to be me feels like being free.

Thanks for reading!

Like all authors I appreciate sincere reviews from readers like you

For more stories like this, as well as early access, sneak peaks, and free books, join my Readers Club: www.willforest.com/newsletter/

ABOUT THE AUTHOR

Author, blogger, and general nuisance Will Forrest writes unusual – and usually queer – Historical and Paranormal Romances with a dash of mischief and mayhem.

Will grew up on a steady diet of Douglas Adams and classic 90s bodice rippers, and has a diploma of fashion design, a degree in social theory, and a bad habit of changing careers, life goals, and continents.

Currently Will lives in a very warm part of Canada with three lovely humans and a succession of martyred houseplants.

willforrest.com

Join the Readers Club for advance access, free books, and (occasionally) recipes.

willforest.com/newsletter/

ALSO BY WILL FORREST

AN INCONVENIENT EARL (M/M)
THE UNTAMED HEART (M/M)
HOW TO RESCUE A BARONESS (M/F)
A PEARL FOR AN EARL (M/F)
A LOVE UNBROKEN (M/F)

SERIES & COLLECTIONS

LONDON HUSTLE (M/M)
HOLLOWOOD FALLS (M/M+)
THE JAIME SKYE CHRONICLES (ACE M/M)
THE LIBERTINES (POLYAM)
SOCIETY WIVES (M/F, POLYAM)

COMING IN 2024

HOW TO INHERIT A HUSBAND
AUTHOR, AUTHOR
STARMAN